MIDWINTER MARRIAGE

MIDWINTER MARRIAGE

Sarah Stanley

CHIVERS

British Library Cataloguing in Publication Data available

This Large Print edition published by BBC Audiobooks Ltd, Bath, 2010.
Published by arrangement with Robert Hale Ltd.

U.K. Hardcover ISBN 978 1 408 47850 9
U.K. Softcover ISBN 978 1 408 47851 6

For Dunster and its castle in Somerset, upon which I have based
Greylake. I am especially grateful to the National Trust and the staff at
the castle for giving me a thorough guided tour in the depths of winter.
And my continuing thanks to Frampton-on-Severn in Gloucestershire,
and Lynton and Lynmouth in Devon.

Printed and bound in Great Britain by
CPI Antony Rowe, Chippenham and Eastbourne

CHAPTER ONE

At sunrise five days before Christmas, a matronly maid peered disapprovingly between the curtains of the bed at the Bell and Fox, convinced of finding its scandalous occupant naked with at least two lovers.

'Begging your pardon, Miss Mannacott. I—I mean, Miss Tremoille . . . but Sir Guy wishes you to join him for breakfast without delay.' She was plump and grey-haired, with a sanctimonious expression that banished joy and goodwill from the festive season.

Pale candlelight shone over her shoulder, casting uncertain light on the twenty-five-year-old lady slumbering alone within. Beth Tremoille's hazel-green eyes opened resentfully. She didn't want to be accountable to anyone, least of all Sir Guy Valmer, yet since last night that was precisely what she'd become. Well, she certainly wasn't going to leap at his command! She watched the maid open the bed hangings, allowing the light from the candle on the mantelshelf to spread more evenly, before going to draw back the curtains at the windows. It had stopped snowing outside, and the low sun suffused everything with a vivid, disquieting blend of blood red, plum and gold. The frozen heights of Exmoor seemed almost on fire, while down here in the

1

small coastal town of Porworthy, where the night shadows were in slow retreat, the white-carpeted streets and roofs were touched with rich dark ruby. Spectacular sunrises and sunsets had become commonplace since early in the summer, before the victory at Waterloo, and many people regarded them as an ill omen, although of what no one could say.

The room was at the rear of the Bell and Fox, with one window looking west, where Exmoor plunged down to the coast, and the other facing north over crowding rooftops toward long-abandoned medieval quays that had once bustled with vessels. Two miles of salt marsh now extended to the Bristol Channel, and Porworthy was no longer a port. The steeple of the parish church rose nearby, as did the smoke-blackened remains of Sir Daniel Lavington's woollen mill, which had been burned in August during a riot over new machines. He was a harsh magistrate and equally harsh landowner, and loathed by almost everyone, his own class included.

Beth glanced around the sparsely furnished room, where embers glowed in a small hearth, and a sprig of holly on the mantel was the only nod toward Christmas. These four walls had been a welcome refuge after her embarrassingly public arrival at the inn the night before, when inebriated carol-singing revellers poured out of the taproom into the snowy night to ogle as Sir Guy Valmer assisted his shocking bride-to-be down from his travelling carriage. She had been humiliated, and longed to be back at the peace and seclusion of her leased home in the fishing village of Lannermouth. Instead she was on her way to Greylake Castle and a forced marriage.

The maid went about her duties, sniffing disparagingly, and generally making no attempt to conceal her puritanical aversion for the woman who had only yesterday been the unprincipled adventuress Miss Mannacott, but today, under her real name of Tremoille, was set to become the most notorious siren in the West Country, if not the entire realm. Beth didn't care for her manner. 'What is your name?'

'Rachel, miss.'

'Well, Rachel, take your pious self off to Hades, and instruct Sir Guy to accompany you.'

The maid was alarmed. 'I can't do *that*, miss!'

Beth relented, for it was unbecoming to resort to sarcasm with servants, even one as presumptuous as this. 'Then simply inform him that I will join him in due course.'

'Yes, miss.' The woman hurried to the door, but then remembered something. 'Begging your pardon again, miss, but I have set out the clothes Sir Guy desires you to wear.' Arranged over a chair were a fashionable peppermint

3

muslin gown, grey silk spencer and elegant accessories selected from Beth's luggage. They had last been worn in London during the summer, when Guy almost captured her, and Beth had no idea why he wished her to wear them now. She remembered how terrified she'd been of being thrown into jail for theft, and how she'd eluded him three times before fleeing to the Dower House at Lannermouth, a remote fishing hamlet some five miles west of Porworthy. But last night she'd finally been cornered, and had submitted. Guy knew too much about her shocking past, although far from wanting to see her punished for theft or worse, as she'd feared, incredibly, he wanted her hand in marriage. But the threat of being held to account for her crimes ensured her capitulation, and so she'd left everything to come with him. The maid intruded upon her thoughts. 'Will you require me further, miss?'

Be dressed by those bony, self-righteous fingers? Beth would as soon be attended by one of the Furies. 'No. I'm accustomed to dressing myself.'

And to being dressed by Mr Haldane, the maid thought, glancing at the gentleman's white kid evening glove that lay upon the bedside table. Whose was it? Mr Haldane's or Sir Guy's? Maybe it was someone else's entirely. Who could say with such a woman as this? After the briefest possible curtsey, she gladly quit the presence of the strumpet of

4

Lannermouth. Hastening to the evergreen-decked staircase that descended to the main hallway on the ground floor, she saw another maid coming up toward her. It was her cousin Letty, who was as warm and worldly wise as she, Rachel, was not. Letty stopped with a broad grin.

'Well, Cousin, what's she like in the cold light of day, eh?' she asked softly, not wanting the indiscretion to be heard by others.

'Comely enough, I suppose, if you like trollops with witch eyes.'

'Your prudish mouth is as pursed as an arsehole,' Letty responded frankly.

'Oh, mock me if you must, but she gave up all respectability from the moment she arrived at Lannermouth last summer. Everyone knows she's been allowing Mr Haldane far more favours than any woman should before marriage. And she's not even a widow, which might have spared some of her blushes. Now it seems she's been using a false name as well! With all her flaunting ways and tempting glances, she snared one of the best catches in Devon, and last night tossed him aside—in public at their betrothal ball!—for the finest catch in the whole south-west of England. Men are such fools. Mr Haldane could have had any lady he liked, but went and chose a jade! As for Sir Guy, well, I don't know what he can be thinking of, wanting to make such a doxy Lady Valmer. She'll *never* be respectable!'

'Hush, you clatter-tongue, or he'll hear you. He's only in the little parlour, the door's open and he's got ears like a cat.' Letty glanced uneasily downstairs at the wood-panelled hallway, with its sporting prints, uneven stone flags and mistletoe bunch. She moved closer to Rachel. 'Be honest now, and tell me true. She's more than just pretty, isn't she? She *has* to be to hook the likes of Sir Guy and Mr Haldane. And they such enemies!'

'I suppose so.'

'My word, Rachel, I wouldn't mind a roll with that Sir Guy. He brings out the bawd in me, that's for sure.' Letty sighed. 'Anyway, thanks to all this, folks hereabouts haven't had so much to chew on since that Topweather fellow was found dead on the Lannermouth road. I know it was supposed to be the work of highwaymen, but they'll take a purse and jewels, maybe, or luggage off a stagecoach, but never do a murder.

'It wouldn't surprise me if *she* had something to do with it.' Rachel nodded back up the stairs in the general direction of Beth's room.

'You can't go blaming her for everything. You'll say she fired the mill next!'

'Well, these things have only happened since she took the Dower House.'

A cool male voice, quiet-spoken and lazy, addressed them from the foot of the stairs. 'When you idle pair have quite finished gossiping about your betters, may I remind one of you that I still await a response from Miss Tremoille?'

Starting guiltily, they whirled about to see Sir Guy Valmer standing there. He was a tall, elegant man in his early thirties, leanly muscular, with tousled, dark chestnut curls that he wore longer than was the vogue, and he exuded such an air of confidence and authority that no man—or woman—of sense would take him lightly. Aristocratically handsome, with pale, clear skin, a straight nose, sculptured lips and memorable grey eyes that were clear and compelling, he also possessed an immaculate sense of style. His superbly cut coat was dark blue, the discreet frills of his shirt pushed through the undone top buttons of his pale blue Marcella waistcoat, and his light grey trousers vanished into gleaming Hessian boots. The trousers were so tight as to reveal his generous masculine proportions in almost shocking detail, a fact of which Letty was most appreciative. *My word, Letty Smith, that's a mighty wick he's got to dip! Mighty enough to make even you squeak. Lucky, lucky Miss Tremoille.*

'Haven't you any work to do?' he enquired, aware of her scrutiny.

She coloured. 'Begging your pardon, Sir Guy.' She hastened on upstairs, leaving her dismayed cousin to face him alone.

7

'Well?' He eyed Rachel. 'Have you spoken with Miss Tremoille?'

'Yes, Sir Guy. She said she would be down directly.'

He raised a cool eyebrow. 'Really? That's all?'

'Yes, sir.'

'The truth now, for such mildness doesn't smack of the lady in question.'

Rachel's thin face became red with embarrassment. 'Well, sir . . .'

'Out with it.'

'She did say she would be down in due course, but before that she told me to go to Hades and take you with me.'

He was amused. 'Ah, that sounds more like it. No doubt she intends to keep me waiting for some time yet. I guessed as much. Please have some coffee brought to the parlour, and serve breakfast when Miss Tremoille eventually deigns to join me. And be warned, although I'll overlook your malicious chattering on this occasion, if I find that you—or any of the servants here—have continued clacking about my private affairs, I'll see you're dismissed.'

'Yes, Sir Guy,' she answered contritely, eyes lowered, and as soon as he'd gone back into the parlour she continued crossly down the stairs. Cousin Letty would get her hanged yet!

Guy resumed his seat at the white-clothed parlour table, which was set for two. So far the only sign of breakfast was a dish of strawberry preserve and another of the costly orange marmalade that was only served to very select persons. It was the landlord's private room, and contained a splendid dresser of green-and-cream crockery and copper lustre ware. Upright wooden armchairs stood on either side of the inglenook fireplace, where fresh flames leapt and crackled, and sprays of holly and mistletoe were fixed above the two faded landscape watercolours on the whitewashed walls. The small square window gave on to the High Street, where few people were to be seen and only a single cart braved the elements. Isolated snowflakes again floated aimlessly on the cold air breathing down from the frozen moor, and new clouds began to mask the unnatural sunrise.

Guy leaned back in the chair, his fingers drumming on the newspaper that had been thoughtfully provided while he awaited the convenience of Miss Elizabeth Tremoille. What was Gloucestershire's most star-crossed heiress going to bring to Greylake Castle? Spirit, certainly, and a quick mind, but what else? Notoriety? Mockery? He needed her for his own purposes, and had no desire to carry out his threat to have her arrested if she didn't obey him, but he wouldn't be taken for a fool either. A nerve flickered at his temple. He was proud of his name and reputation, of his lineage and station in life, and it was bad

9

enough that he'd been obliged to publicly destroy Beth's betrothal to Landry Haldane. The match had already been scandalous, now it was a *cause célèbre* that would reach Mayfair.

He told himself the ends justified the means, but did it? Just how deeply did Beth feel about Haldane? At the ball he'd overheard her insist to her good friend, the vicar's daughter Harriet Bellamy, that she didn't love Haldane and would have ended the betrothal anyway. Had that been the truth? Would she still have given up Haldane if it had not been for the sudden revelation that Harriet was the mother of his illegitimate daughter, Katy? Guy's grey eyes were shaded. What was he to think? That Beth still loved Haldane, but was stepping aside for Harriet's sake? As for Haldane, this unwelcome proof of past misconduct left him with no option but to marry Harriet, but it was Beth he wanted.

Ah, Beth, that entrancing, enigmatic woodland spirit who seemed to cast an effortless spell over every man she met. Oberon's daughter, with hazel-green eyes, a cloud of dark curls, and a figure that was so exquisitely curved and feminine that it seemed to invite caresses. Guy breathed out slowly, recalling how he had forced a calculated testing kiss on her as they left the ball. Her response had astonished him with its intensity and apparent desire, but was it, as she claimed afterward, as calculated as his had been?

Possibly. Oh, what a damning word that was; so slyly suggestive of probably . . .

In the bedroom above, Beth continued to snuggle wilfully between the sheets. She was ashamed to admit that turning her back on Landry had not been as difficult as it ought to have been. Truth to tell, she wasn't unwilling at all, because her dilemma—her very secret dilemma—was that she'd been fiercely drawn to Guy before she'd even heard of Landry. There was nothing pure or admirable about the carnal craving that had threatened to devour her body and soul that day, but Guy must never know that. He was offering a loveless marriage of convenience, and that was what she must remember. For the sake of her dignity and self-respect, her compelling desires must be suppressed and concealed.

She turned to look at the man's evening glove on the bedside table. Guy had dropped it the night before. There was no need to suppress her feelings now, she thought, drawing it slowly beneath the warm bedclothes and slipping her hand into it. How sensuously he flexed his fingers when donning gloves. Everything about him was seductive, and she was so conscious of the glove being his that erotic sensations began to quiver in her loins. Closing her eyes, she ran the supple white silk over her body, as if he caressed her. She imagined his soft whispers of love, his sighs and moans as his need mounted and then his

11

potent weapon, long, hard and strong, pushing deep into the heart of her sexuality.

The glove moved between her legs, exploring the secret moist places where she so yearned to feel him. It was his hand, she told herself, his fingers that breached her defences, gave her pleasure and set the blood racing magnificently through her veins. He was driving satisfyingly into her, making her cry out with gratification! Joyous feelings melted through her flesh, and her breath snatched as the muscles contracted excitedly between her legs. The sensations were rich and warm, and her breath escaped on a long sigh as she stole every delight that she could from their rich bounty, but as they undulated into oblivion, she could not help wondering how much more wonderful they would have been with the man himself.

She lay there for a while afterward, her eyes closed. Sometimes she wished her sensuality had never been brought to life, because being an innocent virgin was a simpler existence. But she had been introduced to the pleasures of the flesh, and now needed a man's love to make her feel whole. No, that wasn't quite true, for it was *Guy's* love she needed for that. He'd kissed her once, last night on leaving the ball, and he'd only done it to prove a point. She taunted him about being cold, and he kissed her to prove she was wrong. All his remarkable skill was brought to bear in a kiss she'd found more irresistibly aphrodisiac than any before. His lips had mastered her, coaxed and teased her, and seemed to adore her in every way.

No man could devote himself to such a kiss without becoming aroused. They were fully dressed, but she'd felt his masculinity, strong and urgent, straining his satin breeches and threatening to reach through the delicate fabric of her ball gown. Sir Guy Valmer might almost have been hers for those few moments, and the feeling was so intoxicating that she almost forgot he was only teaching her a lesson. But even then, caught up in his knowing embrace, enchanted by desire and blinded with love, she retained one important quality—common sense—and knew she had to play him at his own clever game.

He had to be shown that she too could pretend passion and desire if she chose, and so she ended the kiss coolly and dismissively, taunting him that she was his match. But her inner turmoil was unbearable, and she was so needful of final gratification with him and only him, that it would have been easy to blurt the truth. Somehow common sense continued ascendant, and the truth remained buried. As far as he was concerned, Beth Tremoille might be his prisoner, but she wasn't his victim too.

From now on she had to be cool and remote with him, and not betray her love by so much as a flicker of her eyes. The thought was

13

sobering, and suddenly she couldn't lie there any longer. It was time to face her nemesis in the cold light of day. But, as she flung the bedclothes aside and slipped out of the bed, her gaze came to rest on the clothes he expected her to wear. She wasn't about to meekly comply with his commands; she would wear clothes of *her* choice!

A quarter of an hour later, washed and refreshed, she considered herself ready to go down to the parlour. She had chosen a cherry-red woollen gown and a matching pelisse. Both garments were the work of the celebrated London *couturière,* Madame de Sichel, and were as modish as any that had ever graced the Bell and Fox in Porworthy. After fixing a white fur hat at a jaunty angle on her pinned-up hair, she picked up her mantle, muff and embattled pride, and prepared to cross swords with the man she was determined would never know he was the undisputed love of her life.

CHAPTER TWO

Guy heard Beth's light footsteps approaching the parlour and, as he rose to greet her, there was nothing in his manner to indicate his thoughts. She appeared in the doorway, a defiant figure in red. He'd only selected the other clothes to test her mettle, and she'd

14

tossed the gauntlet magnificently on the floor between them.

'Good morning, Beth.'

'Good morning, sir,' she replied, her hazel-green eyes steady, her manner challenging.

'Sit down, please.' He relieved her of the mantle and muff, and then drew out a chair at the table. 'Breakfast will be brought directly,' he explained, as he then resumed his seat and regarded her. 'How are you this morning?'

'Blooming. How are you?'

'In rude health.'

She looked at him. 'Enough beating about the bush, sir. I imagine your need for me has something to do with my father's missing will?'

'Ah, you've deduced that much?'

'Well, you certainly aren't hopelessly in love with me, and yet you want me enough to threaten my arrest unless I marry you. My disputed inheritance seems the likely explanation. You think—or rather, you *know*— that the will reinstates me as my father's sole heir, so by marrying me you will regain Tremoille House.' She spoke of her beloved home in the Cotswolds, near the city of Gloucester.

'Valmer House,' he corrected.

'It bears *my* family name for the time being.' She paused a moment. 'There is something I think you should know: if you marry me, you will have a barren wife.'

'You know this for a fact?'

15

'I was almost a year in poverty with Jake Mannacott, and I conducted a very carnal affair with Landry Haldane, yet have never even been late. You, sir, need an heir. The Valmer name, and all that.'

'Regaining my stolen lands comes first,' he answered.

She watched as he ran a fingertip along one of the table knives on the crisp white cloth. Oh, to be that piece of cutlery. Her thighs trembled and a wavelet of desire lapped her veins. She managed to continue, 'So your sole *raison d'être* is to claw back what you regard as your property?'

'I just want what is mine by right, and what is also yours, Cinderella. Your wicked stepmother, Jane Tremoille, or perhaps I should now refer to her as Lady Welland, suppressed the existence of your father's final will, tossed you out in the streets, and then improved her lot even more by marrying the man she'd always wanted, Lord Welland. Neither she nor Welland has a right to that property, and I mean to haul them through the courts. Don't you want your inheritance?'

'Sir Guy, if you win, it will not be mine. What is yours is yours, and what is your wife's is yours too. Is that not how it is?'

'I'm not offering you a paltry deal, but a very advantageous marriage.'

'If you could prove my father's sleight of hand was the reason the Valmers lost the property in the first place, you would certainly do so. But because you can't, you have to use me instead. I'm a stratagem, that is all.'

'Well, if that is how you wish to view it . . .' He spread a hand upon the table, and the frills at his cuff fell back so that she could see the pulse in his wrist.

'It's too clear to ignore,' she answered, trying not to be aware of his fingers, so fine and perfectly cared for, and the heavy signet ring bearing his family's lion badge. Thoughts of his glove made her avoid his eyes.

He regarded her. 'But you accept what I intend to do?'

'To the Wellands? Yes, why not? He was always a prickly neighbour, quite as disagreeable as his second wife, and with dear Jane now strutting the corridors of Whitend, poor Rowan must abhor visiting home.' Rowan was Lord Welland's son and heir. She'd known him since childhood, and had even been marked to marry him, until his father realized she wasn't going to inherit anything after all. It might have been a successful marriage, she reflected, because although separated by five years and not in love, she and Rowan were certainly fond of each other.

'Rowan knows I've found the will and have been seeking you.'

'I didn't realize you and he were acquainted.'

'He's my distant cousin, and I've taken him

17

under my wing.'

'What is his opinion of all this?' she asked curiously; after all, Lord Welland's marriage to Jane had added Tremoille House and its lands to Rowan's patrimony. Guy's success in court would reverse that.

'He's content for me to win back what he too believes to be mine.'

She was a little hurt. 'He approves of blackmail and coercion?'

Guy lowered his eyes so that his lashes obscured his eyes. 'Well, to be sure, I've been frugal with such awkward details.'

'So, at least you are ashamed of what you do,' she observed quietly.

'No, Beth, I like him and simply see no need to risk any discord.'

'You're ashamed,' she repeated, holding his gaze.

The faintest of smiles turned up the corners of his mouth. 'Think as you wish. Incidentally, he appears to be in love, and not with just another inamorata.'

'Who is she?'

'I have no idea. He's being coy, which leads me to wonder if she is quite, well, acceptable.'

'I'm not acceptable,' she reminded him.

'You have breeding, my dear. I suspect Rowan's sweetheart may not.'

'Good luck to him,' Beth said with feeling. 'If he's truly in love, then I hope they can be happy together.'

Guy raised an eyebrow. 'Amen to that,' he murmured, and was silent for a moment before he changed the subject slightly. 'Did you know that Jane only married your father because his lands abutted Welland's?'

'Nothing about that woman would surprise me.'

'She met both men in the same Worcester brothel. I fear your father was a lecherous old goat, Beth, well known in every bagnio between the Severn and the Thames. I doubt if there was anything he didn't sample at one time or another.'

She didn't appreciate her father being spoken of like that, even though it was the truth. 'Since it is clearly the season for praising dead fathers, yours would appear to have been such a simple-minded, feckless gambler that he was easily duped into parting with valuable property. So let's be fair, Sir Guy, and admit that neither of our sires deserves respect.'

'Esmond Tremoille certainly doesn't, because he cut you, his only child, completely out in favour of his rapacious second wife.'

'But reinstated me,' she pointed out, for her father had told her, as he lay dying of consumption, that he'd made a new will, but he hadn't said where it was. She believed he'd left that information in a mysterious letter he'd lodged with his London lawyers, Withers, Withers & Blenkinsop. She had yet to see that letter.

19

Guy stretched his legs out, and she heard the squeak of his gleaming Hessian boots. It was an oddly warm and evocative sound that again made her sexually conscious of him. He had such lazy grace that her senses were teased by everything he did. Everything. She knew she was trembling, and hoped he could not see. 'Well, whatever his sins in that respect,' she responded, 'he rectified them at the end. Why else did he leave that letter? It contains directions to the whereabouts of the final will, doesn't it? You've read it if you've found the will.'

'No, actually. You see, most infuriatingly, in the letter your father used a code that requires an unidentified book. Certain words on certain pages, you know the sort of thing. Without knowing the book, the letter can't be deciphered.'

'It will be the copy of *Gil Blas* in the library at Tremoille House,' she answered without hesitation, because her father had always liked her to read it to him. 'So, Sir Guy, if you didn't find the will through the letter—which, by the way, you had no business opening—how did you find it?'

'Luck. I chanced to visit the Gloucester home of your father's closest friend, who is now indisposed and confined to bed, and discovered the will hidden at the back of a daub of your father.'

'How very convenient.'

He read her thoughts. 'Oh, no, Beth, I haven't forged anything. I want what is mine, but only within the strict letter of the law. The will's authenticity will be confirmed in court, and with you as my wife, your conniving stepmother will be trounced. By the way, does their marriage make Welland your stepfather?'

'It makes him nothing to me, just as she is nothing to me, and you are nothing to me.' How could she look him in the eyes and utter such a monstrous lie? He was the entire universe to her.

'The feeling is mutual, but nevertheless I am obliged to marry you.'

'Otherwise you'll expose me for stealing money, and maybe even murder.'

'Beth, on your own admission you stole the thousand guineas I paid your stepmother for the stallion, Lancelot.'

'And that is *all* I admit,' she countered, fearing he was about to accuse her of killing Joshua as well. Joshua was an old family servant she'd known since childhood, and Jane had despatched him to the bank in Gloucester with the money, but he'd been thrown from his horse and killed. After being disinherited a year earlier, she, Beth, had returned to look at her former home from a nearby hillside. She'd happened upon Joshua, already dead, and took the guineas she regarded as hers, because Jane had no right to sell Lancelot. No right to anything Tremoille. But then she'd fainted at

21

the roadside, and Guy hadn't passed by on the other side.

Guy watched her face. 'Oh, Beth, I can't help a grudging admiration for the way you sat there in my carriage, clutching that basket stuffed with money. You were a grubby urchin, barefoot and in rags, and I didn't recognize you, even though I'd been seeking you for months. How could I possibly have seen the beauteous Miss Tremoille in the unkempt beggar creature to whom I'd played Good Samaritan?'

'I was terrified you'd look in the basket and find the money,' she admitted.

'Did you love Mannacott?' he asked, with a sudden change of subject.

'He was a good man.' Jake Mannacott was the blacksmith who'd given her a roof over her head when she was destitute. She'd paid her rent with her body—and by teaching his surly adolescent daughter, Rosalind, how to read, write and speak properly. It was a wretched existence from which she'd seized the chance to escape, leaving half the money for Jake. He'd been her first lover, and had adored her. Rosalind, on the other hand, despised her from the outset, and probably danced a jig when she left.

'So he was a good man, but did you love him?' Guy pressed her to answer.

'No. He took me in and was kind to me when I had nothing, so I was—and still am—

very fond of him.'

'He remains besotted with you. I could see that well enough when I spoke to him at Frampney forge, of which, thanks to mysteriously acquiring sufficient money, he is now co-owner.'

Beth didn't answer, and at that moment breakfast was brought, two large plates of bacon, eggs, sausage and fried bread, with tea and toast. As the door closed on the maids, Guy looked at Beth again. 'I trust you like generous helpings?'

'Sir Guy, if there is one thing my time with Jake taught me, it's to appreciate good food.' A wry thought struck her and she smiled to herself.

'Something amuses you?'

'I almost wish Rosalind Mannacott could see me now.'

'Mannacott's daughter? Why?'

'Because she'd hate to know I'm to be Lady Valmer.'

'Why?'

'She sees me as having come between her and her father. I couldn't make her understand that a father's love for his child isn't diminished at all by his love for another woman. Jake made me teach her elocution, reading and writing. She was a very unwilling pupil, which was a shame, because she's pretty, intelligent and quite capable of taking herself out of her present class. Simply to spite me—

23

and her father for taking me in—she deliberately spoke with the broadest Gloucestershire accent imaginable.'

Guy commenced his breakfast. 'So, that was your life with Mannacott, and I can quite understand your eagerness to be free of it, but what of your life with Haldane? Do you love him, Beth?'

Her knife and fork paused. 'Does it matter?'

'Yes. Holy Haldane is—'

'I do wish you wouldn't call him that.'

'Force of habit, my dear.'

'And don't patronize me,' she said tartly.

Their eyes met for a moment. 'Very well, in future I will endeavour not to do either, but I still want to know if you love him.'

'And I'm not going to tell you. It's none of your business.'

'It's very much my business, because this time yesterday you had every intention of marrying him.'

'That was before I learned the whole truth about his brief liaison with Harriet, if liaison it could be called.'

Guy gave a thin smile. 'Ah, yes, Haldane's dishonourable past caught up with him.'

'So did mine,' she reminded him, 'and how can *you* criticize him? Just how honourable is it to compel a woman into submission?'

She was rewarded by the colour that touched his cheeks. 'Beth, I repeat, I offer you a title, wealth, comfort and security. Haldane

24

offered Harriet nothing, until forced to last night. How can you ever have loved such a paltry knave?'

'I ask no questions of your private life, Sir Guy, do not ask of mine.'

'If you think that is how our marriage is going to go on, Beth, you are sadly mistaken. As Lady Valmer you will have no life private from me, and will conduct yourself impeccably. There will be no *billets-doux* exchanged with Haldane, no secret meetings, no contact whatsoever. Nor will there be any other lovers. When my ring is on your finger you become mine, and mine alone. Is that clear?'

'Perfectly.'

'Nor will you do anything else that may reflect badly upon my name.'

She looked at him. 'Such as?'

'Becoming involved in shady matters.'

'I stole money once, that's all.'

'Yes, and if that should ever come out— which won't be through me—you might find yourself charged with Joshua's murder as well. Oh, I accept that you didn't do it, but nevertheless, mud has a very unpleasant way of sticking. Jane Welland will certainly press for it. Then there is the strange matter of Henry Topweather's demise.'

Beth froze. 'Topweather?'

'Don't play the innocent, you know perfectly well of whom I speak. Damn it all, you leased the Dower House through him.' Guy studied her.

'Are you connected with his death?'

She hesitated, but then thought it best to tell the truth. 'Henry Topweather came to the Dower House to blackmail me. He was going to tell you where to find me unless I gave myself to him. I refused, and he tried to rape me. He would have succeeded had not my coachman struck his head with a log.'

'So he was murdered at the Dower House, and then deposited on the coast road?'

'It wasn't murder, but yes to the rest.'

'My, my, Beth, trouble does follow you around.'

'So do you,' she reminded him.

He ignored the remark. 'Is there anything else I should know?'

'Well, I was arrested for rioting outside the Prime Minister's house last summer, and I stole the Prince Regent's handkerchief at the Argyle Rooms. Oh, and I've robbed the Barnstaple mail twice, and the Taunton Flyer once.'

'Very amusing, but please confine yourself to the truth.'

'As you wish. Topweather compelled me to lay illegal bets for him at Belvedere's, on the outcome of the St Clair case. He colluded with Mr Justice Baynsdon, who presided over the matter and happened to be his relative. They needed someone like me to actually go to

26

Belvedere's. If I'd refused, Topweather was going to hand me over to the authorities. He guessed I had something to hide and was probably being sought. So I did as I was told, and used what I had left of the stolen guineas to lay bets of my own. I won a fortune, and was able to lease the Dower House in the knowledge that I could support myself for the rest of my life.'

'How enterprising. And I have now been told all there is?' he asked.

'Yes.'

'So Mannacott and Haldane were your only lovers?'

'Yes, of course they were!' she cried, her indignation so real that he knew it was true.

'Very well, but I needed to know.'

'If I had lain with a whole brigade of guards, I'm sure you'd still marry me to get your hands on my inheritance. Don't pretend that my sexual past matters in the slightest.'

'Beth, it matters a great deal, for I will not have it said that Lady Valmer is no better than a whore.'

'I'm sure it's already being said,' Beth replied quietly. 'I behaved very badly with Landry, it was a midsummer madness that I continued through the autumn up until yesterday. I know we were the talk of the neighbourhood, and that I'm regarded as very shocking. That aside, Jane is certain to know about my months with Jake, and will go

27

around with a bell once she learns you've married me. Be warned that I will be a very embarrassing Lady Valmer.'

'I can weather it, provided you aren't keeping anything else from me, or if you break your marriage vows. Am I clearly understood?'

'You are.'

A resounding silence fell, broken only by the shifting of the fire as they finished the meal. Beth spoke again as she poured the final cup of tea. 'You have been direct about what *I'm* expected to do and not do, but there is one important thing I don't yet know about *your* intentions.'

'And that is?'

'Are you going to share my bed?' Her heart seemed to stop beating as she awaited his reply. She had to know, she *needed* to know.

He tossed his napkin on the table. 'I haven't given it any thought.'

She was nonplussed.

'I would not have thought you'd want me in your bed,' he said then.

'After all you've done, you surely can't think you will stir my desires, sir,' she replied, somehow managing to look and sound as if she meant it.

'I see. Then it seems we are unlikely to awake entwined in each other's loving arms.' He glanced at his fob watch and rose to his feet. 'It's time to leave. Greylake may only be six miles away, but I must call at Culvermine on the way. I'm having the harbour surveyed, with a view to improvements. I won't dally there any longer than necessary, but with so much snow our progress will be slow.'

'Sir Guy . . . ?'

'Yes?'

'I know that you are a great landowner, with interests in many areas, including Culvermine—'

'I *own* Culvermine, lock, stock and barrel of rum,' he interrupted, 'and I intend it to become as fashionable a resort as Brighton itself.'

'And I wish you well in your ambition, but I must return to the matter of our marriage, which apparently is to be in name only. That being so, I wish to know what façade we are to present when we leave this room.' She was apprehensive, because leaving the inn would be her first daylight brush with her new circumstances. And with the full extent of her greatly increased notoriety.

'I'll do whatever you wish, Beth. We can be cold, civil or affectionate. The choice is yours.'

She knew he was recalling last night's kiss, and a blush crept into her cheeks. 'I'm branded a strumpet no matter what, but I will be forgiven a little if they think you've been my true love all along.' *Which you have, God help me.*

'You wish it to be believed that we are reunited lovers?'

'Is such a pretence beyond your capabilities?' she asked provocatively.

'Beth, last night we both proved we are consummate actors. Very well, Beth, in public I will be as loving and attentive as you wish. But in private it will be as we are now. Agreed?'

She nodded, her feelings hidden behind an emotionless visage. 'But there is one more thing, Sir Guy. When we are married, and you have my inheritance, what then? Will you let me go?'

'That remains to be seen. Now, Dickon is just bringing the carriage to the front entrance. Your luggage will be safely on board, so do not think anything will be left behind.' He helped her with the mantle and muff, and then donned his astrakhan-lined greatcoat and top hat, which he'd hung behind the door earlier. 'Are you ready?' As she nodded, he drew her hand firmly over his sleeve and then enclosed it with his. It meant nothing, but was just an outwardly affectionate gesture for the benefit of onlookers beyond the parlour.

The entrance passage was oddly thronged, every doorway having a complement of craning necks. The story of the ruined betrothal ball had spread through the town like wildfire. Whispers abounded, and the atmosphere was so expectant that it seemed to brush Beth's face as she forced a smile to her lips and tilted her head toward Guy. The outer doors were opened, and they stepped out into the snow-decked High Street, where fresh flakes continued to idle through the air.

Dickon, Guy's loyal coachman, was huddled on the box of the dark green travelling carriage, the capes of his brown benjamin coat lifting slightly as a breath of icy moorland air carried through the town. There were several rugs over his knees, and his bushy eyebrows drew together as he saw Beth in daylight. He hadn't recognized her last night at Haldane Hall, but knew her now as the beggar girl his master had helped at the roadside near Tremoille House. Knowing better than to let anything show on his face, he nodded and touched his cocked hat deferentially. 'Good morning, Sir Guy, madam,' he greeted in a Somerset accent.

Moments later he urged the team into action, and the carriage drew away from the inn, taking the road east toward Culvermine and then Greylake Castle.

CHAPTER THREE

In Gloucestershire two days earlier, the Honourable Rowan Welland had ridden to Frampney village, but once there found himself in two minds. As it happened, he'd been in two minds for the few days since

31

attending the Christmas fair in Gloucester, and remained so now he was actually within a few hundred yards of the cause of his dilemma.

He wore an old green greatcoat over his riding clothes, and his top hat was tipped right back on his head, but he had too much natural poise to look disreputable. Romantically good-looking, with wavy dark hair to his shoulders, he was just twenty-one and boyishly slender, with quietly expressive golden brown eyes. But such almost feminine looks were deceptive, because one of his favourite pastimes was prize-fighting, and it was nothing for him to take on much heavier men, even though he knew he'd be trounced and that the watching crowds were gleeful to see a member of the aristocracy beaten into raw steak. He'd once been described as having the charm of an angel, the looks of a dashing pirate captain and the character of a dozen squibs in a fire. All were true.

He leaned one boot on the mounting block outside the George and Dragon, and raised a welcome tankard of strong cider to his lips. He'd ridden down from the snow-covered world of Tremoille House on the Cotswold escarpment, to a frozen grey haze down here in the vale of the River Severn. His gaze was fixed on a skein of smoke rising from the forge at the far end of the vast village green. If he drew back now, nothing more would come of it, but if he rode over to that tempting twist of smoke, he'd be inviting disaster, almost certainly including disinheritance. Oh, he would still eventually be Lord Welland, his father couldn't prevent *that*, but the estates and fortune could certainly go elsewhere. Probably to the as yet unidentified bastard half-brother the old boy was already brandishing like a sabre. A rift of some nature seemed inevitable, even without the thorny problem now exercising Rowan's conscience. His heart—and base male urges—bade him do one thing, but prudence and fear of ostracism urged him to ride away again without delay. He swirled the cider pensively, only too aware that his life was poised at a very important crossroad. But the question was, which course should he take?

At the general store beyond the inn, an ox wagon belonging to the local carrier, a huge, bearded fellow named Johnno Walters, was about to depart for Gloucester, and an altercation arose when one of his passengers tried to take two goats on board without paying extra. The vociferous exchanges brought people out of their cottages and the inn, but Rowan had too much on his mind to take any notice. His horse, a fine chestnut colt, snorted and stamped impatiently, its breath silvery in the brittle air, and Rowan automatically patted its glossy neck. 'All right, boy, all right,' he murmured, but the horse nudged him and capered around irritably, so

33

Rowan sighed, finished the cider, placed the tankard on one of the inn's window ledges, and then vaulted lightly up into the saddle. Indecision still clouded his brow. If ever a man was in a self-made frying pan, it was he. Should he meekly return to his father's gleaming aristocratic table? Or plunge into the all-consuming fire? He glanced once more at the smoke as it wound skyward, and then turned the colt toward it. 'Follow your heart, Rowan, follow your heart,' he breathed.

Frampney lay between the dangerously tidal Severn estuary and the as yet unfinished embankment of the Gloucester and Berkeley Canal. It was a small but pleasing village, with pretty houses and cottages, all in good repair, and well-tended vegetable gardens. The famous village green was said to be one of the largest in England, and boasted three duck ponds. The northern side had fewer properties, being mainly taken up by the redbrick wall and wrought iron gates of Squire Lloyd's manor house. The squire had been much pitied in recent months because of the murder of his licentious son and heir, Robert, who'd been as hated as his father was loved. The squire was the only one to mourn his violent passing.

The closer Rowan drew to the forge, a low, straggling building overhung by leafless trees, the more clearly he heard the rhythmic hammering of the smith at work. Behind the forge stood a neat white house, little more than a cottage, that in summer was drenched in wisteria blooms. He reined in at the forge entrance, through which the fire beamed and flared as if from Hell itself. The old smith, Matty Brown, a huge man well past his prime, with a large belly and unhealthily glistening skin, worked the bellows, while his new partner, Jake Mannacott, whom Rowan now knew to have been Beth Tremoille's lover, fashioned a horseshoe. Jake was a youthful forty, or thereabouts, with a fine, muscular body, narrow hips, and an even-featured face that was twisted into a grimace as he wielded the hammer. His short dark hair, wet with perspiration, had tightened into curls, and his skin was so grimy with smoke that Rowan couldn't imagine him with the dainty, well-bred Beth.

Recognizing him, Jake tossed the hammer aside and plunged the shoe into a bucket of water, before coming out. 'Good morning, sir.' There was no warmth in his brown eyes; in fact they were cold and unfriendly. Had the Honourable Rowan Welland crawled from beneath a cowpat, the blacksmith could not have shown more disdain.

'Good morning, Mannacott.'

'What can I do for you, sir?' The man's voice matched the chill in his eyes.

'I'd like you to change my horse's off fore shoe. It doesn't seem quite as well set as the others, and I can feel it in the ride.'

'As you wish, sir. I'll do it right now.'

'I'm grateful.'

Jake's eyes flickered. Grateful was a word with which he doubted the aristocracy was much acquainted, but he waited politely as Rowan dismounted. The latter paused before handing over the reins. 'Have I offended you?'

'Offended, sir? How could that be?'

'I don't know, which is why I ask. Is it because of what happened at the fair?'

'As I understand it, sir, I owe you my gratitude for looking after my daughter when trouble broke out.'

Rowan shifted a little awkwardly, and hoped he didn't look as guilty as he felt about the very carnal turn of affairs that marked his encounter with Rosalind Mannacott. 'I promise you that no ill befell Miss Mannacott while she was under my protection.'

'I'm sure not, sir, but you must understand that it does Rozzie's reputation no good at all to be alone with a swell such as you, or indeed with any of the village boys.'

'It was unavoidable, and I vow that only Mrs Brown knows of it.' Phoebe Brown was Matty's wife, and had accompanied Rosalind to Gloucester that day.

'Yes, and Johnno Walters,' Jake reminded him, for Rowan had taken Rosalind back to Phoebe Brown outside the Gloucester inn where the Frampney wagon waited.

Rowan glanced back toward the George and Dragon, where the ox wagon was at last moving off from the general store, although whether it was with or without the goats he couldn't tell. 'You don't like my kind, do you?' he enquired bluntly of Jake.

'I have very good reason not to.' The smith curtailed further conversation by leading the colt inside.

Rowan remained tactfully outside, his attention on the little white house to the rear of the forge. Was Rosalind there? Would she come out? Would she even dare? He recalled her words the first time they met, when he'd tried to make her stay with him a little longer. My *father won't like it. I'm not to speak to gentlemen.*

In the house, Matty's wife, Phoebe, put more coal on the kitchen fire, and then put the bucket next to the hearth. She was small, plump and comfortable, with an open, good-natured face and country-pink cheeks. Her white hair was pushed up beneath a simple mobcap, and she wore a corseted, old-fashioned fawn woollen gown, with a clean white neckerchief. An anxious shadow entered her eyes as she looked out of the window at the young gentleman by the forge. She knew him, and that he'd have had a cool reception from Jake. She also knew why.

Phoebe glanced at the girl seated at the scrubbed table, peeling vegetables. Rosalind was seventeen, and such a pretty thing, with long straight silver-blonde hair and forget-me-not eyes set above high cheekbones. She had a dainty figure, with small, upturned breasts, although to be sure, her nipples were always so prominent that it was impossible not to notice them. Still, she couldn't help that, short of binding herself.

Rosalind felt the older woman's gaze, and looked around. 'What is it, Phoebe?'

'Mm? Oh, nothing.'

'I've almost finished these. What would you like me to do afterward? Take the ale out to the forge?' A jug of mulled ale stood waiting by the fire.

'No, my dear, I'll take it in a moment.' Phoebe looked out at Rowan again, knowing it was best to keep the girl inside until he'd gone, but Rosalind noticed the glance, and got up to see what could be of such interest. Her breath caught as she saw Rowan, and Phoebe clasped her arm anxiously. 'No, Rozzie, you're to stay here. Your father is still minded to suspect something went on at the fair between you and Lord Welland's son.'

'Nothing went on!' Rosalind protested, but it was a lie. A good deal had gone on when she and Rowan were separated from Phoebe. They'd done things together on the dark river-bank, and she wanted to do them again. They hadn't lain together, but had been intimate in many ways. It was the first time she'd held a man's most private part in her hand, and stroked it until he came. For those few moments she could have died of delight.

Her first experience of fleshly matters had come when she worked at Poll Barker's tavern in Gloucester. Poll's lump of a son, Ned, was always trying to grope his hands all over her, and press her hand to his crotch, so she'd learned a few things, but it was vicious Master Robert Lloyd who deflowered her simply to be avenged upon her father for some slight or other. Her father found out what had happened, and Robert's body had been found not long after that. She knew her father had done it, helped by foolish Jamie Webb, the village boy who would have married her by now, had it not been that she could not abide him.

The whole business with Robert had frightened her on two counts. First it showed her how heartless men could be toward women, and second it exposed a violent side of her father that she had never suspected before. She didn't want Robert's fate to befall Rowan, who was as different from the squire's son as it was possible to be. The best way to protect him would be to stay here in the house with Phoebe until he'd gone, but now that she'd seen him again, so near and yet so far, all good resolutions evaporated before the heat of her desire. Lying with Robert had taught her to enjoy the feel of a man inside her, enjoying his urgent thrusts and relishing his excitement. And her own. She wanted Rowan Welland inside her like that. Feeling as she did, she knew she had to speak to him, and show with her eyes that she wanted to repeat what they'd done at the fair; that, and much, much more. She turned pleading eyes toward Phoebe, who drew back in dismay.

'I know what you're going to ask, Rozzie, but—'

'*Please*, Phoebe.'

They both looked at the jug of ale, and Phoebe hesitated. It was an error of judgement, because Rosalind always knew the moment to seize her chance. Without waiting for another word, she grabbed the jug and hurried out of the house. She ran down the cinder path between the vegetable and flower gardens, and then out through the gate to the strip of grass that lay between the house and the forge. There she slowed to a more becoming walk, wishing she was wearing the foolish rose silk dress her father had given her on her seventeenth birthday. But it was midwinter, and she must make do with faded blue wool. The closer she drew, the more she succumbed to sexual sensations that made her feel quite weak. Her whole body hungered for him, and it certainly wasn't just the cold that made her nipples crinkle and harden, so they stood out so much they rubbed against her bodice.

Rowan had seen her the moment she left the house, and her haste told him she reciprocated his feelings. A smile lit his face, and she returned it shyly. He was glad his old greatcoat hid the physical evidence of his arousal. Blood pumped so furiously into his loins that the resultant erection throbbed against his thigh, held there by the tightness of his breeches. It was as sudden, fierce and uncontrollable as early boyish excitement, when he only had to think of things sexual to achieve a monstrous pole he'd often had great trouble hiding. Being caught displaying such priapic readiness, especially during his years at Eton, would have been crushingly humiliating; to say nothing of attracting deviant male attention because of his pretty looks. But this was different, because he was in love with an entirely unsuitable girl. He was deliberately stepping into the dangerous unknown . . .

'Good morning, my lord,' Rosalind said, according him a little curtsey.

Her eyes shone as she met his gaze, and for a moment it was as if she were massaging him again, or so his thundering arousal seemed to reflect. He struggled to overcome its overpowering influence. 'Good morning, Miss Mannacott.' He'd given up pointing out to her that he wasn't a lord until his father died.

'How are you?' she asked, but before he could answer, Jake appeared in the forge entrance, his face as dark as thunder as he saw that not only was his daughter speaking alone with a gentleman, but she was without even a shawl.

'What are you doing out here, Rozzie?' the smith demanded.

Rosalind lowered her eyes nervously. 'I—I've brought the ale for you and Matty, Dad.'

'Then hand it over and get back to the house.'

'But, Dad—'

'Now!'

Humiliation reddened her face. 'Please don't be angry, Dad,' she begged.

But Jake was in no mood to be reasonable. 'Get inside,' he repeated, 'and *never* come out in just a dress again! You look no better than a doxy!'

With a choked sob she thrust the jug into his hands and then fled.

Rowan was both embarrassed and angry. 'There's no need to speak to her like that in front of me, Mannacott.'

'I don't need telling how to bring up my daughter,' Jake growled.

'No, of course not, but—'

'With respect, sir, there are no buts.'

Respect? On the contrary, Rowan sensed the spirit of the French Revolution glaring from the blacksmith's eyes.

Jake looked away. 'When I have your horse ready, sir, I'd be obliged if you stayed away from here and had nothing further to do with

Rozzie. Seek female company within your own class, and leave the likes of her to *her* class. Besides, if you think you're going to be the first to have her, you're wrong. Someone else got there first.'

Rowan drew back, appalled. 'Do you *enjoy* belittling and betraying her?' he asked, showing his distaste.

'Just leave her alone, sir, that's all I ask. She's only a lass, and can't be of any real importance in the life of a gentleman. The bastard who ruined her was one such as you, so I must protect her.'

Rowan bit back a cutting reference to Beth's ruin at Jake Mannacott's hands, but thought better of it. Now was perhaps not the time to fall out even more with Rosalind's father.

Jake returned to the forge to finish the colt's shoe, and found Matty falling asleep in his chair, a lighted pipe dangling from his limp fingers. Rowan heard the younger smith's annoyance. 'Matty? Wake up there! You're going to have this place in flames around our bloody ears if you don't take more care!'

Deciding that Jake Mannacott was a curmudgeon without a genial word for anyone, and that the year-long liaison with Beth had to be a myth, Rowan glanced around again. A mile away to the north he could see the five-gabled roof and chimneys of Whitend rising above a windbreak of evergreen trees. It had been his family's home for several centuries, but was now empty because his father and new stepmother preferred Tremoille House up on the escarpment. Their marriage meant that both estates were part of his, Rowan's, heritage, although in his opinion Tremoille House rightfully belonged to his cousin Guy, from whose father it had been tricked in the first place. Rowan knew he himself would forfeit all worldly goods if he embarked on a serious entanglement with Rosalind Mannacott, yet having seen her again he wanted her more than ever. He was bewitched. Enough for the final madness of marriage? Maybe. Just maybe.

He knew that his burning sexual desire was overwhelming him, and that he needed to step back from the brink. After all, it was only a few days since the fair; before which he'd only exchanged a few words with her. Maybe a return to London would cool his ardour. To hell with Christmas at home, enduring the increasing chill between his father and stepmother. Guy had gone to Greylake Castle for the festive season, so his fine townhouse in Park Lane, which was always at Rowan's disposal, suddenly seemed very enticing. But then Rowan thought again. Did he really want to be alone right now? No, he didn't, he'd rather go to Greylake to air his weighty problems with Guy himself. Yes, that's what he'd do.

CHAPTER FOUR

Late that afternoon, Rowan joined his father and stepmother in the drawing-room at Tremoille House, meaning to find the right moment to announce that he would not be celebrating Christmas with them after all, but the stony atmosphere was such that so far he had only lounged silently on a sofa.

He liked Tremoille House, and always had, perhaps because it was unashamedly Tudor. It had never been 'modernised', but remained faithful to its origins in the reign of Henry VIII. The firelit drawing-room had richly coloured tapestries on the oak-panelled walls, and three cartwheel chandeliers depending from the candle-yellowed ceiling. The large carved stone fireplace, big enough to stand in, still bore traces of its original painted decorations, including the blue lion of the Valmers, which was to be found throughout the house. Apart from several sofas upholstered in peach velvet, the chairs, tables, cabinets and portraits were sixteenth-century, and at least four of the chairs were known to have been there since the house had been built. The Valmers had held the property until a very suspect royal flush transferred it to Esmond Tremoille.

The loud rustling of *The Times* turned his

attention to his father, a short, middle-aged man with a paunch, and iron-grey hair that had receded to little more than a monk's tonsure. His cheeks were strangely hollow for such a portly man, and his forehead was very broad, with eyebrows that resembled hairy caterpillars. Cigar ash stained his battered hunting-pink coat, his muslin neckcloth was crumpled, and it was clear that the old tyrant was in a bad mood; not that he was ever in a good one. What was it this time? His usual gripes, from the enforced lowering of rents and the price of corn, to the common people's increasing propensity to riot for their rights? Or might he have learned that Guy had found the missing will, and realized the Tremoille possessions weren't quite as securely his as he'd thought? No, if that were the case, at the very least Jane would be sporting a black eye.

The new Lady Welland stood by a window, silhouetted against the snowy glare. It had to be said that although in her fifties she was still very handsome. The willowy figure of her youth had thickened a little around her waist, but her back was straight and she held herself well. Her salt-and-pepper blonde hair, pinned beneath a decorative lace day bonnet, teetered on the brink of turning fully grey, but her china blue eyes retained both their clarity and their duplicity. He didn't know much about her origins, except for persistent rumours about an infamous Worcester bordello. Be that as it may, she certainly *appeared* to be a lady through and through, dressed in a high-waisted crimson merino gown with lace trimming at the gathered wrists, and a gold-and-brown cashmere shawl draped loosely over her arms. Elegant, yes, but she was a study in gloom.

Rowan wanted to loathe her, not least because of what she'd done to Beth, but she had a wry sense of humour, and was disarmingly honest about regretting her second marriage. Not that she deserved sympathy, as she herself would be the first to admit. She had behaved badly, and was reaping the harvest. For the past two days, however, it had become clear that something else was wrong, and Rowan could not imagine what it was. Jane already knew that the lost will was now found, and there hadn't been any further word of Guy's quest for Beth. Rowan felt guilty about the will, because Guy hadn't wanted anyone to know it was now in his possession, but Jane knew because of the Honourable Rowan Welland's clacking tongue. He hoped Guy didn't discover his lamentable indiscretion. The thought so pricked his conscience that he got up to pour himself a measure from the decanter of cognac on a nearby table.

The Times was shuffled almost deafeningly. 'It's a little early for that, boy!' his father growled.

Provoked, Rowan poured the cognac anyway, bringing further ire down upon himself. 'Damn you, boy!' Thomas cried, gripping the newspaper as if to swat his son like a fly. The simmering dislike on his face should have withered his son and heir on the spot, but Rowan couldn't resist antagonizing him even more.

'Don't worry, Father, I'm about to relieve you of my tiresome presence.'

Thomas's brows beetled suspiciously. 'And what does *that* mean?'

'I'm leaving today. I intend to spend the night at an inn.' From the corner of his eyes Rowan saw Jane turn in silent dismay, but Thomas erupted incredulously from his chair.

'You're what? Before we've had so much as a mince pie?' he cried.

The thought of eating mince pies with his obnoxious sire was so unlikely as to be comical, but Rowan's face didn't alter. 'Yes, Father, before even that.'

'Why bother to come here at all if you intend to fuck off before giving yourself a chance to even fart?'

'Charmingly put. As it happens, a swift departure wasn't my original intention,' Rowan answered levelly. 'I came here meaning to stay for the entire festive season, but I see no reason to suffer because of your ill humour.'

'Damn it all, boy; I have reason to be ill-humoured!' Thomas bellowed, spittle flying. 'You're a feckless ne'er-do-well, sent down from Oxford, and then arrested for driving a curricle so dangerously that you forced Lord Fitzroy-Digby's carriage to overturn. Next you were caught in a compromising position with no fewer than three married women, and throughout all this mayhem, you proceeded to get yourself pulverized in so many prizefights that I marvel you can still draw breath. All this is supposed to make *me* jolly and devil-may-care?' He spluttered with fury, and not a little self-pity, as he added, 'And now your stepmother adds to my burden by announcing her wish to live at Whitend in the New Year, obliging *me* to support two households at the same time.'

So that was the reason for the heavy atmosphere, Rowan thought, meeting Jane's wry glance.

Thomas had not finished. 'The value of my shares fell almost overnight after Waterloo, and I bitterly regret not having capitalized when advanced news of the victory was sent by pigeon to the banker Rothschild.'

Rowan's lips parted. 'Did you say by *pigeon*?'

'Yes. It seems they not only fly home, but can bring messages too. I therefore had a few hours of prior knowledge, but didn't act. Oh, I could have made a killing, but instead I dallied.' He glared at Jane. 'With you, as I

49

recall.'

Her eyebrow twitched, but she didn't rise to the bait.

His complaining continued. 'So I missed my chance, and paid the price. Now my tenants wring their hands about rents, which I've reduced, but *still* they complain. And now, when there is a glimmer of good news because the price of corn has risen to one hundred and three shillings a quarter, my blasted son decides to ruin Christmas by buggering off because staying don't please him.'

'Given your low opinion of me, I'd have thought you'd be relieved,' Rowan answered. 'And if I'm not here, I'm not leeching from your purse. But from whom do *you* leech, eh, Pa?'

'No one, damn it!'

'On the contrary, you suck the very blood out of the poor. While you and other landlords rejoice about the rising price of corn, the poor are weeping because their bread costs even more.'

'So, we have a hedge preacher in our midst,' Thomas observed acidly.

'Maybe even an anarchist,' Rowan replied, enjoying his sport. 'Did you know there was a meeting in Gloucester yesterday? It was attended by farm workers and factory labourers alike, united in their grievances against the establishment. That's you, Daddy. So while you're seated by your roaring fire, your belly full of fine food, bewailing your comfortable lot in life, there's revolution in the air.'

A heavy silence fell upon the room as Thomas wrestled with his speechless fury, but then he found his tongue again. 'If you leave this house now, my laddo, I will disown you.'

'Then disown me, because I'm going.'

Jane gasped. 'For pity's sake, Rowan—!'

'No, Jane, I've had enough of this.'

Thomas advanced, and halted close enough for Rowan to taste his breath. 'You think you can call my bluff and get away with it?'

'No, Pa, because if you recall, you've already threatened to replace me with your by-blow,' Rowan replied, 'so I imagine the moment has come for you to reach into the relevant midden and produce the fellow.'

'Have a care, sir, for I can deny you all future comfort.'

Rowan was beyond caring. 'Do what you want, because I'll be the next Lord Welland whether you like it or not.'

'A threadbare lordling, while your half-brother Edward lives in style,' Thomas taunted.

'Edward? Are we to be enlightened with his surname, which clearly cannot be Welland?'

'Barker, Edward Barker.'

Rowan's lips parted, and he stared. '*Ned* Barker?' he asked incredulously.

Jane looked curiously at him. 'You know

51

this person, Rowan?'

'His mother's tavern is one of the most notorious in Gloucester.'

Thomas rounded on her. 'You keep your nose out of this, madam, for it doesn't concern you.'

As she resumed her study of the view outside, an almost snarling Thomas resumed his bullying of Rowan. 'Yes, sir, Ned Barker, who'll be only too glad to step into your worthless shoes'

Rowan laughed. 'So, you are the lord who dibbled Poll Barker? She has always boasted that her boy has aristocratic blood, but no one believed her because her precious Ned is such a cretinous oaf! Do you *really* imagine you can bring him into your household? He'll probably piss in the fire, scratch his balls at the table, and handle the maids in front of the Bishop of Gloucester.'

For once, Thomas was not drawn. 'If you leave, boy, he'll be installed here, cretinous oaf or not.'

'Then send for him this instant, because I'm going.' Rowan swept his father an insolent bow, and left the room.

Dumbfounded, Thomas gaped after him. For all his threats and bluster, he'd never actually believed Rowan would force a break between them. The drawing-room fell utterly silent, except for the fire in the hearth.

Jane remained motionless at the window,

gazing out as if nothing had happened. She wasn't about to give Thomas cause to tear into her as well, and after a moment Thomas resumed his chair and unfolded the newspaper as if it offended him. He did everything loudly, Jane thought, even lovemaking, except that love did not enter into it. She clasped her hands neatly before her. How she despised him now, and yet, incredible as it seemed, for most of her adult life she had been hopelessly in love with him. Heaven alone knew why, for he was no oil painting, and certainly wasn't a Romeo. She shuddered to think he was now sitting in the very chair where, before their marriage in the summer, she'd been infatuated enough to suck his wretched little dick. Now the mere thought of it revolted her. She wished she could go to Whitend right away, but Rowan had rather stolen her thunder, so it was probably wiser to leave arrangements as they were. The Welland country seat no longer suited Thomas, who had removed up here to Tremoille House after a terrifyingly vivid nightmare that he would die horribly in floodwater from the Severn and the canal embankment. It would be a suitable fate for such a bad-tempered, violent, morose, grasping, libidinous old ram, she thought cordially.

But she herself was hardly a shining example, she thought, recalling her astonishing social climb out of a Worcester whorehouse

53

into the aristocracy. She'd still be there if Esmond Tremoille hadn't offered marriage. As his wife she'd pursued her own greedy goals by determining to get rid of his inconvenient daughter, Beth. Eventually Esmond had believed the lies he was told about the girl, and changed his will in his wife's favour, but then he reconsidered and secretly made another will that restored Beth to everything. It was so secret that no one knew where it was. She, Jane, had searched high and low, intending to destroy it, but it had eluded her. She had even gone so far as to instruct her faithful butler, Mordecai Bolton, to burn to the ground the premises and records of Esmond's Gloucester lawyer, Beswick. It was unfortunate that Beswick happened to be in the building at the time, but there was nothing that could be done about that. How galling that the will should turn up anyway, and was now in Guy Valmer's clever hands. But before he'd found it, she had successfully argued that it had never existed. Thus the courts permitted the previous will to stand, and she had everything. Her first act had been to turn Beth out of the house; the second had been to set about marrying Thomas Welland, who didn't love her but wanted her inheritance. If Guy Valmer found and married Beth, and then produced the infernal will, Thomas Welland's violent fury would descend upon his untruthful Lady Welland.

Looking out of the window again, she tried to put such discomforting facts from her mind by simply enjoying the matchless view over the park. The sun was fast sinking in a nightmarish blaze of red, purple and gold that tinted the Cotswold snow. The park sloped down toward the western edge of the Cotswold escarpment, below which spread the flat patchwork vale. The motionless midwinter air was so cold that distance was hazy, although she could still see Gloucester cathedral, and the Severn winding south to the estuary. Whitend was somewhere down there too. And soon, God willing, would she be.

*   *   *

In his rooms, Rowan was ready to depart. Wearing his old greatcoat, his top hat tapping against the back of his calf, he stood looking at himself in the tall gilt-framed mirror in his dressing-room. What did he see looking back at him? A man of noble principle who refused to prostitute himself in the face of his father's bullying? Or a good-for-nothing who didn't deserve a sou?

Both, probably, he decided ruefully, although there was no denying the honour of his feelings for Rosalind. He was tempted to drive to Frampney tonight and take her away from her brute of a father. They could stay at an inn, and make passionate and beguiling love all night. Even thinking of her lovely eyes and little upturned breasts, aroused him so that a damned tree trunk sprang from his loins.

Hearing his travelling carriage at the front of the house, he left his rooms to go down the staircase, past all the Tremoille portraits that no one had bothered to remove. Bolton hastened to open the front door. The butler was a lanky man of about fifty, with silky light-brown hair and spaniel eyes, and had been with Jane since before her marriage to Esmond Tremoille. The truth was that he'd once been the doorman at the Worcester brothel, but these days only he and Jane knew that. 'I wish you a safe journey, sir,' he said, his voice as deep and guttural as his appearance was soft and smooth.

'Thank you, Bolton.' Rowan pulled on his gloves and tapped his top hat more firmly on his head. 'Oh, and the compliments of the season.'

'And you, sir.'

'Please extend my sincere regrets to Lady Welland, but not within my father's hearing. Tell her I'd like to offer my support, but if I don't leave, my father and I will probably come to blows.'

'I'll be discreet, sir.'

Rowan stepped out beneath the stone porch into the dying day and then entered the waiting carriage. As he drove away, he knew his estrangement from his father was going to be permanent, because no lord, least of all one like Thomas Welland, could be expected to accept a blacksmith's daughter as his daughter-in-law.

*   *   *

Rosalind, Jake, Phoebe and Matty had just enjoyed a hearty meal of mutton stew and dumplings, and a pleasantly quiet evening might have ensued had Jake been able to hold his tongue about Rowan.

'Well, Rozzie, what have you got to say for yourself, eh? Running out in your undress to that Welland swanky?' His brown eyes were hard and accusing, his mood having changed abruptly after laughing at Matty's jokes a moment since.

Rosalind's cheeks flamed. 'I wasn't in my undress!'

'No? Well, as far as I'm concerned, you were just that. If you don't mend your ways, girl, I'll see you married off as soon as look at you.'

Phoebe frowned at him. 'Enough, Jake!'

'No, Phoebe, it's got to be said. After that trouble with Master Robert, I'm not about to take any more nonsense from this silly chit of a girl.'

Rosalind gazed at him with tears in her eyes. Why had he started saying all this? Everything had been good, but now, all of a sudden, he was going on at her as if she went with every man she met.

Jake held her gaze. 'I'll not have any more of it, Rozzie, is that clear? If that Welland swell comes here again, you're to stay in the house, or if he sees you outside, you're to turn from him and go inside. And if you don't, and he persists, then he'll go the same way as that Lloyd tomcat. Do you understand?'

'Yes,' she said in a small voice, hanging her head.

Phoebe couldn't bear it. 'Jake Mannacott, you are a great bully at times, indeed you are!'

'It's not bullying, Phoebe, it's keeping an eye out for my daughter.' Jake continued to look at Rosalind. 'Know this, girl, if I catch so much as a *whiff* of trouble, I'll hand you over to Jamie Webb, who's daft enough to want you to wife.'

'I can't *abide* Jamie Webb!'

'Maybe so, but he can give you a good home. He's the only lad in the village to have made anything of himself. He earns well in Squire Lloyd's employ, more than anyone else of his age. I think he'd suit you very well.'

Rosalind rose with a tearful gasp. 'You wouldn't, Dad! You wouldn't!'

'Look at me! Do I seem to be joking?'

She stared. 'I hate Jamie Webb, and I hate you!' she whispered, then ran to the door to the narrow staircase and ran up to her room.

Jake gazed after her. 'It's for her own good,'

58

he insisted.

Phoebe sighed loudly, and Matty rattled his pipe between his teeth. 'Not well done, Jake, my boy, not well done,' he muttered.

Jake reached for the jug of ale he'd sent Rosalind to bring from the George and Dragon. 'I have to do these things, Matty, otherwise she'll come to a bad end.'

Matty and Phoebe exchanged glances, and nothing more was said.

Up in her room, Rosalind was seated on the edge of her little bed, her fists clenched as she wept bitter, silent tears. She'd never have believed she could hate her father, but she did. He wasn't the kind, gentle man she'd thought, but a vile-tempered brute who thought nothing of choking a man to death. That's what he'd done to Robert Lloyd, throttled the life out of him, then walked away as if nothing had happened. Jake Mannacott had a black side now that he'd never had before Beth Tremoille ruined everything. It had to be Beth's doing, because she'd brought bad luck with her. Well, maybe not all of it was bad luck . . .

Rosalind's sobs died away as she glanced at the chest of drawers in the corner, and at the bottom drawer in particular. Getting up, she listened at the door for a moment, and hearing no sign of anyone coming upstairs, went to kneel in front of the chest. She drew the bottom drawer right out, and set it on the floor, then leaned in to get something she'd hidden right at the back. It was a neatly folded pillowslip, oddly heavy and lumpy because it had something inside, something that rustled and jingled.

Holding her breath, she opened it and looked at the crumpled banknotes and gleaming guinea coins. 480 guineas, and no one knew she had it. There had originally been 500, but the difference had gone to her father for buying into the forge. She could hear Beth's voice now. *The money is for your father.* That was the last they'd seen of her. Rosalind ran a fingertip over the money. She knew she shouldn't have kept anything, let alone nearly all of it, but what Jake Mannacott didn't know he couldn't grieve over. On coming here to Frampney she'd dreamed of spending the rest of her life with Robert Lloyd, and would have used the money as a secret dowry. That hadn't happened, of course, and she was glad of it now, because of Rowan. If *he* were to want her—properly want her—she'd have all this to give . . .

Suddenly she recalled what Beth had said to her before leaving. *I couldn't care less what you want, Rosalind, because I think you are a malicious little spit-cat who should have been drowned at birth.*

Rosalind smiled as she replaced the pillowslip and then the drawer. 'I'm going to do better in life than you, Beth Tremoille. And when I'm a fine lady, I hope you have to drop a curtsey to me.'

CHAPTER FIVE

After leaving Porworthy *en route* for Greylake Castle, Dickon drove Guy's travelling carriage slowly east through uncleared snow. The land was still hilly, and twice he had to engage extra horses to pull up a particularly steep incline, but then, at about midday, they reached the little port of Culvermine, where a string of bathing huts along the beach already heralded the prosperous and fashionable future Guy planned. Beth was accommodated at a quayside inn while Guy conducted his business, and then the journey to Greylake was resumed. Not long after leaving Culvermine, the road skirted a desolate salt marsh that had formed between the Bristol Channel and the northern edge of Exmoor. Meandering rivulets and winter-dead plants marked the marsh, with one or two small pools where seabirds congregated, and the sea was a mile north of the original shoreline. Then, rising as eerily as Glastonbury Tor, Beth saw a prominent outlier of the high moor, topped by what looked like a medieval watchtower.

'That's Coneygarth Hill; Greylake lies behind it,' Guy explained. 'Coneygarth means "rabbit enclosure".'

'I'm aware what it means, sir.'

The ghost of a smile appeared on his lips. 'Well, you may not be aware that the hill once guarded the mouth of the River Evell creek, which was wide enough and deep enough for seagoing vessels. The tides came right in past the town of Greylake to the foot of the castle tor, and there was even a shipbuilding industry of sorts, but over the centuries the sea retreated and a bar of silt, now thickly wooded, completed the abandonment. There's a landlocked freshwater lake that's fed by the Evell and other Exmoor streams and overflows to the marsh by way of a weir. It didn't give Greylake its name, that was due to the fact that the sea was always particularly grey there.'

Like your eyes, she thought, but said, 'I find it hard to picture what it must have been like.'

'Well, we would be swimming now, not driving,' Guy replied mordantly.

'Not a pleasant thought,' she said with a shiver, 'especially as I cannot swim.'

'I can, and I promise you that such is your importance to me at the moment, I would make certain of rescuing you.'

'Leaving me to suppose you'd let me sink if you'd already regained Tremoille House,' she murmured.

'You think me so cynical?' He stretched his legs, placing a gleaming boot on the seat beside her. She was conscious of the slight squeak of leather, and the tautening of his breeches against his lean but strong thighs.

As the road began to curve around the foot of the hill, she glanced up at the summit. 'Is that a watch tower?'

'In a manner of speaking. It's a folly built by my great-grandfather, who was convinced there was a sea serpent in the Bristol Channel, and that it sometimes came ashore on the marsh. It never appeared, but he never stopped hoping.'

She found herself remembering a summer's day on the shore at Lannercombe, when Landry told her the story of the mermaid said to live in the bay. Everything had been so romantic that day that she'd known she would take him as her lover. 'I wonder if the sea serpent story has anything to do with the mermaid legend at Lannercombe?'

'So, you've heard of that, have you?'

'Landry told me,' she replied without thinking.

His eyes cooled. 'Would that be before or after he enticed you to his bed? Let me see now, I'd hazard it was before, because it's just the sort of romantic nonsense he'd employ when intent upon seduction.'

She turned her head away. 'I don't intend to discuss him with you.'

'Look away if you wish, but I know I've touched a nerve. There are many things I should tell you of Haldane, Beth. Has it never occurred to you to wonder why he was on his way home to Haldane at the very time Wellington and the army were confronting Napoleon at Waterloo?'

She didn't respond, because it *had* crossed her mind.

'Let me enlighten you. Your beloved Landry was dishonourably discharged. He lost heavily at cards and accused another player of cheating. He was challenged, and there was a duel. At least, there should have been a duel, but Haldane turned before the order was called, and killed his opponent in cold blood. He tried to abscond, but was caught and imprisoned. Then they cashiered him and threw him out on his scabrous ear. There are also some unsavoury rumours that the Hanoverian horse upon which he pranced in full hussar regalia, even though he no longer had any right, wasn't his at all, but had been stolen from a wounded Prussian officer whom he then left for dead.'

She knew which horse he meant. Landry had given it to her as a present. She could hear his voice now. *'His official name is Sleipnir, after Odin's six-legged steed, but I just call him Snowy.'* 'I don't believe a word of this,' she said at last.

'Why? Surely he's done enough to prove he's not exactly a saint? His conduct toward your friend Harriet Bellamy is evidence enough.'

64

The flush on her cheeks intensified. 'He didn't know about that,' she insisted.

'We've been here before, Beth, and I still say he *should* have known. I wish you would see him for the louse he is.'

She refused to be further drawn, and instead watched the darkening scenery. The road forked, to the left continuing east toward Bridgwater, to the right leading over the wooded bar Guy had mentioned. Then she had her first view of Greylake, which occupied a natural amphitheatre, in front of which, where tides had once rolled, was a white, frozen lake, surrounded by an area of flat meadows and parkland. The little town was sheltered by Coneygarth Hill to the north, then by the eastern flank of Exmoor and a quarter of a mile to the south by a second, almost conical outlier, upon which rose the castle, a partially ruined medieval fortress of towers, turrets, battlements and curtain walls. It was very romantic, even in the depths of winter, but Beth also found it forbidding, because the unknown awaited her there.

The road suddenly turned sharply south from Coneygarth Hill, around the corner of a very old ivy-covered inn and then down the town's wide main street. She would learn that the inn was supposedly haunted, and that Rowan had once slept there for a dare. Next they passed a strange octagonal structure standing on low pillars. It was the old yarn market, and was built entirely of wood, except for the gabled roof.

In spite of the snow, the town was busy, with Christmas in the air and people hurrying about their business. They all, without exception, seemed pleased to see Guy's carriage returning to the castle. The houses were mostly whitewashed and tidy, some low and thatched, others tall with slate roofs. Curls of smoke drifted from chimneys, and bell-ringing practice was in progress at the large spired church. It was all very prosperous, with shops for most needs—a general store, butcher, baker, haberdashery, chandlery and a cobbler—as well as two more inns, a house with a notice in a front window announcing dressmaking services, and an ironmongery of sorts next to a blacksmith's forge, where the sound of hammering brought Jake sharply to Beth's mind.

Closer to the southern hill, Beth saw that a pleasing Jacobean mansion, brick with stone facings and mock battlements, rose elegantly among the ruins of the original medieval fortress. The castle wasn't the highest point of the tor, because a smaller conical knoll rose to one side of the mansion, and its summit had been levelled to accommodate an elegant summerhouse or gazebo.

Dickon cracked the whip, and the carriage jolted forward as the tired horses flung themselves into the steep climb up the hill. At last the hoofs and wheels clattered on snow-cleared cobbles where the road divided into three. To the right lay the stables and the staghounds' kennels, straight ahead was the great medieval gatehouse, and to the left was a relatively new carriage road that provided a much kinder ascent around the side of the hill, past the curtain wall and partly subterranean kitchens. At last the weary team trotted along a wide, flambeaux-lit gravel drive across the snowy lawns of what Beth would later learn was called the Green Court, and then, at last, Dickon finally applied the brakes in front of the castle's three-storeyed porch.

'Welcome home, Beth,' Guy said in the sudden silence.

Home? How could this place ever be that to her?

Two footmen hastened down a short flight of walled steps that were guarded by stone Valmer lions exactly like those at Tremoille House, and Guy alighted. Cold air swept in, bringing the yelps of the staghounds in their kennels further down the hill, and the calls of roosting peacocks.

Guy held out his hand. 'Beth?'

She accepted rather unwillingly, feeling that her fate would be sealed the moment she set foot in Greylake. But then she stepped down, and the deed was done. She looked around as Guy directed the footmen concerning the luggage. There were two towers in the curtain wall, one dilapidated and beyond repair, the other complete in every detail. The door at the base opened and a tall, stooping clergyman emerged. Behind him she saw a candlelit chapel, with a fine stained glass window. Was it being prepared for the wedding? She didn't know if her secret heart quickened with anticipation, or turned over with trepidation.

Guy glanced from directing the footmen in time to observe her face. 'I feel I wouldn't be flattered by your thoughts at this moment.'

'You probably wouldn't,' she replied.

'It is because I've been cruel enough to tear you sobbing from Holy Haldane's undeserving arms?'

'You said you wouldn't call him that.'

'I'm too weak to resist.'

'Weak is one thing you are not.'

He smiled again. 'Would you prefer me to be spineless and vacillating, Beth?'

She turned away under the pretence of looking at the house. She wanted him the way he was, strong, clever, witty, disparaging, single-minded, arrogant and unbelievably desirable; she wanted him to sweep her into his arms and match her desire with his kisses. She wanted, but she wouldn't have. Hers was the hapless role of the unwanted but very necessary bride.

'Smile, Beth, for we must convince the servants we are lovers.' He drew her right hand from her muff and then over the arm of his greatcoat.

Somehow she summoned a happy, upturned curve to her lips, and allowed him to usher her up the steps and into the great hall, where lighted chandeliers banished the gathering shadows, and a small army of servants waited. Among them, wearing a brown coat, his grey-speckled hair tied back, she recognized the sallow-faced agent, Bradfield, whom she had once encountered at Haldane Hall with Landry. Everyone stared at her so obviously that she felt like a specimen under glass, but then the strutting butler, Gardiner, white-haired and possessed of an odd stoop that projected his posterior, cleared his throat and they lowered their eyes as one. Then he stepped forward with a bow. 'Welcome home, Sir Guy.'

'Gardiner.'

The man turned to Beth. 'Welcome to Greylake, Miss Tremoille.'

'Thank you, Gardiner,' she replied, smiling and inclining her head.

The butler turned urgently to Guy. 'Sir Guy, Bradfield wishes to speak to you on a pressing matter.'

'Pressing? Very well, tell him he'll have my attention directly.'

'Yes, sir.' Gardiner assisted Guy with his greatcoat and hat, and then withdrew.

Guy turned to Beth again, took her hand to raise it to his lips, but then decided to pull her into his arms to kiss her instead. She heard the watching servants gasp, and sensed their exchanged glances and low whispers, but he persisted with the kiss, even sinking his fingers into the hair at the nape of her neck. It was a gesture made for the benefit of the staff, who had no idea of its true emptiness.

Somehow she managed to trade him false kiss for false kiss, but found it very hard indeed. This time she felt daunted by this self-imposed punishment. Maybe she was simply tired after all that had happened. Whatever the reason, she struggled to maintain the agreed façade, and when he looked at her in surprise, she couldn't conceal her confusion and embarrassment.

'What's this, Beth?' he whispered. 'Where's your acting spirit?'

'I'm tired, sir,' she answered, 'and I find it embarrassing to kiss you in front of all your servants.'

He studied her, and for a dreadful moment she thought he'd perceived the truth about her feelings for him, but then he smiled apologetically. 'Perhaps I've misjudged on this occasion,' he conceded, and then added, 'I trust it is not another misjudgement to have arranged our wedding to take place in the morning.'

Her eyes widened with shock. 'So soon?'

'I see no purpose in delaying,' Guy replied.

'But, how did you make all the

arrangements? You only found me yesterday.'

'I sent instructions here before I interrupted your betrothal ball.'

'How sure of yourself you were,' she murmured, 'but what of the licence?'

'Oh, that has been in my possession for some time now. They are simple enough to obtain if one has friends in the right places. All that's required now is the relevant date, signatures and so on.'

'And it's legal?'

'I never do anything illegal, Beth. Be assured that the licence will stand up in a court of law. Tomorrow you will become Lady Valmer, and then I will begin in earnest to reclaim what was stolen from my father.'

'How romantic our union will be,' she observed.

'I did not promise romance, Beth, and nor, I suspect, do you seek it.'

If only he knew the truth, she thought unhappily.

Guy took her hand again, this time brushing it only fleetingly to his lips, and then he left her to go to speak with Bradfield.

Beth looked around the entrance hall. It was very grand, with ceiling plasterwork in a delicate 'spider's web' pattern, upper walls of the purest white and lower walls cloaked in fine linen-fold panelling. A handsome octagonal table, superbly inlaid, stood in the centre of the gleaming wooden floor and, as well as several maroon-upholstered sofas, there were some excellent examples of medieval ash bobbin chairs. Elaborate displays of ancient weapons adorned the upper walls, among them Tudor flintlock muskets, and Guy's return had been anticipated with lavish Christmas decorations. Kissing boughs and red-ribbon bows hung between the chandeliers, and garlands were draped around the doors and the immense stone fireplace set into the west wall. A luxuriant arrangement of seasonal foliage graced the octagonal table and in the fireplace flames leapt and crackled around fresh logs, warming a trivet of clove-spiked oranges in the hearth. The rich, spicy aroma hung pleasantly in the air, somehow conjuring thoughts of Christmases long gone, when mummers performed, jesters played the fool and guests celebrated before a dais where the lord and his lady sat in honour.

She was so lost in thought that she didn't see a woman approach her. 'Madam?'

Beth gave a start. 'Yes?'

The woman was about forty, of medium height and comfortable build, with a square, rather stern face, cold blue eyes and heavy brown brows. A plain, heavily starched mobcap was pinned to her hair, and long, unexpectedly thick brown ringlets fell to the shoulders of her high-throated lilac wool dress. 'I'm Mrs Bradfield, the housekeeper, madam, but Sir Guy wishes me to attend you. I will do my best by you until a proper maid can be engaged in London.'

'Bradfield?' Beth glanced at the agent, with whom Guy was now in deep conversation.

'Mr Bradfield is my husband, madam.'

Beth smiled, hoping to soften the other's manner. 'I'm sure there will be no need to look for a replacement.'

The housekeeper displayed no sign of emotion. 'As you wish, madam.'

Beth's heart sank. The woman was clearly the castle dragon, although, on reflection, perhaps she was too cold to breathe flames. Maybe the sea serpent had come ashore after all. *Oh, Mrs Cobbett, how I wish you were here with me . . .* Beth longed for her beloved housekeeper at the Dower House. And Billy the coachman and Molly the maid. What a happy little household they had been.

'May I congratulate you upon your betrothal, Miss Tremoille?'

'Thank you, Mrs Bradfield.'

'I'm to show you to Lady Valmer's rooms.'

'I'm not that yet,' Beth pointed out.

'But you will be tomorrow, madam.'

It would seem that everyone at Greylake Castle was aware of the imminent nuptials, only the bride herself had remained in ignorance, Beth thought.

Mrs Bradfield continued, 'The rooms belonged to Sir Guy's late mother, and are always occupied by the principal lady of the

73

family. Sir Guy sent word yesterday that they were to be aired and made ready for you. If you will follow me?'

She began to lead the way through to the staircase hall.

CHAPTER SIX

Beth followed Mrs Bradfield into the inner staircase hall, where candles shone brightly, and the melodic chimes of a black-lacquered Chinoiserie longcase clock dropped gently into the relative quiet. Family portraits, some of which had probably once hung at Tremoille House, looked down from the shadowy walls, and another fresh log crackled in a massive stone fireplace, which this time had a carved oak overmantel.

There were more spiced oranges in the hearth, and their scent drifted pleasingly around Beth as she was conducted toward a splendid Jacobean oak staircase. Mrs Bradfield lit a candle at a small table of candlesticks and candelabra that stood beside the newel post, and then began to ascend. The staircase turned back upon itself at a half-landing where three graceful gothic tracery windows revealed a twilight of yellow-grey snowclouds, edged with the violent shades of sunset.

At the top of the staircase, a mahogany door gave on to a long gallery, tapestry-hung and spacious. It was unlit, and the housekeeper's trembling candle flame smoked and fluttered so much that she had to protect it with her cupped hand. Halfway along, she opened one of several doors and stood aside for Beth to go inside.

Beth entered a room that was illuminated by the dancing light of the fire and, as the housekeeper attended to more candles, the shadows retreated to reveal furnishings in shades of apricot and rich cream. The soft colours were enhanced by dark wall panelling and a heavily carved four-posted bed. Figured velvet curtains were drawn across the windows, the highly polished oak floor was scattered with several rugs, and the cinnamon scent of carnations floated from a crystal vase of hothouse blooms on the ottoman at the foot of the bed. A glass-domed ormolu clock on the mantelshelf began to whir and then chime prettily. Clearly not all the castle clocks were synchronized, Beth noted.

Mrs Bradfield went to open a door beside the fireplace. 'Your dressing-room, madam.' Two housemaids were inside, discreetly unpacking and putting Beth's clothes away in wardrobes and chests of drawers. They started around as the door opened, and smothered little giggles before hastily continuing their task. The housekeeper frowned at them. 'Miss

Tremoille doesn't wish to be disturbed by your noise, so finish your tasks in silence and then leave in the same manner.'

Closing the door again, Mrs Bradfield began to help Beth out of her travelling clothes. 'Dinner will be served in two hours' time, madam. Would you care for a dish of tea, or some other refreshment in the meantime?'

'Yes. Actually . . .' Beth suddenly felt daunted by the prospect of facing Guy again. It had been a long day and she was tired. Much better to sleep before their next meeting. 'Mrs Bradfield, please bring me some tea now, and then some light supper an hour after that. I wish to retire early.'

'As you wish, madam.' If the woman was surprised, she did not show it. She took Beth's cloak, hat and muff to the maids in the dressing-room, and returned. 'Will there be anything else, madam?'

'No, that will be all.'

There was a noticeable hesitation. 'Is all well, madam?'

Beth smiled faintly. 'Thank you for troubling to ask, Mrs Bradfield, but I assure you that all is as well as it can be.' Take that whichever way you wish, she thought, breathing out with relief as the woman withdrew.

Going to a window, she held the curtain aside. It was virtually dark now, and she saw several snowflakes drift past the glass. The

76

room faced over the Green Court, where the torches still flickered red and gold on the lying snow. Her gaze was drawn to the tower with the chapel. It was closed and unlit, giving no hint of the shining place of worship within. Tomorrow she and Guy would be married there, yet only yesterday she had been dancing the night away in Landry's arms, feeling confident of future happiness. She lowered her eyes, knowing she was sprinkling too many rose petals. Yes, she had been happy with Landry, but she hadn't loved him, not in the way she loved Guy, and she had certainly become increasingly aware of flaws in his character. It hadn't only been because she knew he'd fathered an illegitimate child— she thought by the former maid, Carrie Markham—but because she'd learned he'd ordered poachers on his land to be shot. Now she knew about Harriet, and all that Guy had said about dishonourable discharges, disobeying the rules of duelling, gambling, drinking, and stealing horses from dying Prussian officers. It didn't seem possible that Landry could be so contemptible, yet there was a corner of her conscience that believed it all. Landry's honour was questionable. She wished it were not so, but knew she wished in vain.

The dressing-room door opened and the maids emerged. After respectful curtsies, they hastened giggling into the gallery, leaving Beth alone.

*   *   *

Down in the entrance hall, Guy had waited until Beth passed out of sight with the housekeeper, before nodding at Bradfield. 'See that the young gentleman's carriage and luggage are made ready for immediate departure. He will be staying at the Valmer Arms tonight and, I trust, be gone from Greylake come the morning.'

The agent was perplexed. 'But, Sir Guy, he believes he will be staying here.'

'What he believes is immaterial.'

'Yes, Sir Guy.'

'I will accompany him to the inn, but will dine here with Miss Tremoille, who, by the way, is not to be informed the gentleman was ever here. I have already instructed your wife to ensure silence among the servants, and I expect you to make certain my wishes are obeyed.'

'Yes, Sir Guy.'

The agent inclined his head and then hastened away toward the kitchens. Guy went in the opposite direction, along a passage that led from the southwest corner of the hall. The library lay at the far end, and Guy entered quietly, to find the Honourable Rowan Welland, who had arrived unannounced just over an hour earlier, fast asleep in a comfortable fireside chair. The library was a room of great elegance, with rose silk on the upper walls, a mainly green carpet, and a pink-and-grey marble fireplace. The glass-fronted bookcases, which wrapped all around the walls, were of a height that permitted a man to comfortably take out a book from the top shelf, and above them was a collection of sporting prints and ink drawings.

Glazed double doors opened to the adjacent conservatory, to which Guy adjourned to think for a moment. It was dark and shadowy, and the tropical plants were motionless. The sweet, intoxicating fragrance of potted lilies-of-the-valley filled the air. They'd been his mother's favourite flower, and had always been forced early in the conservatory because she liked to have them in the house. Guy leaned against a leaf-twined pillar. Under any other circumstance Rowan would have been most welcome, but not now, and it wasn't going to be easy to turn him away without giving offence. How was it going to be best achieved?

He glanced back at Rowan, who managed to avoid the unbecoming sins of snoring or sleeping with his mouth open. What had brought him here? Surely old Welland hadn't thrown him out already? There hadn't been time . . . or had there? Guy's lips twitched as he considered the elder Welland. The miserable old bugger was a monstrous parent, but then Rowan was hardly an ideal son. Guy

79

knew of the illegitimate half-brother with whom Rowan had been threatened, and wondered if the fellow had been brought into the family anyway. Yes, it was a distinct possibility.

Well, there was only one way to find out. Guy returned to the library and shook Rowan's arm. 'Wake up, my laddo,' he said quietly.

'Mmmm?' Rowan shuffled in the chair and settled to continue sleeping.

'Wake up,' Guy repeated, this time shaking him more forcefully.

'Huh? What?' Rowan sat bolt upright as if stuck with a pin.

'Welcome to the world of the living,' Guy said, moving away to stand in front of the fire.

Rowan recovered a little. 'Ah, there you are. I was beginning to think I was doomed to a lonely Christmas after all.'

'I fear you are, my friend, because you cannot stay here.'

'Eh? But it's *huge* here, so please don't tell me there isn't room.'

'Rowan, at any other time you would be assured of a warm welcome and even warmer hospitality, but right now, your presence is rather awkward. I will see that you are comfortably accommodated at the Valmer Arms, but I really would like you to move on in the morning. Be anywhere but here.'

Rowan stared at him. 'Why?' he demanded

bluntly, then his eyes changed. 'You have female company? Don't tell me you've found Beth?'

There was a split second before Guy gave him a studied answer. 'My quest for that lady has not yet led to marriage,' he replied diplomatically.

Rowan accepted the words at face value. 'Then you've made up with La Carberry? Good God, I thought you'd had enough of her tantrums.'

Maria Carberry was a leading actress on the London stage, Irish, fiery, quick-tempered and very beautiful; she had also been Guy's mistress until a few months ago, when her caprices finally drove him to end the liaison. The relationship had been long, tempestuous and, Rowan suspected, more than a little addictive.

Guy saw no reason to correct him. 'You know Maria, my friend, for her three would most definitely be a crowd.'

It was another ambiguous answer that wasn't questioned. 'Understood, dear chap, understood.' Rowan got up, but then hesitated. 'I didn't come here just to impose myself, but to tell you I'm disowned, lock, stock and proverbial barrel.'

'So, you and your pa have crossed swords once too often?'

'Yes. He makes me want to puke, and is welcome to his oaf of a by-blow.'

'Oaf?' Guy raised an eyebrow. 'Does this mean you are now aware of this half-brother's identity?'

Rowan nodded. 'A certain Edward Barker, son of a female tavern keeper, and known to one and all as Ned. He's a dolt of the first water, so will certainly fit in well with all things Welland.'

'So you are now penniless and homeless?'

'Well, not entirely penniless, for I have the money my mother left me. It's not a fortune, but is still fifty times more than a labourer will earn in ten years.' Rowan grinned. 'No, I'm not about to touch you for a donation, but I do need a roof over my head.' He eyed Guy hopefully.

'The house in Park Lane is always at your disposal, you know that.'

'Thank you, I appreciate it.' Rowan hesitated again. 'One more thing, your advice, actually. I now have a goal that is as great as yours to regain Tremoille House. Mine isn't bricks and mortar, but something far more personal.'

Guy smiled. 'The female of the species?'

'Yes. I've already told you I'm in love, but—'

'—But you've been very careful not to identify her,' Guy interrupted.

Rowan nodded, and then looked shame-faced. And for reasons of my own, I still mean to keep her name a secret. What I want of you, Guy, is advice as to whether I should follow my heart, or flout convention.'

'*Convention?*' Guy chuckled. 'Since when has convention ever concerned you?'

'Since the thought of marriage entered my head.'

Guy drew a long breath. 'It's that serious? Then I have to wonder what there is about the lady in question that brings flouted convention into the equation. Does she already have a husband?'

'Good God, no!'

'What then? I cannot imagine you have taken up with a doxy or drab, so unless she has some physical deformity, or is prone to doing unearthly things by the light of the full moon . . .?'

'She is young, beautiful and free to marry whomsoever she pleases.'

Guy's brows drew together. 'Then it has to be her background. What is she? A flower girl? A milliner? A hackney coachman's daughter?'

Rowan shifted a little. 'She is none of those.'

But. The small word, a mere conjunction, hung unsaid in the library. There was a 'but' about this young lady, and it must be considerable for Rowan to be so torn. 'Rowan, is there something about her that really puts her beyond the Pale?'

'That depends upon your point of view. She would be beyond the Pale for much of society, but not for me. I adore her, utterly. She's the

83

most delightful, enchanting, adorable creature that ever drew breath, and I want her as I've never wanted before.'

'Does she love you?'

'Oh, yes.'

Guy exhaled slowly. 'If that is the case, my friend, to hell with society. Go after her, make her the next Lady Welland, and have a brood of squealing babies.'

'That is your advice?' Rowan pressed.

'In the absence of further information about her, what else can I say? You love each other, and that is something that must never be overlooked. You may never have another chance, so seize the moment.'

'And if I do, can I take her to your London house?'

Guy paused. 'I will rely upon your good faith and common sense to see that she really is suitable, Rowan, for I will not have anything distasteful or disreputable infringing upon my affairs. I have problems enough of my own on that score, without taking on yours as well.'

'I understand, Guy.' But behind his open countenance, Rowan was uneasy. Guy might have Maria Carberry here with him now, but the actress was never going to be Lady Valmer. That title was set aside for Beth, who may have been Jake Mannacott's mistress but was nevertheless a lady born and bred. Rosalind Mannacott was lowborn, and would still be that if she became Lady Welland. There was also the further complication that Rosalind despised Beth, which would put a considerable strain on his friendship with Guy. It wasn't a good idea to take Rosalind to Guy's London house, but Rowan couldn't think of an alternative. It would do in the meantime, and hopefully he and Rosalind would soon find somewhere of their own.

Guy smiled. 'Is my advice required in any other area?'

'No, I'll toddle off—reluctantly—to the Valmer Arms.'

Guy smiled. 'I'll accompany you, and walk back when you're settled. Rowan, I really am sorry about this, but you do understand, don't you?'

'I understand fully, Guy. Believe me, right now, if our roles were reversed, you too would be staying at the nearest inn. And rest assured that I will hie me to London in the morning.'

CHAPTER SEVEN

There was an uneasy atmosphere in the gold-and-white drawing-room at Haldane Rectory, where Harriet and Landry had joined the Reverend Bellamy. Harriet's clergyman father, white-wigged and black-clad, was seated at his writing desk, and the scratching of his quill was the only sound. It was evening, and the fire had been built up to fend off the bitter cold of the Exmoor winter.

Harriet's father was a tall, heavily built man of about fifty, with a rasping voice and long, rather gloomy face, and was labouring over a new sermon, having realized with some embarrassment that the old one centred upon shouldering responsibility for one's actions. His intention had been to wag an accusing finger at two pregnant, unmarried young women in the village; now, of course, such a theme came uncomfortably close to his daughter's situation. It was hard enough to compose any sermons these days, but having been up for most of the previous night after dosing himself with far too much rhubarb, he was now particularly tired.

Harriet and Landry sat opposite each other by the fire, she with her hands clasped and eyes lowered, and he straight-backed and expressionless. Harriet was twenty-nine years old, pretty, with short golden hair and light grey eyes flecked with gold, and a little mole at the corner of her mouth that gave her an attractive smile. Not that she had smiled much since the drama of the betrothal ball. She hated being at the centre of so much gossip, and was bitter that Landry resented having to marry her.

No one could have guessed the dark, abandoned nature of Harriet's thoughts as she sat there, prim and proper in a high-throated, long-sleeved cream woollen gown that was embroidered in blue and pink. No one could have appeared more modest and demure, but inside she seethed with anger and sexual frustration. Until Beth came to the Dower House, there had always been a small chance of winning Landry, but Beth had turned his head completely. Why couldn't Landry see that she would have left with Sir Guy anyway? Why didn't he accept the impure carnal passion awaiting him in the arms of the clergyman's daughter he chose to blame for everything that had gone wrong in his life?

She glanced across at him. Landry Haldane wasn't strictly handsome, but his face was usually animated by immense charm. Dark-haired, with deep turquoise eyes, firm lips and a manly figure, he wore a dark blue coat and riding breeches, and his neckcloth was embellished with a fine sapphire pin. Civilian clothes. But when he had been a major in the King's Own Light Dragoons, a dashing hussar, courageous and nonchalant, she had found him heart-stoppingly attractive. He had been in uniform the day their daughter was conceived.

Landry felt her glance, and was sure not to meet it. He was thinking of Beth. And Guy. Dear God, he could have borne losing her to almost any other man, but not his most despised enemy. He closed his eyes, gripped by sickening pangs of jealousy and bruised pride.

It was all Harriet's fault. He had convinced himself of this, even though it had been his former mistress, Carrie Markham, now at death's very threshold with consumption, who had told Beth about his daughter Katy's real mother. Nor did he shoulder any responsibility himself for what he'd done all those years ago. It did not suit him to accept that he wouldn't be facing this unwanted marriage if he'd kept the contents of his dashing hussar breeches under control.

Katy hardly crossed his mind at all, but then she never had. It had pleased him when she wanted to live with Carrie at the lodge, instead of being under his feet whenever he was on leave at the hall. Now the child was asleep upstairs here at the rectory, having been brought from the lodge on the Haldane estate, where Carrie clung to life by a tenuous thread. It was fear of Katy's future that had led the dying woman to tell Beth the entire truth. Carrie had always believed he and Harriet, as the child's proper parents, should marry and provide her with a stable life. All he saw was that between them, Carrie, Harriet and Katy were denying his chance of happiness with Beth.

All these powerful undercurrents swirled in the warm air as the Reverend Bellamy's tiredness began to get the better of him. His head nodded. Not only was he tired, but the shock of discovering he was the grandfather of an illegitimate nine-year-old girl had led him to consume too much Madeira. He'd always believed Harriet to be as pure as the driven snow, and had delighted in her engagement to her cousin, John Herriot. The startling revelations at the ball had shaken his comfortable, rather smug world. Suddenly his principles were being challenged, obliging him to share the shame he had always heaped so freely upon his unfortunate parishioners. *As ye sow, so also shall ye reap.* It was a humiliatingly appropriate text for his next sermon, but he preferred not to practise what he preached, and so chose something suitable to the Christmas season. Which, if he were honest, was what he should have done in the first place, rather than denouncing young women who were already suffering enough for their lapses. As he began to snore, the quill slipped from his grasp, leaving a splodge of ink on the words he had managed to compose.

Landry immediately got to his feet. 'I think it's time I returned to the hall,' he announced, anxious to be free of the rectory and its occupants.

'We really ought to talk,' Harriet replied, rising too. 'There have been a lot of words today, but very few of them just between you and me.'

'What is there to say? I will marry you and together we will give Katy as normal a family surrounding as is possible. Under the circumstances.'

Her eyes registered hurt. 'The circumstances being that you want Beth?'

'If you expect me to deny it, you'll be disappointed. I will always love her.'

'Even though she has clearly been deceiving you from the outset?'

His jaw tightened, and there was dislike in his turquoise eyes. 'Do you have knowledge of this? Did she *tell* you about Valmer?'

Harriet drew back slightly. 'Last night was the first time I heard of her connection with him.'

'I only have your word for that.'

'I'm not in the habit of lying, Landry.'

His nostrils flared and his lip curled. 'No? Damn it, Harriet, you've been lying for ten years or so!'

'You felt nothing for me, Landry, and I loved you too much to force you into marriage. Now matters are out of my hands. The truth is out and we will need a very important reason not to marry.'

'You could decline,' he suggested bluntly.

She flinched. 'I could, but I won't. Now that the world knows I'm Katy's real mother, I intend to do what's right by her. And I must consider my father, who is suffering great shock and shame because of what we did. I won't destroy him completely by refusing to marry his granddaughter's father.'

'We won't do well together, Harriet,' he

warned.

'Not if you refuse to even try,' she replied bitterly.

'I love Beth, Harriet. No one else can compare, but because of you—'

Harriet's eyes flashed at that. 'It isn't *my* fault she's marrying Sir Guy! How *dare* you blame me for that! She has a very pressing reason for choosing him over you. I don't know what it is, because she didn't tell me, but I *do* know that even if Katy and I didn't exist, Beth would still have left you.'

The muscles worked in his jaw, and he avoided her eyes.

'What did you really know about her?' Harriet demanded. 'Just how much did she confide in you?' She watched his face. 'Not a great deal, it would seem. Beth has dark secrets in her past, Landry, and clearly Sir Guy Valmer is one of them.'

'No! I won't believe that! Nor will I have you saying it, d'you hear?' He stepped forward suddenly and seized her wrist with a strength that could have snapped it.

'You're hurting me, Landry! And you're frightening me, too!' she cried, and her father grunted and opened his glazed eyes.

Landry released her immediately, and contrived to smile as if nothing had happened. Not that the Reverend Bellamy was aware of anything, for his eyes closed again and after a moment the snores resumed.

Harriet had taken the opportunity to step away from Landry, putting her father and the table between them. She glanced at her father, afraid he might not be as deeply asleep as he seemed, but to her relief he was unaware of anything, so she looked at Landry again. His brief display of violence had aroused something cold and calculating within her. If he thought to bully her into submission, he was going to be gravely disappointed. 'Landry, I will let you go from this match, but first you should consider the consequences. Your character has already suffered because of your antics with Beth, and now it has come out that you once ruined the vicar's daughter by getting her with child. There is already other talk too.'

'Other talk?' His turquoise eyes sharpened.

'Rumours that you have lied about the circumstances of your leaving the army.'

His eyes narrowed. 'What nonsense is this?'

'Sir Daniel Lavington's nephew is friendly with one of your fellow officers. The word "cashiered" was mentioned, something to do with a gambling debt and dishonourable conduct in a duel. There is even an unpleasant rumour about how you acquired Snowy.'

Landry's cheeks went a dull red. 'None of it is true.'

'Maybe, but it wouldn't take much for such whispers to spread far and wide.'

Landry was incredulous, for there was no mistaking the veiled threat. It was the last thing he expected from Harriet. 'Are you blackmailing me?' he breathed.

She gave a faint smile, and didn't answer.

Splinters of ice began to flow through his blood. The truth stared out of her gold-flecked grey eyes; he had to accept the offer on the table, or suffer the consequences. An apologetic smile sprang to his lips, and he spread his hands. 'Oh, come now, Harriet, you know me better than these spiteful tales.'

'No, I don't,' she answered quietly. 'Tonight I have seen your true colours. I should have had the measure of you all those years ago, when you behaved as if our intimate encounter had never happened. You wished to forget it, and so I let you. An honourable man would have behaved very differently. I've made excuses for you for far too long, but that is all over now. Your nasty little show of violence has brought me to my right mind, and I'm a fool no more.' The last phrase was uttered softly.

His mind raced behind his contrite smile. He feared the consequences of calling her bluff. A man in his position—wealthy, landowning and influential—needed a good reputation if he was to maintain his place in society, and Harriet threatened to destroy all that by broadcasting the rumours. Collecting himself, he glanced away suddenly, as if trying to control his emotion. 'Harriet, I—' He took a long, shuddering breath. 'I beg your forgiveness. So many shocks in such a short time have made me less than kind. I would never deliberately hurt you, surely you know that?' When she remained silent, he stepped toward her, and then halted again. 'Please say I am forgiven, and that we can start again?' he implored, squeezing tears to his eyes as he held out his hands to her.

She hesitated for what seemed an unconscionable length of time, but then smiled and came to him. Her smile was as false as his, but she wanted him, and from now on was prepared to do whatever she had to. He thought he was fooling her as he caught her close and placed his parted lips over hers. He told himself that if he imagined she was Beth, he could be convincing enough to make certain of her. And so he remembered his assignations with Beth on the cliffs of Stone Valley, of how they lay passionately together with only the sea and the sky to see them. Thinking of Beth stirred his body, as he knew it would and, as his false kisses became hungrier, he grabbed Harriet to his hips and moved himself against her, enjoying the erotic pressure on his swelling loins.

Harriet gave herself to the moment, however artificial it was. If Beth could throw all caution to the wind and snare him in a sexual spell, then Harriet Bellamy could—and would—do the same. She was so hungry for a repeat of the carnal pleasure she'd known when Katy was conceived, and so determined to be sated, that she caught his hand and drew him into the adjacent room, where her father kept his many books. It was a small chamber, in virtual darkness, and no one saw as her kisses now became an assault. She leaned back against the bookcases, pulling him with her as she devoured his lips and cleaved wantonly close, as if she were the embodiment of ancient fertility.

Such was the intensity of her onslaught that he found control slipping from him. He was haunted by images of Beth, and could even smell her perfume. It was Beth who wanted him; Beth whose flesh craved him. He slid his hands over her buttocks, so small and firm beneath her gown, and when he looked into her eyes, they were hazel-green. His hands trembled as he pulled her gown up around her thighs and then fondled her warm, smooth flesh, sliding eager fingers into the moisture of her most private places. Oh, so moist. She was ready for him.

Still thinking of Beth, he undid the falls of his breeches, and the shaft he released was more than firm and throbbing enough for the job in hand. He lifted Harriet from her feet and slid himself between her legs. Her breath caught with all the pent-up passion of ten years of frustration and yearning, and she wrapped her legs tightly around him, the better for him to penetrate her. She had to stifle a cry that was almost animal as at last she had him inside her again. She felt like a virgin, pierced for the first time, and the experience took her close to ecstasy.

'I love you, Landry,' she breathed, the words barely comprehensible as she nibbled his lower lip and then dragged her lustful lips over his cheek and down to his throat. She clung to him almost parasitically, as if she would suck his life away, and her private muscles clenched and stabbed uncontrollably around the virile pole deep within her. Her moans of passion were primitive and raw, the sounds of a basic coupling instigated out of raw craving. So abandoned did she become that Landry was swept along too, beginning to thrust in and out of her as if he would rip her apart. He moved like a piston, faster and faster, harder and harder, but no matter how rough and thoughtless he was, her ferocious desire was undiminished. All the years of wanting were being banished, and nothing, *nothing*, was going to deny her the exhilarating climax she pursued with such ardour. If there was pleasure, no matter how small and fleeting, to be had from these moments, she feasted upon it as if she had been starved. She was lost in a labyrinth of voluptuousness, a creature formed of sexual need and nothing else, and she squirmed against him with all the crude abandon of the savage and wild. Gratification came hot upon gratification, until she felt as if her flesh could endure no more, but *still* the shuddering rewards engulfed her.

His lips were as savage as hers as he worked into her like a man possessed. He was making love to Beth, as he had only four months ago at the Dower House. He could hear again the gale howling in the chimney, and the high tide breakers on the rocks only yards from the house. He drove his virility into her, exulting in the sheer power of his need, and his entire being was now concentrated in his loins. He was a god of sexual prowess. *Beth, my darling, my love* . . . He was trapped in a world of longing, where euphoria waited to burn his flesh and steal his strength. For a moment his fury obliterated all the pain, and then he came, pulsing again and again as if ridding himself of all the heartbreak.

Harriet didn't want him to come, because that would mean the end of ecstasy, but come he had to, for he couldn't withstand such an assault. The shuddering jets of pure joy weakened him so that he felt he could not hold himself up, but somehow he endured, and gradually they subsided, and with them his erection. He forced Harriet down on him, just to be sure of staying inside her, and still she jerked against him, taken almost to the edge of consciousness by the discharge of so much emotion.

His thighs were trembling too much, and he had to lower her to her feet again and allow his member to be dragged out of her, but she wanted more. There were things she yearned to do, and wished to do now. His seed was running slowly down the inside of her thigh, and his wet member pressed into the hairs at her groin. Oh, how intimate it felt, how freshly exciting and tantalizing. New desire was already beginning to pour through her veins. She knew that she had been Beth to him for these exquisite moments, but it was Harriet Bellamy who'd benefited, and now she wanted more.

He tried to pull away to push himself back inside his breeches, but she stopped him by taking his spent masculinity in her hand. Her eyes were closed as she massaged it, hoping to feel it respond, but it didn't. His few minutes with the clergyman's daughter had left him exhausted beyond belief. He felt almost raped, and suddenly wanted to escape from her. But he did not dare. She had a hold on him in more ways than one, and the last thing he wanted was to risk alienating her.

Realizing that she wasn't going to have him again now, she released his used up organ, but she didn't intend to let him go just yet. Slipping her arms around his waist, she sank to her knees, still holding his legs tightly. At last she was able to put her face against the part of him of which she'd dreamed for so long. She rubbed herself against it, until her skin was damp with him, and then, hesitantly, she sucked him into her mouth. He felt the frissons of new gratification engulfing her, and she experienced such a violent contracting of the muscles between her legs that she had to cling to him to hold herself up. It was too much, even for her, and reluctantly she drew away, her lips keeping his foreskin for a little longer, stretching it and enjoying its softness, before she let him go.

'Sweet Mother, Harriet,' he whispered, shaken yet again by her sexual fervour, and angry too. He loathed the way she made him feel guilty. She looked so strange kneeling in front of him, as if he were a king and she his lowliest of subjects, and at the same time managing to make him feel knavish.

There was slyness in her smile. 'You're mine, Landry. Oh, I know that you were thinking of *her* just now, but I don't care. Your ring is going to be on my finger, not hers, and I will be the vessel into which you pour your desire.'

He pulled away from her and quickly made himself decent, but her smile didn't waver. 'You'll want this again, and I'll be ready, make no mistake of that. It will be me to whom you come, even though you see Beth's shade. Your heart I forfeit, but your body will be mine.'

He gazed down at her, suddenly deeply disturbed by everything about her.

'Go,' she whispered.

He needed no second bidding, and slipped

out past her sleeping father, took his outdoor things from the stand in the hall, and then went out into the freezing night.

In the rectory Harriet still knelt on the floor. She had slipped her hands between her thighs, where his essence was still thick and wet, and then she smoothed it all over her face. Somehow it seemed to keep him with her. Then she got to her feet again, tweaked her clothes and went back into the drawing-room to look at herself in the mirror. How unbelievably tidy she still looked, she thought, and left the room for the kitchen, where she informed the servants that her father had fallen asleep and two men or more might be needed to assist him to his bed.

Then she took herself up to her bed. She didn't wash, but after undressing slipped naked between the sheets. There she pushed her fingers between her legs again, prying deep into the warmth and moisture. After ten long years she had Landry's seed inside her again, and she knew that her monthly cycle was right. She wanted to bear him another child, proof anew of her fertility and Beth's barrenness. Her fingers worked to and fro and she thought of him, and smelled him on her face. New waves of pleasure began to break over her, and her body tingled voluptuously. She was sated and happy again, for the first time since conceiving Katy.

Oh, how bitter these ten years had been,

and how hard to pretend to be demure. Everyone saw her as innocent Miss Bellamy, but she wasn't innocent at all. She knew now that she never had been. She had spent her fertile life yearning for Landry Haldane. Well, he was hers now, whether he liked it or not, and she knew she would have many more such pleasures as this. At last she closed her eyes and curled up, her hand still between her legs, his seed now dry upon her face.

CHAPTER EIGHT

In Gloucester that same night, the cathedral bell sounded midnight, ringing out over a city where the good and law-abiding were soundly asleep, while the less respectable still thronged low taverns, like Poll Barker's mean hostelry in narrow Cross Keys Alley. There was the usual raucous fiddle music, shouting and laughter inside, and the usual inebriated drunkards outside, oblivious to the cold.

Poll was stout, with red-dyed hair and unattractive jowls, and wore a rather crumpled mobcap and a navy-and-white striped fustian gown into which she was squeezed and corseted until her face was permanently flushed. It was hard to believe now that she had once been beautiful. Certainly she had lost her charm, and her smiles revealed teeth like yellow tombstones.

No one believed her claims that a lord of the realm had sired her son, because the young man cut an even less engaging figure than she did. Ned Barker was the result of Poll's questionable notion of motherhood, and his life was further blighted by Thomas Welland's disagreeable looks. Not for him the advantage of his younger half-brother Rowan's elegant aristocratic mother, or the privileged upbringing that assured Rowan a place in society; indeed, Ned expected to spend his entire life at the tavern, taking it over when Poll eventually shuffled off her mortal coil. He was henpecked at home and a bully out of it, and so generally unhappy that he drank too much every day, in the hope that come nightfall his wretchedness would be dulled, if not banished. He wasn't liked, nor did he like himself. Women certainly weren't drawn to him, which meant recourse to whores, particularly those with large breasts. To get them to his bed he bribed them with free gin, a liberty of which his fond mother knew nothing. Poll might dote on him, but not even he could come between her and profit.

A year older and a little shorter than Rowan, he had Thomas's stocky build, wide forehead, bushy eyebrows and hollow cheeks, and when his hair was washed it was thick and blond, but it was usually too lank and greasy for the colour to be discernible. His clothes were always the same, a battered old brown coat that may once have been quite good quality, and vaguely fawn breeches that were several sizes too big for him, bagged at the knees and held up by a leather belt. With this ensemble he wore darned woollen stockings and a pair of wooden clogs in which he stomped around in the same way as his father. Thomas Welland had been reborn in his unappealing bastard firstborn; give Ned wealth and education, and he'd be his father all over again.

As the last note of the cathedral bell died away, he was in his attic room with two plump whores, one young and saucy, the other older and more worldly. An empty gin bottle stood on the floor by the pile of straw that comprised his bed, and a single candle lit the scene as the drunken trio cavorted naked on the straw. The ceiling sagged alarmingly, and the room was freezing, but Ned and his trollops were warmed by the gin. There were giggles and snorts, with here a gartered thigh, there a wobbling bosom, and Ned was lost in pleasure. For a while he was able to forget the wretchedness of his existence, but in his heart he longed to love and be loved.

A horseman, cloaked and hunched, his low-crowned hat worn well down over his forehead, dismounted in the snowy alley by the tavern, and tethered his sweating horse in as much shelter as he could find. He was tired and ill-tempered at having been sent all the way to Gloucester on his master's irrational whim. Snow crunched underfoot as he stepped over the legs of a snoring man propped against the tavern wall, and then went into the smoky, candlelit taproom. There was an overpowering stench of stale liquor and ale, as well as tobacco smoke and unwashed bodies, and he doubted if the straw and sand on the floor had been changed in several months. He glanced around with half-hooded eyes, and his lip curled with distaste as he removed his gloves and hat.

Poll was serving at the trestle in front of two large tapped barrels, and straightened suspiciously, because although not a gentleman, he was better dressed than her usual clientele. She disliked him on sight. 'And what can I do for you, my fine sir?' she demanded sarcastically as he approached her.

'Mrs Barker?'

'Who wants to know?'

'My name is Delaney, and I'm Lord Welland's agent.'

Poll's breath caught, and suddenly she could not have been more helpful. 'Would you care for a jug of ale, Mr Delaney?'

'I'd as soon drink from the Severn.'

She was offended. 'Well, now, you like to give yourself airs and graces, do you? Think yourself more lordly than his lordship?'

'No, I just have standards. My only reason

for being here is to speak to your son, Edward.'

Poll's jaw dropped. After all this time, Ned was being summoned by his father?

'I don't have all the time in the world, Mrs Barker, so the sooner I see him, the sooner I can get home to my bed.'

She recovered from her shock. 'Right, I'll find him right now.' She craned her neck to look all around the taproom, but there was no sign of Ned. In fact, now she came to think of it, she hadn't seen him for some time. Slowly her gaze moved to a shelf where there should have been two full bottles of gin, but there was only one. Next her gaze moved up to the ceiling, above which was her son's bedroom. A furious frown darkened her brow, and she marched to the rickety door that gave to the steep narrow stairs. She swept up to the equally narrow landing like an avenging angel, and the first warning Ned heard was the loud squeak of a telltale floorboard. But it was too late, and his enraged mother had flung the door open before he had time to get up. By the light of a candle Poll saw his excited manhood collapse into an alarmed droop.

'Get out!' she screeched at the whores. 'Get out, you bitches, and never let me see you round here again!' She bundled them to the landing and practically threw them down the stairs, and then confronted her quaking son.

'Ma—' he began.

'Don't you "Ma" me!'

He felt like a rabbit in a poacher's sights. 'Ma . . .'

'Ma? Ma? You sound like a sheep! You're my only child, and I've always tried to do right by you, and *this* is how I'm repaid! I'll serve the likes of those poxy streetwalkers in the taproom, but I won't have them in my house. Is that clear? Why can't you find yourself a *decent* girl, eh?'

'Because no decent girl will have me.'

He raised his arms to protect himself as she crossed the room and cuffed him soundly around the head. Then, almost as unnervingly, she became all sweetness and light. 'Now, Edward, I want you to tidy yourself up. There's someone to see you.'

Bewildered, he lowered his arms. 'Who?'

'Haven't I always told you your father was an aristocrat?'

'Yes, but—' Perhaps now wasn't the moment to tell her he'd never believed her.

'You're Lord Welland's son, and he's sent his agent to speak to you.' She dusted his coat and thrust it toward him. 'Pull yourself together, and put *that* away!' She slapped his genitals and then marched to the door. 'Come right down, and be on your best behaviour.'

He glowered after her as she went out. What best behaviour? He didn't have any, he thought, as he dressed and then looked at himself in the fragment of mirror fixed to the wall. His half-brother Rowan was handsome, refined and pedigree; Ned Barker was a mongrel, and always would be. With a sigh, he went downstairs.

The taproom was unexpectedly quiet, Poll having taken the unusual step of ejecting all her customers. Except one, who was presumably Lord Welland's agent. Ned shuffled self-consciously to join his mother behind the trestle.

Poll drew herself up proudly. 'Mr Delaney, this is my son, Edward,' she declared, as if introducing royalty.

The agent sniffed and rubbed his cold nose. 'Well, I suppose I'd know you in a crowd,' he answered, thinking how unfortunate the young man was to look like his lordship. Was he also as mad as Welland? Did he even have enough brains to be mad?

Poll was impatient. 'Does his lordship wish to see his son?' she demanded.

'That's for his lordship to know and you to wonder,' Delaney replied annoyingly. 'Your boy's to go at Tremoille House tomorrow evening. Have you a horse?'

Poll laughed. 'Do I look as if I can afford horses? His Lordship doesn't pay me enough for that.'

The agent looked at Ned again. 'Then I'll send a pony and trap for you. You'll need to bring your belongings.'

'I . . . I'm to *stay* there?' Ned gasped.

'His lordship hasn't issued specific instructions, but I'm presuming that is his wish.' Delaney donned his gloves and hat. 'You'll be Edward when you're there, is that clear? Lord Welland won't hold with Ned, he'll say it's a name for carthorses.' He turned toward the door, and Ned spoke up quickly.

'Mr Delaney, what am I to do there?'

'Please his lordship. If you don't, you'll be back here quicker than you can fart.'

The cold night air swept in as he departed, and neither Poll nor Ned spoke until the sound of his horse had died away along Cross Keys Alley. Then she turned to her son. 'I've always prayed this day would come, Ned, I—I mean Edward. Why should that stuck-up Rowan have everything just because he's on the right side of the blanket? You're Thomas Welland's *firstborn*, so it's right and fair that he should send for you.'

'Ma, I'm a pig's ear, and no amount of pretending will turn me into a silk purse. I'll probably be back here tomorrow night. One look at me will persuade Lord Welland that I'm best left in the middens of Gloucester.'

'He'll look at you, and think he's looking in a mirror,' Poll answered, seizing him urgently by the arms. 'It may be a long time since I last went with him, but I know him well enough. Something's happened for him to send for you, and that means this is your chance. You've had your last common whore, it'll be fine courtesans from now on.'

'The only girl I ever *really* wanted was Rozzie Mannacott.'

'That little madam? She led you on, then said no. A proper prick-teaser.'

Ned looked away. He'd behaved badly toward Rozzie, and wished he hadn't. But it was too late now, because she and her father had left Gloucester. Not that he particularly wanted to see Jake Mannacott again, having had a good lamming from him one dark night. Jake didn't take kindly to having his daughter pawed about.

Poll put a hand on his shoulder. 'Just take every chance you can in life, Edward, and make sure you're as close on Thomas Welland's hide as a tick on a dog. And don't give your half-brother any credit he's not due. Things have never gone well between Rowan and his father, and it's my guess there's been a real falling-out. Getting your feet under the table is one thing, keeping them there quite another. So you live on your wits.'

'Such as they are,' Edward muttered.

She smiled suddenly. 'You can do it, Edward. Now then, it's late, so you get on up to bed. You'll need some sleep tonight.'

He went slowly back upstairs. Less than an hour ago his life had been simple, now it had changed, and he wasn't sure he liked it. Then it struck him that if Rozzie hadn't wanted Ned Barker of Cross Keys Lane, maybe she'd prefer him as Lord Welland's son.

*   *   *

In Frampney at that moment, Jake suddenly awakened from a deep sleep. He didn't know what had disturbed him, just that he felt rattled. Everything was quiet, except for the distant screech of a barn owl as it flew over the far end of the village green. Flinging the bedclothes aside, he got up, shivering as the cold night air touched his naked body. Something was wrong, although he could not have said what on earth it was. Grabbing his old breeches from the back of the only chair, he began to dress.

The latch squeaked as he went out to the pitch-black landing. There wasn't a sound from Rozzie's room, nor from Matty and Phoebe's, and it was the latter that bothered him now, because Matty Brown always snored fit to raise the roof. He opened their bedroom door and was just able to make out that Phoebe was alone in the bed, her hair twisted with curling papers. Matty's side hadn't been slept in.

With a soft curse, Jake closed the door again and hastened downstairs and, as he opened the door at the bottom, he immediately heard Matty's familiar rattling snores. The room was warm from the banked-up fire, and a guttering candle revealed the old blacksmith asleep in his chair, his head bowed to his chest, his hands relaxed as they rested on the worn wooden arms. Too relaxed by far! His lighted clay pipe had slipped from his fingers and shattered on the rush mat in front of the hearth, scattering its glowing contents. Wisps of smoke were beginning to rise from the smouldering rushes.

Jake's breath snatched as he took the shovel from the coal bucket to beat the nascent fire into oblivion. The loud clangs awakened Matty with a start. 'Eh? What's up? What's going on?' he cried confusedly.

'You darned old liability, you've almost had us burned alive!!' Jake shouted furiously, tossing the shovel back into the scuttle and then stamping on the rushes.

Still muddled with sleep, Matty clenched his right hand, expecting his fingers to close around the familiar clay pipe. His lips parted and he sat forward to look at the floor, where the pulverized clay remains and smoke-darkened patch of matting told a very clear story. 'Oh, darn it, darn it,' he muttered.

'Is that all you can say?' Jake demanded, still angry enough to want to shake the old man. 'How many times have I warned you about that bloody pipe?'

There were footsteps on the stairs, and then Phoebe and Rozzie appeared, both jolted into wakefulness by the noise from the kitchen. Phoebe's eyes were wide and frightened, and

111

Rozzie, her silvery blonde hair tumbling like silk from beneath her night bonnet, peered nervously over her shoulder. 'What's happened, Jake?' Phoebe asked, her curling papers trembling.

'This mad old fart fell asleep again with his lighted pipe. It broke on the floor and would have started a fire if I hadn't come down in time!' Jake ran a hand through his dark curls, shaken to the core. If he hadn't awakened when he had, God knows what could have happened.

Matty was almost in tears. 'I'm sorry, God help me I'm sorry . . .'

Phoebe looked at him. 'Oh, Matty, you promised me you wouldn't light up in the house again.'

'And I didn't mean to, I just forgot.'

She knelt beside him and took his hands. 'You *have* to stop this, my love. If Jake hadn't come down . . .' She glanced around, puzzled. 'Why *did* you come down?'

Jake shrugged. 'I've no idea. I just woke up, realized Matty wasn't snoring like a grampus in your room, and came down just as the mat was catching fire.'

She breathed out slowly. 'The Lord is merciful,' she said softly, then turned to Matty again. 'This must be the very last time you do this, Matty Brown. Do you hear me? You've become a danger to us all.'

Tears shone in her husband's eyes, and he

nodded. 'It won't happen again, Phoebe, I swear it.'

Jake glowered at him. 'It had better be so, Matty, or so help me I'll throttle you!'

Silence fell as the words conjured memories of Robert Lloyd.

CHAPTER NINE

The morning of Beth's wedding day dawned bright, clear, crisp and cold. She awakened slowly from a dream of being lost in a magical rose garden, where the paths led nowhere, and the air was so heady and scented that she wanted to wander there forever. The dream clung around her, and she smiled wryly. To dream of roses was to be fortunate in love, or so she'd heard say. She stretched drowsily in her curtained cocoon, missing the sound of the sea that had greeted her every morning at the Dower House.

A maid crept quietly in to attend the dying fire, and then someone else spoke and Beth realized Mrs Bradfield was in the room as well. The new flames soon took hold, and then the maid dragged a metal wire guard in front of it and left. Then the bed curtains twitched a little and Mrs Bradfield looked in. 'Ah, you're awake, madam. I've brought you a nice cup of tea. Will you take it with the hangings drawn like this, or opened up?'

'That's very kind of you, Mrs Bradfield, and please draw the curtains back.' The woman pulled the hangings back and fixed them with their tasselled ropes, and then brought the tea in a dainty Sèvres cup and saucer. 'I trust you slept well, madam?'

'Yes, thank you.'

Mrs Bradfield looked intently at her. 'And everything is as it should be?'

Beth's eyes met hers. 'Yes.'

'Forgive me, madam, but I do not believe you.'

Beth's lips parted in astonishment. 'I won't be spoken to like that!'

The housekeeper drew back slightly. 'Miss Tremoille, I am not being disrespectful, I'm merely concerned about you. Something is wrong, I can tell it, and if I can help in any way, I would very much like to. I've been told to take care of you, and that is what I will do, but you must believe me when I say that whatever you confide in me will not reach Sir Guy's ears.'

'Mrs Bradfield, you are in Sir Guy's employ,' Beth reminded her.

'But right now I'm answerable to you, Miss Tremoille.' Then the housekeeper smiled a little. It was a warm smile that reached her eyes. 'Just know that I am here if you ever need me. And please, call me Braddy, because everyone does.'

'I'm not everyone,' Beth replied, still uncertain.

The housekeeper nodded. 'I know, madam, for you are about to become Lady Valmer. Sir Guy has told me to advise you that the ceremony will take place at eleven.'

'Very well.'

'When do you wish me to help you prepare?'

'At ten.'

'Very well, madam.' The woman glanced outside at the sunlit snow. 'It's lucky to marry when there is snow lying,' she observed. There was no response, and so she bobbed a curtsey and withdrew, leaving Beth alone again. The warm air was rich with the scent of the carnations on the ottoman, and now that the curtains at the window had been pulled back, she could see snow on the ledge outside. Beyond that was a clear blue sky. Was the sun shining in Lannermouth as well? What were Mrs Cobbett and the others doing at the Dower House? And Landry and Harriet at Haldane . . .

There was another knock at the door, and she lowered the tea cup. 'Yes?'

Guy entered, wearing an unbuttoned floor-length charcoal-grey brocade dressing-gown over a shirt and trousers. His hair was tousled and his grey eyes quick as they rested on her for a long moment. 'Good morning, Beth.'

'Have you no concern about it being ill luck

for a bridegroom to see his bride on their wedding day?'

'Luck has no place in this, Beth. Our marriage will be what we make of it.'

What *you* make of it, she thought, trying not to gaze at him like an adoring puppy. Just seeing him turned her heart over, denying her the will to appear cold and indifferent. The aching desire that washed unstoppably through her was so intense that she felt weak. If he were to come to her now . . .

'I've come to see what attire you intend to wear.'

She had to collect herself. 'Attire?' she repeated a little stupidly.

'For the wedding,' he said, patronizingly as she thought.

'Oh, that,' she answered with a good deal of acidity.

'Do you always awaken with a quip on your lips?'

Her eyes flickered. 'Yes. It's something you'll soon learn to live with.'

'Only if we awaken in the same bed,' he pointed out.

'Will we?' she asked.

'That's up to you,' he replied unexpectedly.

'Me?'

'Yes. I'll consider coming to your bed if you request it, not before.'

'You'll *consider* it? Sir, you flatter yourself!' she replied, so incensed by his male arrogance

116

that she wanted to throw her teacup and saucer at his head.

'Clearly I didn't choose my words well.'

'Clearly.'

He was silent for a moment, and then continued, 'How would you regard it if I came to your bed without asking, and forced my vile self upon you?'

I'd adore your vile self with such passion you'd have a very great shock. But she gave him a cool smile. 'I would regard it as a monstrous assault,' she answered, but her heart and body urged her to fling back the bedclothes right now and beg him to banish the craving that racked her existence. Her head, however, forbade such utter folly, and her temper urged her to hurl the teacup and saucer at him with all her might. She had to say *something*. 'It seems to me, on the evidence of what happened when we were leaving Haldane Hall, that we may do better together than either of us thinks now.'

'You always have the capacity to take me by surprise, Beth.'

'On the occasion to which I refer, *you* took *me* by surprise,' she reminded him. Thrill upon thrill of intense excitement passed through her, congregating almost unbearably between her legs. She was conscious of his attraction, and of the way the rich brocade of his dressing gown outlined his body; that body she yearned for so much that her life had become an agony of repressed desire. His voice caressed her emotions, taunting with its hint of hidden fire, and his eyes seemed to know all her secrets.

He came to the bedside. 'Beth, is there something you wish to say to me?'

Something? She had *everything* to say to him! 'Only that I'm afraid, Guy. The one thing I have come to value is my right to make my own decisions, and yet you have taken that away from me. We are about to enter a loveless marriage of convenience, and the future stretches ahead so coldly that—' She broke off because tears were stinging her eyes and she had to bite her lip to drive them away.

He sat on the edge of the bed, and relieved her of the cup and saucer. Then he put a hand over hers. 'Please don't fear becoming my wife.'

'That isn't what I fear,' she whispered. 'It's the coldness.'

'I'm not cold, Beth.'

She held his gaze. 'Nor am I.'

He hesitated, and she wished she knew his thoughts, but then he said, 'Are you inviting me?'

'Would you accept if I did?' *Why can't you just say yes, Beth Tremoille?*

He smiled. 'Question for question. If you want to know if I desire you, then the answer is yes. You are a beautiful, fascinating woman, and I could very easily make love to you right now. The question is, would it be wise?'

118

'Why does it need to be wise?'

His eyes seemed more arresting than ever as he smiled again. 'Wisdom can make or break the human race,' he said softly.

'Of which we are but two.'

He nodded. 'So we are.'

'Two who are about to marry. Guy, I need you now, because I'm alone, frightened, and I only have you to turn to.'

His fingers tightened around hers. 'Torment into which I have plunged you.'

'It is easily put right,' she whispered, venturing to link her fingers through his. 'Telling me all will be well isn't enough, I need your physical comfort.'

'Sexual comfort,' he murmured.

She nodded. 'Yes.'

He gazed at her, drinking in her loveliness. In his mind's eye he could see her portrait at Tremoille House. Beth, the spirit of tree and meadow, the fairy king's daughter, so fey and delicate that she seemed to be a dream . . . Now she was flesh and blood, and more tempting than he cared to admit. His flesh responded to her, desire driving into his loins in a way it never did with Maria. It wasn't part of his plan to consummate this marriage, for consummation would inevitably lead to complications, and his sole purpose was to use her to recover his lost lands. But she was so alluring, so fascinating and appealing that he could feel his resolve melting away. He wanted her so much, and only had to slip between the sheets to have her.

'Please, Guy,' she whispered, linking and unlinking her fingers between his in a way he found even more arousing. A great shaft now thundered from his crotch, and it was all he could do to conceal it as he sat there, so very close to her.

Suddenly she pulled her hand away and knelt up on the bed to undo the ribbons of her nightgown. Slowly she raised it over her head, and tossed it away. Naked and vulnerable, her hair cascading over her shoulders, she raised herself so that her thighs were parted and her breasts were taut and desirous. Her flesh trembled with anticipation, and she was already so wet between the legs that small tides of pleasure passed through her. But they were as nothing to the ecstasy she knew he could give her. 'Please, Guy,' she breathed again.

His final reservations evaporated. He wanted her so much he felt his climax might come unaided, and so he got up to take off his clothes. Her heart was beating so wildly that she was sure its flutter must be visible in the tremble of her breasts. Everything he did was so lazily attractive, so very sensuous and virile. Her breath caught when at last he was naked, and she could feast her eyes upon the man she loved to the edge of reason itself. He had not lied when he said he desired her, for the proof rose proudly from the tangle of dark hair at his groin. He was strong, perfect, beloved and almost godlike to her, and in a few moments now he would be in her bed, to be hers, if only for a short while.

He came to the bedside and put a hand to her cheek. 'Are you sure of this, Beth? Because if you want to change your mind—'

'I won't change my mind, Guy,' she answered, and raised quivering lips to meet his. The moment their mouths touched again she felt as if her soul were being drawn out of her. Her body felt weak and melting, and her consciousness blended with the voluptuous sensations that engulfed her. No other kisses could match his.

He joined her in the bed, drew her down to the pillows, and then leaned over her. His body was against hers, his leg over hers, his rigid erection hard against her groin. He cupped her breast with one hand, teasing her hard nipple between his finger and thumb. Slowly he bent his head to kiss her other breast, drawing it into his mouth and caressing it with his tongue.

Strands of her hair clung to her damp face, her cheeks were flushed and her eyes dark with desire as she arched with pleasure. This was her dream come true, the intimacy with him she had hungered for since that day he'd helped her at the wayside, and she loved him so much it become a pain keening through her.

Her hands slid over his back, exploring the lines of his body, and all the while she rubbed herself against his maleness, so tantalizingly close, and yet not between her legs. Her hungry flesh quivered with such excitement that she gasped. The truth hung upon her parted lips. *I love you, Guy, I love you with all my heart and soul . . .*

His kisses breathed richly against her breasts, and then beneath them, to descend to her abdomen. As he moved lower, so his iron-hard erection slid down against her thighs. She could feel it throbbing, at once fierce and tender, strong and defenceless, and as he pressed his face into the dark thatch of hair at her groin, she was able to clasp his arousal between her legs. Its sheer size was sweet joy to her, and its vitality so much a part of him that she was enraptured. Euphoric jets of exquisite pleasure fled through her.

Then he eased himself further down her body, gently pulling himself from her clasp in order to tilt her hips, then, slowly and with infinite promise, his kisses moved in between her legs. Her breath escaped on a shuddering sigh as wild new sensations seized her. His lips and tongue were tender jailers, trapping her in an erotic snare that robbed her of everything but sheer, exquisite gratification. There was no part of her too secret for him to storm, no part of her that did not long for more. Her fingers twined lovingly through his hair, that

122

wonderful rich, dark auburn hair that so arrested attention wherever he went. He was beyond the ordinary, beyond the stars themselves, in a class of his own, and she wept as he ministered to her sexual soul. So much had she dreamed, but this was beyond dreams, almost beyond reason itself.

At last he raised his head again, and leaned up on his hands to straddle her. He smiled down into her tear-filled eyes. 'Shall I reassure you more, Beth?' he whispered.

'Yes, oh, yes!'

He lowered himself gently between her thighs and slid his steel-like member into the regions where his lips and tongue had just made obeisance. She cried out as he penetrated her, expanding her flesh so gratifyingly that her heart seemed to sing within her. Let him make love to her forever. Forever. Her breath caught again as at last he drove in to the hilt, withdrew, and then drove in again.

So unstoppable was the sexual joy that she was swept to heaven itself. It was sweet agony, and her body quivered and shook as his relentless strokes continued, each one rewarding her for the months she had craved him. He used his weapon with matchless accuracy, always sliding it against that part of her more sensitive than anywhere else. He was a knowing lover, aware of how to impart the utmost pleasure to his partner, while saving himself until they could both share the climax.

'Look at me Beth,' he breathed at last, and she opened her eyes to meet his steady gaze. 'I must come,' he whispered, 'I cannot hold back any longer.'

'I want you to come, Guy, I want it so much . . .'

He gasped and his whole body jerked as he began to pulse into her. She felt every spurt, and savoured the sensations of his pumping member, so deep within her. Their bodies moved in exquisite unison as he impaled her in the sweetest way imaginable, and she knew the primitive joy of having the man she loved so secretly give up his seed to her. It was knowledge that took her past the heavens to the furthest stars beyond . . .

The act of love ended slowly and richly, each of them absorbing every last nuance of pleasure from the voluptuous aftermath. Still within her, he bent his head to kiss her on the lips. It was a lingering, tender kiss that might almost have been one of love. If only she dared to believe it was, but she was afraid to speak. His tongue pushed gently into her mouth, and slid against hers in a way so erotic that the muscles between her legs clenched again around his softening member. He drew his head back and smiled at her. 'What a creature of passion you are, Beth.'

'Perhaps because you are such a knowing lover,' she answered, closing her eyes again as she gave herself to the fading embers of sensual joy.

He was silent for a moment, and if she'd opened her eyes she would have seen a change come over his face, as if he suddenly had cause to doubt her sincerity. 'How do I compare?' he asked then.

She heard the difference in his voice. 'Compare?'

'With Mannacott and Haldane.'

'Guy, they haven't even crossed my mind.'

'No?'

She gazed up at him. 'They don't matter any more, they're in the past. You are the one I'm going to be with from now on, and—'

'And we'll live happily ever after?' he broke in, easing himself out of her and getting out of the bed. 'Well, at least we seem set to do nicely between the sheets.'

She was on the point of confessing her love, but then remembered his words and tone. *How do I compare?* Suddenly she was afraid to say anything. She could feel the joy slipping away, and there seemed nothing she could do about it. 'Please don't do this, Guy,' she pleaded, 'because you are so very wrong about me.'

'All men enjoy indulging in sex, Beth. We are slaves to our genitals, or had you not heard? You are a woman of experience, and—'

'And therefore to be treated as a whore?' she interrupted.

'I did not say that.'

'You didn't need to.'

He held her gaze. And I did not need telling that my prowess was on trial.'

'Is *that* what you think?' she gasped incredulously.

'What else can I think? I don't appreciate being assessed alongside Haldane and a bloody blacksmith! When I first decided to marry you, I knew the best thing would be to treat you as a matter of business, but I was tempted, and now bitterly regret it.'

She was cut to the quick. 'Well, it's pleasant to know I'm merely a matter of business, Guy, and that you bitterly regret making love to me. Am I supposed to beg your forgiveness? Or maybe you prefer to regard me as a witch who has spellbound you? Yes, that will be it, you're a poor male who cannot be held responsible for his actions. It's all the fault of this wicked female.'

An angry silence descended over the room as he dressed. When he'd finished, he looked at her again. 'Have you decided what you will wear today?' he asked, as if he'd only just entered the room.

She kept a tight hold on her emotions. 'No. Why?'

'Well, if you intend to stand before the altar in your drabbest frock, then I will not bother to dress formally,' he explained.

'Since you set the terms for everything, I will let you decide.' She indicated the dressing-

126

room door. 'The late Lady Harcotleigh's wardrobe awaits inspection.'

'Lady Harcotleigh? What has she to do with it?'

'She was inconsiderate enough to expire and leave her London dressmaker, Madame de Sichel, with an unpaid for wardrobe on her hands. I came along, and—'

'—used stolen money to purchase it?'

'I used money that was mine by right.'

'Mine by right,' he corrected, opening the door and going inside. She heard rustling as he went through the gowns hanging there before coming out with two, an iridescent sapphire blue taffeta she had only tried on as yet, and the emerald silk she'd worn the night she'd been forced by the house agent, Henry Topweather, to place illegal bets at Belvedere's Tearooms in London. 'Have you worn these before?' he asked.

'Only the emerald silk.'

He placed the sapphire taffeta over the ottoman. 'Then wear this, it will certainly do for "something blue".'

'As you wish. But what of "something old" and so on?'

'I will see that a posy of flowers is provided, they will be new. I presume your shoes will have been worn before?'

'Yes.'

'Then they will be something old, and this will serve as something borrowed.' He

127

removed the golden pin from his neckcloth and fixed it to the hem of the gown. 'There, I believe that satisfies on all counts?'

'Oh, yes, sir, you have satisfied on all counts,' she answered. 'Since comparisons apparently mean a great deal to you, let me assure you that you are a far better lover than either Jake or Landry, in fact, I'd go so far as to say you are superb. I will not go so far as to award points, of course, for that would be too vulgar.'

Their eyes met. 'You score quite highly too,' he replied.

'Then we can both feel smug with ourselves.' She regarded him. 'I trust you have remembered the small matter of a ring?'

'Naturally. The same ring has been worn by Valmer brides for centuries.'

'And were all those brides whores too?' she enquired.

He leaned against the bedpost. 'The word is your choice, Beth.'

'So it is, and me a murderous thief as well.'

He nodded. 'So you are. Well, I'm sure you'll reform and live up to my exacting standards.' He didn't wait for her response, but left the room.

Beth closed her eyes. She could still feel his presence, and her heart was pounding urgently, as it had from the moment he came in. She drew a long, steadying breath. No matter what had gone wrong since, she had made love with him at last, and the experience was so wonderful that if she never made love to anyone again, this one occasion would feed her dreams until the day she died.

It would have to, because it seemed very unlikely indeed that he would come to her again.

CHAPTER TEN

Beth hoped in vain for enough time to compose herself before the wedding ceremony, because it wasn't long before a maid, having kept a discreet watch until Guy left, brought some tea, scrambled eggs and toast on a tray. Beth gazed at the fluffy yellow mound, and then pushed the plate away, taking only a slice of dry toast and a cup of tea. The encounter with Guy, and its regrettable conclusion, had unsettled her so much that, try as she would to muster a little calm and dignity, she failed abysmally.

The sun rose higher, the shadow of the castle foreshortened over the snow-covered Green Court, and she saw the clergyman in his vestment walk to the tower chapel. Two peacocks flapped out of his way, and then contented themselves with loud echoing calls. Beyond the castle, curls of smoke rose from the chimneys of Greylake town, and in the northern distance, visible on either side of Coneygarth Hill, was the cold glinting blue of the winter sea.

At just gone ten o'clock, Mrs Bradfield returned to help the bride prepare. She brought a beautiful wedding posy of lilies-of-the-valley. 'The flowers are from the conservatory,' she said, and then added, 'at Sir Guy's instruction, of course.'

Beth was taken aback that he should take such an interest.

The housekeeper looked approvingly at the blue taffeta gown. 'You know what they say, madam? Married in blue, love ever true. We're all so happy for you and Sir Guy. He is a fine man, and well loved here.' She smiled at Beth, who saw in her eyes that everyone in the castle knew the marriage vows had been anticipated.

'Yes, Mrs Bradfield, I'm sure he is.'

The woman paused, concerned. 'Something is wrong, madam, for you do not seem the happy bride. Are you unwell? Is that it?'

'Unwell?'

'Your monthly, madam.'

'Oh, I see. Well, that curse finished yesterday,' Beth replied.

'Then what is bringing you so low, madam? Please let me help you.'

The kindness in her voice at last tempted Beth into indiscretion. 'Things are not as they seem, Mrs Bradfield. Sir Guy is not marrying me for love.'

The woman's eyes widened with disbelief. 'Not for—? But, madam, earlier on he—' She broke off hastily, realizing she was being very imprudent indeed.

Beth gave a sad little smile. 'Don't make assumptions, Mrs Bradfield, because you'll be wrong.'

'But he shows every interest in your comfort, madam, and when he speaks of you we all know that it is with deep affection.'

'It's pretence.'

Mrs Bradfield was thunderstruck. 'But, my dear. I mean, madam . . .'

Beth smiled. 'Please forget I said anything, Mrs Bradfield, for I'm sure Sir Guy would be very displeased if he knew.'

'Not a word will pass my lips, madam, not even to Mr Bradfield.'

Beth believed her. 'Thank you, Braddy.'

The woman beamed at the use of her nickname. 'I'm here for you, madam.'

'Then do what you can to make me seem like a happy bride.'

Three-quarters of an hour later, Beth looked at herself in a floor-standing mirror. She had undergone an astonishing transformation. The sapphire taffeta became her well, her hair was pinned up, except for a number of long ringlets, and Braddy had fixed a tiny knot of lilies-of-the-valley to the side of her head.

The housekeeper beamed at her in the

mirror. 'You look beautiful, madam.'

'Thanks to you, Braddy.'

'It is a pleasure, madam, a great pleasure. I would rather wait all day upon you than a minute upon—' The woman broke off quickly, her face registering a mixture of horror and dismay.

Beth turned. 'Upon whom, Braddy?' she asked curiously.

No one, madam.'

'There's something you know that I don't, and I won't rest until you tell me.'

Braddy was completely flustered. 'Oh, *promise* me you will never tell Sir Guy!'

'You will never be implicated.'

Braddy relaxed a little. 'I was speaking of Miss Carberry, the . . . the actress.' The last word was uttered with a wrinkled nose.

'Maria Carberry?' Beth asked in astonishment, for there could not be many in the land not to have heard of the voluptuous toast of Drury Lane in London.

'Yes, madam.' The housekeeper tried not to meet her eyes.

'She was here?'

'Yes, madam.'

Beth glanced away. 'She's Sir Guy's mistress, isn't she?' she enquired flatly.

Braddy's cheeks burned. 'I believe that is what you would say.'

'When was this?'

At the beginning of the summer, madam.

May, June, or thereabouts.'

Dismay engulfed Beth. How could she have been so naïve? Of *course* a man like Guy would have a mistress! How foolish and doubly used she felt. Today he'd had the gall to find fault with her past, when all the time the Carberry creature was in his present.

'Madam?' Braddy was upset. 'Forgive me. I shouldn't have said anything.'

'I gave you my word I wouldn't say anything to Sir Guy,' Beth reminded her. The clock on the mantelshelf began to chime. It was time to go to the chapel. She drew a long, unhappy breath. This hurtful revelation made no difference to the matter in hand, but she shrank from facing him again. 'Braddy, will you come down with me?'

'I must anyway, madam, because Mr Bradfield and I are to be witnesses.' Braddy looked anxiously at her. 'Madam, you have your reasons for thinking Sir Guy does not love you, but I know he holds you in high regard. Oh, yes, madam, for I have been in his employ a long time now, and I know him. He will treat you well, because he's a gentleman through and through.'

'Is he? Tell me, Braddy, where did Miss Carberry sleep when she was here?' Beth expected to learn that she and Guy's mistress had shared the same bed.

'She had the Honeysuckle Room, just across the gallery.'

133

Beth was only slightly mollified. 'Was she here long?' She couldn't help questioning the housekeeper; she *had* to know.

'A month, and very stormy it was too. She's a very difficult woman. Very difficult. Nothing pleased her, except Sir Guy, of course. She made our lives a misery, and we were all relieved when she left. But there's no gainsaying she's very beautiful, very beautiful indeed. All that red-gold hair.'

Beth raised an eyebrow. 'Two redheads together? How tempestuous.'

Braddy shifted uncomfortably. 'Please remember, madam, that although gentlemen take actresses to their beds, they never marry them. It's ladies they marry.'

And just how much of a lady am I? Ladies didn't give themselves to blacksmiths, steal money, live under false identities, or become tainted by close proximity to two violent deaths. Beth wondered what Braddy would think if she knew the tawdry events that had culminated in Beth Tremoille's presence at Greylake.

Braddy went to get her cloak. 'It's cold outside, madam.'

Beth shook her head. Learning of Guy's mistress made her impervious to the cold.

Followed by Braddy, Beth proceeded along the gallery to the grand staircase, and soon, watched by the entire complement of servants, she emerged into the cold morning air of the

134

Green Court. A path had been cleared to the chapel, and she began to walk slowly along it. A strange sensation overtook her that she wasn't there at all; this was all happening to someone else. Peacocks called, the staghounds were audible in their kennels, and sounds drifted from the town below the castle walls, including hammering from the forge. What was Jake doing now? What would he say if he knew she was moments away from wearing Sir Guy Valmer's wedding ring? She reached the steps to the chapel door. Was Guy inside already? Or would she have to wait at the altar until he arrived? Please, not the latter, for that would demean her still more. Her steps were hesitant as she entered, and for a moment the shadows inside seemed as black as pitch after the dazzle of the sunshine and snow, but then she was bathed in the jewelled light of the stained-glass window above the altar. Candles burned, and the smell of hot wax was thick as she looked around the small, circular chapel, with its Norman stonework and three narrow rows of dark oak pews.

At first she thought there was no one else present, but then saw movement beside the altar, where Guy, Bradfield and the clergyman, the Reverend William Wakefield stood together. Guy was dressed formally, in a plain indigo velvet coat that was dappled with colour from the window. He might almost have been dressed for Almack's, with a pearl pin in his elaborate neckcloth, and the frills of his shirt pushing through his quilted, partially buttoned white satin waistcoat. His lower portions were encased in the snuggest of white trousers.

Braddy immediately drew back out of earshot as he came over to his bride. He toyed absently with the shirt frill at his cuff as he permitted his gaze to move over Beth, and if he disapproved of her uncovered hair he did not say so. 'You are as beautiful as I knew you would be,' he said quietly, so that no one else would hear.

'A compliment, sir?' she answered wryly.

'What else on our wedding day?' He held out a white-gloved hand, but she didn't take it. His hand fell away again and he looked enquiringly at her. 'Beth?'

'Would it not be a fine thing if I changed my mind at this late juncture?'

'I can think of many words to describe it, but "fine" is not among them.'

'You used me this morning.'

He hesitated. 'As I recall, I did nothing that was not at your agreement.'

'You used me,' she repeated. 'You made love to me when all the time you hold me in contempt for having had two lovers before you.'

'Keep your voice down,' he answered. 'Beth, I do not hold you in contempt.'

'I'll warrant you don't . . . not at this precise moment. But you did then. I saw it in your eyes, and heard it in your voice.'

'Please believe me, you are wrong in this.'

'Really? Then tell me, Guy, how did I compare?'

'With whom?' he enquired.

'Maria Carberry.'

'Ah, so little servant tongues have been wagging.' He toyed with his cuff again.

'Are you going to deny her?'

'I see no reason why I should.'

Her eyes flashed angrily. 'I see *every* reason why you should, sir!'

His returning glance was cool. 'Beth, I am not about to enter into a discussion about my private life, which will remain private. You have come here to marry me, and that is precisely what you are going to do.'

'I find you abhorrent,' she breathed, with monstrous falsehood.

He was cynical. 'Indeed? That's not how it seemed earlier. So let's be sensible, Beth. You are a thief who is implicated in murder, so false vows will be easily made.'

She drew back. 'So you hold the threat of arrest over me again?'

'Beth Tremoille, you are enough to turn a saint into a sinner. Why are you quibbling now? Is it foolish female revenge for an imagined slight this morning? You gave yourself to me, and now regret it?'

'I regret being made a fool of. You had the unspeakable nerve to find fault with me for

137

having had lovers in my past, and now I've learned that you keep a mistress. I expected more of you, sir, and you've sunk in my estimation as a result. You may be sure there will not be a repeat of this morning's weakness.'

'As you wish, but for the moment, do you intend to marry me?' Interpreting the ensuing silence as assent, he gave her posy to Braddy, and then drew Beth to the altar.

The clergyman gave no sign of thinking there was anything irregular about this almost clandestine marriage. He wasn't about to question the actions of the master of Greylake, to whom he was most likely greatly beholden. If Sir Guy Valmer wished to be married hastily, in virtual secrecy, with an unorthodoxly acquired licence and a bride who looked apprehensive about the entire business, the Reverend William Wakefield was content for it to so be. Tall and inclined to hunch over, he cut a rather nervous figure, and kept looking anxiously at Beth over his large, hooked nose, as if fearing she would suddenly try to stop the ceremony by claiming to be there against her will.

He began to intone. 'Dearly beloved: We have gathered here together in the presence of God to witness and bless the joining together of this man and this woman in Holy Matrimony . . .' She paid full attention only once, when he said, 'I require and charge you both, as ye will answer at the dreadful day of judgement when the secrets of all hearts shall be disclosed, that if either of you know any impediment, why ye may not be lawfully joined together in matrimony, ye do now confess it.'

Silence hung. I should speak up, she thought, because this isn't going to be a proper marriage, but will fly in the face of these sacred vows, but then Guy requested the clergyman to continue, and the moment was lost. She paid attention again when it was time for Guy to make his pledge. 'Wilt thou have this woman to thy wedded wife, to live together after God's ordinance in the holy estate of matrimony? Wilt thou love her, comfort her, honour, and keep her in sickness and in health; and, forsaking all other, keep thee only unto her, so long as ye both shall live?'

'I will,' Guy answered, and met her gaze for a moment.

Then the same pledge was required of her, with the additional pledge that she would also obey. She gazed at the Book of Common Prayer in the Reverend Wakefield's pale, beautifully kept hands. Obey Guy? Be subservient to him in everything? *Don't do it, Beth!* Her long silence became noticeable, and Guy leaned his head toward her. 'Beth?'

She glanced up into his eyes. Oh, such eyes, such power and magnetism; eyes to deny her the will to resist. 'I . . . I will.'

139

She heard Guy speak below his breath. 'The day you obey me in everything, Beth Tremoille, will be the day hippopotami dance around the Yarn Market.' Then he was slipping the ring on her finger. 'With this ring I thee wed, with my body I thee worship, and with all my worldly goods I thee endow. In the Name of the Father, and of the Son, and of the Holy Ghost. Amen.'

She became aware that, unseen by anyone else, his thumb was caressing her palm. It was time to kneel, and he drew her down gently. The taffeta of her gown rustled softly, and the colours from the window seemed dazzling. She saw the clergyman in silhouette only, but hardly heard the rest of the ceremony. Then Guy was raising her to her feet, and drawing her left hand to his lips. 'You are now Lady Valmer,' he murmured.

'And your property,' she replied.

'I look after my property, Beth. Believe me, you will be treated well, and shown all the respect your position warrants. I didn't use you this morning, and I'm disappointed that you think I did.'

'And I'm disappointed that you took such pains to tell me that it meant nothing.'

'Beth—'

'You said it, Guy, and you meant it.'

'Words mean little, Beth, it's actions that matter.' He kissed her hand again. She felt the warmth of his touch, lingering a little before he released her.

'What does that mean?'

He smiled faintly. 'Think about it,' he said softly, and then turned away to speak to the Reverend Wakefield.

Braddy immediately came up to Beth, whose face was a study of mixed emotions. The housekeeper pressed the bridal posy back into her hand. 'It is done now, madam, you are Sir Guy's wife.'

'Yes, God help me,' Beth whispered sadly. Her glance stole toward Guy, and in that moment Braddy saw the truth written on her face.

'Oh, madam, my lady, you love him, don't you?'

'Shh! He may hear!' Beth drew the housekeeper aside anxiously. 'He doesn't know, nor must he ever find out.'

'But, my lady, what if you are wrong to think he doesn't love you?'

'Wrong? When the queen of London's theatres is in his life?'

The housekeeper fell silent.

'Don't pity me, Braddy, I beg of you, or I will start to pipe my eyes, and that will not do at all.' Beth laughed, but it was all bravado.

A few minutes later, the bride and groom emerged from the chapel to find the servants and many townsfolk waiting to applaud. An old woman came forward to press a little crocheted net of hazelnuts upon Beth, who accepted with a smile, although she didn't know the gift's significance.

Guy explained. 'It is to ensure your fertility.'

Colour swamped her cheeks. 'Then it is wasted,' she replied.

'Beth—'

'All things considered,' she interrupted, 'I will not expect you in our marriage bed tonight.'

'Very well.'

She'd wanted him to try to persuade her to change her mind. But he didn't. He just bowed to her wish, as if he could not have cared less.

CHAPTER ELEVEN

Edward Barker's arrival at the gabled, stone-tiled Tudor splendour of Tremoille House was not what he'd anticipated, because he didn't even see his father, let alone speak to him. The servants were aware of Edward's parentage, because Thomas Welland's confrontation with Rowan had been heard throughout the house, but although most of them looked down on the illegitimate son of a tavern keeper, they did not dare to show it. They had their own livelihoods to protect and, as yet, no one knew precisely what Thomas's intentions were. Beyond summoning his bastard son, he had not issued any further instructions, and no one wished to approach him, not even Bolton, who would have walked on burning coals for Jane, but shrank from going anywhere near Thomas Welland, unless expressly summoned. Like the rest of the staff, Bolton believed the new master of Tremoille House was more than a little mad.

Unaware of what to do about Edward, Bolton took the precaution of asking Jane what was to be done. She, being in a particularly disgruntled mood because she wished to be out of the house and back at Whitend, and also being more than a little on Rowan's side, answered that Edward was to be dealt with as would any other newly arrived servant. Thus Edward found himself bundled off to sleep in a hayloft above the stables. It was certainly not the feather bed and lavender sheets for which he'd been hoping. The desultory reception made him feel very unwelcome, and the only thing that prevented him from walking home to Gloucester through the snow was the thought of the thrashing he'd get from his mother. So he settled to sleep, listening to the horses in the stalls below, the night breeze in the eaves and the mice scuttling along the rafters.

As the rose-coloured dawn filtered into the loft, a young kitchen maid with nut-brown hair awakened him. 'Mr Bolton says you're to come for breakfast.'

He gazed up at her, thinking how dew-fresh

143

she was, and how she smelled of soap and starch. He'd awoken with a pounding erection, as he always did. It was the sort of arousal that could be swiftly satisfied, so he grabbed her by the arms to pull her down on top of him, intending to roll over and force her to lie there while he slipped himself between her legs. Just between the legs would do, no need to go inside. He'd shoot his load in a few seconds, and feel much better for it. There was no thought of her, just that she provided the means for his release. He clamped one hand over her mouth and struggled with the other to open his breeches. She couldn't move, because he had her trapped, and her stifled screams increased as he pushed himself between her thighs and began to rub.

He grunted with pleasure, intending to be over and done with in a few seconds. It was nothing to him. He treated her as he did his whores. His own relief was all that mattered, to quench the urgent desire that gripped him. He saw nothing wrong. After all, if he didn't come inside her, she couldn't get pregnant. She might even enjoy it, if she loosened up a little and stopped struggling. He was big enough to satisfy her; big enough to satisfy six of her! He groaned as he came close to a climax. The shaft that he rubbed to and fro between the softness of her thighs was so engorged and sensitive that he was in ecstasy. *Come on, Ned, come on, give her a good shagging!*

His exposed backside was bumping up and down almost dementedly, and the rosy dawn seemed blood red as at last he uttered several loud, jolting grunts as he and his load parted company. The separation wasn't quite complete when suddenly a broom handle jabbed him savagely between the buttocks, almost subjecting him to penetration.

'Get off her, you bloody animal! Get off, I say!' growled an angry male voice.

Edward screeched with pain and rolled swiftly away, exposing his instantly deflated genitals to the end of the broom handle, which was immediately pressed warningly to their vulnerable softness. He saw a man looming over them, with a kerchief tied across his lower face and a wide-brimmed hat that cast his eyes in complete shadow.

The maid gasped, half with relief, half with fresh fear, and clambered away while she had the chance. When she couldn't go any further, she cowered back into the angle between the roof and the wall, watching what happened. Down in the stalls, the horses were unsettled by the disturbance, moving nervously in their stalls.

The newcomer prodded Edward's testicles. 'Put your miserable pizzle away, or I'll put it away for you!' The kerchief muffled his voice, and all the girl could tell was that he was tall and fairly young.

145

But when Edward tried to obey the instruction, the broom handle stabbed cruelly anyway. Edward screamed in agony and curled up, clutching his crotch. 'You madman!' he gasped, almost sobbing. 'Just wait until my father hears about this!'

'Learns about what, tavern muck?' the anonymous man taunted. 'That someone stopped you from raping one of the maids?'

'She wanted it!' Edward lied.

'No, she didn't, not Maggie. She's a good girl. You, on the other hand, are a worthless pile of dog shit.'

'My father—'

'Is unhinged, and so will you be if you've got his blood! You're from the wrong side of the blanket, a slop-bucket who'll never amount to anything. Her ladyship has no time for you, and you mark my words, Master Rowan will be back before long, and you'll be kicked back to your whore of a mother!' The man laughed. 'Everyone in Gloucester knows Poll Barker always parted her legs for anyone who'd pay a halfpenny!'

A cry of fury was wrenched from Edward as he hurled himself at his sneering foe, who was caught off balance and fell backward over the edge of the loft. Edward's breath snatched with horror. The bastard must be dead! How was he going to get out of this? Belatedly pushing his floppy tackle back inside his breeches, he leaned fearfully forward to look down, and was just in time to see the hooded man dashing out of the stables, having had the luck to fall on a pile of old hay. The horses were now thoroughly alarmed, whinnying and moving around.

Edward whirled about toward Maggie, whose hands were pressed to her mouth, her blue eyes huge and terrified as she pressed even harder against the unforgiving wall. 'He's shown a clean pair of heels,' he growled, 'but I want to know his name!'

'I—I don't know.'

'Oh, yes, you do, because he knows you! Give me his name, or I'll give you more of the same.' He reached threateningly inside his breeches.

'I don't know!' she cried. 'I've only been here a few days and I don't know everyone yet!'

Edward hesitated. He was smarting with humiliation and fury, his balls were causing him agony, his arse felt as if he'd been serviced by an elephant, and he needed to strike out. She was the only one within reach, but he'd never hit a woman in his life. He'd done everything else, but never hit one. Besides, if she went back in even worse shape than she was now, he'd probably get a thorough drubbing from his recent assailant—and however many 'friends' the fellow had. Ned Barker was many things, but not an out-and-out fool. He'd realized on arriving that he

147

wasn't going to be popular; now he knew it for certain. They all, Lady Welland included, favoured his brother Rowan!

He moved away from the ladder. 'Get out of here,' he breathed. 'Go on, get out of here!' She remained where she was, so he stepped further away.

Terrified, she edged forward, at first on her hands and knees, and then, when there was room, getting to her feet like a hunted animal. Her wide eyes didn't leave his face until she at last reached the ladder, which she scrambled down as fast as she could. At the bottom she turned to look up again. 'Tavern muck!' she cried, and then spat on the floor before catching up her skirts and fleeing.

Almost immediately Edward heard the murmur of angry male voices in the stable yard, and his mouth ran dry. They'd come to get him! The colour drained from his face, and he felt sick. He couldn't stay up here all day, but if he ventured down . . . His stomach heaved, both with dread and emptiness, and when the spasm passed he straightened again. He was here because he had aristocratic blood! He was better than them, and he knew all about dirty fighting. He wouldn't win, but he'd beat hell's bloody bells out of some of them before he fell!

Straightening his clothes, he slipped his stockinged feet into his clogs and climbed down the ladder. At the bottom he took a deep breath and then marched out into the yard as cockily as he could, given that his crotch and backside were wincingly painful. The morning sky was vibrant with red and gold, colouring the snow on the surrounding hills, and bathing everything with an unworldly glow. He was right, they were waiting. About eight of them, all wearing kerchiefs and hats, and brandishing sticks of one sort or another. Safety in numbers, eh? Well, he'd show them what Lord Welland's other son was made of! Gritting his teeth, he launched himself at the nearest man, kicking, biting and gouging like a fiend. He'd reached the second one before they gathered their wits to set upon him *en masse*. Within seconds there was a scrambling, heaving mass of bodies struggling in the middle of the yard, with Edward buried at the bottom. The racket upset the horses again, and even Thomas Welland's wolfhounds in their kennel beyond the yard wall.

Suddenly Thomas's enraged voice bellowed above the noise. 'What in *God's* own name is going on here?' He'd come to the yard to see how his favourite hunter was improving after a bout of colic, and had been greeted by the astonishing scene. Edward's assailants leapt fearfully away and scattered in all directions, disappearing as if by magic, all safe in the knowledge that their identities were unknown.

A nerve pulsed at Thomas's temple as he advanced upon the bedraggled figure on the ground. 'Your name, sir!' he demanded furiously, his leather gloves taut across his knuckles as he gripped his ebony walking stick. He wore his battered old hunting pink, and leather breeches that shone with age.

Edward scrambled to his feet. 'Ned— I—I mean Edward Barker,' he replied, trying to look dignified, but failing miserably.

Thomas's cold eyes cleared a little as he realized he was gazing at himself when younger. 'What was all that about just now?'

Edward's mind started working. He knew to whom he was talking, and that this was the perfect moment to commend himself. 'They resent my coming here, my lord, and made me sleep in the stables. They were waiting to set upon me when I came out. I gave as good as I got.'

'Did you indeed? So they resent you?'

'They like my brother and don't want me here.' It was true enough, but Edward also knew it would instantly place him on his father's side of the matter.

Thomas's brow darkened. 'Don't mention that good-for-nothing ne'er-do-well!'

Edward lowered his eyes respectfully.

'Well, my boy, you've acquitted yourself well, and from now on your place will be in the big house. You'll be at my right hand, known everywhere to be my favoured son. And you will be known as Edward *Welland*, is that clear?'

Edward's heart leapt with joy. 'Yes, my lord.' Now he'd get those hooded bastards, and make sure they got their just deserts, especially the one in the loft.

'Well, come on, we'll take breakfast together! But first we must find you something to wear. It will have to be from my wardrobe for the time being, but as soon as possible, I'll see that clothes are made for you.' The sick horse forgotten, Thomas beamed at his new son, flung an arm around his shoulder and ushered him toward the house.

Jane had observed everything from a window, including the dishevelled maid running out after clearly being mauled, at the very least, by Thomas's oafish offspring. She gazed down at Edward, her lips twitching with distaste. If the unwashed, uncivilized dolt was being ushered back with smiles, then she was going to have to endure his presence at mealtimes. She shuddered at the prospect, and wished for the hundredth time that she had never married Thomas Welland.

Breakfast was all she feared it would be. Edward had been scrubbed, but he still looked exactly what he was, a tavern slut's brutish pup. What was worse, his likeness to his loathsome sire was underlined by his wearing Thomas's clothes. He proceeded to live down to her expectations when he shovelled devilled kidneys into his mouth as if he hadn't eaten for days, and then was only just prevented from wiping his greasy lips with the sleeve of Thomas's exquisite corbeau-coloured coat, stitched by one of the most admired tailors in Bond Street. He sniffed and belched, and once, by the aroma, he farted as well. There was no doubt about it, Edward Barker—er, no, it was to be Welland from now on—was a chip off the obnoxious old block.

Jane found out just how much of a chip when Thomas was called away by a messenger from Whitend. As soon as the door was closed, she eyed Edward. 'Sir, your table manners are atrocious, and I trust will be improved upon without further ado.'

'I'll learn quick enough,' he replied, 'after all, I'm here to take Rowan's place.'

She stiffened. 'You, sir, aren't fit to mention his name, let alone take his place!'

'Oh, yes, I will. My father says as much, and it's his orders I take, not yours.'

'How *dare* you speak to me like that!' she breathed, quivering from head to toe.

'I'll speak how I like. Who are you to look down your nose at me? I've heard things, whispers about a whorehouse in Worcester, or somewhere like that. I've a bone to pick with you, because you're the reason I had to sleep in a hayloft last night, and why a gang of servants wore masks and tried to beat me.'

'Oh, no, you slimy little toad, that's not why you were beaten. What did you do to that maid?' Jane was within a hair's breadth of grabbing Thomas's walking stick, which was hooked over the back of his empty chair, and clouting his impudent byblow around the head with it.

Edward was all innocence. 'What maid?'

'You know very well. I was watching. I saw her go in, and then saw her running out looking, to say the least, a little dishevelled.'

'Oh, that maid. Yes, she came in, because she fancied me. I gave her a good seeing to, and then she changed her mind, said I'd forced myself on her. She's just a lying little trollop, as I'll tell my father if he asks.'

Jane was speechless that such a guttersnipe could have the audacity to treat her in such a manner. The maid wasn't the only one he saw fit to give a good seeing to!

Edward grinned. 'My father hates the sight of you, that's clear enough, so don't expect me to show you any respect. Bugger you, lady.'

She saw Thomas Welland looking out of his sly bumpkin eyes, and in that second decided to return to Whitend immediately, whether or not Thomas liked it. Spending Christmas with two Thomas Wellands was simply too much to cope with.

*   *   *

In Haldane, helped by Katy, Harriet was just putting the finishing touches to the Christmas greenery in the parish church. Nearby, the

153

Reverend Bellamy was discussing Carrie Markham's funeral with the verger and several prominent parishioners, whose frequent sly glances at Harriet and her daughter were a reminder of the scandal's continued prominence.

Katy, a solemn child, with long, straight blonde hair and blue eyes, looked pale and nervous. She wore a royal blue pelisse trimmed with honey fur, a white merino dress, blue leather gloves and tan ankle boots, and appeared very much Landry Haldane's daughter, but her eyes were bewildered as she went through the motion of selecting another ivy spray for Harriet to add to a garland twined around a stone pillar. Only once did she show any interest. 'Why can't there be mistletoe?'

Harriet smiled and looked down at her. 'Because it's pagan,' she explained.

'What's pagan?'

Harriet didn't know where to start, and chose the coward's way out. 'Grandfather Bellamy doesn't like mistletoe.'

'Is he really my grandfather?'

'Yes, of course, because he's my father.'

The child's bewilderment resumed. 'Is he Mama's father too?'

Harriet paused. 'I'm your mother, Katy, and I always have been.'

'But my mother went to sleep last night and will not wake up again. She's gone to play with the angels.'

The moment wasn't right to press the point. 'And that's what she's doing now,' Harriet said gently.

'The next time you hear thunder, you'll know that she and the angels are playing skittles up in Heaven.'

That brought a smile. 'I hope she wins.'

'I'm sure she will.'

The smile faded uncertainly. 'But Papa is still my Papa, isn't he?'

'Yes, of course he is, and he loves you very much. I love you too.'

'Do you, Miss Harriet.'

'You can call me Mama, if you like.'

'Mama is with the angels,' Katy reminded her.

Harriet sighed inside, realizing that it wasn't going be a simple matter to replace Carrie. Just as it wasn't a simple matter to replace Beth. Why did someone else always stand between Harriet Bellamy and what she wanted?

The sound of excited barking came from outside the church, and Katy gasped delightedly. 'Pompey! It's Pompey!' And before Harriet knew it, she'd run off down the aisle, past her grandfather and his companions, and out into the morning sunshine and snow, where she halted, looking around. There was a movement beneath the lych-gate and she saw her father, in a navy-blue greatcoat and top hat, starting up the churchyard path with her adored pet, a King Charles puppy, on a little leash.

'Papa, Papa! You've found him!' She ran headlong down the path to fling herself into his arms.

'Yes, sweeting,' Landry replied, struggling to hold her and at the same time keep a tight grip on Pompey's leash.

She looked earnestly at him. 'You *are* still my Papa, aren't you?'

'Of course I am! Why ever would you doubt it?'

'Because Miss Harriet says *she's* my mama now.'

'Ah. Well, she is. Your other mama was just looking after you for her. But she loved you as much as if you really were her little girl, never forget that.' He put her down slowly, and gave her the leash. 'Now then, you keep a tight hold of that pup, because the next time he runs off he may keep running.'

'Pompey wouldn't do that.'

'Maybe another dog has told him that the pavements in London are piled with golden bones.'

Katy gave him a pert look. 'That's silly, Papa.'

'Can you be sure?'

'Well . . .'

'You see, sweeting? You can't, so you really must keep Pompey close to you, in case he discovers a fancy for one of those golden

156

bones. Take him for a toddle around the churchyard, but stay on the cleared paths, otherwise poor Pompey will be in snow right over his head.'

Katy gave a screech of laughter, and then dashed off, with the overjoyed puppy bounding at her side. Landry tilted his top hat to the back of his head. Katy was good for him, there was no doubt of that. He'd been in a foul mood when he left the hall, but now the weight seemed to have slipped from his shoulders. Well, some of it. A resentful scowl returned to his face as he remembered standing at the top of the staircase at the hall, listening to the indiscreet conversation of his visitors. Squat, ugly Sir Daniel Lavington and his lean, affected nephew were unaware of the unusual acoustics of Haldane Hall, which permitted even the softest of whispers to carry up to the next floor. At first they'd passed lascivious comments about Guy and Beth, accompanied by conjecture as to what the facts really were in their case, but then their attention turned much more scathingly to Landry himself. They gleefully assassinated his character, beginning with his having a mere maid as his mistress, then his vile deflowering of the vicar's daughter, followed by his disgrace in the army, his abandoned affair with the equally abandoned tenant of the Dower House, and then his final humiliation at the ball. The word 'pantomime' was used, as well as various

157

expletives that gave the full flavour of their contempt for their host.

Landry could only listen in almost apoplectic silence. To go down and make a scene now would do him no favour, so he remained where he was, struggling to master his fury. Sir Daniel was hardly a shining knight, and his nephew's reputation was tarnished by an unsubstantiated charge of rape, so they had no business criticizing anyone.

The undercurrents during their brief visit had been almost tangible, and had been due warning of how he, Landry, was going to fare in society for the foreseeable future. How much worse would it become if Harriet carried out her veiled threat to spread even more of the scandal far and wide? Damn her! She was never meant to be anything more to him than a friend, but now he was burdened with her as a wife! And all he really wanted was Beth. Only Beth.

At that moment the Reverend Bellamy and his three companions emerged from the church. Seeing Landry, the verger and parishioners exchanged glances that further fuelled his ire. Damn it, he'd become the laughing stock of the bloody county! It was all Harriet's fault, hers and Carrie Markham's. They'd conspired to spin him a tissue of lies, and the world blamed *him!*

Harriet's father beamed at him. 'Ah, Landry, good morning to you.'

'Good morning,' Landry replied, doffing his top hat.

'Did you wish to see me?'

'Actually, I came to return Pompey to Katy. He came to the hall again.'

'Ah, yes. Well, if you wish to speak to Harriet, you'll find her inside.'

Under the circumstances, there was little Landry could do but enter the church, for it would have been regarded as most curious if he'd declined to see his bride-to-be. At first his eyes were still dazzled by the snow outside, but they soon adjusted and he saw Harriet by the garlanded pillar. She was wearing a ruby-red quilted velour cloak over a long-sleeved fawn woollen gown, with a neat little bonnet on her short golden hair. She turned and smiled. There was a time when he'd have thought how attractive she looked, but now she simply grated on him, although when it came to things sexual, for a clergyman's daughter she had proved astonishingly intuitive and voracious. He'd been shocked by what she'd been prepared to do while her father was asleep in the adjoining room, and now could not help wondering how far she'd go in the church, when the old boy might walk in at any moment. The thought of taking such a foolhardy risk excited him, and he was filled with the urge to test her. Yes, he would see how far she would go to satisfy her lust for him. Driven by his own arousal, he strode over to her and without so much as a greeting grabbed her into his arms to kiss her savagely on the lips.

Startled, she dropped the fronds of ivy she was holding, and slipped her arms around his neck to return the kiss. He had already noted a particular dark, shadowy alcove nearby, and he lifted her from her feet to carry her into it. He'd fuck her like a St James's whore! His lips were harsh over hers, his tongue forcing between her lips in a way that wasn't loving or tender. He grabbed her skirt with one hand and hauled it up almost to her waist, and then wrenched her undergarments aside. But if he thought to alarm her with such ferociousness, he was disappointed, for her fingers fumbled with his trouser falls and then with his genitals. Her hand encircled his erection, and then her palm slid adoringly over the knob, massaging it with erotic delectation.

It was graceless and thoughtless sex, solely motivated by the element of danger. They were both aware that at any moment they might hear footsteps enter the church, but at the same time they were both ravenous for a swift release from the lust that engulfed them. Her bruised lips moved against his as she whispered his name. 'Landry, oh Landry . . .'

He lifted her a little more, and then forced himself cruelly into her. Her legs wrapped around him, and he heard her excited gasps. Harder and harder he drove, trying to hurt her, trying to make her gasp with pain rather than pleasure, but nothing seemed to touch her. All she wanted was to receive him, and to take delight in his ferocity. The knowledge that he both loathed and desired her was intoxicating, and she closed her eyes in elation as waves of gratification broke unstoppably through her, and the more powerfully he penetrated her, the more she wanted it to continue. Violent sexual congress brought exquisite reward, and she didn't want it to stop. 'More,' she panted, 'more . . .'

He gave one final thrust that should have split her in two, and suddenly his climax burst within her. His member pumped violently, and with such enervating force that he had to cling to her to prevent himself from sagging at the knees. Harriet ceased to exist, because at this ultimate moment it was Beth's name he breathed.

Harriet didn't care. Let him long for the unreachable. Her eyes were closed as she leaned her head back against the cold stone. She heard her father and his friends outside, and Katy laughing. The thunder of her heart found an echo in Landry's, and slowly she bent to put her trembling lips to his. He didn't pull away, but accepted her long, lingering kiss. It wasn't an eager response, but neither was it rejection. Maybe he was still thinking of the woman he'd lost. Well, let him. He could yearn all he wanted, he'd remain in Harriet

CHAPTER TWELVE

Darkness fell early in Frampney on Christmas Eve, and the village green was almost deserted as Rosalind went out in the early evening to fill another bucket with coal from the pile in the forge. She was well wrapped against the cold, and hurried the few yards from the house to the forge, where she knew Matty had gone to have a crafty smoke of his pipe. He was supposed to have gone to the George and Dragon, Phoebe having forbidden him to smoke in the house and Jake having forbidden him to smoke in the forge, but he couldn't bring himself to trudge all the way to the public house.

Rosalind was almost there when suddenly she heard a male voice calling her softly and urgently. She glanced around, and then a figure moved from the shadows by the old apple tree that in summer was sweet with honeysuckle and climbing white roses. 'Rowan?' She glanced nervously at the forge, fearful that Matty might hear.

'A moment, that's all,' Rowan begged, and putting the bucket down, Rosalind stepped into the snow to go to him. He almost snatched her into his embrace, burying his face

162

in her hair and pressing her against his body. He had only thought of her since leaving Greylake, and with each unsatisfied moment his desire had increased. He was past the point of no return. Rosalind Mannacott was the one for him. The *only* one. He pushed her back against the apple tree, finding her parted lips in a kiss so filled with love and passion that in spite of the bitter cold she felt he might melt in her arms. *Rosalind, Rosalind, Rosalind . . .* He could hear her name echoing across the dark skies, and through his heart, and the taste of her upon his lips was ambrosia itself.

He pulled her from her toes, and she wrapped her legs around him, supported on the mound of intense excitement that swelled the front of his riding breeches. His eyes closed with pleasure as she squirmed against it. He buried his face against her throat, aware of how her skin warmed and her breath came in little gasps of delight as her eager flesh shuddered with gratification. Their lips met in a long, lingering kiss, before she drew back. 'Let me do what I did before, the night of the fair.'

He smiled and lowered her to the ground again. She began to open his breeches, but just as her slender little fingers touched his bursting masculinity, they both heard a sound from the forge. She gasped and moved back from him as if scalded, and he cursed under his breath as he fumbled to straighten his clothes again. But no one came out of the forge, and all went quiet again. The moment had gone, however, and she didn't offer to finish what had so nearly begun.

He cupped her face in his hands. 'Come away with me, Rosalind.'

'Away? But . . . Rowan, I haven't seen you for days, I hardly know you, and—'

'Do you love me?' he interrupted.

She stared, and then nodded. 'Yes, of course, but—'

'No buts, Rosalind, no buts. I want you, you want me, and there is nothing to prevent us from being together.'

'There's my father to begin with,' she said, still with half an eye on the forge.

'He'd prevent you from one day being Lady Welland?'

Her eyes widened and her lips parted. 'What are you saying?' she breathed.

'That I want to marry you.'

'You're mad!' she gasped, but the prospect was beginning to sing through her veins like a romantic melody. This was what she wanted, what she'd dreamed of since first seeing Robert Lloyd, who'd been nothing more than a squire's son. Rowan was the son and heir of a lord of the realm! She felt almost dizzy with excitement, and as the moment threatened to fly away with her, she struggled to keep a cool head. 'You know you can't marry me, Rowan. I'm nothing, and if you make me your wife, you'll be nothing too. Society won't accept me, and will look down its nose at you.'

'My stepmother was reputedly a brothel whore in Worcester, yet she has made two very fine marriages. You are a sweet innocent, and I love you. Society will love you too.' But he knew that although such a state of affairs might indeed come true, it would be an uphill battle all the way.

For once Rosalind wasn't entirely selfish. 'You don't have to promise to marry me, Rowan, I will come with you anyway.'

'As my mistress? My doxy?'

She hesitated, but then nodded.

He kissed her adoringly on the lips, and then whispered a line from a Shakespeare sonnet. *'Thy love is better than high birth to me.'*

Rosalind didn't know where the words came from, but listened, rapt. 'Oh, Rowan, that is so romantic.'

'Your love *is* more important than my high birth. How many people are fortunate enough to encounter true love? Not as many as wish they did. That's why we must be together, whether or not our classes are different. I can even be certain of a clergyman to perform the ceremony. My uncle, Oswald Welland, loathes my father enough to gladly make us man and wife. All we have to do is present ourselves at his parish in north London.' He pressed his lips to the tip of her cold little nose. 'I may be the Honourable Rowan Welland, and the future Lord Welland, but I'm not rich now. I have an inheritance through my mother's family, but the allowance I once received from my father has been terminated. I'm disowned. The rest of what was once to have been heaped on me is now to be heaped upon my bastard half-brother, Ned Barker.'

Rosalind was startled. 'Ned Barker? Poll Barker's Ned?'

'You know him?'

'I worked at Poll's tavern, and he was always trying to get hold of me.'

'What did he do to you?' Rowan demanded hotly.

'Not as much as he'd have liked.' Rosalind smiled. 'Don't look like that, Rowan; I could always move faster than he could.'

'If I thought he'd so much as—'

She slipped her arms around his neck and stretched up to kiss him again. 'I lay with Robert Lloyd and it was a terrible mistake. When next I lie with anyone, it will be with you, my dearest love. And maybe we have a little more money than you think. I do not come without a dowry.'

He was taken aback. 'A dowry?' He couldn't imagine Jake with either the resources or the will to provide for his daughter's marriage to a blue-blooded swell.

'Not from Dad,' she laughed. 'I just have a little money of my own. No one else knows about it, just me . . . and now you as well.'

'Where did it come from?'

'It was given to me.'

'Given?' He tilted her chin to make her look at him. 'By whom?'

'A woman. That's all I'm going to say.'

Rowan searched her eyes in the darkness of the night. 'How much is it?' he asked curiously, able to tell by her voice that she meant what she said.

'Four hundred and eighty guineas.'

An oath escaped him. 'Sweet God!'

'It's mine, Rowan, and I've been keeping it for just such a time as this. We can manage for a while, can't we?'

'I rather think so,' he breathed, 'especially as we already have a fine London house to go to.'

'We do?'

He nodded. 'My cousin's house in Park Lane.'

'Is that Mayfair?'

'Yes,' he replied with a smile.

Her eyes shone. 'I'll be living in Mayfair,' she said softly, hardly able to believe it was true. Then she looked at him again. 'When do you want me to be ready?'

'As soon as you can. I've taken a room at the Lamb and Flag on the Bristol road, and my travelling carriage is there. I hired a saddle horse to come here.'

She shook her head. 'I can't go to the Lamb and Flag, Rowan, the landlord is Matty

Brown's brother and he knows me.'

'Then we'll go to Whitend.'

'Your *father's* house?'

He smiled. 'The old boy is up at Tremoille House with his new son. Jane intends to return there, but not until the New Year, so the house is empty at the moment.'

She hesitated, and then nodded. 'I can't leave until after church service later this evening. They'll all be asleep by midnight, and won't know I've gone until tomorrow morning, and by then it will be too late.'

'Midnight it is. I'll return to the Lamb and Flag to dine, and then come back here with the carriage.'

'Wait outside the village,' she urged. 'There's a place among the trees, where the lane leads off to the Bristol road, no one will see you there.' She gasped as she heard Matty moving around in the forge. 'I'd better get the coal bucket filled, and then go back inside.'

He pulled her close for a final kiss, gripping her little buttocks through her clothes and holding her on to his loins. She sighed with fresh pleasure. 'Will we sleep together tonight?' she whispered.

'Yes, oh yes,' he answered.

She hurried away into the forge, and he heard her greeting Matty as she began to fill the bucket.

Rowan hurried away, consumed with such sexual frustration that when he reached the horse he had to lean against it and push his hand and handkerchief inside his trousers to relieve himself. It did not take long, just a few deft strokes and a few pulsing seconds of climax. Ashamed, he closed his eyes and rested his forehead against the saddle. What was happening to him? Only days ago he would never have dreamed of doing such a thing outside, even in the dark. Now he was so enthralled by Rosalind Mannacott that his cock had power over everything.

*   *   *

At ten o'clock that evening, Jake, Rosalind and Phoebe emerged from the Christmas Eve service at Frampney parish church. With them was Jamie Webb, the village lad who'd fallen in love with Rosalind, although she couldn't abide him. He was going on nineteen, fresh-faced and burly, and had wiry brown hair that he cut back as and when he remembered. His clothes were nondescript, although of reasonable quality, because he had secured a position in Squire Lloyd's employ. He'd done better for himself than the other young men in the village, but even so, his real ambition—after marrying Rosalind Mannacott—was to learn blacksmithing. His eye was upon joining Jake and Matty at Frampney forge, and eventually living in the forge house with Rosalind as Mrs Webb, but she regarded him as a half-witted clod, who certainly could not stand comparison with someone like Rowan Welland. Or even the late, unlamented Robert Lloyd.

The black velvet sky was clear, and twinkled with thousands of stars. There would be another freeze before morning. Jake paused by the church porch to light the lantern that would see the way safely back to the forge. A lot of lanterns were being lit because of treacherous patches of ice that could upend even the most careful walker. The atmosphere was festive and happy, with friends calling out Christmas greetings and well-wishing as Jake and his party began to walk back to the forge.

Much to Rosalind's annoyance Jamie remained with them, Phoebe having made a point of asking him to their little supper of minced pies and hot, spiced cider. Phoebe was of the opinion that Jamie was a good prospect for Rosalind, and that a match would come of it if she thrust him upon the girl frequently enough. Jamie tried to walk alongside the object of his desire as they trudged through the crisp snow, but Rosalind immediately quickened her steps and pushed herself between Phoebe and her father. Phoebe was grumbling about Matty. 'He's getting to be next to useless these days, and he keeps moaning about not being able to smoke that old clay pipe.'

'If he smokes in the house again, I'll break

the pipe over his head,' Jake muttered, still alarmed about what might have ensued if he hadn't stirred when he did.

Phoebe sighed. 'He promised he wouldn't, and to be fair, he goes to the George and Dragon when he fancies a smoke.'

Rosalind shook her head. 'No, he doesn't, because it's too far for him. He goes in the forge.' She didn't like telling on the old man, but even she knew he was a danger.

Jake lost his temper. 'Damn it, he can't be trusted to do anything he says!'

Phoebe's face had fallen. 'Oh, Matty,' she whispered sadly.

They didn't have far to go now, and everything at the house—and the forge—seemed quiet and as it should be, and a pale wisp of smoke rose lazily from the house chimney into the still winter darkness. Nobody thought anything could possibly be wrong, until Jamie moved closer to Jake. 'Can you smell smoke?'

'Darn it, Jamie, every chimney in the village is—'

'Not that sort of smoke. Something that shouldn't be.'

Jake glanced around urgently. Jamie was right, there was a fire somewhere, and not in any hearth. Looking more particularly at the forge, he saw smoke swirling from the entrance, and with a curse, he pushed the lantern into Phoebe's hand. 'Yell for help!

171

Give it some lung, because we'll need all the hands we can muster!' Then he began to run, with Jamie at his heels. Phoebe and Rosalind stood in dismay for a few moments, but soon recovered their wits to scream at the tops of their voices. 'Help! Fire! Help!'

The two men reached the forge, where the stench of burning had intensified, and leaping flames could be seen through the billowing swathes of thick smoke. The air was searing, and the dancing glow of sparks could be made out along the rafters. Then there was a splintering sound as part of the roof caved in, and flames began to leap up through the roof toward the stars.

Jake ventured into the entrance, trying not to inhale the acrid smoke as he cast around for Matty. 'Matty! *Matty*!' he yelled, but was beaten back as the flames strengthened, and sparks and splinters began to fly through the air.

'There he is!' Jamie cried, and pushed past Jake toward the old blacksmith, who lay motionless on the ground in front of his old chair, which was now alight.

Jake ran as well, and together they dragged the heavy, inert figure well away from the forge. But even as they turned Matty over on to his back, his dull, staring eyes told them he'd gone. There was a look of agony on his face, yet he wasn't burned. He may have gone to the forge to steal a smoke in the warm, but it wasn't sleep that caused the lighted pipe to fall from his fingers, it was more likely a seizure.

Figures were beginning to run across the green from all directions, most of them with buckets. Jake straightened. 'For Christ's sake get to it, lads, or Frampney won't have a forge!'

Phoebe hurried toward Matty's body, followed by a reluctant Rosalind, who was afraid of the dead. With an anguished wail, Phoebe sank to her knees, and put the lantern down in the snow. Then she tried to gather her husband into her arms, but he was too big and heavy, so she curled over him in grief, her tears wet on his smoke-stained cheek as she put her face next to his, whispering his name over and over, as if to breathe life back into him. Rosalind stood there in a daze, too frightened to do anything.

The men of the village formed a long line from the nearest duck pond, the ice of which was soon broken to allow buckets to be dipped in the freezing water beneath. The buckets were swung along the line, and there was a lot of hissing and spitting as the contents of each one were hurled on to the blaze. Steam joined with the smoke, but the flames did not seem to be checked, crackling greedily as they consumed the forge.

Some of the women began to pull Phoebe away from Matty's body. At first she resisted, still holding on to him, wild in her grief, but they persisted, and at last she was persuaded to go back to the house, where she was plied with the hot, spiced cider that had been intended for a much happier occasion. Rosalind had begun to follow them to the house, but Jamie caught her arm. 'You'll be more help out here,' he said, shoving a bucket into her hands.

'Don't *you* tell me what to do!' she cried.

'But Rozzie—!'

'And don't call me that either! I'm Miss Mannacott to you, Jamie Webb, and don't you forget it!' She thrust the bucket back at him, then caught up her skirts and ran after the women. But she didn't intend to comfort Phoebe. She edged around the crowded kitchen when all the women were distracted, and slipped upstairs to her room, where her things were packed and ready, tied up in two shawls. She didn't care about Matty's death and Phoebe's pain, nor did she give a second thought to what her father would do without the forge. All that concerned her was her own happiness. Dropping the bulging shawls out of the window, she slipped downstairs again, and managed to avoid being seen as she left the house. After collecting the shawls, she hurried around the house and then out behind the forge toward the boundary wall of Squire Lloyd's property. No one saw her move stealthily from shadow to shadow, making her way down the long village green to where the lane led out toward the Bristol road.

She didn't expect Rowan to be there yet, but he'd been unable to contain his impatience until midnight, and his travelling carriage was already drawn up where she'd suggested. He climbed down as soon as he saw her. 'I feared you wouldn't come.'

'Why?'

'Because there's clearly something going on in the village, a fire, by the smell of it. I can't see from here.'

'Oh, that. Yes, one of the cottage thatches is on fire, and everyone's helping. I don't know the people very well.'

'I thought by the direction of the smoke that it might be the forge.'

'No.' She smiled and linked her arms around his neck. 'Let's go, for we have our lives to get on with.'

'So we do,' he said softly, brushing his lips to hers, and then he swung her up into the carriage and climbed in after her. Within moments they were on the way to Whitend.

CHAPTER THIRTEEN

Beth was in her dressing-room at Greylake Castle, waiting for Guy to take her down to join the traditional Christmas Eve celebration

175

that would take place at midnight, when a procession of people dressed in animal costumes would accompany Father Christmas from the town to festivities at the castle. She wore a moss-green velvet gown, long-sleeved and high-throated, with a silver-threaded white silk shawl around her arms, and she was surprisingly calm and composed, considering this was to be her first appearance in public since the wedding. She and Guy would be under very close scrutiny from all and sundry, and she was determined to conduct herself as the perfect bride, even though she clearly wasn't.

She looked at her pale, solemn face in the dressing-room mirror. A smile was needed, she thought, trying to appear more light-hearted and happy, as befitted her new position, but it was very hard to smile when her marriage was already in disarray. Guy had abided by her wish, and left her well alone, so much so that she might as well have not existed. Except that he needed her tonight, and so had been obliged to request her presence at his side. Preparations had been going on apace all day, and if the occasion wasn't successful, it would not be because Guy had stinted on anything.

Hearing sounds in the Green Court, she went to the bedroom window to look down. Torchlight illuminated an astonishing procession streaming beneath the gatehouse, led by Father Christmas, wrapped in a bright green cloak with a holly crown on his flowing white locks. His attendants were garbed as bears, bulls, horses, stags and goats, and cavorted among the accompanying townspeople, teasing the children and demanding kisses from the women. A flute, fiddle and drum played as the unlikely revellers, laughing and singing, streamed across the snowy court. It was so medieval and pagan that Beth felt she might have been transported back through the centuries.

As the merrymakers entered the castle, Beth heard steps approaching, and turned expectantly toward the door. It must be Guy, she thought, but the anticipated knock at the door didn't come. Puzzled, she took a lighted candle from the mantelshelf and went to look out into the gallery, which was deserted. Thinking she must have misheard, she was about to draw back into her room when the wavering light revealed an open door opposite. She knew it was the door of the Honeysuckle Room, which had been occupied by Guy's mistress, Maria Carberry. It had been closed ever since she'd arrived, and she'd resisted the temptation to look inside, but now that it was so invitingly ajar she gave in to her curiosity.

The candle fluttered and smoked as she went inside, and she had to pull her shawl up over her shoulders because the room was unheated. It was elegant, decorated in Chinese silk of a honeysuckle design. The bed was richly hung with fringed golden velvet, and the gilded furniture might have come from Versailles, but the room was nevertheless not as fine as her own. The discovery was oddly reassuring, and Beth smiled to herself as she held the candle high in order to send shadows into retreat.

It was then that she saw a tiny flash from the floor immediately beneath the window. Going closer, she saw that it was an earring, a diamond drop. She retrieved it and held it closer to the candle. The diamond was superior and beautifully cut, and twinkled at the slightest movement. There was a long red-gold hair caught upon it.

The light of another candle appeared in the doorway, and Guy spoke. 'Beth?'

She whirled guiltily, instinctively concealing the earring.

He looked curiously at her. 'What are you doing in here?'

'I thought I heard someone.' How perfectly attired he was, in a black brocade coat, tight white silk pantaloons and a quilted waistcoat, with a profusely laced neckcloth at his throat. Was he *ever* less than perfect?

'And so you came into an unused bedroom?' he observed.

'It's a charming room,' she murmured, glancing at the bed and struggling not to imagine him there with his mistress.

'You are perfectly at liberty to have it.'

'No. Thank you.' A flush leapt to her cheeks.

He studied her a moment longer. 'Are you ready to accompany me into the fray?'

'I . . . I think so.'

'Is there something you are burning to say to me, Beth?' he asked curiously.

'Why do you ask that?'

'Intuition.'

She mustered a little wit. 'Intuition is a woman's weapon.'

A brief smile played upon his lips as he took her candle and extinguished it before putting it on a table. 'I am a great respecter of women, Beth, no matter what you may think to the contrary.' Transferring his candle to his left hand, he offered her his right arm, and they proceeded from the room, she with Maria Carberry's earring still clasped tightly in her hand.

They proceeded down toward the noise of Christmas merriment, and halted unobserved on the half landing, to await the actual stroke of midnight. Both entrance halls were filled to overflowing with townsfolk, and the atmosphere was quite magical. Greenery adorned every corner and shelf, and fresh bundles of ash twigs crackled, spat and smoked in the hearths. As the hazel whips binding the ash burst apart in the heat, the gathered company drank toasts with strong beer and ale. Mince pies and other Christmas delicacies were circulating, and the flute, fiddle and drum still provided jaunty music. Carolling and dancing was in progress, and men in animal masks and skin capered amid the gathering. Only Father Christmas himself appeared to be missing.

'Can you face this?' Guy asked, as they paused unobserved on the half-landing.

'I must.'

'It will be worse tomorrow and the day after.'

'What do you mean?' she asked apprehensively.

'In the morning we attend Christmas service in the parish church, and then dine here with forty of the poorest people in the town. I will give them each a shilling, there will be much eating and drinking, and it will be some time before they have all gone and we have time to enjoy our own Christmas Day. If enjoy it we can.'

'I'm sure we can be civil to each other, sir.'

'We can try.'

'And the day *after* tomorrow?' she prompted.

'That is the Christmas meet of the Greylake Staghounds.'

Her heart sank. 'Are you telling me I will be expected to participate?'

'I fear so. It may not be generally fashionable for ladies to ride to hounds, but

it's expected in this neck of the English woods.'
He held her gaze. 'You looked decidedly underwhelmed, my lady.'

'I don't care for hunting of any kind.'

'Man once required to hunt in order to live,' he pointed out.

'Now he hunts for pleasure,' she returned.

'Ah, do I detect Holy Haldane's preaching?'

She flushed. 'No, it has nothing to do with him. I have *never* liked hunting.'

'I trust you hide this when you follow my staghounds. It would not do for this devoted hunting society to perceive that Lady Valmer is opposed to their sport.'

'I won't let you down, sir, just do not expect me to join the hounds at the kill, for my teeth are by no means sharp enough.'

'Madam, the picture you paint is really rather stimulating.'

'That, sir, is a typically male response.'

'True.'

The longcase clock downstairs began to chime and an expectant hush fell. Everyone turned as Guy escorted his wife down. The assembly parted like the Red Sea as he placed his candle on the table at the foot of the steps and then led Beth to the outer hall, where the centre of the floor had been cleared in readiness for something, Beth knew not what. The air suddenly became much colder, and she realized that the outer doors had been opened to the icy night. Then she heard someone shouting from the Green Court. 'Christians awake! Salute the happy morn!' Then came silence, before the same thing was shouted again, this time much closer, and then Father Christmas marched in, green cloak and silvery locks flowing. He carried a brimming tankard that he raised in toast. 'Hail to thee, good people!' he cried.

'Hail to thee, Father Christmas! Hail to thee!' everyone shouted back. He swaggered across the hall to Guy and Beth and proceeded to speak in verse.

'You've opened your doors and let me in,
Now I hope your favours for to win;
Whether I rise, or whether I fall,
I'll do my best to please you all.
I welcome you, my lady Valmer,
And pray that I your smiles incur;
I pray still more that come next year
You'll greet us all with a son and heir!'

Beth was embarrassed and had to lower her eyes, but Guy responded with a broad grin. 'Be assured I'll do my best!' he declared, to a roar of approval.

The figure in green sketched a very fancy bow. 'If you should require a little help, I'll happily step into the breach,' he offered, much to everyone's amusement.

Guy shook his head. 'It's something I can attend to myself,' he said.

182

Father Christmas pointed up at a mistletoe bough suspended above them, and spoke in verse again.

'Then, Sir Guy, you should make a start,
On such sweet matters of the heart,
So buss your bride beneath this bough,
And show us all that you know how!'

The drum began to beat, with everyone clapping in time to it. Beth's face was aflame with embarrassment as Guy turned her to face him. The drumbeats and clapping quickened spontaneously, but she knew they were all aware that until a few days ago Lady Valmer had intended to become Mrs Haldane. They would all be wondering what truth lay behind the hasty, secretive wedding. And they would be wondering about her character. She was suddenly face-to-face with how trapped she'd become, and how little control she had over her own existence.

Guy's fingers tightened around hers. 'If I did not know better, I'd say you were about to blub, my lady,' he whispered, under the guise of smiling tenderly into her eyes.

'Maybe I am.'

'Am I permitted to ask why?'

'For things that have gone forever,' she replied bitterly.

He misinterpreted her words. 'Think of Holy Haldane if you must, madam, just be

183

outwardly convincing as my bride.' He bent his lips toward hers.

'It will be a struggle, sir, now that I realize I have to measure up to Maria Carberry,' she whispered and, as their lips met, she pressed the earring hard into his palm. She felt his fingers close around it, but he continued to kiss her as if she was the only woman of importance to him. A breathless silence descended over the scene, so that the crackle of the ash twigs might almost have been the crackle of electricity as he pulled her body to his and kissed her so ardently that unseen currents swirled in the warm air. He conjured a magnetic force that should have held them together forever, but then he released her and turned to the gaping crowds.

'That will have to do, ladies and gentlemen,' he said with a light laugh, 'because to go further would be to invite you into my marriage bed, and *that* I have no intention of doing!'

This good humour was received with laughter and a resumption of the steady clapping, but then Guy nodded at the musicians, who struck up the old carol, 'Good Kind Wenceslaus'.

Only then did Guy look at Beth. 'My dealings with Maria Carberry are none of your concern, is that clear?'

'Perfectly.'

'And you had better advise Mrs Bradfield

that any further tittle-tattling from her will result in dismissal. Is that also clear?'

'It wasn't Mrs Bradfield,' Beth lied. 'Guy, how on earth did you expect to keep your mistress a secret? Especially when she stayed here for a whole month.'

'My, you *are* in possession of the facts, aren't you?' he answered, smiling through gritted teeth. 'Well, it doesn't matter what you think you know, because you are not to mention this matter again.'

'You, who are always so free with your criticisms of my private life, demand silence when it comes to your own?'

'You disappoint me, Beth.'

'*I* disappoint *you*?' she began, her voice becoming raised, so she immediately dropped it to an angry whisper. 'You are absolutely beyond belief, sir. How dare you stand there and say that!'

'Enough, Beth.'

'Why? Are you afraid your adoring tenants might see you for the wolf in sheep's clothing you really are?'

He managed to keep a fixed smile. 'I think it is time you discovered a headache and took yourself to bed, don't you?'

'With pleasure. But don't forget to kiss me an affectionate goodnight.' She stood there defiantly, so deep into her own anger that she was incapable of withdrawing sensibly.

'Never push me too far, Beth,' he breathed,

and embraced her again. This was a kiss to put its predecessor in the shade, to kindle flames from ice, and to breathe life into stone. Beth's lips had never been so tenderly but wilfully assaulted, never been so pitilessly raided by sensual skills that should only exist in the realms of fantasy. If mere lips could tear out her soul, then his did now, and with it her self-respect. She forgot everything as she plunged into the carnal trap that was Guy Valmer. Her lips matched his in the wild game that lured them both away from common sense. They hardly knew that the music had died away on a straggling note, or that everyone was staring. Even Father Christmas's jaw dropped as Sir Guy and Lady Valmer indulged in a kiss so laden with desire and eroticism that onlookers felt seared by its heat.

It was Beth who cried craven first. Her face was flushed and her eyes dark as she drew from his clasp. The blood skimmed wildly through her veins, and her skin seemed to tingle with new vitality. Never, *never* had she so wanted to complete what had begun; never had she so yearned for the simple right to tell her husband she loved him 'Good night, Sir Guy,' she whispered, trusting she would be able to ascend the staircase without her knees buckling beneath her.

'Good night, my lady,' he responded softly, but when she looked up into the greyness of his eyes, she saw nothing. If he had any

186

fondness for her, he kept it hidden.

She glanced down at his hand, and saw it was still clasped around the earring. Keeping a steely control of herself, she turned, inclined her head and smiled at the still stunned gathering, before catching up her green velvet skirts and walking slowly back toward the staircase. She forgot to take a candlestick, and it wasn't until she entered the dark sanctuary of the gallery that she realized she needed a light, but somehow she managed to make her way to her room. Then she was inside, where the flames of the fire were warm and low, and she had the privacy to sob her heart out into her pillow.

Braddy found her a little later and, after offering what comfort she could, left her asleep, alone, in the bed. The housekeeper was thoughtful as she went down to the kitchens, where she drew her husband aside. 'Mr Bradfield, I think I have to do something,' she declared in a way that sent his spirits plunging to his toes.

'*Do* something?' he repeated warily.

'Yes. The course of true love must be helped along a little.'

He was appalled. 'Oh, no, woman, not your darned herbs and potions!'

'Why not? You and I both know I can mix a rare brew that will send Sir Guy to her ladyship's bed with all the ardour of a rampant stag.'

'Your pesky magic will see you burned by the Yarn Market!' he warned.

'It isn't magic, Mr Bradfield,' she answered primly, 'just a knowledge of which plant will do what. You don't accuse doctors of magic, do you, just because they can mix this with that to cure an ailment?'

'No, but—'

'It's settled then. Tomorrow, I will prepare a love philtre for Sir Guy and her ladyship. It will be a rare Christmas present.'

'I hope you know what you're doing,' he grumbled.

'If there's one thing I know, Mr Bradfield, it's herbs and potions,' she answered primly. 'In fact, I'll make a start right now.'

'You have tomorrow's grand dinner to consider,' he reminded her.

'I've been overseeing the preparation of the grand dinner for as long as I can remember, Mr Bradfield, so I know *exactly* how much time I have for what. I'm going to prepare my potion first.'

'You're meddling in dangerous waters, woman,' he grumbled, but she ignored him and went to collect a lighted candle, which she took to the little storeroom that was her secret lair. She alone held the key, and she alone knew what lay inside. After carefully locking the door behind her, she held the candle up and went to some shelves that were fixed to the opposite wall. They were laden with jars, dishes, bottles, boxes and bowls. Beneath them were sets of little drawers, as might be used by an apothecary, and it was upon these that her gaze came to rest. With a smile, she placed the candle on the rickety little table in the centre of the room, and then went to lift down a pestle and mortar from one of the shelves. Next she selected various items from the drawers, and a bottle of rather dirty looking green liquid from a shelf. Among other more mysterious things, it contained the juice of crushed asparagus, and was her special concoction. It was a sexual stimulant second to none.

From the drawers she had taken ash, laurel and nettle seeds, as well as rosemary, thyme, cloves and ginger, and finally dried nasturtium flowers gathered at dusk from a growing plant upon which she had placed her right foot. That right foot was all-important, and now it only remained to get something that was particularly special. Taking a small metal box from its hiding place up the chimney, she unlocked it with a tiny key worn on a ribbon around her neck. Inside the box were secret things about which only the wisest of wise women knew anything. She took out a little linen bag that contained . . . no, better it should be nameless, for its dark secrecy was half its power. She took two withered, anonymous stamens from the bag, one for Guy, one for Beth, and whispered a strange charm as she began to mix it all together in a very special sequence.

*   *   *

Frampney seemed much more than a mile away as Rowan's carriage approached Whitend along the snowy drive. The park was flat and, some might have said, uninteresting, but the vale of the River Severn was incredibly rich and productive, having in the distant past been washed by a shallow sea. A full moon now hung among the stars, making it possible to see the unfinished embankment of the Gloucester and Berkeley Canal behind the house, while a quarter of a mile in front was the Severn itself, its serpentine course marked by pollard willows and the wild pear trees that made the vale so famous for perry. On the horizon beyond the river, shining silver in the moonlight, were the rolling hills of the Forest of Dean.

The carriage negotiated the wide gravel area at the end of the drive, and drew to a halt next to the ancient stone bridge that spanned the moat surrounding the house. Whitend dated from the sixteenth century, and was not a handsome building. Grey and rather imposing, it rose through four storeys to a stone-tiled roof that had five gables and very ugly chimneys. A narrow porch hunched against the wall as if propping it up, and the arched doorway seemed almost sulky. It had been the home of generations of Lords Welland.

Alighting, Rowan felt no stir of pleasure on seeing it again, and before even stepping over the threshold was looking forward to departing. Everything was in darkness inside, as he'd expected, but then he noticed other wheel tracks in the snow, and knew with a sinking heart that his was not the only carriage to have come here today. He turned quickly to Rosalind. 'Stay here, I'll make sure the coast is clear.'

She drew back into her corner seat, and he closed the carriage door before crossing the bridge to the porch. Someone was aware of their arrival, he thought, seeing the trembling light of a candle shining beneath the door. Keys were turned and bolts slid back, and at last the door opened. To Rowan's surprise, it wasn't his father's old butler who stood there, but Jane's faithful servant, Bolton, who had donned a brown coat over his nightshirt. He was taken aback. 'Master Rowan?'

'Bolton? I thought—'

'Lady Welland returned here today,' the butler explained, standing aside for Rowan to enter the panelled hall, where the fire had burned low in the ornate stone fireplace.

'Just Lady Welland?' Rowan prompted.

'Indeed so, sir.'

Rowan grinned with relief. 'Well, that I can

191

endure. Merry Christmas,' he added, for midnight was well and truly past.

'And you, Master Rowan.' Bolton placed the candlestick on the octagonal table in the centre of the oblong, stone-flagged hall.

'So, the old girl couldn't put up with any more of my festive pa, eh?' Bolton maintained a respectful silence, but gave a barely perceptible nod. Rowan handed him his top hat, and then teased off his gloves. 'Perhaps you had better awaken her ladyship and inform her she has unwelcome visitors.'

'Visitors, sir?'

'There is a lady in my carriage.'

'I see, sir.'

Rowan grinned. 'I don't think you do, Bolton, for I hardly see myself. Off you toddle to break the glad tidings.'

The butler relieved him of his greatcoat as well, placed everything on the table, and then lit another candle before going up to Jane. The staircase was wide and shallow, and squeaked with every step, and as he disappeared at the top, Rowan went out to Rosalind. 'Come, my stepmother is in residence, but I can handle her.'

'Your stepmother? The woman who had Beth Tremoille turned out?'

Rowan tightened his fingers encouragingly around hers. 'Don't be afraid.'

'I'm not afraid, just anxious. She'll know my surname, and will look down on me.'

He hesitated, but only for a split second. 'Just be yourself, my darling,' he whispered, brushing his lips to her forehead. But as he ushered her over the bridge toward the house, he was ashamed that he wished she wasn't a blacksmith's daughter. How much easier would it be if he'd fallen in love with someone like Beth.

They entered the hall, which in daylight was flooded with light from a magnificent oriel window, but now the panes were black against the night sky. Rosalind's heart thumped in her breast as she glanced around. The house was so big, and when she looked at herself in the tarnished mirror above the fireplace, she was so very, very small. Would she soon open her eyes properly, and know she'd been dreaming?

A voice spoke from the top of the staircase. 'What's all this, Rowan?' They turned to see Jane, her blonde hair plaited beneath a night bonnet. She was wearing a quilted brocade robe of luminous kingfisher blue, and there was a quizzical look in her eyes as she came down toward them.

Rowan grinned and went to greet her. 'Merry Christmas, Ma.'

'Call me that at your peril,' she murmured, her glance moving to Rosalind.

'And who, pray, is this?'

He cleared his throat and extended his hand to Rosalind. 'This is Rosalind Mannacott. Rosalind, allow me to present you to my

193

stepmother, Lady Welland.'

'Mannacott?' Jane repeated faintly. 'Rowan, are you *utterly* mad?'

'Don't be unkind,' he answered, his smile fading.

'By your tone, I take it this is serious?'

'Enough to be an elopement.'

Jane glanced at Bolton. 'Is the fire still alight in the drawing-room?'

'Yes, my lady.'

'Then see that some refreshment is brought there. I have need of a good, stiff brandy, but I don't doubt that Miss Mannacott would prefer hot chocolate. Is that not so, Miss Mannacott?'

Rosalind started like a frightened rabbit. 'Yes, my lady.'

Bolton hurried away, and Jane conducted them into the drawing-room, where she lit several candles and then turned to study the runaway lovers. Now that she looked more closely at Rosalind, she remembered seeing her in Frampney during the summer. The girl had been wearing a pink dress; no, a rose dress. Taffeta, and therefore totally unsuitable for everyday tasks in a country village, but then so also had been Rosalind Mannacott's nubile swagger. Jane had recognized her as Trouble with a capital 'T', and now here the creature was, all innocence as she ruined Rowan's life. 'Well, I imagine my presence here has intruded upon your plans,' she observed to him.

'It's an unforeseen complication,' Rowan admitted, going to pour two large measures of his father's prized cognac. 'But let's speak of the family first. How is my adorable sibling?'

'So far beyond redemption as to be at Satan's right hand.'

'And so you scurried back here *tout de suite*?'

'Even quicker than that, I assure you,' Jane replied with a shudder. 'He and Thomas are like two pigs in a midden. I was an outcast in my own house.' Jane took a seat by the fire and accepted a glass from Rowan.

He raised an eyebrow. 'Rather as Beth felt, eh?'

'You can't resist, can you?' she said wearily. 'I now deeply regret what I did, but still you keep sniping.'

'What's this, Jane? A soft underbelly?'

She smiled wryly. 'I'm not the one whose underbelly is going to prove soft,' she observed quietly. 'You and your sweetheart are going to have a very difficult time of it. Forgive me, Miss Mannacott, but these things have to be said.'

Rosalind met her gaze. 'I know I'm not worthy of Rowan, my lady, but we love each other.'

'Love can be very cruel.' Jane looked away, recalling her long years of unrequited yearning for Thomas Welland. 'And sometimes it's far wiser to turn away from it,' she added with

195

feeling.

Rowan was annoyed. 'I don't appreciate being compared with you and Pa.'

'I'm sure you don't, but if you can't see the problems piling up ahead of you, I certainly can. Don't forget, I've learned the hard way, and whatever you may think, I have your best interests at heart. Blind foolishness has led to me being in a very unenviable position now. I like you Rowan, and I don't want you—or Miss Mannacott—to do something you will later regret.' But she was really thinking only of Rowan; Rosalind Mannacott could go to hell.

'You can't stand in our way, Jane,' he pointed out.

'Nor am I attempting to, but I would not be much of a friend to you if I stood by and said nothing. For instance, what will you do for money? You have the limited income from your mother's family, but you've already kissed farewell to anything from your father.'

'We can get by, and Rosalind isn't without money.'

Jane was taken aback. 'You expect me to believe that a blacksmith's daughter is an heiress?'

'Not quite, but she has four hundred and eighty guineas.'

Jane was startled. '*How* much?' she gasped.

'Methinks you heard. Suffice it that we can live well enough for a while.'

'Where?' Jane demanded.

'Guy Valmer's London house,' Rowan replied.

Jane's startlement deepened. '*Valmer* knows of this?'

'In a manner of speaking.'

'And what, pray, does that mean?' she enquired.

'He knows I'm eloping, but not with whom.'

'You daren't tell him, do you? Because of Beth,' Jane answered tartly.

Rosalind's mind raced. This was the first time Rowan had mentioned whose Mayfair house they were going to, and Guy's name was known to her for two reasons: first that Beth had said he'd rescued her when she fainted, and second that he'd come to the forge to ask about Beth. Had more gone on between this Sir Guy and Beth than the latter had let on?

Jane's loyal bloodhound, Mordecai Bolton, had sniffed out a great deal of information about Beth's time in Fiddler's Court with Jake Mannacott, so she knew there had been ill feeling between Beth and Rosalind. Now she could see by the girl's face that Rowan had been very sparing with the facts concerning Guy Valmer's interest in Beth. She frowned at him. 'Rowan, if you're going to take Miss Mannacott to Guy's house, you should tell her everything. If you don't, I will.'

Rosalind turned urgent eyes on him. 'Tell me, Rowan, please. If this has something to do with Beth, I—'

He interrupted. 'My cousin Guy is looking for Beth for his own purposes, and it has no bearing on us. He knows I intend to elope, and offered me the use of his London town house. He didn't ask for any names or any explanations, and I saw no reason to enlighten him.'

Jane was scathing. 'Do stop tiptoeing around it, Rowan! You know full well that Guy Valmer would change his mind if he knew about Rosalind. Perhaps it will lubricate your tongue if you know that he has found Beth.'

Rowan was shaken. 'He has?'

Jane got up to go to the desk by the window, and took the letter that had arrived that day. It had finally pulled the rug from under her artful feet, and she was faced with the awful prospect of having to tell Thomas that she hadn't inherited Tremoille House after all. She gave the letter to Rowan.

Midwinter, Haldane Hall, in the County of Devon

Lady Welland
I have the missing will and the missing heiress, so Valmer House and its lands are as good as mine. Tell your husband what you will, but be warned that he is bound to learn that your fine dowry us no more. Be assured that our next meeting will be in

198

Valmer

Rowan exhaled slowly. So it had been *Beth* at Greylake Castle, not Maria Carberry. No wonder Guy hadn't welcomed him. 'Jane, I don't know what to say.'

'I realize your loyalty is with Valmer.'

'I'm not your foe any more, Jane. My father's, yes, but not yours.'

'Now *there* is a turnabout,' she declared wryly. 'So, you and Miss Mannacott can now be absolutely certain that Beth is part of Valmer's life. He certainly won't support you and Miss Mannacott at Beth's expense. He wants Tremoille House, and nothing is going to stand in his way.'

'Does my father know yet?'

'Dear God, no!' Jane shuddered. 'I feel faint at the thought.'

'I don't envy you.'

She pressed her lips together in a regretful smile. 'I only have myself to blame. I schemed and lied to get my own way, and now I must wallow in the cesspit I've created. Beware that you are not creating a cesspit of your own, because, believe me, *nothing* is worth it.' She closed her eyes for a moment, recalling how she'd unwittingly caused the death of the Gloucester lawyer Beswick. It had been murder as surely as if she and Bolton had stabbed him to the heart, and they would undoubtedly swing for it if their guilt were ever discovered. She pushed the awful thought away, and looked at Rosalind for a moment, before returning her attention to Rowan. 'Sooner or later all this will tumble about your ears, and you will lose Valmer's friendship,' she warned quietly.

Rosalind had been listening with growing dismay. Beth was to marry Sir Guy Valmer? She turned anxiously to Rowan. 'We can't possibly go to Sir Guy's house. You know how I hate Beth.'

Jane was curious. 'Hate is a very strong word. May I ask why you use it?'

'Because she came between my father and me, because she tried to force her high and mighty ways on me, and because I just can't stand the sound of her name.'

'Well, aren't you the spoilt little girl with her nose pushed out of joint?' Jane murmured acidly, unable to conceal her instinctive dislike for Rowan's love. Rosalind flushed and looked daggers, but fell silent.

Agitated, Rowan turned on Jane. 'Rosalind and I love each other, Jane, and that is the end of it. All I ask of you is a roof over our heads tonight, and we'll be gone in the morning.'

'To London?'

'Yes. Firstly to my uncle Oswald.'

Jane smiled. 'Ah, yes, the Welland family's sole contribution to the Anglican church, and venomous enough toward Thomas to marry you to a nanny-goat if he could get away with it.'

'He can marry us in the eyes of God and the laws of the realm, and that's all I want,' Rowan replied.

'Marry where you will, but if you value your friendship with Guy Valmer, and I think you do, then you'll go anywhere but his house. Heaven help me, you can even stay here until Thomas shows his snout again.'

'I won't put you in that position, Jane. We'll only trouble you tonight.'

'In one bed, I presume?'

'I'm sure you can overlook the want of a wedding ring.'

Jane's lips twitched. 'With my history, I'm hardly in a position to be coy.'

Bolton returned with a cup of hot chocolate for Rosalind, and Jane nodded at him. 'See that the guest room is prepared as quickly as possible.'

'Yes, madam.'

When he'd gone, Jane surveyed Rosalind again.

'And what does your father have to say about this?'

'He doesn't know.'

'Oh, dear.' Jane drew a heavy breath. 'So you two really are thinking only of yourselves.' She held up a hand as Rowan's lips parted. 'Oh, don't trouble to lecture me that I am hardly one to complain of that in others. Just think very hard about the step you are about to take. It will change your lives forever, and it may not be for the better. In fact, it probably won't.' She put her empty glass aside. 'Now, I will leave you. Rise whenever you choose in the morning, for Christmas Day or not, it is hardly likely to be a matter of formality here.'

'Will you wish us well?' Rowan asked.

'You know that I do, Rowan, because whether you and I like it or not, we have hit it off.' Jane reached up to press a cool kiss to his cheek, and then nodded at Rosalind before sweeping from the room like a kingfisher galleon.

Rosalind looked at Rowan. 'She hates me.'

'Rosalind, why must everything be a matter of hate? Jane doesn't hate you at all, she's simply anxious for us. You have to face it that Beth is going to re-enter your life, because I intend to stay as close to Guy as I can. If you have difficulty with this, then we will have to think again here and now. I love you, Rosalind, and I love Guy as my cousin and dearest friend. I want to be happy with you both, and I'm sure that you will be able to overcome your loathing for Beth.'

Rosalind's lower lips jutted a little, but she didn't say any more.

CHAPTER FOURTEEN

The Frampney forge was a smouldering ruin on Christmas Day morning, although perhaps not quite beyond redemption. But it would need money, and that was something Jake did not have. He and a few men from the village, including Jamie, had kept a watch on things through the night, but now everyone had gone home. Matty's body had been taken to Ben Wilcox's cottage, to be laid out properly and with dignity. Ben was the village undertaker, and always did things as they should be done. Nothing, no matter how small, was ever overlooked.

Now Jake sprawled on his chair in the kitchen, a large mug of hot, sweet tea on the floor by his stockinged feet. He was exhausted, and his face was grimy with smoke. He could taste it in his mouth, and feel it stinging his eyes. His spirits were low and wretched, but he looked with compassion at Phoebe, who'd fallen asleep in her chair, having been plied with spiced cider. She was in oblivion for a while, and spared the heartbreak of Matty's terrible death.

'You were a darned fool to the end, Matty Brown,' Jake muttered, thinking that it had taken death itself to finally come between the old smith and his bloody clay pipe.

Phoebe shifted a little, and her shawl fell from her shoulders, so Jake got up to tuck it back in place, but she awoke. For a moment she smiled at him, but then she remembered. 'Oh, no, Matty—'

He poured her the last of the cider. 'Drink this, my lover, and then you go to bed. We both must. Rozzie's been up there since the small hours, and now we must too.'

Phoebe glanced up at the ceiling. She ought to be glad that Rozzie had managed to sleep after such a terrible thing, but she wasn't. Resentment curdled her stomach, because she'd begun to think that Rosalind Mannacott didn't have a heart. All the little chit ever did was put herself first.

Jake rested his hand gently against her white hair. 'I'll look after you, Phoebe, don't you fret about that,' he murmured, although right now he hardly knew how he was going to look after Rozzie and himself, let alone Phoebe as well. But he'd manage somehow. 'Drink up, and then get to bed.'

'It will be the first time I've gone to bed without Matty,' she whispered.

He looked kindly into her eyes. 'I know how you feel, Phoebe, because I've twice lost the woman I love, first my wife, and then Beth.'

'And it's losing Beth that matters most, isn't it?' she asked quietly. He didn't answer, and after a moment she finished the cider and then went unsteadily upstairs.

A few minutes later footsteps approached the house, and Jake recognized the tap at the door. 'Come on in, Jamie.'

The young man bent his head to enter, and then quickly closed the door again, to keep the heat in. 'All right, Jake?'

'What sort of darned fool question is that?'

Jamie flushed awkwardly. 'Well, you know what I mean.'

Jake nodded regretfully. 'Reckon I do. I'm sorry, Jamie.'

'Ben Wilcox says to tell you that he'll keep Matty in his cellar until they can dig a grave in the churchyard. Right now the ground's too hard to get a spade in at all, let alone dig anything out. He says Matty will keep a good while when it's like this.'

'Poor old Matty, he just *had* to go puffing that bloody pipe.' Jake sighed. 'I just feel at a complete loss. How on earth am I going to continue after this? The forge will need a small fortune spent on it.'

'That's partly why I've come. Everyone in the village is ready to pitch in to help rebuild it.' Jamie lifted out a chair and sat down at the table. 'How's Rozzie?'

'Still asleep. I haven't seen her since we discovered the fire.'

'Nor me.' Jamie glanced away, remembering how she'd refused to help. There were times when he disliked her with all his heart; but there were others, much more plentiful, when

205

he worshipped the ground upon which she stood.

'It's good to know folk will help with the forge,' Jake observed, 'but it still leaves me with the problem of buying what's needed to do the fixing. I have to find the money from somewhere, because I now have Phoebe relying on me too.'

'That might be where I come in,' Jamie said tentatively.

'Oh?' Jake's brows drew together. 'What do you mean?'

'Reckon I've saved a bit.'

Jake's eyes cleared. 'This is about Rozzie, isn't it? You're offering your money if I offer her?'

'I wouldn't put it quite like that. I've asked you before if I can be a partner in the forge, and I stand by the offer. Yes, it will bring me closer to Rozzie, but I know she'll never love me. Dang it, she *loathes* me! But, Jake, I do want to learn your trade, and there's nothing I'd like more than to learn it at your side, with an interest in the business. You can't go on alone forever, any more than Matty could. You take me on, and I'll give you my savings to put the forge right again.'

'Jamie, you can't possibly have enough to—'

'I have my cottage as well,' Jamie put in quickly.

Jake stared at him. 'What are you saying?'

'That I'll sell it to Squire Lloyd, and then

come and live here, just as you and Rozzie came to live with Matty and Phoebe.'

'You've thought about it all, haven't you?'

'Yes, and believe me, it's not just because of Rozzie. Yes, I love her, but right now I don't like her much.'

'I know what *that* feels like, lad, and she's my daughter. I went wrong somewhere with her upbringing, but God alone knows where.'

'Jake, about my offer,' Jamie pressed, anxious to keep the conversation on the right subject.

Jake sat forward. There was no denying that what Jamie wanted would be of immense benefit, in fact it would solve the problem entirely. If everyone in the village helped, the new forge could be doing business again within weeks.

Jamie watched his face closely. 'Is it a deal then?' he ventured.

Jake nodded, and held out his hand. 'You've made an offer I can't refuse,' he said, but as they shook on it, Phoebe's anxious steps were quickly descending the stairs, and she emerged into the kitchen, her face pale and anxious.

'She's gone, Jake, Rozzie's gone.'

'Eh?' He rose slowly from his chair.

'You heard me. Rozzie's gone. Her clothes and everything she could carry.'

Stricken, Jake sat down weakly. 'That can't be . . .'

'It's true. Your daughter has just upped and

gone.'

He closed his eyes, for that was what Rozzie had accused Beth of doing.

Jamie felt like two left legs. 'Do you want me to look for her, Jake?'

Phoebe gave him an exasperated look. 'Use your brain, Jamie Webb. If she's taken all her things, then you can guarantee she hasn't just run off on her own. She's gone with someone, and I don't think we need look all that far for a name.'

'Who?' Jake demanded, bringing his fist down on the arm of his arm.

'Why, Lord Welland's son, of course. It's plain as plain that something has been going on between Rozzie and him.'

'I'll go after them and wring his bloody neck!' Jake growled.

'And kill another one?' Phoebe's voice fell coldly into the sudden heat. 'You can't go murdering every man who goes near her, Jake, nor is she worth it. That little cat will always be trouble, as I think you, in your heart of hearts, know as well as me. There are some people in this world that you just can't help, and your daughter's one of them. She has to be left to make her own mistakes, it's the only way she'll ever learn.'

'Is that what you really think of her?' Jake asked in a broken voice.

'Yes, I'm afraid it is, Jake. I tried to be a mother to her, but she was only interested in

208

herself. No one can keep showing love to someone like that.'

It was too much for Jake, who hid his face in his hands and wept like a child.

*   *   *

At that very moment, only a mile away to the north, Rosalind was stirring in a luxurious feather bed that smelled of lemons and lavender. The plight of her father and Phoebe didn't cross her mind, because Rowan was her future now.

She was naked, and wrapped in his arms. They had spent the night making love, and now that she had slept a while, she wanted more. Her body tingled with desire, and her nipples crinkled against the sheet as she wriggled around to look at him as he continued to sleep. He was so handsome, with his tousled dark curls, his lashes long and dark against his cheeks, and his lips parted just a little, as if he knew she wanted to kiss them. No, there was something else she wished to kiss first. With a secret smile, she slid further down, the bedclothes turned back so that she could see his pale, lithe body; in particular to see that most exciting part of him. It was limp and pliable now, springing from a forest of dark hairs, the tip concealed in the soft folds of his foreskin.

She smiled. 'Merry Christmas, Rosalind,'

she whispered, the muscles quivered between her legs as she slid herself down to press her face into that dormant masculinity. It was so intoxicating that her senses reeled, and the muscles between her legs were so affected that they stabbed with excitement. She moved her face lovingly against the delicious virility that had pleasured her so much in the night. The joy she'd known with Rowan put her experience with Robert Lloyd entirely in the shade. Her lips enclosed his foreskin, and she sucked it gently into her mouth, her tongue sliding inside to the smooth knob beneath. At first he slept on, vulnerable and unknowing, while she took liberties with his body, but at last he began to awaken as his loins responded to her sensuous assault. He hardened and lengthened in her mouth, and she was so excited she could hardly contain herself.

She had no thought at all for what had happened at Frampney the evening before; no thought of anything that had preceded this moment. That had been another Rosalind Mannacott, not her. The Rosalind Mannacott of now was plunging into erotic ecstasy that she prayed would never end. And one day, she didn't know when, she would be Lady Welland. She closed her eyes and submitted eagerly to the tide of luxury.

*   *   *

The Greylake Singers did more than justice to the exhilarating words and music of 'Adeste fideles'. The old carol rang out as the residents of both the town and castle attended the Christmas morning service, and the atmosphere could not have been more celebratory, or the church more festive, clad as it was in a mantle of seasonal greenery. The Reverend Wakefield had placed a large candle on the altar, its single flame catching reflections in the highly polished plate, as did the sunlight streaming through the medieval glass of the windows.

It was just what a Christmas morning service should be, Beth thought, as she stood with Guy in the central pew of the gallery. She was wearing a sky-blue merino gown and three-quarter-length pelisse, with cream accessories, and beneath a cream fur hat her dark hair was pinned so that three long ringlets fell down over her left shoulder. The marks of last night's tears had been concealed—well, almost—by judicious bathing with cold water and then the application of Chinese cosmetic papers. Braddy had reassured her that Guy wouldn't notice anything, but Beth knew he did. Had he realized that *he* was the cause of her tears? Would he even care if he did? She didn't know the answer to either question, but wished it could be 'yes' to both.

Today she wished so many things that her head seemed to spin. A strangely emotional

211

and capricious mood had overtaken her as they entered the church, so that a sense of confusion and strange excitement pervaded her, and she was so acutely sensitive to Guy that the air seemed to crackle between them. The invisible current danced upon her skin and tingled into her very heart, unsettling her to such an extent that she found it hard to concentrate on the service. She longed for another little glass of the punch Braddy had given them before they went out to the waiting carriage. It had been delicious, a wonderful blend of herbs, spices and other things the housekeeper declined to disclose, but it was quite the most delightful punch Beth had ever tasted.

The Greylake Singers were so accomplished that the wonderful Christmas music brought tears to her eyes. What *was* the matter with her? She seemed set to pipe at the slightest thing. Suddenly Guy nudged her gently and proffered his handkerchief, which she took gladly. The scent of southernwood clung excitingly to the square of fine cambric, which was also warm from his touch; from his body . . . Her gloved fingers closed tenderly over it. She might be constantly at odds with him, but she still loved him so much; so very much.

He took her hand suddenly. 'Are you feeling unwell, Beth?' he asked in concern.

'. . . I'm overcome by the music.' Why had he taken her hand? Why did he still hold it?

212

'Ah, yes. Of course.' His thumb moved briefly around her palm. 'I won't go down to read the lesson if you're distressed.'

She looked at him in surprise. Such consideration? Her emotions threatened to slip even further beyond her control. 'I'll be all right,' she said, praying that her face gave nothing further away.

The singing stopped at that moment, and he released her. 'If you're sure, I'll attend to my Christmas duty,' he said, and left her to go down to the pulpit.

She watched as he emerged from the gallery stairs, a graceful figure in a wine-red coat and pale-grey trousers. His auburn hair was fiery and almost defiant as he passed a stained-glass window, and yet he seemed peculiarly vulnerable. Why? Vulnerable was a word she would never normally have applied to him, but today it seemed well chosen. There was something different about him; about them both.

A hush descended over the congregation as he mounted the pulpit, and then his beautifully modulated voice echoed through the church. 'I read from Isaiah, Chapter Nine. *For unto us a child is born, unto us a son is given; and the government of the land shall be upon his shoulder: and his name shall be called Wonderful, Counsellor, The mighty God, The everlasting Father, The Prince of Peace . . .'*

Later, when the service was over, they

emerged into snow-bright sunshine. The air was still sharp, for it seemed that no matter how much the sun shone, the temperature did not rise sufficiently to cause even a slight thaw. The church bells rang out joyously, and as the forty poor men of the parish began to make their way up the castle hill for their grand Christmas dinner, the townspeople crowded around to watch Sir Guy and Lady Valmer set off as well. It was only a short drive, but for Beth every minute was a new and exquisite torture. She wanted to kneel at Guy's feet and confess her deepest secrets, throwing herself on his mercy so that her soul was bared and nothing remained hidden, and then she wanted his mercy to be tender, loving, and oh, so very carnal. Yet she remained mindful of everything that came between them, including Maria Carberry, and so said and did nothing. She alighted at the castle without uttering a word of confession, although, to be sure, she *had* mentioned the quality of the singing in the church, and the continuing cold weather. Nothing wildly unrestrained.

The annual grand dinner was a splendid affair, with a dais at one end of the outer entrance hall, and a line of tables extending before it. Guy and Beth sat at the dais, with the Reverend and Mrs Wakefield, and the meal commenced with the clergyman saying grace. Next, Guy drank from a large, two-handled, chased silver loving cup, which he passed to the clergyman, who drank from it and passed it to Mrs Wakefield on his left. It went all around the tables and finally came to Beth. She drank from it and then handed it back to Guy. He turned it slowly until he could take a final sip from the same spot her lips had touched. This brought approving murmurs from the diners, and an especially fiery blush to Beth's cheeks, beset as she was by increasingly wayward emotions. She and Guy had taken two more small glasses of the punch on their return from the church, and now she felt uncannily warm. It didn't occur to her that the punch was more than it seemed, because all she could think of was Guy, whose name seemed to whisper endlessly through her head. And her body.

She did not know much about the meal, which was lavish and excellent. It commenced with split pea soup, and then there were rousing cheers as two thirty-pound sirloins of beef were borne in and served with mustard, horseradish and ample vegetables. The traditional delights of plum puddings and mince pies followed, and finally, for those who could manage it, there was a cheese board that positively groaned. Strong beer and ale flowed, although there was wine for those on the dais. The jovial occasion was finally brought to an end when Guy handed each diner one shilling, and they all tottered back down the hill to the town, many of them carolling at the tops of their lungs. 'Hark! The herald-angels sing' had surely never sounded so discordant.

Guy breathed out with relief. 'Enough is enough,' he murmured, 'and now I look forward to a little peace.'

Braddy appeared before them with a little silver tray, upon which stood two glasses of the delicious green-hued punch. 'By your leave, Sir Guy, I think you both deserve a little something to restore your strength,' she said with a twinkling smile.

CHAPTER FIFTEEN

That night, after enjoying a light supper, Beth and Guy adjourned to the candlelit drawing-room, where pots of lily-of-the-valley filled the air with bewitching fragrance. The gold-and-white drawing-room was furnished with graceful Hepplewhite chairs and sofas, and had a fine marble fireplace that was garlanded with Christmas leaves. A particularly handsome French bracket clock had pride of place on the mantelshelf, and was flanked on either side by garnitures of exquisite blue-and-white Chinese vases. Gilt-framed mirrors and delightful watercolours adorned the wall, and there were glass cabinets containing collections of patch boxes, porcelain figurines and Chinese jade. The large bay window enjoyed panoramic views inland up the Evell valley toward the grandeur of Exmoor, but the heavy curtains were closed now.

The room was pleasantly intimate, as indeed were its unwitting occupants, now very much under the influence of Braddy's love philtre. Sexual tension hung in the air between them, but Beth still held her tongue about her feelings. Silence still seemed by far the wisest option. She got up from the sofa and went to hold her hands out to the fire. 'Do you realize that we haven't exchanged a snappish word today?'

'Which proves that anything is possible if we put our minds to it,' he replied.

'Guy—'

'Yes?'

'I . . . I know it's unbecoming to mention Maria Carberry—'

'Then please do not,' he interrupted, 'for it is a topic that is bound to lead to ill feeling, and I do not want today to be spoiled.'

'She is part of your life, Guy,' she reminded him, 'but so am I. How do you feel about me? I mean, how do you *really* feel about me? Am I only a necessary evil?'

He smiled. 'Beth, whatever else I may have said, I'm sure I've never described you as a necessary evil.'

'You came as close to it as makes no difference.'

'Then I retract every word.' He got up as

217

well and joined her before the fire.

She searched his face. 'Do you, Guy?' she asked softly.

'Yes, of course. Beth, I needed you so much in order to regain Tremoille House, that I would have said almost anything.'

'Do you love Maria Carberry?' she asked.

'Beth—'

'Please tell me, Guy.'

He hesitated. 'No, in fact, she isn't my mistress now.'

Startled, Beth gazed at him. 'She . . . isn't?'

'No, nor has she been since that day I played Good Samaritan to you, although the day is just coincidental.'

Joy swept over her. 'Then why did you let me think she was?'

'Because you angered me, and it didn't please me to speak of her, least of all with you. And that is how I still feel,' he added, then drew a long breath. 'And while embarrassingly direct questions are on the table, perhaps I might mention Haldane again.'

'The embarrassingly direct question being . . . ?'

He looked at her. 'How can you be so sure that what you felt for him wasn't love?'

At last she took her courage in both hands. 'I've probably consumed far too much of Braddy's green punch, because I feel oddly uninhibited. I know I didn't love Landry because I know how I feel about you.' There, it

218

was said at last. Her heart felt as if it hung quivering in her breast, afraid to beat again until he had answered.

For a moment he was silent. 'Beth, is this you speaking, or that damned punch?'

'Both,' she replied honestly, and then became embarrassed. 'I've said the wrong thing, haven't I?'

'Did I say that?'

She looked up into his eyes, uncertain of what to say next, but at last the words came. 'If . . . if you want to come to my bed again tonight, I'll welcome you,' she said quietly, and then her nerve broke and she snatched up her skirts to hurry out.

A maelstrom of confusion and regret swirled within her as she reached her room and leaned back against the closed door. What a pathetic fool she'd made of herself. She'd spoiled the entire day and embarrassed him as well as herself. Tears trickled down her cheeks as she began to undress by firelight, having earlier given Braddy the rest of the day to herself. After washing in cold water from the jug, she sprinkled herself with soothing rosewater and then slipped naked into the bed, to curl up into a ball and nurse her wretchedness. The happiness she'd felt on learning that Maria Carberry was no longer his mistress might as well have never been. Far from behaving like a woman of the world, she'd acted like a silly miss from school, and

219

now felt so mortified that she couldn't imagine facing him again. How she wished she hadn't taken so much of Braddy's punch, because inhibitions would have been preferable. If only it were all a daydream. But it wasn't, and now she had to face up to the consequences of her actions.

She remained in a ball of self-comfort for what seemed like ages, and was just relaxing on the point of drifting into sleep when a step in the gallery made her open her eyes with a snatch of breath. She turned to look at the door. Had she *really* heard something this time? Yes, she could see the faint flicker of candlelight. Her heart began to race, like that of a pathetic virgin who was afraid to hope, and even more afraid of being disappointed.

There was a gentle tap at the door. 'Who is it?' she asked, still a silly miss.

'Well, I trust you are only expecting your husband,' was the reply.

Her heart lurched incredulously, and suddenly her skin felt so sensitive that the touch of the bedclothes was a torment. Every nerve and sense was fixed upon the door, and the man who stood beyond it. 'Come in,' she whispered, and then cleared her throat and said it again, this time so that he stood a chance of hearing. 'Come in.'

The door opened, and he was there, wearing his paisley dressing-gown, his eyes and hair lit by the candle flame. 'As you see, I accept your invitation,' he said quietly, closing the door and then coming to the bedside.

She hadn't ruined everything after all? She looked at him in disbelief.

He hesitated. 'Have I misinterpreted, Beth? You do want me to be here?'

'Oh, yes,' she breathed, 'I want you here.'

He moved the candle to see her face more clearly. 'You've been crying.'

'I thought I'd spoiled it all.'

'By telling me how much I mean to you? How could that spoil anything?'

'Very easily, if you feel nothing for me. After all, you *did* say that ours is a cold, calculated marriage of convenience.'

'That *was* my original intention.' He smiled. 'But there is very little that is cold and calculated between us; in fact, I'd say we were unpredictable and very . . . sensual.'

'Sensual?'

He raised an eyebrow. 'How else would you describe it? We seem incapable of being together without sparks flying, very sexual sparks on my part, because I cannot look at you without wanting you.'

The confession, so frank and unexpected, made her feel weak. Could it be true? Did he really feel desire whenever he looked at her? She gazed at him. 'Do you mean that?' she whispered, not daring to believe.

He put the candle on the beside table and then removed his dressing-gown. He was

221

naked beneath, and an impresssive erection jutted from his loins. 'Yes, Beth, I mean it, and right now I cannot conceal it either,' he said with a smile.

Slowly she drew the bedclothes aside to reveal herself, and he gazed down at her. 'Oh, what you do to me, Beth,' he whispered as she reached out to him.

'I didn't think—'

'That I felt anything?'

She nodded. 'You hid it very well.'

'Because I could not bear to think of you and Haldane. You and Mannacott I could endure, but not . . . ' His voice trailed away, and he smiled a little ruefully. 'Enough of that, because I now accept that he is in the past.' His fingers linked with hers, and as he got into the bed beside her, her loins trembled with delicious anticipation. She moved into his arms, her flesh against his, her warmth to his. Wonderful sensations passed through them both as his ample arousal pressed urgently against her. Oh, such potency and power, such irresistible masculinity, she thought as her soul soared high into sexual elation, and when his lips claimed hers, it was in a kiss that shackled her to him forever.

Her questing fingers explored his erection, sliding around its base and testing its steady pulse. Slowly her hand moved up the thick shaft until she could tease his foreskin to and fro, rejoicing in the aching hardness of the exposed extremity, so smooth and lubricious, so inviting of her touch. She massaged it, gliding her palm richly over the silken surface until he moaned with pleasure. He kissed her again, at the same time moving his erection against her hand, and she submitted rapturously as his knowing lips and tongue took her to the very edge of reason. She slipped her hand down him again, sinking her fingers richly into the warm forest of hair at his crotch, and then even further, to caress the two sensitive spheres that were now enclosed so tightly they seemed offered up to her.

He leaned up on his hands, his striking grey eyes dark with emotion. 'You have more power over me than I ever thought I would permit any woman,' he said softly.

'And you are everything to me,' she whispered. 'I think I was created to be with you.'

'I cannot believe that the Almighty fashioned such beauty and perfection just for me,' he breathed, still gazing down into her eyes. 'I want to kiss every part of you, Beth, every sweet part.' Slowly he moved around until, like before, he could press his face between her legs, only this time her lips could explore his masculinity too. Oh, how good it was to kiss the steely shaft, and take him into her mouth to sample the strength and taste of him. Her arms slid adoringly around his hips, and they savoured each other in a way she had dreamed of before, but never done. At last she could satisfy her ravenous hunger for such intimacy with him, a hunger that had racked her since the first day she saw him. She was so jubilant that she could not believe it was happening. Ecstasy gripped her time and time again, until she felt sure she was too weak and sated to endure, and yet time and time again she sought more. She could never have enough of this man. Her love for him was unbridled, and there was nothing she would not do in the pursuit of their sexual happiness.

At last he eased himself around again, until he could straddle her, his erection above her spread-eagled thighs. He gazed down into her love-filled eyes and slowly lowered himself to press to the entrance of her wantonly aroused body. She arched passionately beneath him, and was now so wet between the legs that she could barely endure the suspense of waiting. But wait she did, because he was a masterly lover, knowing how to prolong the moment, and with it their suspenseful excitement. It was agonizing joy, made all the more exquisite by knowing that soon he would be inside her again. But for now he only slipped his straining shaft between the glistening folds of her femininity, moving gently to and fro until she cried out with orgasmic delight. Then she gazed up into his eyes. 'I love you, Guy. I always have, and I always will.'

'Oh, Beth . . .' His breath caught as he kept

a rein on his climax.

'Come into me now, Guy,' she whispered, 'come into me now, please . . .'

Slowly, and with a gasp of ravishment, he pushed forward, distending her flesh and imparting immeasurable gratification. There was nothing hurried or selfish about this enchanted moment; even now he thought of her, knowing each tiny movement that would indulge her more. Her intimate muscles gripped him and then softened, then gripped him more, and with each helpless reaction she came close to sobs of elation.

Her hands moved adoringly over his back, and then down to his taut buttocks, and she pulled him into her until he could penetrate no further. She could feel him deep within her, pressing to the very mouth of her womb, and suddenly she sensed her own fertility. She wasn't barren after all, she wasn't!

'Love me, Guy, love me,' she begged, moving against him so erotically that at last he could not hold back any longer. He began to thrust, long, delicious strokes that raised them both to almost unendurably exquisite emotion. They were no longer of this earth, but soared to the heavens, weightless beings of primal pleasure. His body shuddered as he reached a climax so profound and joyous that he cried out. She shared the moment, clinging to him with such complete capitulation that it seemed they should be joined together until time itself ended. This was perfect, so perfect.

He gasped as his member continued to pump into her. The pleasure was almost savage, and he felt the elixir of life itself flowing between them. This was different, so very different. Beth, his beloved Beth, his adored and adorable Beth . . . His mouth found hers again, and they kissed long and slow, embracing each other so luxuriously that each was aware of even the smallest curve of the other's body. Neither of them made any move to become separate entities again, they just lay there together, exquisitely joined, his member softening inside her and nestling there, for that was where it belonged.

'I love you, Guy, I love you more than life itself,' she breathed, her lips brushing his, her flesh lazily satiated, her heart beating in time to his, her soul still lost somewhere in Heaven.

An answering confession hung on his lips, but he couldn't quite say it. What did he know of love? Against his will—and his common sense—he felt more for her than he had for any woman before, but was it love? Damn it, he felt as unsure of himself as a milksop boy of fifteen! So he concealed the missing response behind another kiss, almost bruising her mouth with his passion. God help him, he wanted her again already; and again, and again.

*   *   *

It was thawing outside the next morning when Guy opened his eyes. The bed was warm, and so was Beth as she curled against him, deeply asleep. He rested his cheek against her dark curls, and inhaled the scent of her, so fragrant, feminine, and faintly floral, as if she had been walking in a rose garden. He wanted these moments to go on forever, and certainly did not want the noise and inconvenience of the staghound meet! Damn it, that was the last thing he felt like now.

He moved his cheek on her hair again. That Beth Tremoille was a creature of passion was something he had always sensed. She was a woman who needed sexual loving, and who needed to give of herself in the physical act. He'd had passionate, abandoned lovers before, but none had given him what she gave. She was the very personification of carnal desire, rewarding, vibrant and utterly adorable. She had wanted him physically, worshipped him physically, drained him physically, and satisfied him physically. Her kisses had stolen his willpower and his heart, and rendered him helpless to resist her allure. But he had never given his heart before, and remained afraid of giving it now. Even after such a night.

His lips brushed her forehead, and she sighed in her sleep, her body soft and pliable, completely relaxed and vulnerable. Her thirst had been slaked, and her hunger satisfied, so

227

that she was warm and comfortable, sleeping in that perfect way that was only possible after absolute sexual gratification. Beneath the bedclothes his hand moved softly over her, a loving touch that even yesterday morning he would never have dreamed could happen. She sighed again, moving closer, but still not awakening. He wanted her again, as his own body was bearing witness. A lazy arousal had begun to reach out from his crotch, throbbing gently, expectantly, and moving the hot blood around his veins. *Oh, Beth, want me again as I want you . . .*

His fingers slid to her breast, cupping its fullness and then toying with her nipple. The stolen intimacy made his desire more urgent, so that his member was now rigid, thick and long, eager to penetrate and adore her, as it had many times in the night. His hand moved down to massage himself a little, just to heighten his mounting pleasure. Each gentle, self-administered stroke was exquisite, almost painfully so, because he had spent his virility so freely through the night.

Beth began to stir, a warm bloom of colour coming to her cheeks. A smile curved her lips as pleasurable sensations reached through her, gathering voluptuously between her legs. Sleep was reluctant to release her, and dreams still coiled around her. It was the summer again, and she was with Landry in their secret place on the cliffs above the Stone Valley at

Haldane. She was in his arms, on the brink of making love with him for the first time, when she still saw only the good in him. *'If you wish me to stop now, you have only to say,'* he breathed softly.

'Never stop, Landry, never stop.'

Guy froze, and his heart squeezed in dismay. His desire was no more, and he felt so cold and sick that his stomach heaved. He flung the bedclothes aside and got up, shivering as the cool air struck his nakedness. He had to lean his hands on a table and bow his head, taking deep breaths to try to restore a little calm to the chaos of his senses and mind. She made a fool of him after all, a trusting fool! He'd allowed her to invade his heart, but in spite of all she said, she still yearned for Haldane.

Salt stung his eyes, and he gritted his teeth as he strove to overcome the devastation that she'd wrought with the single word. *Landry.* He took another long, shuddering breath, and then exhaled slowly. Control was returning, and with it a determination never to repeat the madness of the night. He'd made the supreme error of following while his cock led the way. 'You bloody halfwit,' he muttered, determined to *force* his head to rule his actions from now on. How he wished there wasn't to be the meeting of the staghounds today, for he had no desire to face country society when his emotions were in such flux.

'Guy?'

Beth's voice intruded, and he raised his head without turning. 'Yes?'

'Come back to bed.'

He made himself look at her. Sweet Jesus, she was so beautiful, her dark curls tumbling over her shoulders, her full breasts firm and inviting, her eyes eloquent with what seemed to be love and desire. She sensed something was wrong. 'What is it? What's happened?' she whispered.

He gazed at her, wishing with all his heart that things could be as they had been in the night. But he was sensible again, and would remain so from now on. 'There is nothing wrong, my lady.'

My lady? Her heart plunged. 'Yes, there is, Guy. Please tell me.'

'You and I have nothing to say to each other, madam. Last night I was moonstruck, but I am cured by the cold light of day.' He reached for his paisley dressing-gown and donned it, making himself move at leisure, as if indifferent to her.

She stared at him. 'I . . . I don't understand . . .'

'But I do, madam, and that's enough.'

'Am I to be punished *again?* What is it, Guy? Do you have to whip yourself—and me—whenever we've made love? Tell me, because this is the second time now, and as God is my witness, I don't understand.'

'God isn't your witness, Beth, but I am.' Buttoning the robe, he went to the door.

'Please, Guy!' she called after him. 'Don't I at least deserve an explanation?'

'You deserve nothing, my lady.' He glanced back at her. 'Just see that you present yourself at the staghounds, because the *monde* of Somerset and Devon will expect it. It will also expect you to be all that Lady Valmer should be, and so I hold you to your word that you won't let me down.'

He closed the door softly behind him.

Beth sat where she was, devastated, and barely able to cope with the misery of what had just happened. What had changed him this time? Tears welled from her eyes and she hid her face in her hands. At least last time she knew what it was; this time she had no idea in what way she had upset him, because the mischievous dream had fled as she opened her eyes.

Guy walked back to his own room with as much dignity as he could muster. But he felt as if he'd been stabbed in the heart, and the pain was so piercing and savage that he was hardly aware of putting one foot in front of the other. He passed a housemaid in the gallery. She bobbed a curtsey and was about to smile, as all his servants did on encountering him, for he was that sort of master, but on seeing his face this time she hastily bowed her head and remained silent as he walked past without

231

acknowledging her. When he'd left the gallery, she turned to look toward Beth's room. Things had not gone well. Gathering her skirts, she abandoned her duties in order to hurry back to the kitchens, where Braddy greeted the news with the utmost dismay.

The housekeeper went straight to see Beth, and found her weeping inconsolably. 'Oh, my dear, my dear, whatever is it?' she cried, going to gather her into her arms and hold her close. 'I thought you and Sir Guy were— Well, you know what I thought.'

'We were, at least, I thought we were. Then this morning, when I awoke, everything had changed. He has become as cold as ice again, and I don't know why.' Beth tried to collect herself, and gladly accepted the handkerchief the housekeeper pressed in her hand. 'Oh, Braddy, last night was wonderful, and I went to sleep thinking we loved each other, but when I opened my eyes this morning, he seemed to hate me.'

Braddy pushed the curls back from Beth's. hot, tear-stained face. 'I don't profess to know what has gone wrong, my dear, but I can promise you that last night was everything you remember.'

Beth didn't think of asking her how she knew such a thing. 'He is so precious to me, if only he knew it. Last night I thought he *did* know it, for I told him how much I love him.' Beth looked away. 'But he didn't say he loved me,' she added, remembering.

'All will be well again soon, I'm sure,' Braddy murmured, but with more conviction than she felt. She was mistress of her herbs and potions, and could guarantee their efficacy, but she had no control over what happened when her philtres wore off. The housekeeper could not begin to imagine why such a passionate and fulfilling night should end in such a cruel morning.

CHAPTER SIXTEEN

A thaw set in overnight, although not between the master and mistress of Greylake Castle, and the snow was turning to slush as the keepers let the staghounds out of their kennels. The pack swarmed down the castle hill, yelping and whining excitedly, and then streamed into the town's wide main street, which was crowded with carriages, riders and onlookers. Everyone who was anyone had attended the Christmas hunt.

Sir Daniel Lavington, as disagreeable as ever, and very rotund in hunting pink, manoeuvred his mount next to Guy, who was riding directly behind the hounds. 'How d'you like my horse, eh, Valmer? He's a grand goer, and I can flatter myself that I bred him. Darley Arabian line, out of a dam with pure

Lavington blood. By Gad, I'll be showing you a clean pair of hoofs today. And speaking of such things, you've caught us all on the hop, eh? Snatching Haldane's sweetheart from under his nose.'

Guy's grey eyes flickered coolly toward him. 'That isn't something I wish to discuss, Lavington.' He kicked his heels to move his horse away, because the hounds were milling around impatiently.

Sir Daniel gazed after him. 'Supercilious bastard,' he muttered, rubbing his chin thoughtfully as he twisted in the saddle to look at Beth. She was with elderly Lady Bettersden, and looked as cheerful as a wet Sunday in November. Why had she tossed Haldane aside in favour of Valmer? Money? The title? Love? He gave a wry chuckle, because the latter seemed highly unlikely. He'd watched her with Valmer at the castle a few minutes since, and it was no exaggeration to say they were frosty with each other.

With West Country hunting society subjecting the new bride to its almost cruel interest, Sir Daniel doubted if Good Queen Bess herself would remain poised. She was trying very hard to conduct herself well before so many curious eyes, but the fact was that she looked ill, pale and tense, as if she'd spent the night crying. She claimed to have a cold, but he wasn't fooled. Something was wrong between Sir Guy and Lady Valmer, and Sir

Daniel Lavington, arch troublemaker that he was, dearly wished to know what it was.

He continued to study Beth. She wore a mustard-coloured riding habit with black military frogging, and a carefree hat with a curled ostrich feather, hussar cords and tassels. Damn, but she was a sultry little thing, inviting in a way that made his balls itch. He'd like to get her on her back, spread her legs, and shag her until his heart stopped. Or hers. His tongue passed regretfully over his thick lips. There wasn't much he wouldn't do to gratify his urges, but not when a man like Valmer was involved.

Unaware of Sir Daniel's unpleasant scrutiny, Beth rode quietly at the side of Lady Bettersden, whom she had first met at the Haldane House ball. The lady was a childhood friend of Landry's mother, and had purchased a fine new villa on the edge of Haldane village, close to Stone Valley. A tall, forbidding woman, with a straight back and Roman nose, she was tired of the London hothouse, and wished to enjoy the peace and quiet of the countryside. But her stern exterior was misleading, for she was warm and earthy, and Beth liked her.

As the riders reined in to await the hunt's commencement, Beth watched Guy moving around among the crowd, greeting friends and tenants alike. To her surprise she saw him stop to converse with none other than Harriet's father. The Reverend Bellamy appeared all that was amiable toward him, giving no hint that he shared Landry's dislike for the master of Greylake. Guy smiled and nodded, seeming collected and unconcerned, as if nothing untoward had occurred in his private life overnight. She shared his talent for dissembling, but today such art was simply beyond her; she felt crushed and indescribably unhappy, and it did not help at all to see the man she loved behaving as if nothing were wrong.

Lady Bettersden looked kindly at her. 'I don't know what's happened, my dear, but you look as if you've lost ten guineas and only found a farthing.'

Beth tried to smile. 'That is how I feel, Lady Bettersden.'

'It won't do, you know. You've set the entire West Country by the ears, d'you see? And now we all look to you to play the part of dazzling temptress.'

'Is that what you think of me?'

The other studied her. 'I don't know what to think of you, my dear, and that is an honest fact. When I first met you at the ball, I would have laid odds that you were happy with Landry Haldane, yet you left with Sir Guy, and are now his wife. Now I find you in what I can only describe as a decline. Tell me honestly, my dear, have you been forced into this marriage?'

Beth's eyes swung to meet her gaze. 'No, Lady Bettersden, I have entered this marriage because I love Sir Guy with all my heart.'

'Indeed?' Lady Bettersden was momentarily taken aback, but then she smiled again. 'Then I'm glad, for I like him immensely, d'you see? Oh, I know my allegiance should be firmly with Landry, who is the son of my dearest friend, but one cannot help one's feelings. Sir Guy is the most decent and honourable man I have ever encountered, and I should have been greatly dismayed if he had imposed himself upon you.'

'He had no need to, Lady Bettersden, because I have wanted him since our first meeting early last summer.'

'Good heavens, you are smitten. So Landry was second best?'

Beth looked away, and didn't answer. Her longing gaze went to Guy again. She might as well not exist for him, whereas he had become existence itself to her.

'Have you had a lover's tiff?' Lady Bettersden ventured.

'Yes,' Beth replied, her tone discouraging of further questions.

Lady Bettersden smiled. 'Don't fear I'll pry, my dear, because I won't, but if you ever require a sympathetic ear, then I will provide it. Other than that . . .' she spread her gloved hands. 'By the way, my name is Cleo, and I wish you would use it. And before you ask, yes,

I fear it *is* short for Cleopatra. One grin, madam, and I will cordially wish you a tumble at the first ditch.'

Beth was able to smile at last. 'Please do not do that, for I am already attracting too much unwelcome attention.' Then she added, 'Please call me Beth.'

A stray breeze, cold and damp, wafted along the street, and Cleo shivered. 'Oh, dear, I fear the effects of the stirrup cup are wearing off. I do wish they'd get on with it. The sooner we have this over and done with, the sooner I can get back to something resembling warmth and comfort.'

Beth managed a smile. 'Sir Guy told me the tufting would begin at nine, and it's almost that now.'

'Well, before we have to charge off like a brigade at Waterloo, let me ask you if you will attend a little tea party I intend to hold in order to raise money for war veterans? They are all being cruelly discharged and have nowhere to go and nothing to live upon. It is up to us to do what we can.'

'Of course I will come.'

'Good, for it will give me a chance to show off my fine new villa, which I vow is the most bang-up-to-the-mark residence in the vicinity of Exmoor. And so agreeably close to Stone Valley, where I am able to walk every day.' Cleo gave her a wicked look. 'Not that there is any really interesting wild life to be seen there at the moment.'

Beth's eyes brushed hers. 'One needs to go up on the cliffs for that.'

'Ah, so that's the secret.'

'As you know full well,' Beth observed.

'True, but I could not help twitting you a little.' Cleo stiffened suddenly. 'Curse it, I do believe that odious Lavington beast is about to speak to us. Come, Beth, let's mingle elsewhere, for I cannot bear to even look at him, let alone pass the time of day.'

Beth manoeuvred her bay mare, named Gentian, after Cleo, and they soon managed to make it more trouble than it was worth for Sir Daniel to engage them in conversation. Taking refuge close to the Yarn Market, the two women gazed back down the thronged street, where it seemed that all Somerset and Devon must have congregated. Beth glanced at Cleo. 'Why do you dislike Sir Daniel so much?'

'No one *likes* Lavington. He's execrable, and after last week I know I'll be disgracefully rude if I'm obliged to speak to him.'

'What happened last week?'

'Oh, it's a despicable mess, of which I know because the young woman at the centre of it happens to be my new maid, Tess Hawksworth. She spurned Lavington's lecherous advances, and so he had her two brothers arrested, supposedly for poaching in Granleigh Woods, which partly abuts Lavington's land. As the sitting magistrate, he accepted false evidence against them, and now they are almost certain to hang. He's punishing her through her brothers.'

Beth was disgusted. 'How loathsome!'

'Indeed. I've tried speaking to the judge, but was lectured on attempting to tamper with the King's law, so now my only hope is your husband. He is the one person I can think of with enough clout to make a difference. Oh, I know he won't be able to save them entirely, but at least he might be able to persuade the judge to reduce the eventual sentence to one of transportation. Sir Daniel Lavington's base male urges and injured pride should not be permitted to cost innocent men their lives.'

'I'm sure Sir Guy will help, Cleo.'

'I'm sure too, the question is whether he can bring sufficient pressure to bear.'

There was a surge of excitement in the street as horns sounded and the hounds set off at last, trotting out past the church and then up toward the moor. There must have been over a hundred horsemen, all in hunting pink and mounted on superb horses. There were quite a few ladies too, mostly riding toward the rear, and Beth and Cleo were among these. The excitement was almost tangible, and then the hounds' noise swelled to a deep-throated roar. Someone shouted, 'They've roused a stag!' Horns rang out, the trot increased to a canter, and horses and hounds streamed up over the moor. Hoofs thundered, horns wavered, men shouted, and the staghounds were in full cry.

Beth could only give Gentian her head. She lost track of time as the pace continued relentlessly. Cleo soon dropped out, as did many of the other ladies, and Beth saw the Reverend Bellamy fall in a stream at the bottom of a combe. The remaining riders became strung out as the hounds sang over hilltop and valley. The scent was lost for a while, the hounds trying to work out the difficult route the stag had taken, moving up and down the banks of a mere, where the thawing ice was now almost transparent. A wind gusted over the moor, moaning through the gorse bushes and the clumps of heather that were now exposed as the snow melted. Gentian's ears pricked and twitched, and Beth could feel her quivering. The mare was as excited as the hounds.

Sir Daniel suddenly appeared at her side. 'A good run so far, eh, Lady Valmer? Your husband knows a thing or two about hunting.'

'Yes.' As Guy's prey, she should know, she thought.

'Hold now, for they have the scent again!' Any further questions he may have intended to put to her were forgotten as he kicked his short, stout legs to urge his horse after the hounds again.

The stragglers among the riders, mostly elderly and infirm gentlemen, and a thin scattering of ladies, were only just catching up as the full-blooded baying rang out once more. These trailing horses, and their riders, were all exhausted, and precious few of them elected to continue. Enough was enough, and flasks of fortifying spirits were much in evidence as they called it a day.

The fleeing stag was possessed of strength and stamina, seeming to taunt the overexcited hounds by remaining out of sight ahead. Guy was among the leading riders, but Beth had fallen well back. She hardly knew what she was doing, except that she had to remain in the saddle and somehow be there at the end. She didn't want to witness the kill, but had promised Guy to be all that Lady Valmer should. On and on she rode, clinging to the saddle and willing herself not to give in. It wasn't until the hounds surged up out of a dense wood to the high moor, and lost the scent again by an isolated signpost, that Beth realized where she was. As the hounds and riders milled around in confusion, she looked north, and her heart almost turned over as she saw the cleft in the cliffs that marked Lannermouth. Looking north-west, she saw the white splendour of Haldane Hall. The woodland through which they had just ridden was Granleigh Woods, where Tess Hawksworth's brothers had been caught poaching, and which marked the boundary between Guy's land, Landry's and Sir Daniel's.

She sensed Guy watching her, but then the hounds surged away again, this time uncontrollably, with a blood-curdling racket. Their blood lust was up as they caught a scent. It wasn't the stag, but they were intent upon a kill. She heard Guy shout to the whippers to collect them, but it was useless. The famous Greylake staghounds bayed wildly as they spread down into a sheltered valley, where penned Haldane ewes were grazing on hay. The ewes scattered in alarm, but the hounds leapt over the pens and fell upon them. Beth watched in horror, for it was slaughter on a grand scale, with Landry's sheep soon littering the ground, their blood running into the remains of the snow. Glancing behind, she saw that the carnage was visible from Haldane Hall, but there seemed to be no reaction.

Guy called to Bradfield. 'Get on up to the hall, and put right what you can.'

'Yes, Sir Guy.' The agent touched his hat, and then turned his sweating horse to ride toward Landry's residence.

Guy glanced at Beth, and their eyes met for a long moment before he rode off again to help the whippers round up the sated hounds. 'Get them set!' he shouted, 'we've time yet to rouse another stag!' The horns faltered along the valley as the huntsmen swept the hounds toward the south, away from Haldane, and Beth wearily urged Gentian to follow.

Of the hundred or so riders who'd set out

from Greylake, only a dozen remained at the end, and Beth was the only woman. As she bent forward to pat Gentian's neck, the mare was foam-flecked and dark with sweat. She was an unwilling witness as the terrified, exhausted stag turned to stand his ground in a clearing. The valiant animal screamed once as the hounds ripped it apart, and Beth was almost sick with revulsion and distress. She wanted to ride away, yet somehow found the willpower to remain where she was. But she hated every blood-drenched moment. No living creature deserved to be torn to shreds. It was barbaric, and she vowed never to follow the staghounds again, no matter what the pressure from Guy.

She didn't notice him ride to her side, until he leaned across to put his gloved hand over hers. 'It's nearly done now.'

'I've kept my promise to you,' she said in a voice that trembled, 'but *never* ask this of me again.'

Sir Daniel reined in before them, his face red, mud-spattered and grinning. 'Five and a half hours from lay-on to kill, eh, Valmer? Damned good day. The North Devons couldn't improve. A quart of good claret in the stag's mouth tonight, eh? He's ten years, I'd hazard. And the antlers! Seven on one top and five on the other. He'll make a splendid trophy. What a blooding for you, Lady Valmer, and I claim the honour of marking you!' He

244

heaved himself from the saddle.

The hounds had been hauled from their prey, so he was able to go up to the stag's lifeless body and dip his podgy fingers in its gaping throat. Beth had to lean down for him to smear the blood on her forehead. There were appreciative cheers from the other huntsmen, but she couldn't summon a smile, and when she straightened in the saddle she looked reproachfully at Guy. He avoided her eyes.

*   *   *

Later, when everyone had returned to the castle, there was a celebratory supper. Braddy and the kitchen staff had once again been obliged to work hard to produce a fine repast, and the noise in the entrance hall was tremendous as the feast was enjoyed to the full. The stag's head was borne in on a platter, and placed before Guy and Beth. Guy took a glittering crystal decanter of claret and placed it momentarily in the stag's mouth, before pouring glass after glass for his guests. The decanter was filled and refilled, until everyone was able to toast the day. He gave a glass to Beth, and their fingers brushed as she accepted it, but still he did not meet her eyes.

A little later, when Sir Daniel had distracted Guy's attention, she noticed Bradfield enter the hall from the direction of the kitchens, looking rather apprehensive about something. Guessing that it was connected to the Haldane sheep, she beckoned the agent to her side. 'Is something wrong?' she asked quietly.

'Er, yes, my lady. I approached Mr Haldane earlier, but he was not at home, and so I left a message. Now he has sent his head groom to demand full recompense, and I admit to being loath to approach Sir Guy about it.'

'Mr Haldane is justified in his demand,' Beth pointed out.

The agent was shocked. 'My lady?'

'The Greylake staghounds do not have the God-given right to do as they please. Mr Haldane's land was hunted against his express wish.'

'But it wasn't intentional, my lady,' the agent protested. 'The hounds were out of control.'

'Which does *not* excuse anything. Is Mr Haldane's head groom still waiting?'

'Yes, my lady.'

'Then take me to him.' Aware that what she planned to do would make things infinitely worse for her with Guy, but determined to do what was right, she rose from her seat and followed the bemused agent from the hall.

He took her to the kitchens, where the head groom, Johns, whom she had met before, waited uneasily. His eyes cleared when he saw her. 'Miss Mannacott! I—I mean, my lady.'

'Good evening, Johns. May I ask why you

are here and not Mr Haldane's agent?'

'Mr Carter's unwell, my lady.'

'I see. Now then, how many Haldane ewes have been destroyed?'

'Twenty-three, my lady, and Mr Haldane isn't pleased!'

'I can imagine. Perhaps he will be placated if you tell him that first thing tomorrow thirty prime Greylake ewes will be sent to him. That should be ample recompense for his losses and inconvenience.' And more than sufficient to put Guy in such a towering rage that he should all but combust.

Bradfield's jaw dropped, and Johns blinked, before smiling with relief. 'Thank you, my lady! I'm sure that will be the end of the matter.'

No, it wouldn't she thought, well aware that her high-handedness would result in another disagreeable confrontation with her husband. But she was unrepentant. Guy and his rampaging hunt had been in the wrong today, and no matter how much he loathed Landry, the damage should be put right. Magnanimously.

* * *

That night, Beth was seated at the dressing-table in her bedroom as Braddy brushed her hair. She wore her lace-trimmed nightgown and was weary after the long day. Guy hadn't

247

spoken to her about the ewes, although she knew Bradfield had told him what she'd done. It was hardly likely that he would say nothing on the matter, and this guess was proved correct when the door opened without ceremony, and he came in. Braddy hurriedly put the hairbrush down and left the room, leaving Beth to face her furious husband.

He came to stand behind her, meeting her gaze in the mirror. 'It has come to my attention that you have seen fit to issue extraordinary instructions on my behalf.'

'Extraordinary?'

'For *thirty* of my best ewes to be sent to Haldane.'

'Yes, I did.'

'By what authority did you so presume?' His voice was taut with anger.

'The authority of being your wife. I *am* Lady Valmer, am I not?'

'Oh, yes, madam, you are, but I will not suffer you to make free with such orders. *I* am the master here, and you had best not forget it.'

She picked up the hairbrush and drew it slowly through her hair. 'I only did what any true gentleman would do. Face it, Guy, your rage is solely due to it concerning Landry. Spite does not become you.' She was goading him, but could not help herself.

'Enough, Beth.'

'Or what, Guy? What more can you do to

me than you already have? You've spoken of admiring my spirit, well this is what that spirit entails. I will stand up to you, and if I think you are in the wrong—or will fail to do the right thing—I'll put it right.'

'Don't presume too far, Beth, because I will not stand for it.'

'What will you do? Beat me? Well, why not? You've done everything else!'

'You, madam, are descending into the realms of the ridiculous!' he snapped.

'I've been down there since I met you, sir.'

'No, you've been there since you let a damned blacksmith bed you,' he corrected.

She rose, quivering. 'There goes the last of your honour, sir. Well, think on this. I'm now your wife, wedded and bedded, and you are rather saddled with me. How inconvenient for you that I don't intend to be crushed by you or your moods.'

He laughed derisively. 'You think I mean to crush you? Oh, think what you will, for it's immaterial to me.' Turning on his heel, he left the room.

She stood for a moment, shaking with emotion, and then crept into her bed to cry herself to sleep. He hadn't laid a hand upon her, but he might as well have done, because his final contempt had been a dagger in her heart. It didn't matter how wonderful their lovemaking had been, because she had to finally accept that she would never be more to him than a chattel. She didn't understand him and ought to despise him; instead she still loved him. The former Beth Tremoille was the original fool.

The following morning she learned that he'd left for London at dawn, and would not return for at least two months. As she sat on her own at the breakfast table, she began to wonder what she had to lose if she disappeared, as she had before. He was now assured of regaining Tremoille House, because she was his wife and he also had her father's last will. Her inheritance was all he'd ever sought. Her physical presence was no longer necessary.

CHAPTER SEVENTEEN

Jane thought of tossing a coin to decide whether her dreaded visit to Tremoille House should be on New Year's Eve or New Year's Day, but in the end the choice seemed obvious. As the disagreeable news Thomas had to hear would most definitely signal the end of her long career of scheming self-interest, New Year's Eve seemed much more appropriate. The first day of 1816, could then herald a fresh start. Or so she prayed.

She dressed with care for the occasion, steeled herself with a number of glasses of cognac, and then drove out of Whitend. The Severn had burst its banks because of the thaw, and floodwater reached across the park almost to the house, but the drive was still passable, as were the roads beyond, but only just. It took quite some time for her carriage to negotiate the puddles and ruts of the roads down in the vale, and then the slippery climb up into the hills, where rivulets poured down the lanes to join the river below.

The silver flask of cognac in Jane's russet velvet reticule was empty by the time the Tremoille House gatehouse came into view. She took a long breath to calm herself. At least she looked good, she thought wryly. Her fawn merino pelisse and gown were just right for a woman of her age, and her narrow-brimmed hat was set at a rakish, almost defiant angle. Dressed like this, and fortified by an alcoholic backbone, she felt as ready as she ever could for the daunting interview ahead.

She gazed down at the house as the carriage followed the drive down the side of the valley. It was sad to accept no longer being its mistress. In all the years of her marriage to Esmond Tremoille, she had been queen here, and oh, how she'd exulted in such privilege. Now, when things had come to this sorry new pitch, she could understand how Beth had felt on being ejected so cruelly. 'Oh, Jane, Jane, in your time you've been a bitch and a half, and no mistake,' she murmured.

The servants greeted her unannounced arrival with obvious disquiet, and as she entered the hall she knew that something was very wrong. She glanced around at the familiar panelling and paintings. Visually, everything seemed as she would have expected, with the Christmas greenery beginning to look dry and unattractive, ready for Twelfth Night, but there was an atmosphere that seemed to reach into the furthest, darkest corners of the house. It wouldn't do to question mere footmen, however, so she was almost relieved when she saw Edward coming down the stairs, dressed in hunting pink, as was his custom now, as well as his father's. He was no easier on the eye than before, she decided, at the same time noting that he too seemed disquieted.

She waylaid him at the foot of the stairs. 'What's going on, Edward?'

'Why are you here?'

'The last time I looked, I was Lady Welland,' she responded coolly:

'If you've come to see my father, you'd do better to go back to Whitend.'

'Why?'

'He's drunk and stuffed full with laudanum,' was the flat reply.

Jane's lips parted. 'Drunk I can understand, but *laudanum*—?'

'It was bad enough when he just had the trouble on the estates, but now his bank's closed and he's in a very tricky financial situation. All he can think of is how he missed his chance. He says something about Rothschild's pigeon, but I don't know what he means.'

'Oh, dear . . .' That wretched pigeon, which may or may not even exist!

'He turned to laudanum when spirits weren't enough,' Edward continued, 'and has taken more of the stuff in a few days than I'm likely to take in an entire life. Then, today, a letter came from his London lawyer.'

'Tulliver?'

Edward nodded. 'That's the one. I don't know what the letter said, just that it concerned Sir Guy Valmer. The news was bad, and Father took himself off to the library with more laudanum. He's been there ever since, and to be frank, everyone hopes he'll stay there.'

Jane breathed out slowly. Well, at least her task was going to be easier if Thomas had already learned about Guy, the will and Beth. 'Has he enough sense to know what's being said to him?'

Edward ran a hand through his hair. 'Maybe, but he's restless and weak, sometimes confused, and last night he had a fit.'

'A fit?' Jane was shocked.

'Yes. And his heart's beating nineteen to the dozen, he's got a rash and he keeps wanting to pee, but can't.' Edward looked away for a moment. 'He's all but lost his wits, but at the same time is dangerously sensible, like a firework that's been lit, but hasn't gone off. Maybe he'll explode, maybe he'll just fizzle out.'

'I had better see him,' she declared, collecting her skirts to mount the staircase, but Edward caught her arm.

'It's wiser not to, believe me.'

'I fear I must, Edward, and right now have consumed enough Dutch courage to face Genghis Khan himself, so I'll get it over and done with.'

'Then I'll come with you.'

'It's none of your concern, sir,' she replied coldly.

He held her gaze and said, 'You'll need me.'

His tone made her think again. 'Very well, if that is what you wish,' she said, and made her way toward the library, with Edward following.

From the moment she entered the room she wished she'd heeded Edward's advice, because on seeing her Thomas erupted from his chair at the desk, and ran at her. His eyes were glazed, he was unsteady on his feet, but he had the strength of a team of oxen. He flailed his fists, raining blows upon her, and then he grabbed her by the arm and flung her against the desk. Winded, she collapsed on the floor, her strength frozen in its tracks. She felt Thomas kicking her, calling her every foul name under the sun, and clearly intent upon killing her.

Then she was vaguely aware of Edward's voice as he hauled his maniacal father off her. 'Get out, my lady, get out now!' he cried, grappling with the demented Thomas as she managed to find the wit and the willpower to crawl across the floor and out into the hall, where anxious footmen hastened to help her. Thomas continued to shout and scream in the library, and Edward endeavoured to placate him, but at last there came the crack of a strong fist reaching its target, followed by a dull thud as Thomas fell unconscious. Then Edward yelled for help, and two footmen ran to him.

Jane struggled to her feet. She was bruised and battered, and in a great deal of pain, but still managed to compose herself. 'Send for the doctor,' she instructed weakly, 'and see to it that there's absolutely no laudanum beneath this roof. Hide all the spirits as well, and everything else with a modicum of alcohol.'

'Yes, my lady.' Maids and footmen hastened away, glad of sensible orders to carry out.

A few minutes later Thomas, still unconscious, was carried up to his bed, and Jane followed with Edward, to whom she turned at the top of the staircase. 'I am in your debt, sir,' she said.

'That drew a few of your fine white teeth, eh?' he replied with a fleeting grin.

'I don't deny it, but on today's showing I realize that perhaps Beelzebub doesn't yet have you completely in his clutches.'

'My mother was never much of a mother to me, but one thing she drummed into me was that a man should never hit a woman. I never have, nor will I stand by and let another man do it, even if he is my father. But don't think I'm to be saved, Lady Welland, because I have scores to settle and punishments to deal out. I intend to use my position here to right all the wrongs I think have been done to me. You won't like me at all after I've finished, and you'll soon forget anything I've done today.'

'You're determined to be obnoxious?'

'It's my right to be avenged for all that I have suffered,' he answered, and walked on toward Thomas's room.

The following days were an ordeal. The doctor arrived promptly, and instructions were given for the still senseless Thomas to be strapped into his bed. When he regained consciousness he was like a man possessed, a shrieking, foul-mouthed monster that vowed to heap torture on all its persecutors. When he wasn't violent, he was a slack-mouthed imbecile, talking to people who weren't there, or grinning at something unknown. But gradually, as the grip of the laudanum began to slip away, he became more rational; or at least, as rational as he seemed likely to be from now on. He was a shadow of his former self, sunk in gloom and despondency, convinced he was being persecuted, and terrified of having to return to Whitend, where the Severn lay in wait.

Edward was true to his word, and bullied his way through the days. He was hated by maids and footmen alike, and Jane found it harder and harder to remember how beholden she was to him for saving her from Thomas, but even so, it was due to Edward's insistence that she sent for Thomas's London lawyer, Mr Jethro Tulliver of Tulliver and Partners in Naismith Street.

A tall man of almost cadaverous appearance, with a snub nose and receding grey hair, he came with more bad news, having been in touch with Guy's lawyer, Mr Arthur Withers of Withers, Withers & Blenkinsop in Caradine Street. 'I fear, Lady Welland, that you and his lordship are expected to have handed this property over by the end of January. Sir Guy is most insistent.'

'I'll warrant he is,' Jane murmured. She and Edward received the lawyer in the library, Thomas not being in any condition to understand the interview, let alone take part. She looked at Tulliver. 'Is there any way we can fight this?'

'In my opinion, no.'

Edward was about to wipe his nose on his sleeve, but remembered in time, and sniffed noisily instead. 'What about the new Lady Valmer, eh? She was on her back for a blacksmith for nearly a year. Maybe Sir Guy wouldn't like that sort of scandal to get out in nob society.'

Tulliver's lips twitched with distaste. 'Mr Welland, I fear that we can besmirch Lady Valmer's character as much as we like, but it will make no difference, and please remember that the other side can as easily lay bare your situation. With all due respect, Lady Welland, the blunt facts are that you have much to hide in your background, and you, Mr Welland, have no say at all, not being born in wedlock.'

Edward flushed, and his fists clenched as if he would punch the lawyer for his impudence, but to Jane's relief he refrained. Tulliver continued, 'What matters in all this is the plain fact that the former Elizabeth Tremoille is Esmond Tremoille's heir and now Sir Guy's wife. Nothing we say or do can change it, and the end result remains the same. This house and its lands will go to Sir Guy.'

Jane was nothing if not plain-speaking. 'So, Mr Tulliver, Sir Guy can hang us by our pubic hairs.'

The lawyer stared at her, momentarily at a loss for words, but then he nodded. 'Aptly expressed, my lady.'

Edward banged a fist on the desk. 'What about the will? Who's to say it's genuine? Sir Guy could have had it forged!'

Tulliver was patient. 'It has not been forged, Mr Welland, but has been examined thoroughly, and its authenticity is beyond

258

doubt. Challenging it in court would delay things, but not change the outcome. Whichever way we look at it, Sir Guy is the winner. My advice is that you cut your losses, and simply hand this property over to him. You still have Whitend, and will have no option but to return there.'

'And that is that?' Jane enquired quietly.

'It is.'

'Very well, inform Mr Withers that we surrender without a shot being fired.'

Edward was outraged. 'No, damn it!'

Jane was long-suffering. 'Edward, whatever my husband may have promised you, and however important you have been led to believe you are in the Welland scheme of things, there is nothing in writing to confirm your position. You therefore remain what you have always been, Lord Welland's illegitimate son. As Lady Welland, and in your father's present incapacity, I have the say in what happens now.'

'So, it's out with Ned Barker, eh? Just like Beth Tremoille?' he replied bitterly.

She was tempted to confirm his fear, but had learned her lesson after Beth. 'No, Edward, you can remain in the family, but make no mistake, my instinct is to eject you, because you are here to usurp all you can of your brother Rowan's birthright. I have many sins in my past, but I have the benefit of hindsight. I wrongly did all I could to deny

Beth what she was due, and I find it hard to stand by and permit the same to be done to Rowan, whom I like immensely. But my husband wishes to acknowledge you as his son, which means that you have rights too. So you will stay. It's what your father would wish, were he able to make the decision. All I'm saying is that legally *I* must decide what ensues from this legal dilemma.' She turned to Tulliver again. 'Do as I said before, Mr Tulliver, and we will vacate Tremoille House as close to the end of January as we can.'

'Taking nothing with you that does not belong to you,' the lawyer warned.

'You think I will steal teaspoons, sir?' she answered coldly.

'I am just being cautious, Lady Welland. The best way to keep this matter away from society gossip is to let it proceed as quietly as possible. Do not give Sir Guy any cause to make a noise, and when—if—Lord Welland recovers, impress upon him that you have really had no choice in all this.'

'Mr Tulliver, as far as my husband is concerned, I am the Devil Incarnate. He will blame me for everything, even a cold cup of tea, until the day he dies, but in this particular matter with Valmer, I probably deserve the disapprobation.'

The lawyer spread his hands understandingly. 'The best laid plans of mice and men,' he murmured.

260

'Of mice and women, sir, mice and women.'

*   *   *

Maria Carberry was the undisputed leading lady of Drury Lane, and enjoyed the privilege of a dressing-room of her own. It was small, poky even, but private, and gave her precedence over every other actress, as well as most of the actors. Excluding Kean, of course, for he was treated like a king. Night had fallen outside, and rain dashed the grubby little window. She glanced toward it. Was there to be no end to the abysmal weather? Right now spring seemed to have been postponed forever.

The evening's performance had been so astonishing that it would be talked of for years to come. It was due to Edmund Kean, of course. So intense and powerful was his presence and his acting, that women in the audience screamed and fainted. 'Silly cows,' she murmured, wiping the last of the stage make-up from her face. The play had been Massinger's dark comedy, *A New Way to Pay Old Debts*, and Kean had been Sir Giles Overreach. She had played Lady Allworth, and although she said so herself, she too had shone. 'Kean may be king here, Maria,' she said to herself, 'but *you* are queen!'

Now the performance was at an end, she had removed her costume, her hair was loose and she was dressed only in a transparent lacy white robe. She was enjoying the few quiet minutes before sending for her new dresser to help her prepare for the gauntlet of hopeful gentlemen crowding at the stage door. Sometimes she chose one to service her like a bull, but no man could compare with Guy Valmer, whom she'd lost.

'My matchless English rover,' she breathed, as she sat in front of her dressing-table. Thoughts of him aroused delicious sensations, and she pushed a hand between her legs, fingering herself into further excitement. It was easy to make herself come, but the only climaxes that had ever mattered to her were those shared with Guy. She watched herself in the illuminated mirror, observing the flush on her cheeks and the dark glow in her eyes as waves of self-administered pleasure washed pleasingly through her loins. As the feelings dwindled into a comfortable warmth, she studied herself more critically. It did not do for actresses to age. Her figure was still firm and curvaceous, and her hair as flaxen as ever, although Scandinavian when it ought to have been dark and Hibernian. But maybe her eyes, soft and inviting, like amber moss deep in an Irish wood, were filled with the mist and mystery of her homeland. Such great beauty ought to have kept Guy in her bed, but it had not been enough. She only had herself to blame, for she'd been so headstrong and

262

determined that she'd overlooked the small fact that he hadn't been as besotted with her as she had been with him.

Her dresser tapped at the door. 'What is it?' Maria was in no mood to have her rare moments of tranquillity interrupted.

'There is a gentleman to see you.'

Maria's brows drew angrily together. 'Then tell him to go to hell! He can take his chances with the rest of the pack at the stage door!'

A familiar male voice answered. 'Now, now Maria, is that any way to address your English rover?'

Maria's heart lurched. Guy? *Guy?* She leapt up from her chair and hastened to fling the door back. 'Oh, Guy, my handsome, handsome darling,' she cried.

Guy smiled and allowed his glance to move slowly over her robe. 'I see your knowledge of etiquette and manners hasn't improved.'

'Would you prefer it if it had?' she enquired, placing her hands upon her hips so the robe slipped from her shoulders and was held up only by her crooked arms. There was nothing he could not see, from her full breasts, narrow waist and flaunted hips, to the thick, dark hairs clustering at her groin. The moment was only spoiled by the venomous look she cast at the dresser. 'I'll call you when you're needed!' As the woman hurried away, Maria said, 'This is a most unexpected pleasure, sir.'

'I confess I had reservations about coming.

263

After all, we parted on ill terms.'

'I was stupid then. I'm sensible now.'

'Not too sensible, I trust.'

'Certainly not.' She smiled earthily. 'Do you intend to give me a good seeing to?'

'Well, I won't say no,' he said, entering the room and closing the door behind him, before tossing his outdoor clothes, hat and cane on a chair.

She moved away, searching his face. 'I'm told you're married.'

'Word does travel,' he answered.

'Is she the one you told me you were looking for?'

'Yes.'

And do you love her?'

'That, Maria, is none of your business.'

She smiled a little. 'Well, I suppose the answer is no, or you wouldn't be here so swiftly upon the heels of your marriage vows.'

'Guess as you wish.'

'How many times have you fucked her?'

He didn't reply.

'I can't bear to think of that fine weapon of yours being inside someone else.'

'Then don't think of it.'

'Oh, you're as cruel as ever, my English rover,' she said softly.

'I haven't changed, Maria. What I've been in the past, I still am now.'

'So I can't say I haven't been warned?'

He spread his hands briefly. 'If you wish me

to go, I will.'

'Go? Guy, you are my delight, my joy and my lodestar, the opium to which I am an addict. Seeing you again like this has repaired my broken heart, so if you go now, that heart will be shattered once more.' Her amber eyes were shrewd as well as adoring. 'I don't know why you've come to me again, nor do I care. You're using me, that much I do know, but I have no pride or vanity where you're concerned. I'll always be here for you.'

'Don't put me on a pedestal, Maria, because I'm definitely not worthy.'

'I'll be the judge of that,' she answered softly, and then nodded toward the door. 'Push the bolt across, for this is one shag that isn't going to be interrupted.'

He obliged, and then she went closer to him. 'I've been waiting and waiting for this, Guy. I've dreamed about you, yearned for you, *willed* you to return to me. I know I was at fault before. It was stupid of me to keep picking arguments and try to wheedle you into a marriage you clearly didn't want. And nor do I, if I'm honest. There would be far too many shackles in being Lady Valmer, or lady anyone else, for that matter.'

He gave a short laugh. 'Maria, we couldn't have married anyway, because you're already married to the theatre manager who contracted you in Dublin. You left him to make your fortune here, and you reverted to

265

your maiden name, but for all that you're *still* Mrs Ambrose Malone.'

She pursed her lips philosophically. 'I seem to recall that the last time you reminded me of that, I called you a slavering, misbegotten English hellhound.'

'Ah, yes, the words have a familiar ring.'

She shrugged the lace robe to the floor, and then eased her buttocks on to the dressing table, her legs apart. 'Puss has missed you, my rampant tomcat. Puss needs you so much that she's in danger of withering up.'

'Puss has always found more than enough elsewhere to avert such a peril,' he replied, moving closer until he was between her thighs.

'That's a wicked lie, sir,' she whispered, beginning to undo the front of his trousers. 'Show me what you've got, sir, let me see the fine rod that has pleasured my Puss so often in the past. Oh, my, what a big, big boy you are.'

'There's more of me to the pound, and that's what you really like.'

'Oh, I won't argue with *that*,' she answered, putting her arms around his neck and wriggling until she presented herself to him. Her breath caught as his member pushed between the lips of her most intimate parts. 'Stop there, my darling boy, stop there,' she breathed, her whole body trembling with anticipation. 'Kiss me, Guy, let me taste your lips again, for they are sweeter to me than the finest honey.'

266

'And from which role is that a quote?' he teased, bending his head to put his lips over hers.

'*The Life and Loves of Maria Carberry.* Puss wants you now, my beloved, but slowly now, so that she can lap up every morsel. Oh, yes, that's the way. Holy Mother, how I adore you, Guy Valmer,' she breathed, the words barely intelligible as she surrendered to his kiss. Her flesh felt about to burst into flame, and her limbs lacked all substance as their mouths joined erotically.

She wriggled further on to him, then off the dressing table to be supported by their physical joining. Her hidden muscles gripped him almost ferociously, and he could feel the flush of desire consuming her whole body. Her lips slid longingly over his, and her breasts pressed against his shirt so that her nipples caught on the rich folds of lace. Her hands moved over the back of his coat, and then descended to his firm buttocks so that she could pull herself on to him even more, and force his ardent member further inside her.

Suddenly she lost all control, writhing against him like an animal, and kissing him so savagely that she seemed to want his lips bruised and bleeding. 'Holy Mother! Holy Mother of God!' she gasped, her fingernails clawing his back through his clothes. He could feel her intimate flesh willing him to give up the essence that would bring them both to the wild heights of gratification. She had no shame and displayed no restraint. She wanted one thing from him, and nothing was going to prevent her. Her moans and groans must have been audible on the stage itself, he thought, letting her do as she would. He wanted her to cleanse him, to make everything as it had been before Beth. That was all he'd come here for, to be cleansed of Beth.

Maria's feminine craving tugged at his soul as she worked against him until he felt he would burst. Suddenly she pulled her head back to look in to his eyes. 'You're mine at this moment, Guy Valmer, mine!' She worked her hips urgently to and fro, and he capitulated. As his weapon pumped deep into her, she cried and groaned, raising the very roof with her noisy gratification, but he didn't care. *This is all I think of you, Beth, this and no more.* He could feel her ravenous flesh sucking every last drop of his potency, and his pleasure should have been intense, but Beth's name still rang through his head, echoing with regret.

Maria was almost beside herself with love and wild excitement as she tried to keep him to her, but he pulled his loins away. Knowing she wanted more, he slid a hand down between her legs and stimulated her again. She rocked against his fingers, her eyes glazed with delight, and then she found his lips in a kiss so filled with longing and adoration that he hated himself for using her like this.

'You know that I love you, don't you?' she whispered, her flaxen curls damp against her forehead and cheeks.

'Yes, I know it, Maria.'

'But you will never love me.'

'I have never lied to you.' He took out his handkerchief to wipe his fingers, and then he pressed it into her hand. 'A little mopping up would seem to be necessary.'

She smiled regretfully. 'That's one handkerchief I will not be returning. So what do we do now, my English rover? Are you taking me to supper at some fine Piccadilly establishment? The Pulteney Hotel, perchance?'

'Tomorrow, maybe. Tonight I have to return to Park Lane.'

'To your wife?' She couldn't hide the edge in her voice.

'No, she is at Greylake.'

'Then why must you go to Park Lane?'

'Because I have two guests, one of whom needs taking down a peg or three.'

Maria searched his face. 'But tomorrow we will dine together?'

'If you wish.'

'You know that I wish.' She smiled. 'Have you returned to me, Guy?'

'It would seem so.'

'I don't know whether to pity your wife, or hate her.'

He retrieved his things from the chair. 'My

wife is immaterial,' he murmured, and then kissed her again before leaving.

But as he slipped out of the stage door, past the eager throng of gentlemen still waiting in the rain, he did not feel cleansed at all, but cheap and ignoble. And as his carriage conveyed him away, he despised himself for wanting to punish Beth, because all he'd done was punish himself. And Maria.

How ironic it all was, and how pathetic. He resented Beth's unknowing slip of the tongue, as if saying Haldane's name amounted to adultery; yet he, Valmer, was the one to have broken the Seventh Commandment.

CHAPTER EIGHTEEN

After leaving Maria, Guy drove straight to Park Lane, and his fine house opposite Hyde Park. The park was lost in a gloom of rain, and the street lamps shone feebly as his carriage turned in through the gates and drew up beneath the *porte cochère.* A footman hastened out, and Guy climbed down reluctantly. He was in no mood to confront Rowan about Rosalind, but confront him he must, because that young lady's presumptuousness had to be dealt with. Taking a long breath, he entered the soothing grey-and-white vestibule, where his prized collection of classical Italian

270

landscapes was arranged on the otherwise plain walls. As another footman divested him of his outdoor clothes, he glanced toward the closed double doors of the drawing-room facing the top of the staircase. The fact that they were closed informed him that Rowan and his new wife were within.

He didn't care for Rosalind, whom he'd decided was a lowborn adventuress who would always put herself before any other consideration. Maybe she loved Rowan, she certainly seemed to, but she loved herself more. And there was the puzzling matter of her money. Blacksmith's daughters simply did not have money unless they'd inherited it from a wealthy relative, which this one certainly had not. Therefore the mysterious money excited curiosity . . . and suspicion.

Allowances had been made for Rosalind's youth and inexperience, but at dinner earlier tonight her host had finally had enough. There had been one snide comment too many about Beth, who was apparently the bane of Rosalind's life, and the time had come to draw a line. Guy hadn't wanted to react in anger, which was why he'd said nothing before going out to renew his liaison with Maria. Now he was composed, and knew exactly what must be done. He turned to a nearby footman. 'Request Mr Welland to attend me in the morning-room.'

'Sir Guy.'

271

As the footman went up to the drawing-room, Guy adjourned to the ground floor morning-room, which faced the gardens at the rear of the house, and on sunny mornings was bright and cheerful. Tonight, however, there was only firelight to keep shadows at bay. He went to the mantelshelf and reached for one of the cigars he kept there in a silver box. Smoking wasn't often one of his vices, but he felt in need of it now. Lighting a spill at the fire, he held it to the end of the cigar, and then tossed the spill on to the glowing coals.

For a moment he didn't think of Rowan and Rosalind, but of the letter he'd sent to his lawyer, Withers, that very morning. It had been very brief, a few sentences, but said everything that was necessary.

My dear Withers,
See to it that I become the new owner of the Dower House, Lannercombe, in the County of Devon. I don't care what the price, just that the property becomes mine. Please accept this undertaking as a matter of urgency.

Valmer

Hearing Rowan's tread on the staircase, he turned reluctantly, uncomfortably aware that this wasn't going to be an easy interview. Rowan came in, a warm smile brightening his handsome face. 'Guy? I trust the theatre went

272

well?'

'I wouldn't know, I didn't actually watch the performance.'

'Not watch La Carberry? I admire your restraint.' Rowan nodded at the silver box. 'May I join you?'

'By all means.' Guy extended the box, and even kindled another spill. Rowan drew the cigar into life, and then glanced shrewdly at him. 'You're too attentive, Guy, so I imagine something's up?'

'We need to talk, my friend.'

Rowan drew back a little, guessing it concerned Rosalind. 'Guy, I haven't criticized or questioned you about Beth, and so I expect the same consideration from you regarding Rosalind.'

'How defensive you are, for I haven't mentioned any names.'

'I just know.'

Guy nodded. 'Yes, because you also know that things have to change if you and Rosalind are to remain beneath my roof.'

'Rosalind is green to our ways, Guy, but she will learn.'

'She had better do so, because if she continues in her present vein she'll ruin you before this coming Season even commences.'

'That's a little harsh,' Rowan replied resentfully, and went to the window to look out at the rain-distorted darkness.

'You, sir, are letting your cock do the

thinking,' Guy observed.

'Oh? And what, pray, were you up to this evening with Maria? Playing cards? Discussing the price of bread?'

'Maria occupies a certain part of my life, Rowan, and that part has nothing to do with my social standing. You, on the other hand, have made Rosalind Mannacott your wife, and therefore the future Lady Welland. She needs to temper her conduct and learn how to hold her tongue. If she had behaved like this beneath almost any other roof than mine, you would long since have been requested to leave.'

Rowan turned, flushing. 'She's very young, Guy, and—'

'—and thinks herself the Queen of the May. She certainly appears to think she has the God-given right to pass witless and derogatory remarks about Beth.'

Rowan couldn't deny this charge. 'I know, Guy and I'll speak to her about it.'

'Yes, you damned well will, because if it happens again, you and she will find yourselves out in the street. I mean it Rowan, because while you mean a great deal to me, your wife means nothing.'

'It won't happen again, you have my word.' Rowan left the window to flick ash into the fire. 'But you have to admit, Guy, it is curious why you should leave your new bride at Greylake and then come here for some unspecified period.'

'Is it your business?' Guy snapped.

'Well, but, but—'

'Is it Rosalind's business?'

'No.'

'Then why does she see fit to comment upon it?'

Rowan couldn't reply.

Guy's anger had stirred. 'She does it because she has fixed upon Beth as having bloodied her adorable little nose. If anything impinges upon Rosalind Mannacott's self-centred little world, she reacts with more spite and venom than is natural.'

'I say, Guy, steady on, for although I admit Rosalind has faults, I won't have her insulted so cruelly.'

'But you'd have my wife insulted,' Guy retorted.

'Look, you've made your point on that score. I'll speak to her, and promise you it won't happen again. I regret that things have got off to such a sorry start.'

Guy searched his face in the firelight. 'Rowan, have you *really* considered what you've done by rushing into this marriage?'

'If you are about to lecture me on class—!'

'Don't fly off the handle, because class isn't what I'm getting at in this instance.'

'Then what?' Rowan faced him. 'Go on, state your point.'

Guy paused, and then went to sit down in a

275

fireside chair, hoping to restore calm to the situation. 'Sit down, Rowan, please, because we begin to resemble fighting cocks.'

Rowan obeyed, but unwillingly. He felt as if Rosalind was in the dock, and his every instinct was to protect her.

Guy regarded him. 'How much money does Rosalind have?' he asked bluntly.

'It's none of your business!' Rowan cried, beginning to rise again, but Guy waved him back down.

'For God's sake, Rowan, I want to *help* you. Now then, if you know the sum she claims to possess, then—'

'She doesn't claim it, Guy, she has it!'

'How much?' Guy repeated.

'Four hundred and eighty guineas.'

Guy breathed out slowly. 'Then I trust you can put two and two together, my friend, because I know that Beth left five hundred guineas for Jake Mannacott. Yes, she shared the money equally with him. All he required was twenty guineas to buy into the forge in Frampney, and that is what he received. Now what does the mathematician in you say was left from that five hundred guineas?'

Rowan stared at him. 'What are you hinting, Guy?'

'Hinting? Damn it all, Rowan, it's plain as the nose on your face. I doubt very much if Jake Mannacott handed such a fortune over to his loving offspring.'

'Guy, I won't let you accuse Rosalind of stealing from her own father!'

'Very well, then leave. Do as you damned well like, but please be warned of the true character of that sweet, fresh-faced little angel you are pleased to call your wife.'

'You malign her, Guy, and you insult me.'

'I just want your eyes to be fully opened. You've chosen a perilous road, and Rosalind is not the sort to extend a helping hand unless it's of benefit to her.'

Rowan tossed his unfinished cigar into the fire and got up. He started to stride from the room, but then paused, head bowed, to place his hands on the breakfast table. 'Are you sure, absolutely sure, that Beth left five hundred guineas for Jake Mannacott?'

'Yes, she told me she entrusted the money to Rosalind. And she told me that Mannacott only required twenty. You've seen that forge at Frampney, it hasn't had anything spent on it, nor has Mannacott suddenly blossomed into Gloucestershire's dandiest blacksmith. Face it, Rowan, your wife, no matter how much you worship her, is capable of immense falsehood. She not only failed to give her father what he was due, she then left him and took the funds with her. You've heard her boasting about how she just packed her things and left without a word of explanation. She wants it to be seen as proof that her love for you overcomes everything else. I see it as callousness on a grand scale. So please be cautious from now on, Rowan.'

Rowan remained as he was for a long moment, then straightened and went out. Guy leaned his head back and closed his eyes. He'd said what he could, now it was up to Rowan . . . and the unpleasant little vixen with whom he'd so rashly encumbered himself.

*　　　*　　　*

Jake and Phoebe were walking home after Sunday morning service. It was the middle of February, and for the moment the rain had stopped. Spring seemed to have retreated sulkily behind the winter skies, and even the snowdrops, usually so brave and delightful in this month, were little more than timid green leaves that were afraid to peep up too high above the ground.

The ducks sheltered where they could around the village-green ponds, and the ground was still so waterlogged that crossing the grass was out of the question. Huddling in their winter clothes, Jake and Phoebe walked swiftly home to the roast mutton that had been left cooking slowly by the hearth. Jamie wasn't with them today, having decided to visit his mother, who lived near Whitend. He was proving a good pupil, eager to learn the blacksmith's art, and even Phoebe had to admit that he seemed set to one day be as fine

278

a smith as Jake was and Matty had been.

Phoebe glanced across at Squire Lloyd's mansion. 'I will never understand how the squire could have a son like Master Robert.'

'Or me a daughter like Rozzie?'

She looked at him. 'I didn't say that.'

'No, but you thought it.' Jake hunched his shoulders against the cold wind that blustered from the east. 'It's been weeks now, Phoebe, and not a single word from her.'

'You and I no longer exist in her new life, Jake, you had best accept that.'

He halted, stretching his neck to look at the roofs and chimneys of Whitend, a mile away to the north. 'Reckon I'll have to go there and find out what I can.'

'Go to Whitend? With mad Lord Welland in residence? You'd be a madman too. Haven't you heard how he sobbed like a baby when he came back to Whitend and saw the floods? Now I've been told that all the shutters and curtains have to be kept closed, so he doesn't see the water. That dismal old house must be like a great coffin.'

'I know all that, Phoebe, but I can't just stay here and do nothing. Whatever you may think of Rozzie, she's still my flesh and blood. I need to know she's all right.'

'If she's with Master Rowan, then she is,' Phoebe pointed out.

'It's all very well to *guess* that, I need to know it for a fact.'

Phoebe looked unhappily at the distant chimneys. 'Go if you must, Jake, but there's not only Lord Welland to be wary of. You and that Ned Barker have a history.'

'Ned Barker? Don't you mean the fancy new Edward Welland?' Jake laughed. 'Dear God above, I still can't credit that such a grubby lout is now swaggering around the countryside as the son of a lord. Well, my past dealings with him were short and to the point, I thrashed the living daylights out of him for groping around my daughter. He couldn't stand up to me then, and he won't now.'

'He wasn't Welland's darling then,' Phoebe reminded him.

'I'll be all right.'

Phoebe couldn't leave it at that. 'Let me go there instead. I haven't upset anyone, and—'

'I'll do my own dirty work, Phoebe. Settle down now, girl, or you won't be able to enjoy your own roast mutton!'

*   *   *

A little later that same morning, the Welland carriage drove back to Whitend from Gloucester Cathedral, where the attention of the congregation had been upon Thomas and his bastard son. Even Jane, with her notoriety, had faded into the background in comparison. She sat deep into the corner seat, and kept her eyes averted, determined not to catch

Thomas's eye. Or Edward's, for that matter.

She wore indigo and cream, and felt she had acquitted herself well throughout the service, which was more than could be said for the others. Edward had picked his nose and trumpeted into a dirty handkerchief, and Thomas had laughed moronically and encouraged his disreputable byblow.

Moronic was the best word for Thomas these days, she thought. He did not have to be restrained, as had happened at Tremoille House, and he even appeared to have accepted the decision she had made not to contest Sir Guy Valmer's lawsuit, but he had reverted to a disquieting form of second childhood. He laughed over childish things, stamped his foot pettishly, and sometimes even sucked his thumb. Other more repugnant ways had appeared as well, from scratching his balls in public, to urinating in the fireplace rather than bother with the correct office. He lacked interest in anyone and anything, except Edward, whom he appeared to regard as a paragon.

The servants went in fear of father and son alike, and estate labourers were treated with callous unconcern at a time when there was already unrest in the countryside. On top of this, prices were high, work was scarce, and winter crops had either been frozen in the ground or destroyed by the floods. Like the alarming sunsets and sunrises, the atmosphere across the land was generally so oppressive and filled with foreboding that Jane sometimes thought she could not bear it. But where could she go to escape? She had nothing, not even the smallest cottage to call her own, and Beth would no doubt say it was no more than she deserved.

It began to rain more heavily as the carriage neared Whitend, and as the coachmen set the horses along the drive to the house itself, Thomas began to lower the blinds, fearful of seeing the floods that rippled in the park. The horses splashed through deep puddles, and Jane saw how he shuddered with terror. Suddenly his porcine little eyes swung balefully to her. 'Lower your blind too, madam!' he snapped.

She began to obey, but Edward sat forward suddenly, seeing something outside that made his eyes gleam unpleasantly. 'Wait a moment, I do believe that's—' He looked out at a small group of men sheltering beneath a tree. 'Yes, it's that bugger Don Bryant.'

'Who's he?' Thomas enquired.

'No one you'd know, but I've several scores to settle with him.'

Thomas ventured to glance out. 'Who are you talking about?'

'The tall one with the wide-brimmed hat,' Edward answered.

'Oh, him. He's one of my keepers.'

Edward's eyes were cunning. 'Oh? Then

282

you've employed a poacher to guard your game.' He grabbed Thomas's cane and rapped it loudly against the carriage grille. The coachman immediately dragged the horses to a standstill.

'Eh?' Thomas looked blankly at him. 'Poacher?'

Jane knew Edward was lying. 'Don't listen to him, Thomas. Let's just drive on.'

'You keep out of it, woman,' Thomas snapped, before returning his attention to Edward. 'You've scores to settle? And he's a poacher?'

'He was. Robbed you blind, he did, and boasted about it all over Gloucester.'

Jane was appalled. 'Stop it, Edward! There isn't a shred of truth in your accusations. You just want to get your own back for something in the past.'

He gave a sleek smile, and looked at his father again. 'Is he in a tied cottage?'

'Of course, all my keepers are.'

'Then I want him out.'

Jane's dismay deepened. 'Bryant has a wife and four children!'

'That's his problem,' Edward answered, and opened the door to climb down. Thomas shuffled eagerly along the seat, the better to watch. His face was gleeful, and he scratched his genitals to quicken his excitement, but then he saw the floods again, and his face fell. 'The blind, woman! The blind!' Jane obeyed, but by

283

sitting right back she could see what happened as Edward approached the group under the tree. And as the carriage door hadn't been fully closed, she and Thomas could hear what transpired.

Edward's sneering voice was an echo of his father's. 'So, Don Bryant, we meet again, eh?'

Bryant's face, raw-boned and bearded, went pale, and his tongue passed uneasily over his lower lips. 'I don't want any trouble, Master Edward.'

'I'll bet you don't, but you've got it anyway. You're out of work as of this moment, and you're to be out of your cottage by the end of this week.'

Bryant stared at him in dismay. 'But I haven't done anything!'

'You've poached off my father's estate.'

The other men in the group sprang to Bryant's defence. 'No, he hasn't, sir! Don Bryant is a keeper, and an honest one!'

'Not in my book.' Edward turned to make his way back to the carriage.

'Like father, like son,' Jane said softly. 'I only pray I'm there to witness it when your odious seed eventually meets his nemesis.' She looked at Thomas, who had averted his head throughout in order not to see the floods.

'Hold your tongue, or it might suit me to throw you out as well,' he answered.

'You and dearest Edward have given tongues enough to wag about already, without

284

adding to it by turning me out.'

He scowled. 'I abhor you, madam,' he breathed.

'The feeling is more than reciprocated.'

'If you hadn't capitulated to Valmer—'

'I had no choice in the matter. Valmer holds all the trumps. Tulliver advised me not to contest, and I accepted his advice.'

'You crumbled, madam. If I had been there—'

'But you weren't, were you? You were a dribbling, hysterical lunatic, and clearly in no position to make a rational decision about anything.'

Utter hatred gleamed in his small eyes. 'I wish to God I'd never met you. If it weren't for you—'

'I've made no real difference to you,' she interrupted. 'What you've always had is still yours. You're here at Whitend, as ever you were, and when it comes to your pathological dread of drowning, well, that has nothing whatsoever to do with me.' She calmly released the blind so that it lifted to reveal the acres of flooded land outside. Her reward was to see the dread draining white across his face, and the way he sucked in his lower lip to chew upon it like a bedlamite.

The carriage drove on when Edward had resumed his seat, and several minutes later it halted by the moat bridge. Thomas hardly waited for a footman to open the carriage door, before alighting. Cane tapping, he hurried over the bridge into the house as fast as he could. Jane remained exactly where she was until he'd had time to take himself into the library, where she hoped he'd drink himself into oblivion. How good it would be if he never awakened again.

Edward was about to follow Thomas when something new seized his attention. 'Well, if it isn't Jake Mannacott,' he muttered, leaning out into the rain to look through the entrance arch of the nearby stable yard. He could just make out two men by the door to the stalls, and the big blacksmith was impossible not to recognize, even at such a distance.

Jane's interest was also captured. Beth's former lover? She glanced at Edward. 'Don't tell me you also have scores to settle with *him*?'

'There is unsettled business, yes.'

'Is there anyone in Gloucester with whom you do not have bones to pick?'

He smiled grimly. 'He beat all hell out of me for daring to look at his daughter.'

'Fair Rosalind?'

Edward sat back. 'You know her?'

'In a manner of speaking.'

I hear tell she's disappeared the night the Frampney forge burned down.'

Jane was startled. 'Burned down?'

'Didn't you know?'

'No, actually.' Jane's mind was racing.

286

Rosalind had left the night the forge burned down? So, not only had she run off without telling her father anything, she'd done so when all he had was burning down around him. Rowan's bride was repellent, and no mistake. One wondered more and more how she had obtained 480 guineas.

Edward alighted and made for the stables. Jane allowed the footman to hand her down, and then followed. Torrential rain or not, she was going to observe what transpired when Edward and the blacksmith met. Halting beneath the entrance arch, in a spot where as much shelter could be gained as possible, she watched Edward stride through the puddles, wet straw and horse excrement littering the yard. Oh, how unnervingly like his father he was.

Edward halted in front of the two men by the stalls. 'What are you doing here, Mannacott?'

Jake straightened warily. 'Well, Ned Barker, I do declare,' he replied.

'I'm Edward Welland now, especially to the likes of you!' Edward snapped.

'Ned Barker you were, and Ned Barker you remain.'

Edward's eyes narrowed. 'We've got unfinished business.'

'Don't tell me you think you can give me a beating?' Jake laughed.

His companion backed away nervously,

gradually blending back into the shadows of the stalls. Edward's face was angry. 'You think you can give me lip now, Mannacott?'

'Nothing's changed, Ned, you're as worthless now as you always were.'

'Worthless, am I?' Edward began to strip to the waist.

Smiling, Jake did the same, but before he'd finished Edward darted for a horsewhip coiled over a wall hook. In a trice he'd swung it at Jake, slicing the front of his half removed shirt as if with a knife, and drawing blood. It happened so quickly that Jake had no time to collect himself before another crack saw the whip coil around his leg. Edward tugged viciously, and Jake went down like a felled tree.

Edward laughed gleefully, and tried to whip Jake again, but the latter caught it with such a wrench that it was Edward who went down, falling so heavily that he was winded on the wet, dung-stained cobbles. Jake seized full possession of the whip, and got up to toss his coat and shirt aside, before standing over his prone opponent.

Jane gazed at him with approval. What a fine body he had, and how nobly handsome his looks. She saw how the rain glistened on his exposed chest. His breeches were wet too, and clung to his hips and thighs as if wishing to be fashionable. He was no Guy Valmer when it came to the size of his tackle, but he was ample enough, she thought, aware of stirrings in her lower portions. She could certainly envy Beth her nights with him. How very good it must have been to be serviced by such a prize stallion.

Edward began to recover from his momentary winding, and gazed up in horror as the large blacksmith loomed above him. 'Don't hit me!' he cried. 'Don't hit me, please!'

Jake threw the whip away in contempt. 'You'll always be a snivelling nobody, Ned Barker, no amount of fancy borrowed clothes will change that.'

Edward scrambled to his feet, glancing around to see if anyone had witnessed his whimpering disgrace. A number of grooms and stable lads drew hastily out of sight, but not before he knew word would be out within the hour. Humiliation stained his face as he grabbed his clothes and walked back toward Jane, who said nothing as he stalked by.

CHAPTER NINETEEN

Jane waited until Edward and his wounded vanity had gone into the house, before approaching Jake. 'That was well done, Mr Mannacott.'

He turned quickly. 'Lady Welland?'

'I have that dubious honour.' She looked

intently at him. 'You didn't answer Edward's question. Why are you here?' she asked.

'I came to see if I could find out anything about my daughter.'

'I should think that by now she is Mrs Rowan Welland.'

'That's daft,' he muttered.

'But true.' She watched a raindrop make its slow way from his throat, down his chest, to soak into his breeches. The temptation to gaze down further, to his crotch, was too much, and she did not fight it.

'You know about her and your stepson?' he asked, aware of her interest.

'They came here the night they eloped, stayed overnight, and left in the morning. They were going to Rowan's clergyman uncle, who will not have hesitated to make them man and wife, because he despises Lord Welland almost as much as I do.'

Jake gazed at her. 'You believe in speaking your mind, eh?'

'For my sins. As far as I know, they are now staying at Sir Guy Valmer's London address. That was their ultimate destination.'

'Valmer? Oh, I know him,' Jake replied.

'Indeed?'

'He came to see me about Beth Tremoille. Thought I'd know where she'd gone. I didn't, because she'd left me.' He smiled self-consciously. 'There wasn't a forwarding address,' he added.

'She will be Lady Valmer by now.'

Jake lowered his gaze. 'Well, she was always a lady, one way or another.'

'Whereas I have never been one,' Jane said briskly. 'Let's be honest here, Mr Mannacott, all you know of me is that I was the very wickedest of stepmothers to Beth. But if it weren't for me, you would never have met her.'

He was astonished. 'So I'm in your *debt*?'

'If you wish.' She couldn't help watching the rain on his skin. What a muscular giant he was, and so active . . .

'Well, my lady, I have to admit that you aren't what I've been led to expect.'

'Oh, I was, sir, make no mistake of that. I was the most of a bitch you could encounter, but marriage to Lord Welland is the greatest cure-all since Merlin's magic.'

'*Did* you play tricks with your late husband's wills?' Jake asked bluntly.

'No, and that is the truth. I suspected there was another will, but I had no idea where it was.'

He nodded. 'You were a hard woman, though.'

'Yes, and I've more than paid the price, I promise you that.'

'Ned Barker *and* Lord Welland? Yes, I believe you have.'

She allowed her approving gaze to move over him. 'I wondered what it was that Beth saw in you, sir, but now that I've met you, I can see why. You're a comely figure of a man, Mr Mannacott. I vow that if I were younger, I might try to seduce you myself.'

'Would you now?' Jake was unfazed by her. 'And maybe I'd let you.'

'What a very pleasurable thought.' *Almost too pleasurable.* She smiled at him, but then became serious. 'I am truly repentant about Beth, but I do not think she will ever forgive me for the things I did. Nor will your daughter forgive Beth for whatever it was that passed between them.'

'Rozzie's not an easy spirit, Lady Welland. Once she gets a bee in her bonnet—'

'I gathered that when I met her. Well, you need not worry about her, because in Rowan Welland she has snapped up a treasure among gentlemen. I like him immensely, and know that he will do all he can to protect her and make her happy.'

He smiled. 'Then I think my mind is at rest. At least he is well off, and can afford to keep her in luxury.'

Jane shook her head. 'He isn't a rich man, Mr Mannacott, and only has a small inheritance from his mother. The Welland title and lands are his true inheritance, but his father has, at the moment, decided to withhold the latter. The title Rowan will have, so your daughter will eventually become Lady Welland. Sir, as far as I can tell at the moment, it is *Rosalind* who has the money.'

Jake stared, and then laughed. 'That's nonsense!'

'No, sir, it's true. They told me that she had four hundred and eighty guineas.'

Jake's jaw dropped. 'Never! Where would Rozzie get that sort of money?'

'If you do not know, I certainly don't,' Jane replied.

He turned weakly away. 480 guineas? It was madness! And yet he knew Jane was speaking the truth. He didn't want to think it, but couldn't prevent himself. He thought Beth had left him twenty guineas for the forge, but had there been much more money than that? Had his own daughter stolen from him?

The rain stopped, and Jane suddenly felt uneasy. 'I think you would be wise to leave now, Mr Mannacott. Edward won't take lightly his latest defeat at your hands.'

Jake nodded. 'Yes, I believe you're right. Lady Welland, if you hear anything of Rozzie . . .?'

'I'll be sure to tell you.'

She watched him walk away, putting on his clothes again as he went. She admired the set of his shoulders and strong, narrow waist. He was the well-endowed swain for whom she'd long yearned, with the stamina of an ox and the ability to swive her until she was witless with pleasure. Oh, to see him as naked as the day he was born; to ravish him when he was

293

helpless to fend her off. The notion appealed so much that hungry desires washed through her. Maybe it was time to take herself up to the privacy of her own room. Yes, indeed. 'Thank you, Jake Mannacott,' she whispered, 'for you've done this libidinous old hag the power of good.'

*   *   *

On a fog-shrouded, frosty afternoon toward the end of February, Guy was in his London study, attending to various estate documents. Hyde Park disappeared into an icy haze, and carriages passing along Park Lane were obliged to light their lamps even though darkness was hours away. A footman entered with a letter on a small silver tray. 'Begging your pardon, Sir Guy, but this has just been delivered.'

'Mm?' Guy glanced up, and then at the letter, which he saw bore his lawyer's seal. 'Ah, yes,' he declared, taking the letter and nodding to the footman to withdraw. The moment the door had closed again, he broke the seal and read.

Felicitations, Sir Guy, and congratulations too, because you are now the new owner of the Dower House. All that is required is your signature and seal upon the deeds, which I can bring at your earliest convenience. I will go into the fine financial points when we meet, but it may interest you to know that someone else was attempting to purchase the property. I refer to Mr Landry Haldane of Haldane Hall, also in the County of Devon. As instructed by you, I continually outbid him until he withdrew. There is no doubt that he was anxious to purchase the property, but it would seem his funds were insufficient.

I await your summons to Park Lane.
Your obedient servant, Arthur Withers.

Holy Haldane wanted the little nest where he'd rolled his darling Beth on her back? Guy smiled as he folded the letter again. 'Poor fellow,' he murmured, 'how galling it must be to know that I have the lady and the property. Well, the time has now come for me to go home to Greylake.'

His darling Beth? Was she? Guy knew he had no firm ground for suspecting her of anything, just his own insecurity. She'd sworn never to have loved Haldane, and that he, Guy Valmer, was the one she had wanted all along, but when she'd whispered Haldane's name . . . He closed his eyes, finding it hard to credit how little confidence he had where she was concerned. It was something he had never had to deal with before. He tried to tell himself he'd been driven to his mistress by a faithless wife, but the excuse simply didn't wash. His behaviour was contemptible. Rationality was beyond him when it came to Beth.

Sighing, he returned his attention to the documents he'd been studying before the arrival of the letter from Withers, and came upon a clause that was not quite as he would have wished. It wasn't a matter of any huge importance, but nevertheless he felt it needed clarifying. Getting up, he went to the bookshelf immediately next to the library door, lifted down a dusty old tome, and began to sift through it for the reference he wanted. He was still thus engaged when he heard a light tread outside the door, and then a timid tap. 'Sir Guy?'

It was Rosalind, and so he did not respond. She was the last person he wished to see, and he hoped she would simply go away. But to his astonishment, instead of going away, she opened the door, which swung in a way that hid him from her view. 'Sir Guy?'

Annoyed at her persistence, he remained silent, and then his annoyance turned to anger and outrage as she calmly went to his desk and began to inspect the paperwork that lay in profusion. She looked so dainty and innocent, in a primrose velvet gown, her fair hair pinned up beneath a lacy day bonnet, but her eyes were sharp and clever as they skimmed the first document she picked up. It wasn't until she went so far as to open a drawer and go through its contents as well that he spoke.

'May I ask what you think you are doing?' he said suddenly.

She gasped and recoiled, her eyes filled with guilty dismay. 'Sir Guy!'

'The very same.' He went to the desk and slammed down the heavy legal book he'd taken from the shelf. 'Well? And please don't tell me you were looking for a pencil!'

'That's just what I *was* doing, Sir Guy. Truly.'

'And need of a pencil requires you to read my private papers?'

'I wasn't.'

'Madam, I watched you.'

Her chin came up in that way he'd come to loathe. 'If you accuse me of such a terrible thing, I will deny it.'

'What did you hope to find? Information that would enable you to dip your sticky little fingers into my money?'

He'd found a target, for a flush swamped her cheeks. 'I wouldn't do that!'

Guy smiled. 'We both know you would, because you've already purloined money to which you do not have a right.'

She stared at him. 'I have no idea what you mean! How dare you accuse me of such a terrible crime!'

He was unmoved. 'I am sure that my wife will confirm having left five hundred guineas for your father.'

Rosalind was defiant. 'Beth would say

anything to get at me.'

'It's more likely to be the other way around, madam. Well, you have now gone too far. I want you out of here.'

'Rowan will take my side,' she warned.

'That is no threat, my dear, because he already knows what I think of you. He also knows the likely source of your fortune. If he hasn't mentioned it to you, it's because he's sparing your non-existent feelings. You are the coldest, most unprincipled, grasping creature it has ever been my misfortune to meet, and the sooner you leave this house, the better I will like it.'

'I hate you,' she breathed.

'You hate everything, except yourself. Now, please don't compound the felony by defying me in this. I am prepared to lose Rowan's friendship in order to be rid of you, so don't think to play him off against me. Now, get out.'

Rosalind looked at him, longing to run at him and sink her fingernails into his face, but then she thought better of it. 'I'll get you back for this,' she vowed.

'Grow up, madam. You are no longer your father's sweet little moppet, but a married woman with all the responsibility that position entails. I wish to God Rowan could see through you, but it seems he cannot. I can, however, and I'm dealing with you appropriately. If you and Rowan are not out of this house within the hour, I will have you both thrown out.'

She knew she had no option, but had no intention of doing it quietly. Catching up her skirts, she fled sobbing from the room, and up to the drawing-room, crying Rowan's name. Guy resumed his seat at the desk, and waited for the inevitable angry confrontation with Rowan. It was not long in coming. Rowan stormed downstairs and into the library.

'What have you been saying to Rosalind?' he demanded, eyes blazing.

Guy sat back, his fingertips placed together as he maintained an air of complete calm. 'I witnessed her going through this drawer, and requested her to leave.'

'She said that you made advances!'

Guy raised an eyebrow. 'Well, I didn't, but if you wish to believe her, please feel free to do so. I'll meet you at dawn at any place of your choosing. But please think carefully before taking such a rash step. You know exactly what I think of your wife, so the thought of my having laid lustful hands upon her really is laughable. You have made a dreadful misalliance, Rowan, and I have done my utmost to make allowances for Rosalind's conduct. But in this she has overstepped the mark by a yard, and I am withdrawing my hospitality. I realize that this will alienate you as well, and that is something I do regret. One day I trust we will be close friends again, but for the moment I accept that this is impossible.

Please let the scales fall from your eyes sooner rather than later.'

'Damn it all, Guy, she's in floods of tears, and the bodice of her gown is ripped! Do you honestly expect me to—?'

Guy rose to his feet. 'Rowan, do you *really* believe I would do such a thing?'

Rowan met his eyes for a moment, and then looked away.

'I think that answers my question,' Guy observed. 'Rowan, where she is concerned you seem to have lost your wits. She ripped the gown herself, and invented my so-called advances in an attempt to pre-empt anything I may say of her. It is all too much, and I want you both to leave.'

'I will find it hard to ever forgive you.'

Guy spread his hands. 'That is your problem, not mine. My regard for you has not diminished, but I cannot abide your wife. Now, please go.'

'Where?' Rowan demanded.

Guy raised an eyebrow. 'That, my friend, is also your problem. You married her, therefore you provide for her. Besides, didn't she steal a tidy little sum that could secure you a more than adequate residence?'

'Damn you, Guy,' Rowan breathed, and turned on his heel to walk out.

*　　　*　　　*

It was the first of March, St David's Day, and Beth was walking by the lake at the foot of the castle tor. The weather was cold, but at least the wind was light and the rain was holding off. There should be daffodils on St David's Day, she thought, instead there were snowdrops, and then only in sheltered places. Where was spring? And where was Guy? She still had no idea when he intended to return from London, and felt very lonely and unhappy as she huddled into her fur-lined cloak and glanced across the choppy grey water. Oh, for a crystal ball, and the ability to see the future. At least then she'd know something. As it was, she knew nothing, except, incredibly, that she was carrying Guy's child.

Only Braddy knew she'd missed her January bleeding, and that her February bleeding was overdue. There wasn't any doubt in her mind, because she felt strange as well, as if she weren't really there, and the thought of some foods had become very disagreeable, but it was the smell of coffee that actually wrenched her stomach over. That morning she had been horribly sick, which in Braddy's opinion was final proof of her condition, if any further proof were needed.

So convinced had Beth been of her barrenness that she hardly dared to believe she had conceived, although she was sure of the exact moment it had happened, and remembered her instinctive knowledge that she was fertile after all. Now she was confused and felt more isolated than ever. After all the times she'd lain with Jake, and then with Landry, she had never even been late, but Guy had proved her fruitful after all.

She was past crying now, and just felt very tired. The baby had been conceived when she'd been ecstatically happy, believing they were joined in love. But it had all changed since then. Would Guy want a child with her? Or might he accuse her of trying to foist Landry's brat upon him? She knew the child was Guy's, and that it prevented her from any notion she may have had of running away again. Her son or daughter would be the rightful heir to the vast Valmer estates and fortune, so it was her bounden duty to stay here, no matter what.

The distant sound of hoofs made her turn, and she saw a horseman riding down toward her from the castle hill. For a split second she thought it was Guy, but then was dismayed to recognize Landry. Her heart lurched unpleasantly. Was he mad? Had he no thought about compromising her? She began to walk quickly in the direction of the steep, winding path that led down through the castle gardens, but Landry only changed his direction and reined in so she could go no further.

'Beth?'

'Please leave me alone, Landry. If Guy should discover—'

'He's in London,' he pointed out, dismounting and then tipping his top hat back as he looked at her. He was thinner, and there was something in his eyes that told her he'd changed, and not for the better. There was no spark in his turquoise eyes, and his lips no longer seemed ready to break into a charming smile.

'And Harriet is at Haldane Hall, with your daughter,' she reminded him.

'I don't want to speak of them, just of you and me.'

She glanced away. 'Did you or did you not marry Harriet a week ago?'

He exhaled a little impatiently. 'And if I did?'

'Then your duty is to her. I am Guy's wife, and therefore nothing to you now.'

Her words were ignored. 'I believe I have you to thank for the prompt and generous replacement of my slain sheep.'

'I only did what Guy would have done.'

He was disdainful. 'Greylake might have grudgingly replaced twenty-three, not thirty, and certainly not with his finest stock.'

'We will never know, because I interfered.'

'Yes, and I'll warrant he was sweet and understanding about it.'

She looked away. 'Is that why you've come? To thank me for the sheep?'

'No, I've come to ask you why you tossed me aside for the owner of all this.' He swung

303

an arm to encompass their surroundings. It was a contemptuous gesture, and as insulting as he could make it be.

'All this? No.'

'Then why? Why did you crush my heart and my honour so publicly, and then leave with a man I despise?'

'I never concealed the fact that there was someone else I loved first.'

'So it was *Greylake* all along?' Bitter resentment lit his eyes. 'Is that why you came to the Dower House, to be near him?'

'The ball was the first time I knew Guy was the man you call Greylake.'

'You expect me to believe that?'

'It doesn't matter whether you do or not, Landry. I was honest with you when I agreed to marry you, because I didn't think anything could ever come of my love for Guy.'

'And suddenly, out of the blue, he offers marriage? Come now, Beth, it's hardly likely. There was obviously something going on between you.'

'It's of no consequence now. You and I have ceased to be, Landry. Your duty should have been with Harriet from the moment you first seduced her.'

'Damn it, Beth, *she* seduced me!'

'And that makes it honourable?' Her glance was almost contemptuous. 'Be more of a gentleman than that, Landry. If you continue like this, I will believe all the terrible things I have heard of you.'

He flushed. 'So Greylake has been pouring his poison, has he?'

'You, of course, heap compliments on him,' she countered. 'Enough of this, Landry, I was honest with you about having secrets in my past.'

'The greatest of them being Valmer.'

'No, but he knows all about me.'

'You have other secrets too? What a dark horse you are. And the Haldane fool was never worth telling,' he said bitterly.

'I didn't *tell* Guy, he found out. Landry, our marriage became impossible the moment I learned that Harriet was Katy's real mother.'

'Harriet?' He gave a cold laugh. 'If you only knew how I despise her.'

Beth was dismayed. 'How cruel you are.'

'You've made me thus,' he replied.

'You blame *me*? Landry, if you had not lain with her all those years ago, you wouldn't have had to marry her now. You behaved badly then, and you still behave badly. Chivalrous you are clearly not.'

'Whereas you have behaved impeccably?'

'I have never claimed to be perfect.'

A light passed through his eyes. 'Beth, I told you what had happened with Harriet. I told you everything.'

'And it did not make pleasant hearing. But what you never mentioned was your history of drinking and gambling, of conducting yourself ignobly at a duel, and of being cashiered from the army. You even stole Snowy from a dying Prussian officer!'

'So, you've heard all that, have you? And if I deny everything?'

'Do you?'

He drew a long breath. 'The drinking and gambling is public knowledge, the rest is malevolent fiction.'

But his eyes gave the lie to his claim. It was all true, Beth thought sadly, unable to believe she had come so close to marrying him. What a disaster it would have been. And what a disaster it must now be for Harriet. She couldn't bear to be near him a moment more. 'Landry, I want you to leave now. Go back to Harriet and Katy and start living again. Forget all about me, just as I will forget all about you.'

'You expect me to go home and play the contented husband and father?'

Her anger sparked. 'I expect you to *try*!'

He gave her a thin smile. 'Your sympathy for her is misplaced. Gone is the clergyman's demure little daughter, and in her place is a rabid predator. She is insatiable, and will have me wherever and whenever the urge takes her. There is nothing she will not do and no degradation she will not sample, and if ever a parasite sucked its prey dry, she does.'

Beth stared at him, both shocked and repelled.

He continued, 'The Reverend Bellamy's

sweet daughter was never the innocent she pretended. She knew what she was doing when Katy was conceived, she made all the advances, and she seduced me into completing the act when I would have stopped. She wants my body, and doesn't care how she takes it. I feel raped, and perhaps I am. Don't weep over her Beth, because she hates you.'

Beth couldn't bear to stay with him any longer. 'I'm going back to the castle now, and I think you will understand if I don't invite you to accompany me.'

'So, it's come to that? You can't even be hospitable?'

'You despise my husband, and he certainly has a low opinion of you, so would you really have the gall to enter his home?'

'But like that, perhaps not. But he isn't here, Beth.'

Her gaze turned to ice. 'How dare you!' she breathed. 'How *dare* you hint that I should entertain you in his absence! You've become unspeakably shabby.'

'Then, for old time's sake, perhaps we should part with one last kiss.'

Before she realized what was in his mind, he reached out for her elbow and swung her into his embrace. His lips were as cold as the winter itself, and as unforgiving. He crushed them over her mouth, and pulled her tightly to him, taking her hand and forcing it against his crotch. She could not mistake his arousal, or

307

her own revulsion. She struggled to be free, but he was strong enough to make it seem as if she shared and welcomed the kiss.

She managed to drag her lips away from his, although remaining tightly in his embrace. 'Let me go, Landry, let me go or so help me, I'll—'

His eyes were dark with desire. 'Come to me one last time, Beth, just one last time. Please!'

'No! I don't want you, Landry! I don't even *like* you any more!'

He released her, but slowly, so that to all intents and purposes it seemed as if they were parting fondly. 'I still love you, and my heartbreak is your burden.'

She didn't wait for him to say anything more, but turned and ran toward the path through the gardens. When she was halfway up she paused to look back. He was urging his horse away around the lake. With a sigh of relief, she continued up to the castle, but halted with renewed dismay on reaching the Green Court, because Guy's travelling carriage was drawn up by the porch. Might he have seen? *Could* he have seen?

Steeling herself for confronting him again after so long, she entered the castle and tried to appear relaxed and unconcerned as a footman divested her of her outdoor clothes. Guy was in the inner hall, in conversation with Bradfield and the butler, Gardiner, and did not seem to have noticed her as she lingered in the outer hall. He wore a charcoal coat, too tight to be buttoned, and therefore left open to reveal the elaborate frills of his shirt pushing out from his oyster silk, single-breasted waistcoat. There was a shine on his Hessian boots in which one could no doubt see one's face reflected, and had his trousers been painted upon his person they could not have fitted more. His signet ring caught the light as he toyed with the frills at his cuff, and nothing seemed to have changed his grace and poise. He seemed to have been touched by frost, and therefore immune to passion, and yet she knew differently; she knew differently.

He addressed her suddenly. 'My lady?'

'Sir?' She started out of her reverie, striving to conceal how her spirits plunged when he greeted her formally.

He approached in that lazily sensuous way that quickened her blood and aroused her deepest, most erotic cravings. No man should be so desirable, or so beloved . . . He drew her hand vaguely toward his lips, and then released it again. Again he toyed with his cuff. 'What was Haldane doing here?' he enquired coolly.

Her courage halted in its tracks, and she knew that honesty was her only wise course. 'He came to ask me why I left him as I did.'

'You invited him?'

Her eyes brightened angrily. 'No. I went for a walk, and he waylaid me, knowing that you have been absent for so long.' She was pleased to add that, for it made Guy at least partly responsible.

'What did you say to him?'

'If I am to be interrogated, sir, at least have the courtesy to do it when we are private.' She nodded past him to where Bradfield and Gardiner waited. There was a footman nearby too, and she did not doubt there were other servants lurking, all eager to spy upon what happened when the master returned after such a lengthy absence.

'As you wish. Let us adjourn to the drawing-room.' He offered her his arm, and they walked across the hall. Once in the drawing-room, he turned to face her again. 'Very well, madam, we are private. Now tell me the truth about Haldane's visit.'

'I've told you the truth.'

'Have you?'

'Yes. I told him I wanted nothing more to do with him, and he left.'

'Just that?' he murmured lightly, going to the window to look out over the lake.

'Well, other things were said, of course, but the outcome is just that. He came, we spoke, he left. Oh, and to convince him that I was no longer interested in him, I told him I had always loved you.'

'Really?' He didn't look around.

She decided not to comment. Two could be enigmatic, she thought. 'Then why did you kiss and embrace so tenderly?'

Her spirit rose. '*We* didn't kiss and embrace tenderly, *he* forced me!'

'I'm expected to believe that?'

'Believe as you will, there's nothing I can do to change you,' she answered defiantly. 'But tell me, sir, were you true to your marriage vows while you were away?'

'No. I have resumed my acquaintance with Maria Carberry,' he replied cruelly.

Pain stabbed her. 'Then of what possible concern can it be to you whether or not I have kissed Landry Haldane?'

'You are my wife, madam, and you are *never* to forget that.'

'Sauce, goose and gander,' she said softly.

He feigned not to hear. 'I observed your loving farewells with Haldane. If I learn that he has been here on other occasions, so help me I'll wring his unholy neck.'

'Today was the only time I've seen him, and it certainly was not of my choosing. And do you honestly think I would keep a clandestine assignation in full view of the castle and probably the entire town? Allow me a little more sense and discretion than that. But think on, my husband, if you'd taken me with you to London, you'd have known exactly where I was and with whom. Instead you chose to scurry off to your mistress and leave me here alone for eight weeks or more. Perhaps I should take an armed footman everywhere with me in future, with orders to shoot anyone who speaks to me.'

'You think you are amusing?' he enquired coldly, turning from the window and coming back to face her.

'No, I think myself wronged, sir. By Landry Haldane and by you! I still don't know why you left so suddenly, or why you despise me. I didn't ask to become your wife, you pursued me and gave me no choice in the matter. I have served my purpose, have I not?'

'Indeed you have, my lady, because I have now lodged all the necessary documents with Arthur Withers, and now the law will take its course. Withers is of the opinion that the Wellands will not fight. Tremoille House will soon be mine.'

'I'm delighted for you. What will happen to me when you have the deeds?'

'I haven't given it any thought.'

'Then please do.'

He held her eyes suddenly. 'Do you swear you didn't invite Haldane's advances?'

The change of subject confounded her. 'I have already told you the truth, so go to Hades, Sir Guy.' Turning, she walked out of the room with her head high and her eyes awash with sorrow.

CHAPTER TWENTY

Things had not improved when, on the last Sunday of March, Guy obliged Beth to accompany him all the way to Haldane for morning service. It wasn't her idea—far from it—but he insisted, so they breakfasted early in order to set out in good time.

Beth had taken care about what she wore, and chose cherry red trimmed with white fur, a matching hat, and her white fur muff into which she sank her gloved hands. Guy was in a dark mustard coat and dove-grey trousers, with his greatcoat resting around his shoulders. His top hat, gloves and cane lay on the seat beside him, his gleaming Hessians were placed on the seat next to Beth, and not a word had passed his lips since breakfast, except to comment on her pallor. He gazed out at the passing scenery as if daydreaming. Perhaps of Maria Carberry, she thought unhappily.

She had yet to tell him about the baby, even though Braddy urged her most strenuously. His reaction to Landry's brief visit had taught her a very sharp lesson, and she knew she'd be accused of having been with child before coming to the castle, and so she held her tongue. Sooner or later her increasing waistline would force her to tell him. She would weather the outcome, at no matter what the cost to herself, because whether he liked it or not, the child she carried was his heir. Her glance encompassed him. He was all she wanted and could never have. But at least she carried part of him within her, a son or daughter to be half Tremoille, half Valmer, to inherit everything and thus put right all the bitter quarrels and injustices of the past.

The carriage swayed and jolted over the winter-damaged road. It wasn't raining, but remained cold and windy when at last the carriage began the steep descent of Rendisbury Hill in the gorge-like creek of the conjoined Lanner rivers. Beth couldn't help craning her neck for her first glimpse of Lannermouth, the little fishing village that had been her home. On the cliff top on the opposite side of the gorge, some 500 feet directly above Lannermouth, was the large village of Haldane. It was such a picturesque and quaint part of Exmoor that it had inspired famous poets like Coleridge, Wordsworth, Southey and Shelley.

Her beloved Dower House was at the bottom of the hill, right on the sea shore in the north-west corner of two acres of flat, tree-dotted lawns of almost bowling-green perfection. The little Gothic house had arched, trefoil windows, a thatched roof and veranda, and its seaward foundations were washed by the tides. The garden was drab now, but in the summer became a riot of flowers and shrubs of almost tropical lushness. Roses and honeysuckle climbed the veranda, drenching summer nights with scent, and to her it was the most idyllic place on earth.

Guy observed the longing on her face. 'So, this is still preferable to Greylake?'

'I'm lonely there.'

'Because Holy Haldane is here?'

'Oh, do stop it, for I have no interest at all in Landry Haldane. If I wanted I could have run off with him by now, but I've been well and truly cured of any affection I once had for him. He has become unkind and selfish.'

'He was always like that,' Guy murmured.

'I had not witnessed it for myself.'

'And now you have?'

'Yes.'

The carriage reached the foot of the hill, and Guy lowered the window glass suddenly. 'Dickon? Go to the Dower House, if you please.'

'Yes, Sir Guy.'

Beth was puzzled. 'Why are we going there?'

'So that I can see my own property.'

She stared. 'You own the Dower House? But . . . how? I thought the previous owner had returned to Jamaica.'

'Fortunately for me he was delayed, and more than pleased to part with it.'

'Are you sending me back here?' she asked.

'Back to Haldane's clutches? Hardly.'

The carriage moved sedately along the straight drive that had the elegant little park to one side and the Lanner in spate on the other. Dickon halted the team at the house, and Guy alighted just as Mrs Cobbett, all of a fluster, opened the front door. She wasn't dressed for church, Beth noticed with concern. Was something wrong?'

The housekeeper, plump and comfortable in a large mobcap, brown woollen gown and crisp apron, gaped on seeing Guy, but then she saw Beth. Her face broke into a delighted smile, and she dipped a little curtsey. 'Sir Guy. Miss Beth. I . . . I mean, Lady Valmer.'

Guy was unsmiling. 'Mrs Cobbett, I'm the new owner of the house, and have come to see if I've purchased a pig in a poke.' He assisted Beth down, and then reached into the carriage for his hat, glove and cane, before setting off to inspect the outside of the property first.

The housekeeper looked at Beth in fond concern. 'You're too pale, and no mistake,' she said, ushering her into the little hall passage and then to the spotless whitewashed, red-tiled kitchen, where there was the remembered scent of dried herbs. Blue and white crockery adorned dresser shelves, the scrubbed table was as pale and clear as ever, and Mrs Cobbett's potted geraniums still stood on the window ledges. A kettle sang gently on top of the unexpected modern luxury of a range by

Count Rumford.

The other two servants, Billy Pointer and the maid, Molly Dodd, leapt up from the table in delight on seeing Beth again. Billy was small and almost monkey-faced, with a broad grin and warm heart, and was the coachman and former jockey Beth had hired at the famous Swan With Two Necks inn in London. Molly was a rosy-cheeked girl of about twenty, with delphinium-blue eyes and a figure that was almost as well upholstered as Mrs Cobbett's. She was also Billy's sweetheart. 'Miss Beth!' they cried in unison, but the housekeeper wagged a stern finger.

'It's Lady Valmer now, and don't you forget it.'

Beth smiled. 'Miss Beth will do.'

Mrs Cobbett waved the others outside. 'Off with you. Go out for a walk or something, anything that keeps you from listening to her ladyship and me.' As soon as they'd gone, the housekeeper ushered Beth to the table, made a cup of tea, and then sat down with her. 'Are you happy, Miss Beth?' she asked bluntly.

'I could be, if things were different.'

'Different? With Sir Guy, you mean?' Beth nodded and blinked back easy tears, and Mrs Cobbett stretched out a comforting hand. 'I saw the way you looked at him. Nothing gets past me, Miss Beth. You love him, don't you?'

'I cannot deny it. Unfortunately, he doesn't feel the same about me. So there you have it, indifference on one side, unrequited love on the other.'

'Oh, my dear . . .'

'Don't sympathize, Mrs C, or you'll have me piping.'

The housekeeper smiled sadly. 'I can see why you love him. Oh, he pretends to be cold, but he's not that at all. There's a hidden fire in him.'

'I know, and I've been horribly singed. I love him so much, you see, and for two wonderful nights he was everything I could dream of. But now he's distant and the very opposite of loving. I don't understand him.'

'Are you coming back here to live?' the housekeeper asked hopefully.

'No.' Beth smiled a little wanly.

'Then why has Sir Guy purchased this house?'

'I don't know.'

Mrs Cobbett shifted uncomfortably. 'So, it's not because . . . of the baby?'

Beth glanced hastily at the door. 'Hush, Mrs C, for I haven't told Sir Guy.'

'Has he no eyes to see? You're as white as a sheet, there are shadows under your eyes, and you look as if anything other than a plain biscuit would turn you inside out.'

'He hardly looks at me at all, Mrs Cobbett, let alone with sufficient interest to notice my appearance. And before you ask, yes, it *is* his child.'

318

'I know, my dear, for I remember you had your monthly around the time of the ball, so unless you've lain with someone else in the meantime, it has to be Sir Guy's.'

'I've been true to him.' Beth glanced around the kitchen. 'No church today?'

'I'm not in the mood to face more gossipy questions.'

'I'm still so notorious that folk want to know the details of my private life?'

'I fear so.' Mrs Cobbett changed the subject. 'This winter has been a terrible time. We've had the sea in the garden, although luckily not in the house. It's never happened before, not that I know of. Most things have died in the garden on account of the cold, and those horrible sunrises and sunsets have been giving me the shivers. The Devil's daubs, that's what I call them.'

'A good name,' Beth replied with a faint smile.

Guy's tread sounded in the passage, and Mrs Cobbett got up nervously. When he appeared in the kitchen doorway, she cleared her throat. 'Do you wish me to show you the house, Sir Guy?'

'No, I've seen enough.'

She twisted her hands anxiously. 'What of us, Sir Guy? Billy, Molly and me?'

'You all remain secure here, Mrs Cobbett, for the house needs attending to.'

'Will you let it again?' the housekeeper

319

ventured.

He looked at Beth, whose eyes were fixed upon the table. 'I don't know yet, Mrs Cobbett, but if you continue to care for it as you do now, I will be content.' He addressed Beth. 'Are you ready, my lady?' he murmured, extending his hand.

They went out to the waiting carriage, and Dickon urged the horses back down the drive to the road, which wound over a bridge over the roaring white waters of the confluence of the East and West Lanners, and after skirting the village, led up through the long, deep gorge toward the high moor. Another road led off to the right just after leaving Lannermouth, climbing up through hairpins to Haldane on the cliff top. Beth was careful not to look at Haldane Hall as they drove past the fine gates, where stone basilisks topped the posts. Carrie Markham's lodge was closed and shuttered, as if no one had ever lived there. Nor did Beth look at the Jacobean rectory where Harriet had lived with her father. She didn't want to look at anything here, because it was in the past for her now, and that was where she wished it to remain.

The usual clutter of traps, gigs and carts had drawn up before the church lych-gate, as well as saddle horses, cobs and ponies. Beth could not see anything that might indicate whether or not Landry and Harriet had already arrived. Other worshippers were about to go beneath the lych-gate into the churchyard, and their eyes widened when they recognized Guy's crest on the carriage. By the way they hurried on toward the porch, it was clear to Beth that word of the illustrious visitors would have spread throughout the church by the time she and Guy finally took their places.

Guy alighted and put on his greatcoat, before turning back to her. 'Very well, madam, let us put ourselves on display.'

'Why are you doing this, Guy?'

'To prove to you once and for all what a hollow, disagreeable, vicious weakling you might have married.'

'I already know it.'

But he could hear her voice, still warm with sleep. *Never stop, Landry, never stop.* 'I don't think you know it enough, but by the time we return to this carriage, you will have learned a great deal more.'

'And what will I have learned about you?' she enquired, reluctantly allowing him to help her down. 'For instance, will I know why you have purchased the Dower House?'

'I bought it because it seemed a sensible idea.'

'In what way?'

'My way,' he replied, drawing her hand over his coat sleeve and conducting her beneath the lych-gate.

She kept her eyes fixed upon the path. 'Why do you hold me in such contempt?' she asked suddenly.

'I don't feel contempt for you, Beth.'

'Then what *do* you feel for me? I don't understand you.'

'No? Then let me explain that you talk in your sleep.'

'I do? What did I say?'

'It is of no consequence now.'

'But clearly it *is* of consequence, or you wouldn't mention it. Tell me, Guy.'

'It really is of no consequence,' he insisted.

'Yet it was sufficient to send you off to London in high dudgeon.'

He raised an eyebrow. 'You flatter yourself. I had business to attend to, not least commencing legal proceedings to regain Tremoille House.'

'Which was so astonishingly urgent that you didn't even have time to tell me you were going? So amazingly complicated and time-consuming that you didn't write a single note? Oh, I was forgetting, you wouldn't have access to pen and paper, London being so much at the back of beyond.'

'Did you *want* me to write?'

'Only if you had something pleasant to confide.' She searched his eyes. 'Certainly not when you are a stranger to me.'

'I have never been anything else,' he said, continuing to the church.

Whispers circled the congregation as they took their places toward the front of the nave.

The sudden stir was so noticeable that even the organist faltered and played a number of false notes. Beth felt her face reddening, and as she and Guy knelt to pray, she hissed bitterly, 'I trust this is worth the effort!'

They knew when Landry and Harriet arrived, because there was renewed whispering. Beth began to turn to look up at the gallery, but Guy stopped her. 'If you turn now, madam, there will be even less understanding between us than before.'

'The only understanding there ever appears to be between us, sir, is between the sheets.'

'I shall take that as a compliment,' he replied, and thrust a Prayer Book into her hand. 'Now do your best to appear meek and pious.'

Beth could feel eyes upon her from the gallery. Landry and Harriet would have seen Guy's carriage by the lych-gate, and so couldn't have entered the church in ignorance. She wondered what was going through their minds.

Somehow she endured the entire service, lengthy sermon included, without dashing out to hide in the carriage with the blinds lowered. Not that Guy would have allowed it. His attention was on her throughout, and from time to time he took her hand. It may have seemed a tender gesture to anyone else, but she knew it was a reminder to behave as he wished. When the service ended and the

323

congregation filed out, she was at last able to steal a glance at the gallery. Both Landry and Harriet were gazing down, he in coldness, she in dismay. Katy was with them, leaning on the balustrade with her chin on her hands. She wasn't interested in Sir Guy and Lady Valmer, only in the richly decorated altar. Then they began to leave the gallery.

Guy delayed until the rest of the congregation had left, and then conducted Beth toward the church door. 'Now we will see the true mettle of the man you almost married.'

Landry and Harriet were conversing with the Reverend Bellamy just outside the porch, and Harriet's quickly averted face showed that she was as reluctant as Beth to be present when their husbands came face-to-face. Guy was suddenly all geniality and charm as he smiled at the clergyman. 'An excellent sermon, sir.'

'Well, thank you, Sir Guy.'

'I trust you've recovered from the rigours of the hunt?'

'I have indeed, sir.' The Reverend Bellamy looked uncomfortably at his daughter and son-in-law, and then bent to make much of Katy in order to escape the awkwardness.

Guy turned to Landry. 'And speaking of the hunt, I must express my regret for what happened on your land. The hounds were out of hand, and we weren't up to the task of

324

containing them in time. But I trust you are adequately compensated?'

A nerve twitched in Landry's right cheek. 'You know that I am, but I trust in future you'll stay off my land.'

'Every effort will be made.' Guy turned his attention to Harriet. 'I believe congratulations are in order, Mrs Haldane?'

Harriet's face flushed with embarrassment. 'Er, yes, actually. But how—?'

'Such word soon travels,' Guy answered, glancing at Beth's shocked face, before continuing, 'May I ask when the happy event is anticipated?'

'Sept— I mean, October.' She corrected herself hastily as the simple mathematics of the situation did not require a great intellect.

Guy smiled. 'I trust all goes well, and you are safely delivered.'

'Thank you, Sir Guy.'

Landry held Guy's eyes. 'Are there no similar tidings from you, Greylake?'

Guy shook his head. 'Alas, not as yet. Now then, Haldane, about next year's apportionment of the Royal Forest of Exmoor. I think it would be wise if you and I get together to discuss which acres we want, otherwise we risk losing out to Lavington and Sir Thomas Acland.'

Landry nodded, and then added, 'Not that I'm in the market for much new land.'

'No? I would have thought you'd leap at this

opportunity.'

'The present situation has squeezed my finances a little.'

Guy smiled. 'Ah, yes,' he murmured, managing to conjure images of gambling, drinking, cowardice in the face of a duel, horse stealing and dishonourable discharge.

Landry's fists clenched, but otherwise he did not rise to the bait. 'You are fortunate, Greylake, in that you have such vast resources.'

Guy nodded. 'So I do. But if your finances are in such a parlous state, I'm surprised you tried to buy the Dower House, which, incidentally, is now mine.'

Beth was shaken anew, and Harriet's lips parted, but Landry was spared having to reply because the Reverend Bellamy, running out of things to say to Katy, straightened reluctantly to rejoin the conversation. 'Oh, my aching bones. I vow this vile weather has put years on me. Did you see the sunrise this morning? I fear Beelzebub is preparing a sinners' path to the portals of Hell.'

Landry looked sourly at him, but Guy was interested. 'Maybe you are right, sir, but maybe there is a more earthly explanation? When I was in London, I was told that the fascinating skies of late might conceivably have something to do with a volcano on the other side of the world. Now, having once seen Vesuvius in eruption, I find such a theory far-fetched, because surely no volcano can possibly be big enough to affect the skies around the entire world? Yet this one—Mount Tambora on the island of Sumbawa in the China Seas—is said to have killed hundreds of thousands of people last spring, and turned day into night for weeks on end. Ships that sailed back to Europe from that area reported dark clouds following them like the Angel of Death, causing winter storms where there should have been summer sunshine.'

With Landry merely listening, but not contributing, the two men continued to discuss the possibility of a volcano being behind the abominable weather, and Beth took her opportunity to speak to Harriet.

'I'm so pleased that you are expecting, Harriet,' she said, managing to turn away from Landry so that he couldn't hear.

'How you feel is immaterial to me,' was the chilly response.

'Please don't feel like that, because I still want to be your friend.'

'Why? In order to gloat?'

'Gloat? Why on earth would I do that?'

'Because you know Landry stills love you.'

Beth gazed earnestly at her. 'But I don't love him, Harriet. I love my husband.'

'How very *nice* for you.'

'Harriet—'

But Harriet turned to Landry and her father. 'If you will excuse me, Katy and I will return to the hall.'

Guy took Beth's hand again, and placed it gently over his sleeve. 'And we must leave as well, for it's a fair drive back to Greylake.'

Landry looked at him. 'Why did you come here, Greylake? Doesn't your own parish church sing the right hymns?'

'I came to speak to you in person about the sheep business. It seemed the only correct thing to do.' The lie was uttered glibly.

'Really.'

Guy inclined his head, and then led Beth down the path toward the lych-gate. They could both feel Landry watching them, a dark presence, brooding and poisonous. Beth was glad when Guy assisted her into the waiting carriage, and Dickon stirred the refreshed horses into action again. The church slipped away behind as they commenced the journey home, and the ascent of Rendisbury Hill had been accomplished before Guy spoke.

'I think you now know more about him, hm? In spite of the hurt he would undoubtedly have caused to Harriet, he elected to spend money on the Dower House, money he clearly cannot spare. And knowing that his wife is with child, he still came to Greylake to confess his love for you. Well, he did, didn't he? He wanted you to leave me and return to him. Where would that leave Harriet and her child? Katy even? He is beneath contempt.'

'As are you, sir, for mentioning his interest

in the Dower House in front of her.'

He declined to respond.

Suddenly she needed to tell him of her condition. It was probably the worst moment she could happen upon, but still she had to say it. 'I'm carrying your child.'

There was utter silence for a moment, and then he answered, 'My child?'

'Yes.'

'How can I be sure of that?'

'Because I'm telling you.' She looked steadily at him.

'Maybe you were carrying Haldane's brat when you married me.'

Her cheeks flared almost guiltily, because this was what she feared he would say. 'You think me that devious?'

He held her gaze. 'I have little reason to think otherwise.'

'You have my word, sir, which either you accept or you do not. The child I carry is yours. I truly believed I was barren. You, however, have changed everything.'

'I am the Great Impregnator?' he said cynically.

'It would seem so, Guy, unless, of course, I can blame my sudden fertility on a surfeit of hazelnuts. As you are the more likely source of my condition, I hope you will believe me when I insist that you are the father. That is the truth.'

'And when do you anticipate this blissful

329

event?'

'September.'

He regarded her steadily. 'If Haldane had not come to see you, in the belief that I was still absent, I might have accepted the situation, but as it . . .'

The moment had indeed proved the worst possible and she could almost feel the splintering of the remains of her heart. She had to strike back at him. 'I tell you this, sir, if it weren't for the child, I would leave you and disappear as I did before. You have what you wanted of me, and are hardly likely to bother pursuing me again.'

'Oh, but I would, Beth, because you are now my wife.'

'And my child is your child,' she said again. 'Like it or not, you are about to have a legal heir, and I don't intend to let you deny your own flesh and blood. I will put up with you for the child's birthright.'

He looked at her for a long moment, and then out of the window again. Silence endured for the remainder of the drive home, and on reaching the castle Beth hurried up to her room. Within moments Braddy came to assist her, and found her standing by the window struggling not to cry.

'Madam? Oh, madam, what is it?'

'I told him about the baby, but he suspects that it is Mr Haldane's,' Beth replied, wrapping protective arms across her belly.

'But it isn't Mr Haldane's, my lady. It can't be. When you arrived here you were coming to the end of your—'

Beth interrupted. 'Yes, I know.'

Braddy was perplexed. 'Did you not tell him so? Perhaps *I* should tell him . . . ?'

'No!' Beth turned upon her. 'For it will smack of *begging* him to accept his child.'

'That surely is not so, my lady, because it will open his eyes to—'

'No, Braddy. I prefer to say nothing more to him.' Beth didn't really know why she was being so obstinate, because it flew in the face of common sense, but her instinct was so fierce that she bowed to its command.

CHAPTER TWENTY-ONE

Jane felt far too awake to even contemplate sleep. Wearing her nightdress and kingfisher robe, and sipping a little Madeira, she stood by her bedroom window at Whitend, looking out at the bright, moonlit night. It was the end of April, and late daffodils bloomed in the park, but a winter chill lingered in the air. The floods had subsided over a month earlier, but the ground was still wet and muddy, and the Severn remained high. If there were more rain now, it would surely burst its banks again. Another dark thought came to her, for it was on a night like this that she'd sent Bolton to fire Beswick's premises in Gloucester. Even after all these months, she still suffered nightmares of being arrested and brought to account.

A vixen screamed outside, concentrating her attention on the park. A ghostly white barn owl glided toward the stables. Everything seemed quiet, and as normal as it could be in these restless times, but the hairs on the back of her neck stirred unpleasantly, and every sense told her something was very wrong. The whole day had been bad. Threshing machines had been destroyed on farms, and rioting workers had ransacked a woollen mill at nearby Stroud. But it was only partly due to anger over machines robbing them of work, the rest concerned food prices. Gangs of armed men prowled the countryside at night, and now, glimpsing faint lights moving in the park, she knew Whitend was about to receive unwelcome attention. Perhaps especially Whitend, because Thomas was hated above all other landowners, even her. He had seen to it that a number of his labourers were sent to Gloucester jail, but some of them had escaped, and were bent upon a savage revenge. Don Bryant was prominent among them, and who could blame him after the treatment he'd received? The wealthy wailed about taxes, rent, tithes and mortgage interest; the poor just wanted to fill their starving bellies and keep a roof over their heads. There was a time, quite recently, when she would only have seen the landowners' point of view. Not now.

Someone knocked at the door behind her, and she turned with a start. 'Yes?'

Edward entered. He was still fully dressed, and came quickly to her side to look out at the lights. 'We're in for some trouble,' he said then.

'I know, although they don't seem to be getting any closer.'

'They will, when they're ready.'

'Where's your father?' she asked.

'Drunk and senseless.'

'Very useful in a time of need,' she murmured drily.

'He'd be more hindrance than help.' Edward opened the window slightly. Another vixen screamed, or so she thought, but Edward's ears were keener. 'That's no vixen.'

'Are you sure?' Jane put down her glass nervously.

'I'm one of them, remember? I don't belong here, but out there. I've poached from time to time, and I know what sounds they make to each other. There, see? They're beginning to move in on the house.'

Jane was suddenly very afraid. 'What will they do to us?'

'I don't know. They hate my father, and I've done little to endear myself since leaving the tavern. You're a woman, so maybe . . . ' He shrugged. 'I just don't know, Jane.'

'Well, I was hardly a model landowner at Tremoille House,' she observed, recalling some of her harsher acts. Suddenly a ground floor window was shattered, and she clutched Edward's arm.

He placed his hand over hers, and squeezed it reassuringly, a startlingly gallant gesture. 'You stay here, Jane. I'll go down and see if I can reason with them.'

'Are you mad?' she cried.

'Probably, but it's time I showed myself as more than a bullying oaf.'

Jane caught his hand. 'I don't know you at all, do I?'

He grinned. 'I've seen the light, like St Paul on the road to Damascus. Now then, you stay here and be very quiet, all right? With luck my father will sleep on, and I'll be free to talk to the troublemakers in their own language.'

'I wish you luck.'

He slipped away again, and she remained by the window. Torches bobbed all over the park, most of them closing in on the house. She trembled. Was this how the French Revolution began? With death stalking the aristocracy in the middle of the night? What could she do if they burst into the room? How could she defend herself?

Edward went downstairs and found the drawing room filled with men, overturning furniture, slashing paintings with knives, and

334

ripping curtains and upholstery, but there was sudden silence as he appeared in the doorway. He fixed his gaze upon one man in particular. 'So, here you are, Don Bryant. I thought you'd be a ringleader.'

Bryant's lip curled back sneeringly. 'You're not so high and mighty now, Ned Barker, and you're the one we want the most. How thoughtful of you to come to us.'

Edward held his ground. He knew these men could be intimidated in strange ways. A single unexpected act could throw them and make them leave, or it might boil them over into worse violence.

Bryant spat on the floor. 'We're going to have you for the things you've done since coming here.'

'Touch me and you'll regret it to the end of your days, which won't be far off,' Edward replied.

'What can you do that you haven't done already, Ned? You've robbed me of my work and my home, so I think I'm justified in taking your scum of a life.'

The men parted as Edward moved further into the room, to stand face-to-face with Bryant, whose tongue passed nervously over his lower lip. Edward glanced around with commendable calm, and then looked at Bryant again. 'I haven't seen anything tonight, Don, not a single thing, because no one came here while I was asleep. Leave now, and that's how

335

it will stay. Continue as you do, and you'll all hang. Damn it, can't you see what I'm offering? Don't you think I know how you're feeling? I've behaved badly, and don't deny it, but I've learned my lesson. Can you learn yours?'

A tall man with a patch over his eye pushed forward. 'You? Learn a lesson? That'll be the day, Ned. Yes, you were one of us, but now you're worse than the rest of the nobs put together. Thanks to your old man, I was sentenced to death for machine breaking a while back. I'm here for revenge, and revenge is what I'm going to have!'

Jane's shadow suddenly fell across the doorway. She had a loaded rifle in her hands, and raised it threateningly. 'Lay one hand upon Edward and I'll shoot,' she said, having found the wit to go to where Thomas kept his guns.

Edward turned and shook his head. 'Lower the gun, Jane,' he said quietly.

'But—'

'Lower it, for it's not needed.' He looked back at the crowded room. 'Leave now, and nothing will come of all this. You have my word.'

'How can we trust you?' Bryant demanded.

'You can, because I have a plan. There's a Welland ship in Gloucester docks, by the name of the *Cicely B*. She's bound for St Malo, to collect a cargo of wine, and I can take you to her right now. You can hide in a Welland ox-wagon to get there, because no yeomanry or army will search my father's property. I can get you over to France, where you'll be free to start again.'

An element of uncertainty spread through the room, and Jane saw exchanged glances. Would they accept Edward's incredible offer? She glanced at her unlikely stepson. Once before she had thought there was more to him than met the eye, but he'd soon shattered that impression. Now she was forced to think yet again, and she began to like what she saw.

Don Bryant turned to her. 'What of you, Lady Welland? Will you hold your tongue as well?'

She nodded. 'Yes, and you need not concern yourself with my husband, because he is completely in drink.'

One of the other men made up his mind. 'Well, I reckon I'll take what's on offer,' he said, and there were some murmurs of agreement. Don Bryant remained suspicious. 'Ned, there's only one way I'll believe in you, and that's if you come to France with us. Oh, you can come back here afterward, but I want to see your ugly bloody face every minute of the voyage.'

Edward nodded. 'That's all right with me.'

Now Jane became suspicious. 'Mr Bryant, do I have your word that Edward will be permitted to return?'

'You do.' Bryant nodded at Edward. 'It's settled. We'll go along with your plan.'

The ugliness in the room suddenly melted away, and Edward turned to smile at Jane. 'I'll be back soon enough,' he promised, and then accompanied the men out into the night. And so the armed gang that had earlier come to attack every Welland it could lay hands upon, left in smiles, assured that a new future lay ahead.

*   *   *

Two weeks later, Jane waited in her carriage at Gloucester docks. The *Cicely B* was expected this evening, and she had been waiting since darkness fell. A thin mist was curled low over the river and harbour basin, the vapour swirling eerily in front of the oil lamps on the lock keeper's lodge. Damp cobbles gleamed on the wharves, trucks clanked on a tramway, and the smell of stale hay was strong enough for Jane to put her perfumed handkerchief to her nose.

There were numerous vessels in the basin, their rigging lacing across the night sky, and a string of packhorses clattered past the carriage, laden with bales of wool, and men shouted by a barque that was being hauled toward the lock gates, beyond which lay the Severn, its muddy waters still high in the narrow, deep channel. It was a silent river, with few ripples to break its surface, except when the tidal wave known as the bore swept upstream, and she always found it menacing, as if at any moment a watery arm might reach out and drag her down into its heartless bosom. The lock keeper emerged, and came to stand by the open carriage door, his head cocked, listening.

'The bore's on the way,' he observed.

'The bore? What of the *Cicely B*?' The tides of the Severn were treacherous, and the bore had caused many a foundering.

'She'll ride the tide, to get upstream as quickly as possible.' The lock keeper tilted his head again. 'Listen, it's almost here.'

Jane sat forward to listen, and soon detected a rushing, hissing, bubbling sound that was drawing closer. She had seen the bore before, but never after dark, and the experience was alarming. Her heart leapt as the wave appeared, breaking on the far bank as it swung around the curve by the lock gates before striking the near bank in a shower of muddy water that spattered the cobbles of the river quay. Willow fronds on the opposite shore were tugged upstream by the inrushing tide, and the Severn was suddenly loud and intrusive after its earlier silence. The waters of the dock basin remained calm and unruffled.

The lock keeper was called away, and Jane leaned out to close the carriage window. How long would it be before the *Cicely B* arrived?

She glanced at the hamper she'd brought. Among other things, it contained a bottle of white wine, a glass of which would be welcome right now, but she'd wait until Edward was here to enjoy it too. Even now she marvelled at what he'd done on the night of the raid, displaying such quick wits and courage that it hardly seemed possible he was the same Ned Barker who'd given her such insolent lip at the breakfast table. Thomas still knew nothing about what had happened when the gang broke in, and when he'd been sober enough to ask for Edward, she'd told him Poll Barker was unwell and needed her boy for a while.

Removing her wide-brimmed straw hat, she leaned her head back against the rich leather upholstery and closed her eyes. It wasn't long before she was fast asleep, although she thought she had hardly dozed off when suddenly the door was flung open and Edward was there. 'So I get a personal welcome home? I'm honoured, and no mistake.'

She had awakened with a start. 'Good heavens, I must have fallen asleep.'

'And there you were, in the middle of the docks, snoring and catching flies,' he said, flinging his coat over his shoulder.

'I wasn't!' she gasped, sitting up in dismay, but then realized he was teasing her. 'Oh, most amusing,' she said tartly.

He climbed in and flung himself on the seat. 'Sweet Lord, I'm glad to be back.'

'Did it go well?'

'I let them loose in France, if that's what you mean. God help the Frogs, that's all I can say, because a few of them are rogues through and through.'

The carriage moved off, out through the dock gates and uphill past the remains of the ancient Norman castle toward the main Bristol road. Edward noticed the hamper. 'Please tell me that's full of good British food.'

'It is. Help yourself. And please open the bottle of wine, with your teeth if necessary, because I long for a glass.' The bottle broached, he handed her a glass, and she sipped it before smiling. 'I've actually worried over you, Edward.'

'Really? Well, that's a turn-up, eh?' He grinned.

'When you're like this you're most agreeable.'

'I suddenly saw myself for the maggot I'd become. Then, that night when they raided us, I realized you only had me to defend you, and—forgive me—the feeling was good. I felt like a man instead of a clod.'

'Because you were, Edward, and I now think very highly of you.'

He met her eyes. 'As highly as you think of my brother?'

'In a way, yes, but you and Rowan are very different.'

'Because he's always been a gentleman?'

Jane shook her head. 'No, not at all. Edward, I certainly haven't always been a lady, as you once so memorably observed. I like you *and* Rowan, just in different ways.'

'I suppose I'll have to be satisfied with that.'

She smiled. 'Better an admirable Edward Welland, than an imitation of Rowan.'

He drained his glass and poured another. 'Can we change the subject? Look, I'd never spent much time with horses before I was sent for, but I have since being sent for. I've got a talent with them, Jane, and would dearly like to learn enough to have charge of my father's stables.'

'Well, I can help. I'll instruct Sam McCullogh, the head groom, to take you fully under his wing and teach you all you should know and, as he is also your father's jockey, he can introduce you to the whys and wherefores of the racing world. Not that Thomas has been involved a great deal of late. I think the closest a Welland horse has come to the winning post recently is a challenge between McCullogh and Robert Lloyd of Frampney. Lloyd was murdered before the match could take place. Anyway, if you're really serious about this, you can rely on my support.'

*　　　*　　　*

That same night, Rowan and Rosalind drove back from Drury Lane to their new address near the Trinity Chapel in Conduit Street, on the eastern extremity of Mayfair. They used his travelling carriage, which they were obliged to employ for all purposes, it being out of the question to go to the expense of a vehicle simply for the streets of London. The home to which they were returning took up one bay of a large house that had recently been divided into three separate properties. Designed by the great James Wyatt, it was stuccoed, with Ionic pilasters on the first floor, and it stood amid stylish shops, superior furniture manufacturers and many residences of eminent physicians. But one bay or not, Rowan knew it was still too expensive. He'd wanted to please Rosalind with a Mayfair address, but it soon become clear that such addresses attracted bills too large for his lean purse. There was no question that he'd overreached himself, and he had to find a way out of his problems. The last thing he wanted was to use Rosalind's money, for he felt it would demean his position as her husband. He had to support her, and her money—if hers it was—must be kept for dire emergencies.

A move to pastures new—maybe even to the colonies—seemed the only viable option, but Rosalind would not want to live anywhere but fashionable London. The matter would have to be broached, however, and he was guilty of putting off the evil moment. She adored her elegant new life in the capital, brushing shoulders with dukes and earls, and even on one occasion a member of the royal family. They were ambrosia to her, even though she was definitely not ambrosia to them. Rowan was hurt that the superior circles in which he had hitherto moved without hindrance should endeavour to exclude his wife, but in his heart he knew the difficulty lay with Rosalind herself.

At first society had been prepared to tolerate her as a beautiful novelty, a blacksmith's daughter who would one day be Lady Welland, but no one cared for the spiteful, snappish character she foolishly failed to curb. He'd tried to reason with her, but she saw nothing wrong in her conduct. What everyone else regarded as the dissatisfied complaining and posturing of a vulgar, ill-bred upstart, she saw as wit and aplomb. But in spite of her demonstrative faults, his love for her remained constant and their lovemaking was passionate and inventive; indeed, sometimes he found it difficult to satisfy her astonishingly ravenous sexual appetite.

But Guy's warning couldn't be ignored, and Rowan knew that Rosalind had almost certainly stolen the 480 guineas from her father. Yet, knowing all this, he still wanted to spend the rest of his life with her, have children with her, and grow old with her. This dream could not be realized in Mayfair, which was why he'd been so astonished and relieved that morning when a communication arrived from a solicitor in Dublin. It contained news that could very well prove the salvation of everything—but only if Rosalind were receptive.

Rowan hadn't mentioned the letter to her yet, deciding instead to see what transpired at the theatre. They'd been to see La Carberry and Kean, an outing of which Rosalind had originally enthused, until she learned that Maria Carberry had been, and maybe still was, Guy Valmer's mistress. From that moment on her face became long, and her petulance obvious. She'd made ill-educated observations that gave rise to sniggering among other theatregoers, and by the time the final curtain came down Rowan had wished himself anywhere but the Theatre Royal. The whole sorry occasion had left him with no choice; he had to drag his embarrassing wife away from London's glare.

The carriage halted at the kerb in Conduit Street, and he alighted to help Rosalind down. She was wearing a pale blue silk gown, and her hair was twisted into a simple style from which a single ostrich feather floated prettily. She looked every inch the fine lady, he thought unhappily, but the moment she opened her mouth . . .

He drew her hand over his black velvet sleeve, and escorted her into the main entrance, where the door to their portion was immediately on the left. Inside, an elderly woman servant waited to see if they wished her to prepare any supper. Rosalind was eager, but Rowan shook his head. 'That will be all, Griffiths,' he said, ignoring Rosalind's protests and waving the woman away.

Rosalind was annoyed. 'But I'm hungry, Rowan!'

'We need to talk.'

'Talk?'

'Yes.' Taking her elbow, he ushered her up the narrow new staircase to the former bedroom that was now the drawing-room. The original small fireplace had been replaced by one more suited to the principal reception room, which was simply furnished and still smelled of new paint. Closing the door behind them, he faced her. 'This London life will not do, Rosalind,' he said bluntly.

'Not do? Why? I love it, Rowan!'

'We cannot afford it.'

'Only because you will not use my money!' she cried, stamping her foot.

'How long do you think those guineas will last? Face the facts, Rosalind, we can't afford Mayfair. Damn it, we can't afford any fashionable part of London.'

'My money—'

'—is not enough. And it isn't just a matter of money. Society is against us.'

She tempered her voice. 'Against me, you mean.'

'It doesn't matter against whom, just that we do something about it.'

'Such as?'

He wanted to tell her that if she modified her behaviour and conducted herself with more modesty and charm, he might have struggled on for longer, but when she spoke so softly and looked at him so trustingly, he couldn't bring himself to say the cruel words. 'I had a letter this morning, Rosalind, from a solicitor in Dublin.'

'What has that to do with it?' she asked.

'It seems I had a maternal cousin named William Palmer. My mother's family is vast, and I don't know of the half of them. Nor did the late William, who knew he was dying without an heir. So he had the solicitor find all the cousins' names he could, and put them in a hat. Mine was the one William drew out.'

Rosalind stared, and then a gleam entered her eyes. 'You've inherited a fortune?'

'Not exactly. I am now the owner of a small lakeside estate, called Coolisk, somewhere in Fermanagh.'

'How much will it fetch?' she asked, ever mercenary.

'Nothing, actually, because I rather hope we will go there to live.'

She flinched, as if he had suggested a move to Hell itself. 'But, I'm so happy here, Rowan.'

'Our finances and social standing are decidedly unhappy, Rosalind, and I want to go to Coolisk,' he said quietly, meeting her eyes squarely to show he was in earnest.

'Do I have a choice?'

'You can refuse to come. Stay here, spend your money, and then see where you are. Coolisk is our deliverance, if you will only see it.'

Rosalind summoned a shimmering veil of unshed tears, behind which her mind raced. She wanted to defy him, but knew that he was right. She wrestled with herself for only a few moments, before giving a sorrowful, melting smile and allowing the tears to fall. 'If it means that much to you, I will come with you,' she said in a little voice.

Breathing out with relief, he went to gather her into his adoring arms. 'It will be the best thing that's ever happened to us, my darling,' he whispered, and kissed her.

CHAPTER TWENTY-TWO

Almost midnight on the second day of May, Guy was returning from Carlton House in his town carriage after attending the evening wedding of the Prince Regent's heir, Princess Charlotte, to Prince Leopold of Saxe-Coburg, and even at such a late hour the streets of London were packed with well-wishers. The royal couple had been fortunate with the weather, which for once had relented sufficiently to allow a little watery sunlight to shine upon their great occasion. The rain had held off as well, and even though it remained cool for the time of year, it had nevertheless been a reasonably pleasant day.

He wore court dress, a single-breasted coat of deep purple velvet, richly embroidered in gold, with white silk breeches, stockings and waistcoat. Black, gold-buckled shoes completed his lower portions, while his hair was hidden beneath a powdered bagwig. His white gloves and cane rested on the seat beside him, as did his folded cocked hat and the dress sword he'd been obliged to sport all day. He was alone in the carriage; indeed, since coming up to London again in April, he had led a very solitary existence. Now he was returning to an empty house. Maria would have been there had he permitted it, but he didn't want her actually beneath his roof. He was using her quite ignobly in order to be avenged upon Beth, but Maria wanted him regardless of the terms, and he was ungallant enough to follow his urges.

Rowan and Rosalind had left his house rather promptly after the great falling out and, as Rowan was clearly deeply offended about the things that had been said of his wife, Guy could only presume that he and his cousin wouldn't meet again as friends. He was sorry for it, but there was nothing to be done. The advent of Rosalind Mannacott had changed everything irredeemably. She was a conniving, self-centred little thief, and it was to be hoped that the light of truth dawned sooner on Rowan rather than later.

Guy leaned his head back and closed his eyes, reflecting that perhaps he wasn't in a position to really criticize, because profound changes had been brought about by the presence of Beth Tremoille. Who was he to tell Rowan that Rosalind's word wasn't to be trusted, when he didn't trust his own wife's word? He dreaded the thought that Landry Haldane might have fathered Beth's baby, and such was his private anguish that he hadn't even been able to face Beth, choosing instead to rush back here to London. Like a cur with its tail between its legs, he thought scathingly. Ostensibly he'd come to complete one final legal formality with Withers, and to attend the royal wedding, to which he'd been invited before there had been a Lady Valmer to include, but it had also been to escape the further humiliation of knowing that if it weren't for the child, Beth would have already left him.

The baby was a complication that he, Guy, hadn't anticipated. He hadn't intended to consummate the marriage, but then there had been Beth's assertion that she was barren. Now, because he had not been able to resist her, and because she was wrong about herself, he was plunged into the most wretched of quandaries. He closed his eyes, tortured by the fear that by disbelieving Beth he might spurn his own child.

The carriage drew up beneath the lamp-lit porte cochère, and a tired footman emerged to open the door and lower the rung. The scent of jonquils drenched the cool night air as Guy entered the house, where he gave orders for a hot bath to be prepared in his dressing room, before adjourning to the library to enjoy a final glass of cognac. He'd had more than enough already, but told himself it was in celebration of the royal match, and nothing to do with his problematic private life. Flicking back the richly embroidered tails of his court coat, he sat down at the desk and reached for the decanter and glass that stood on a handsome silver tray. He had to consider when he would return to Greylake. All documents had been examined and signed, and he'd seen to other outstanding estate matters, so any further dilly-dallying in the capital would be an obvious display of cravenness.

His glance fell on a letter that Withers had charged him to give to Beth. The seal, which should have been intact but was not, belonged to Esmond Tremoille, and the letter had been lodged with the London solicitors to give to Beth after his death. It was a simple guess that it contained directions to the final will, and in Beth's absence he, Guy, had persuaded

Withers to open it. What a memorable moment that had been. Guy could see again the splinters of sealing wax falling on the green leather surface of the lawyer's desk, and remember the abject dismay of finding the letter was in code! Draining the cognac, he savoured the heat of the liquid in his throat. The letter was Beth's by right, and he would take it to her when he returned. Whenever that was. At that moment a footman came to inform him the bath was ready, and he got up from the chair, hoping that a good soak would restore his spirits.

His bedchamber enjoyed pride of place above the *porte cochère,* with connecting doors to a dressing-room that was large enough to be a bedchamber in its own right, and in which the bath had been set. Both rooms had gilded dove-grey walls and rich crimson velvet curtains that hung at balconied French windows facing across Park Lane to the park. There was no valet to attend him, because he had never felt the need for one. It was his opinion that if a man could not take care of himself he wasn't much of a man. Provided his clothes were laundered and in readiness, he could do the rest.

Once undressed, he stepped into the citrous-scented bath, and leaned back luxuriously to savour the moment. The soap bobbed on a little wooden float, and fluffy towels waited on a chair beside the bath. The surfeit of cognac had taken the edge off him, and he felt hazy and relaxed. It was a more honest and pleasurable sensation than any he'd had recently.

Detecting a stealthy sound in the adjacent bedroom, he sat up. 'Who's there?' No one replied, but then the connecting door to the bedroom was pushed further ajar and Maria came in, completely naked, her thick flaxen hair loose about her shoulders. Her breasts shone in the candlelight, her nipples casting little shadows, and her curvaceous body was sweetly inviting. She slid a hand down to her crotch, sinking her fingertips through the dark thatch of hair. 'Don't be cross and churlish now, because poor Puss is hungry. You've stayed away for two whole days, and now nothing will do but that she's satisfied.'

'Puss is always hungry,' he murmured, leaning back again. He was too lethargic to face a scene with her now, so let her do what she would.

Smiling at the unspoken invitation, she crossed to the bath and stepped in to sit astride him and slide herself intimately over his loins. 'Mmm, that's nice. Let's make Puss purr,' she breathed, bending to put her lips to his.

She took the soap and lathered it, before sliding her slippery hands beneath herself to massage him. He found it only too easy to slide into sexual pleasure, and closed his eyes as she manipulated him. 'Let's see what you have for me, my love,' she breathed. 'Oh, yes, you have a lovely big dick, the sweetest, most potent and most puissant dick in all the realm.'

'You flatter me, I think,' he murmured, sighing as her hand moved to and fro.

She noted the slight note of inebriation in his normally measured voice, and her eyes shone a little more. 'My, I do believe you're a little fuddled.'

'It helps.'

'Helps what?' She was curious, because he just wasn't a man to ever be in drink.

'Everything.'

She caressed his erection, which was now more than ready for her, but she did not move herself on top of it. Instead she slid a knowing fingertip over the tip. 'Why are you in drink, my English rover? I might have expected you to be drunk with joy, but not drunk and quiet like this.'

'Joy?'

'Why, because you are to be a father, of course.'

He caught her by the wrist to stop her caressing him. 'How do you know about that?' he demanded, his voice suddenly sharp and clear.

'I make it my business to know all about you, my love.'

'That's no answer.'

She winced as his fingers tightened. 'All

354

right, I'll tell you. I pay one of your servants at Greylake to pass on everything I ought to know.' She pursed her lips reproachfully. 'You've impregnated your wife, Sir Guy, and didn't tell poor Puss.'

'Because it's none of your business. Who is the servant?'

She laughed. 'You don't honestly think I'll tell you, do you? Not when I am told such titbits as your bride's meeting with her former lover—or is he *still* her lover? I know they shared a kiss in front of the castle, while you were looking the other way, presumably. Well, now, might *that* be the reason for your glumness? Are you afraid dear Beth is *enceinte* by her lover?'

'Damn you, Maria!' He stood to get out of the bath, but she caught his arm.

'Take it out on me, Guy,' she urged, 'do what you will to me, pretend I'm her and you're punishing me!'

'I'm not in the mood for this, Maria.'

'Yes, you are,' she breathed, and suddenly knelt up to wrap her arms around his thighs and take his now soft virility into her mouth. She sucked him deep, rolling him ecstatically around her mouth while at the same time sliding her soapy hands over him.

He began to pull away from her, but his body betrayed him. The prospect of sexual relief triumphing over mental torture was sinfully inviting, and his defences were in

355

disarray. Hating himself for his shabby weakness, he surrendered to her expert seduction, and his body responded just as she wanted. She made delighted little noises as she enjoyed his renewed erection, and then she gradually drew him back down into the bath before kneeling to straddle him with her thighs. Smiling down into his eyes, she held his now potent member upright in order to sink down upon it. How slowly she engulfed him, easing herself inch by sweet inch until Puss could go no further. Her breath escaped on a long sigh of exquisite pleasure, and she closed her eyes. 'Oh, Guy, if you only knew how much I love you.'

'Don't love me, Maria, for it will do you no good.'

'I know that,' she whispered, 'but the pleasure of having you inside me like this is so exquisite that Puss would not care if I died right now, for she would die with you as the very last experience of her wicked life.'

'Maria—'

'Shh.' She put a soapy finger to his lips and began to move up and down on him. 'Oh, Holy Mother,' she gasped, as gratification gripped her. He felt her muscles undulating strongly as she continued to work herself on him. 'Slow but sure, Puss, slow but sure,' she whispered, forcing herself to take her time.

He closed his eyes, wishing she were Beth. It was a moment of clarity amid the mist of his life. He wished she were Beth because he wanted Beth to be his. All his. *To have and to hold, from this day forward, for ever and ever . . .*

Maria's pulsating desires were beginning to overwhelm her, stealing her control and sweeping her away into the sexual oblivion that seemed to shine brightly before her. New surges of joy swamped her, and she began to jolt up and down on him, crying out and cursing in a way that would have pleased a Billingsgate fishwife. She was so frantic for the ultimate satisfaction that she virtually bounced upon him, and when at last he came, she gave such screams of unbelievable delight that he feared the servants would rush to see if there was murder being done.

Her racket dulled his pleasure; or perhaps it was simply that he too wished to cry out. *'Beth! Oh, dear God, Beth!'* The words remained unsaid, but they rang through him so clearly and sweetly that he was close to tears. It was too much to endure, and suddenly he scrambled up out of the bath.

Maria was spent, her cheeks flushed, her eyes like molten velvet as she rolled around in the bath to look up at him. 'Oh, Puss has never purred so much.'

'Or made so much damned noise,' he answered, reaching for a towel to wrap around himself.

She laughed at such inappropriate modesty. 'Come now, sir, there is nothing that I haven't

357

seen—and had—before.'

'Maybe.'

She sensed his sudden distance. 'Can I stay with you tonight?' she asked.

'You can have a room, but I think you should leave in the morning.' He spoke reasonably, and with a smile, not wanting to needle her.

'So, now it's out with poor Maria?' She pouted, not entirely playfully.

'No, it's simply a matter of what's right and what's wrong. I shouldn't have permitted you to come here at all this evening.'

'Why?'

'Because I'm married now, damn it, and I think it's shabby of me to permit my mistress beneath my wife's roof. Any meetings with you should take place elsewhere. It's my fault, Maria, not yours.'

'I notice you only think that now, when you've slaked your lust. Now, all of a sudden, you have a married man's conscience? And all because of a faithless wife? You disappoint me, sir. Well, damn you, Sir Guy Valmer, damn your conscience, and damn your harlot of a wife.'

The words touched a nerve. 'That's enough, Maria.'

Perceiving a chink in his armour, she twisted the dagger a little more. 'Will you dare to acknowledge the brat?'

'Get out,' he said softly.

358

'The thought makes you smart, does it?' she taunted.

'Get out, Maria, before I throw you out.'

Resentment lit her face, and she erupted out of the bath, breasts wobbling. 'You English bastard!' she cried. 'You take my love and then hurl it into my face.'

He ceased to care. 'I didn't invite you here tonight, Maria, you came because you wanted to be—'

'Fucked? Is that what you were going to say?'

'Does the word matter?' he asked.

'I'd prefer it to be loved.'

'Well, it isn't, nor has it ever been between you and me. I have never lied to you on that point.'

'No, you haven't, nor have you finally rebuffed my advances. Don't you know that while you let me in, I will keep coming? I want you more than anything else in the world, Guy Valmer, and one day, so help me, I will have you. Completely. In a marriage bed. Your wife had better take care of herself, my English rover, because I intend to be the second Lady Valmer.'

'Are you threatening my wife?' he demanded.

'Me? Now, would I do such a thing?' she answered, slipping past him to the bedroom, leaving wet footprints on the floor. She dressed in silence, and then left the house without another word.

*   *   *

On the last night of August, when a storm in the Bristol Channel threatened to inundate the salt marshes of the Somerset coast, Landry numbered among a group of gentlemen at the gaming table in Sir Daniel Lavington's hillside mansion behind the town of Porworthy. There were two lawyers, a doctor, a judge, two clergymen and several landowners, including Sir Daniel himself and Landry. The latter was playing very deep, and the water threatened to close over his head at any moment.

The house dated from the 1750s and was elegant and symmetrical, an unexpected jewel for a man as ignoble as Sir Daniel. There had never been a Lady Lavington, so the interior of the house lacked the feminine touch, although if there was one room that would surely please any woman of taste, it was the gaming room. Decorated in the Chinese manner, with crimson walls and lavish white plasterwork of exotic oriental design, it was really quite exquisite. The mahogany doors were carved with scenes from Chinese life, there were trellises around the doors, and a pagoda-shaped lantern was suspended low over the green baize table. A fire flickered in the hearth of a white marble fireplace that was fashioned like a temple on the banks of the

Yangtse river, and the whole room was a masterpiece that would not have been out of place at the Regent's magnificent pavilion in Brighton.

Before play began, conversation had been taken up with failed crops, an eternally bad spring, financial disasters and so on, but silence had reigned from the moment the cards were shuffled. The storm raged outside, but few draughts found their way into the sumptuous room, and the faces of the gentlemen glowed in the arc of light from the lamp over the table. It was almost midnight, vast sums were being wagered, and Landry was desperate for his luck to change. Like all reckless gamblers before him, he believed that his present hand would see the relentless tide finally turn in his favour. In the far recesses of his mind he knew the hand was weak, but he had to win! His pulse raced as he concealed the cards and waited for his moment. Perspiration marked his forehead, and his mouth was dry. He was a fool and knew it, but a devil had perched on his shoulder, urging him on into further madness. This time, *this time*, he would emerge victorious. It had to be so, for surely the law of averages must favour him at some point?

He glanced up at the mirror on the overmantel, and saw his candlelit face, pale, tense, and not a little frightened. His fine evening clothes told one story, but that face told quite another. He was diving into the depths of his purse, and seemed hell bent upon crashing to the bottom. The Haldane diamond, which had been worn by every Haldane bride for several centuries, and had briefly graced Beth's finger, had been sold for a fraction of its true value, as had many of the paintings, antiques and various parcels of land that he had been obliged to sell to cover green baize debts. He had even sold Snowy, his cream Hanoverian horse, once a gift to Beth. Not that the horse had been his anyway, because it was true that he'd stolen it from a dying Prussian officer. *What next, Landry, what next? You only have Haldane itself now, because you're out of control, my boy, and it's all because of Beth.*

Sir Daniel, seated opposite, was intent upon his own hand, and at last raised his small eyes to Landry. 'Very well, Haldane, let's see what you've got.'

Landry could taste his own fear as he hesitated, the cards still tight in his hands, but then he could delay no more, and placed them face-up on the green baize.

Sir Daniel's mouth drew back sleekly. 'You went so far on *that* miserable hand?'

An expectant stir passed around the table, and Landry's heart seemed to miss a beat. Lavington could clearly top him. Grinning triumphantly, Sir Daniel did just that, and everyone gasped at the array of aces. Everyone except Landry, who stared down at the cards that finally ruined him.

Sir Daniel grinned again. 'I trust you can meet the debt, sir?'

'I will have to sell Haldane.'

There was utter silence, during which the storm could be heard outside, and then Sir Daniel nodded. 'I'll give you two months to complete, otherwise you'll hand the entire estate over to me, lock, stock and barrel. And be clear, I want it in writing now.'

Landry nodded. 'Very well.'

Sir Daniel nodded at a footman lurking in the shadows, and pen and paper were brought. Landry was in a daze. What *had* he done? What had he done? Sir Daniel eyed him curiously. 'What are you going to tell your wife, eh? There she is, about to be brought to bed, and you must toddle home and tell her you've lost everything. You're such a bloody idiot. No woman, least of all a whore like the Mannacott woman, is worth the ruin you've brought upon yourself.'

'It's not a subject I intend to discuss, Sir Daniel.'

'You should have accepted your defeat. It was as plain as a pikestaff that she always intended to go with Valmer. You were a plaything, Haldane, a prick to soothe her itch until her real love found her again.'

Landry leapt to his feet and tossed the IOU across the table. 'You'll have your money, sir,' he said through gritted teeth, and then turned so sharply to leave that he almost overturned his chair. As he went out, he heard a babble of conversation and laughter break out behind him.

The drive back to Haldane was prolonged by the storm, and all the more miserable for it. Landry huddled in his seat, listening to the howling gale, and wondering how he was going to break the grim tidings to Harriet. She wouldn't say much, but the accusation and reproach in her eyes would drive a dagger deep into the remnants of his pride. That was how it had been when he'd asked her to return the Haldane diamond. *You're such a bloody idiot.* Sir Daniel's taunt echoed so loudly that he might have been in the carriage. 'I know, damn it, I know,' Landry whispered, closing his eyes and seeing only Beth. She was his obsession, his punishment and his salvation. If he could win her back, then the sun would shine again in his world.

It was well into the small hours when the carriage at last drove through the gates of Haldane Hall. Landry tried to glance up at the stone basilisks on top of the gateposts, but it was too dark. It was said that the fabulous reptiles had been hatched by a serpent from a cock's egg, and their breath and glance was fatal. Maybe Beth had been a basilisk disguised in the sweetest of human forms. Yes, it was something like, and he was her victim.

As the carriage neared the house he saw a number of lights in the windows, and then noticed Dr Carter's cob waiting by the steps. What was happening? Was it Harriet? He alighted the moment the carriage halted, and hastened into the house to find the servants waiting around in anxious groups. Then a childish sob made him turn. Katy was seated on a sofa in her nightgown, weeping disconsolately. Seeing her father, she ran to him. 'Papa, now I've lost my new mama too. I must be a very bad girl!'

'Lost?' After a shocked pause, Landry swung her up into his arms, and turned enquiringly as the doctor, his face grey and sorrowful, came downstairs.

'I'm sorry, sir. I did all I could but Mrs Haldane was too weak after the birth.'

Landry stared at him. It couldn't be! Surely it couldn't be! 'And . . . and the baby?' he asked at last.

'A healthy little girl, born early, but strong enough to prosper.'

Another girl? The thought passed only fleetingly through Landry's mind, and he kissed Katy's cheek as she sobbed against his shoulder.

She raised her hot, tear-stained face. 'Is it my fault, Papa? Have I done something wrong?'

'No, of course not, sweeting.'

She was reassured. 'Can we call the baby

Emily, Papa? After my dolly?'

'Yes, of course. It's a very pretty name.' He was too shocked to argue, and if it was what Katy wanted, he was sure Harriet would have wanted it too. He couldn't absorb it all. Harriet was dead? He'd known her almost all his life, and been fond of her for most of that time, but she had ruined everything for him, and he could not help being thankful that she'd gone. He was free again, and maybe—maybe—he could still win Beth.

*   *   *

Two days later, Landry and Katy stood in the silent ballroom, watching the dawn spread over the eastern skies in bloody and unsettling colours. The sound of seagulls flying inland seemed like the cries of lost souls, and the smell of lilies was almost cloying, because there were so many in and around Harriet's coffin.

Landry gazed down at his wife's body. Harriet in death was so much more peaceful than the tormented creature he had driven her into becoming. He knew he had to take some of the blame, because she had been so different before he'd blamed her for losing Beth. But it was barely half a conscience.

Katy placed a little bunch of white roses by her mother's cheek, which was as pale and clear as the petals. 'I want her back again,

Papa, I want her back.'

He pulled her up into his embrace again. 'There now, sweetheart, don't upset yourself so. Mama wouldn't want you to be unhappy. She has left us to take care of little Emily, and that is what we will do.'

'Now both my mamas have gone.'

'It isn't your fault, sweeting. Such things as this just happen.'

Katy wriggled down to the floor again. 'Cover her now, Papa, we've said goodbye.'

He nodded at the men waiting nearby, and then he and Katy left the ballroom. Behind them they heard the coffin lid being lifted into place.

The funeral was sombre, as it could not help but be, and was attended by almost everyone in the village. The glances that Landry perceived were not friendly, as they once had been, and he knew he was being held to account for Harriet's demise. After the ceremony he departed for Ilfracombe, where he faced a very disagreeable meeting with his banker, Nathan Theodore. It proved worse than disagreeable, because his finances were more parlous than he thought. He'd been hoping, rather wildly, that there would be some way of keeping Haldane after all, but there was nothing more to sell. The coffers were empty, and he had no option but to make arrangements with Theodore for the swift sale of his estates.

On the return journey to Haldane, Landry gave substantial thought to his future, and that of his daughters, and by the time he was home again, he had a plan firmly in mind. As soon as Haldane was sold and legal matters settled, he would leave for America, but Katy and Emily would remain here in England, adequately provided for by the residue of the estate. They would be deposited at the Dower House, in Mrs Cobbett's capable care, and as Beth was still officially the tenant there, he could not imagine she would permit her husband to throw Katy and Emily out, simply because they bore the Haldane name. He knew he was behaving basely again, but it all seemed so clear and obvious in his mind. All he had to do now was hope that a buyer would soon be found.

CHAPTER TWENTY-THREE

It was a warm but sunless day in mid-September, yet in Lady Valmer's room in Greylake Castle, the curtains were tightly drawn at the windows. A fire blazed brightly in the hearth as Beth tossed and turned in the bed, beneath half-a-dozen blankets and coverlets. She bit her lip, drawing blood as the agonizing pain galloped through her again, seeming intent upon cleaving her flesh.

'Something's wrong, Braddy! I know it is!' she sobbed, terrified by Harriet's death.

'Wrong? Nonsense, my dear,' Braddy replied soothingly, 'it's always like this with the first baby. The next one will slip into the world before you know it. For now, though, you need all your strength, so let me bring you something to eat.'

The thought made Beth feel sick, as did the excruciating contraction racking her body. At last she found breath to speak again. 'How long is it since Bradfield went to Culvermine for the doctor?'

'He went five hours ago, but Dr Halnaker is probably out on another emergency. Don't fret now, because all will be well. Babes have arrived this way since Eden.'

Beth's contraction reached its peak, and began to fade again, but she knew it wouldn't be long before it returned. A minute, maybe, certainly no longer. This was physical stress and anguish on a scale she would never have believed. And she was so unbearably hot. 'Please take the blankets away, Braddy,' she implored.

'You must be kept as warm as possible, my dear, it's the way of it. Now then, will you at least sip this gin? There now, sit up. That's my girl. Sip now.'

Beth made herself drink a little. The smell was revolting and her stomach heaved, but enough stayed down for her to feel its fiery

369

effect in her empty stomach. She seized Braddy's hand. 'Can you at least open a window?' she begged.

'Oh, no, my dear, for windows *must* be closed during labour and the birth itself.' Braddy replaced the gin on the bedside table. 'Lie back again, my dear. Here, let me cool your poor face.' She dabbed Beth's forehead with a damp cloth.

Beth closed her eyes and turned her head away, her damp, tangled hair dragging on the crumpled pillow. If ever she had needed Guy, it was now. But he had not come near her. He'd returned to Greylake over a week ago, but they had barely exchanged a word. Nothing had changed. He was still cold and aloof.

The few moments of respite were over, and the pain was already returning. Beth could only whimper and drag her knees up to try to lessen the ferocity, but it was in vain, for the contraction was so brutal that it stopped her breath. Braddy looked uneasily at the clock on the mantelshelf. The pains were very close together now, yet Beth wasn't ready yet. Nowhere near ready. Realizing that she herself was going to have to attend to this lying-in, she gave Beth a much more thorough examination. What she found filled her with horror.

She turned to two maids who waited by the door, and instructed one to untie every knot and ribbon she could find in the house.

Nothing, *nothing*, must hamper the babe's passage into the world. To the other she simply said, 'Bring Sir Guy.'

The girl ran out, and it seemed an age before she returned with Guy. 'What is it, Braddy?' he demanded as the housekeeper drew him out of Beth's hearing.

'Is there any sign of Dr Halnaker?' she asked.

'No. I've sent another rider. Bradfield had an accident and was found at the wayside with a broken leg. No, don't worry, he'll be well again soon. But now—I need to know about my wife.'

'Sir Guy, the baby is lying the wrong way around. His feet are where his head should be. She's in a bad way, and I don't know how you wish me to proceed.'

'What do you mean?'

'I can make things easier for her, but at the expense of the baby. If I do nothing, both might be lost.'

Guy gazed at the bed, and then looked at the housekeeper again. 'Save my wife.'

Braddy nodded. 'Very well, sir.'

He went to the bedside. Beth's suffering affected him deeply, and he put a gentle hand to her cheek. 'Beth?' But the pain was so merciless that she couldn't reply. Her tear-filled eyes were dark with misery, and her fear was so palpable that he reached for her hand and squeezed her fingers kindly. 'The doctor will be here soon.'

Her fingers coiled pathetically in his. 'Something isn't right, Guy,' she managed to gasp, 'and I'm afraid for the baby.'

'Everything possible is being done for you.'

Even in her present condition, she knew he still doubted her. He might be showing kindness now, concern even, but he was no nearer accepting his child. 'I have never lied to you about this,' she managed to say, then wrenched her hand away, and turned her back to him, giving in to a welter of sobs that twisted Braddy's heart.

The housekeeper suddenly forgot herself completely. 'Many years I've served you, Sir Guy, and never found fault with you, but you sadden me now. The babe is yours, and yours alone. I can vouch for this because I know women's things. You lay with her twice, and this baby is the result. Mr Haldane only called that one time, and the truth is that he forced the kiss upon her. She did not invite it or return it, yet you have punished her as no true gentleman should ever punish his wife. If you continue to doubt her and make her pay for imagined sins, then I will not remain in service here a moment longer, because you will not deserve my loyalty.'

'You've said enough, Braddy,' Guy answered, turning on his heel to leave.

'Don't run away again, Sir Guy. I beg of you,' Braddy pleaded.

The housekeeper's accusing words rang in his ears as he walked away along the gallery. If what she said was true—and his conscience told him it was—then beyond doubt he was the father of Beth's baby. Emotion pricked his eyes with salt.

Beth had been too lost in pain to hear anything. She just wanted her appalling travails to stop, for the baby to be born safely and well, and for her to be able to sleep in a cool, fresh bed, but it seemed that none of these things would be granted her.

Braddy was anxious. She'd spoken out of turn, and would probably be dismissed for her presumptuousness. But now was not the time to dwell on that, for there was a baby to be brought into the world.

*　　*　　*

The curtains had been drawn back at last, and dawn was spreading across the ruddy morning sky as Braddy wrapped the weak baby boy in a warmed sheet and cuddled him for a moment. He made little snuffling noises as she placed him gently in a cradle by the fire. His eyes were tightly closed, and he had a fuzz of dark hair like his mother's. He wasn't strong, and the housekeeper knew that he'd have to struggle to cling to life, but at least Beth was safe. A maid was tending to her, brushing her dark hair and touching some lavender water to her temples. It had been a harrowing ordeal for mother and child, and now Beth was too exhausted to do anything but lie still. Her face was pale, there were shadows beneath her eyes, and she looked so helpless and lost that the housekeeper's heart went out to her.

Braddy nodded at the maid. 'Tell Sir Guy it's over, his wife is well, and he has a son,' she said, 'and then you can go down to the kitchens to have a cup of tea.'

Guy came quickly, and Braddy noticed how his first glance was for Beth. It was a glance that spoke a whole volume, she thought. 'How is she?' he asked.

'Well nigh worn out, but she'll be better by and by. I'm not so sure about the baby. He's really very frail.'

Guy went to the bedside and put his hand to Beth's cheek, as he had before. Her eyes flew open. 'Guy?'

'I'm here.'

She caught his hand. 'Is the baby . . . ?'

'He's alive and well,' he replied reassuringly.

'I want to hold him,' she said, trying to struggle up in the bed.

Braddy hurried over. 'No, my lady, let him sleep by the fire. He needs a rest as much as you do.'

Beth's eyes became suddenly fearful, fleeing from the housekeeper to Guy and then back again. 'You're both lying to me, aren't you? I can tell you are. Jonathan is dead, isn't he?'

'Jonathan? Is that what he is to be called?' Guy sat on the bedside and took her hands firmly in his. 'Look at me, Beth. Our son is alive and well.'

She stared up at him. 'Our son?' she whispered.

He nodded. 'Yes.'

Her lips shook and her eyes welled with tears. 'You believe me?'

'Yes. Forgive me for doubting you, Beth.'

'How low you must think me to have imagined I would try to make you the father of another man's child. Women have honour too, Guy, I have honour, but you prefer to hold it in contempt.' She turned her face away, and closed her eyes.

Within seconds he could tell by her breathing that she had fallen asleep. He pushed a stray curl back from her forehead, and Braddy looked accusingly at him. 'Look at her, Sir Guy. How could you ever have disbelieved her? Why? Why hurt her so?'

'I have no answer to give you, Braddy.'

The housekeeper studied him in the dull light of daybreak. 'Yes, you do,' she said quietly, 'you can admit that you love her and that everything you've done has been guided by your jealousy over Mr Haldane.'

'That's enough, Braddy.'

'Just admit that you love her,' she pressed.

'Much good would it do me to love her, Braddy.'

*   *   *

Eight weeks later, on a frosty day in November, Dr Halnaker, very experienced and sure of himself, arrived from Culvermine to see how Beth and Jonathan had progressed. He was a stout, elderly man with several double chins and a large belly, and sported a powdered, precisely curled wig that would have been the height of fashion a quarter of a century earlier. Accompanied by Guy, he visited Beth first, and then adjourned to the nursery to see the baby.

Guy watched as he examined Jonathan. 'How is he?'

'Better than expected, Sir Guy. He may have been weak at birth, but he's coming along nicely now. Mrs Bradfield did well to see both mother and child safely through their ordeal. Even had I not been called away to another difficult lying-in—twins—I could not have served Lady Valmer better.'

Guy glanced at the maid in charge of the nursery. 'Leave us,' he said, and when she'd gone he spoke frankly to the doctor. 'You've seen my wife again now, Doctor. She shows no interest in the baby, and just sits in her room all day. What is your opinion?'

'Well, physically she is well enough.'

'But mentally?'

The doctor lowered his eyes. 'Sir Guy, it is

376

not uncommon for newly delivered mothers to sink into a low humour. It is usually short-lived.'

'But occasionally not?'

'Occasionally,' the doctor admitted.

'What is your considered opinion where my wife is concerned?'

'I will be honest, Sir Guy. Lady Valmer's condition appears to be only partly due to the rigours of childbirth. In my opinion there is something else behind it, but she refuses to confide in me, or indeed to Mrs Bradfield, whom she trusts.'

Something else? Guy turned away. Yes, there was something else . . . or rather, someone else. He knew he was greatly to blame.

The doctor cleared his throat. 'Sir Guy, perhaps you, as her husband, could probe further?'

Guy smiled a little wryly. 'I'm probably the last person with whom she'd wish to share her secrets.'

'Then we can only hope that the ailment runs its course, and normality is restored in the fullness of time.'

As the two men spoke in the nursery, Beth remained in her fireside chair, staring into the lazy flames licking around the coals. Her eyes were dull, and her face without expression. Braddy had dressed her in her green merino gown and pinned her thick hair up into a carefree knot on top of her head, but she might as well have been carved from marble. She felt nothing, and the future seemed empty.

Her love for Jonathan was overwhelming, and yet she couldn't bring herself to even hold him without immediately wanting to return him to Braddy. Before the birth she had wanted to flout convention by feeding him herself, but either he did not nurse properly, or she didn't have the milk. Whichever it was, he remained hungry and she felt she was failing him. So a wet nurse had to be found anyway. She, Beth, was locked in fear and wretchedness, oppressed by shadows that seemed forever on the edge of her consciousness. She was a mother without hope—or perhaps a hopeless mother—and of no use to her baby.

And then there was Guy. Her love for him had not diminished, but something had frozen deep within her. It lay beyond the emptiness, and beyond the remnants of her spirit. Even though he now made a point of being gentle with her, she couldn't forget what had gone before. She would always treasure their lovemaking, for it had been so magical that it would shine forever, but which was the real Guy Valmer? The passionate lover, or the cold stranger?

She watched the curling flames and glowing coals. Did it really matter which he was? After all, it no longer made a difference to her. She failed as a wife and a mother, and was utterly worthless.

*   *   *

On that same morning in Whitend, where it was raining heavily, Jane, Edward and Thomas were in the drawing-room taking coffee. At least, two of them were, because Thomas had fallen asleep and was snoring in his chair, his newspaper having slipped to the floor. He wasn't drunk, and hadn't been for several weeks now. Nor had he seemed in his second childhood, although he remained a shadow of his former self. It was certain that he—if not his finances, the political situation or the ruinous weather—had taken a turn for the better. He had resented having to leave the safety of the escarpment to return to the watery dangers of the vale, but at least he accepted it. An air of resignation to the inevitable had now settled around him, and the atmosphere at Whitend had improved accordingly.

Edward's improvement continued as well, much to Jane's delight. He had set about learning his trade with the Welland stud, where his natural talent had already won the grudging admiration of the grooms and stable boys, and of Sam McCullogh. This new Edward warranted their respect, and for the first time in his life he was really happy.

Horses now meant everything to him, and he had discovered a flair for assessing racing thoroughbreds. Some men could sniff wine; Edward Welland could detect a prospective winner at an almost passing glance.

He drank the coffee, wishing it were a tankard of strong ale, and turned to Jane, who was neat and fresh in softly draped aquamarine muslin sprigged with white daisies, her hair dressed up beneath a day bonnet. 'Jane, last week Father asked me to find a new horse, a good goer.'

'He did? My, he *is* making a recovery,' she murmured, glancing at her almost comatose husband. 'He hasn't really been interested in racing for a long time now.'

'I've found the very nag in Squire Lloyd's stud, a two-year-old filly.'

'Fillies can be fickle.'

'Not this one, Jane. She's by Lancelot, and goes like the bloody wind.'

Jane glanced away. Hearing Lancelot's name reminded her of Guy Valmer.

'Lloyd's asking a good price, as well he might,' Edward went on, 'but I have a strong feeling about her. Her name's Sabrina, and she'll be good for our stud.'

Thomas cleared his throat suddenly, and looked across the room. 'Purchase her,' he said.

'Yes, Father.'

'She'll be new blood when we move.'

Jane and Edward stared at each other and then at him. 'Move?' she repeated.

'I can't stay here another month, I loathe every acre, and so wrote to Williamson a month ago. He came here when you were both out.' Williamson was his Gloucester banker.

'And?' Jane prompted, sensing a momentous revelation in the offing.

'I told him I was unlikely to retrieve my losses while I stay here, and I asked him if he'd heard of a smaller estate, on high land, preferably with the owner in financial straits, that might suit me. Banks keep in touch, you know, and always get sniffs of property on the market.'

'And?' Jane said again.

'And he went away to see what he could find. He learned of a place called Haldane, on the north coast of Devon, fast on the border with Somerset.'

Jane was confounded. 'You wish to leave Gloucestershire?'

'What is there here?'

'But your family have been at Whitend since Noah's flood!' It was an unfortunate choice of words, for he scowled.

'That is the very point. I will not sit here and let the Severn have me.' He glowered at Edward. 'And that filly's damned name must be changed.'

Edward was at a loss. 'Why?'

'Because Sabrina is another name for the

381

Severn, and I'm damned if I'm taking that evil river with me. Haldane—thankfully—is on a cliff top.' He scowled, his lower jaw jutting in the truculent way of old. 'It seems the present owner's finances are even worse than mine, but it's self inflicted. He gambled it all away, and then his wife died in childbed, and he has decided to leave for America to remake his fortune.'

Jane was bewildered. 'But Thomas, how on earth will you raise the money for this new estate?'

'Ah,' he said, rubbing the side of his nose in as conspiratorial a way as he could manage. 'I told you that banks know what's going on, well, there's a buyer for Whitend, *nouveau riche*, with a desire to suck up to the Duke of Beaufort. He'll pay over the odds. It's too good an opportunity, so I've accepted.'

Jane swallowed. 'And Williamson was prepared to do all this, knowing how ill you've been?'

'It must be clear, even to you, that I'm much better of late.'

'Yes, but—'

'Enough, woman, just believe me that it's a deal well done. Later today I will tell the staff here and all the estate workers. Some I will take with us, but most will be retained by the new owner.'

Edward spoke up quickly. 'Can I have a say about those working with the horses?'

'I suppose so, since you are such a prodigy. Have you anyone in mind?'

'All of them,' Edward replied promptly.

'*All?* Oh, I don't know—'

'Father, I can make the Welland stud great again, and I know these men are the ones to help me.'

Thomas gaped. 'You amaze me, boy. Very well, keep them all if you must.'

'And I want a really good blacksmith.'

'We have one.'

'He's getting on now, and I still want him, but there's another man who's probably the best farrier you'll ever find.'

Jane knew what was coming, but Thomas didn't. 'Who?'

'Jake Mannacott.'

Silence fell, and then Thomas glared. 'The fellow who spawned that little whore who's got Rowan by his prick? Never!'

'Father, I can tell you that Mannacott disapproved of that marriage as much as you. He hasn't seen or heard from his daughter since she left, and he doesn't expect to. He's the best, I swear, and I'd like to try for him. I just need your consent, Mannacott hardly being your favourite name.'

Thomas's mouth worked a little, as it had done when he was in the depths of his collapse, but then he nodded grudgingly. 'If you must.' Then he gave a cold laugh and looked at Jane. 'I'm tempted to leave you

383

behind instead, madam, but that would deprive me of something to heartily despise.'

She drew a cross breath and rose elegantly from her chair. 'You can leave me if you wish, Thomas, but I will require a house and a good allowance.'

'Precisely, so you must come. I'm not lavishing more on you than I have to.'

'You were ever the gallant, sir,' she answered. 'When is this great upheaval to take place?'

'Christmas. I can't go before then because the purchaser cannot sign earlier. As I'm unlikely to get a better offer for this place, I have no option but to go along with it.'

'Have you overlooked the fact that Sir Guy Valmer lives somewhere on the coast of Somerset, close to the border with Devon?' Jane enquired.

'What does that matter?'

'Well, perhaps it doesn't, but I wouldn't have thought you wished to have him as a neighbour.'

'More to the point, madam, you probably don't wish to have him as a neighbour. After all, if it weren't for him, we'd still have Tremoille House.'

Her blue eyes flickered disdainfully, and she swept from the room.

*   *   *

Edward and Jane dismounted outside the rebuilt Frampney forge. It had stopped raining, and now a cold south-westerly blustered up from the estuary, bringing screeching seagulls that glided white against the lowering clouds.

The sound of voices and hammering told them Jake was at work, and as they entered it was a moment or so before their eyes became accustomed to the glare of the fire. Jamie was fashioning a particularly difficult horseshoe under Jake's tutelage, and both men turned as their grand visitors appeared. Jake's expression was guarded on seeing Edward, but he smiled and nodded at Jane. 'Lady Welland.'

'Mr Mannacott.' She tried not to look too hungrily at his gleaming muscles. Seeing him again opened her eyes to just how fiercely attracted to him she was.

Edward picked up the pincers and examined them. 'So this is your kingdom, eh, Jake?'

'So I'm Jake now? Seems to me the last time we met I was plain Mannacott.'

'And I was Ned Barker then, but I'm truly Edward Welland now.'

'Oh?'

Jane nodded. 'Please believe him, Mr Mannacott, because he has changed greatly since your stable yard encounter.'

Jake's gaze moved over her for a moment, and then directly into her eyes. He smiled, just a little, and there was something warm in his knowing brown gaze, but then he nodded at Edward. 'Very well. What have you come to say?'

'Did you know my father's selling up and moving to Devon?'

'No.'

'Well, he is, and I'm to have charge of his entire stud. Our present smith would have come too, but I've just learned that he prefers to end his days here. I'd have asked you anyway. The money will be good, certainly better than here.'

'Why would I want to put such a millstone around my neck, eh? I'm my own master here.'

'You'd be your own master there, too. I'd see to it that neither the forge nor the attached house or cottage is tied to the estate. You have my word on it. I just want you to hand, because you're the best smith I know.'

'Compliments too? My, I'm all a-quiver,' Jake muttered drily, before turning to Jane. 'Does his lordship know about this? I can't think he does, not since Rosalind—well, you know.'

'He knows, Mr Mannacott,' Jane replied. 'This is a very good offer. So please think on it.'

Again their eyes met, again he smiled . . . just a little. It was enough for her to know his idle comment in the Whitend stable yard had been honest. He wouldn't spurn her advances. His body could be hers. She felt almost faint with excitement, her body quivering with craving. He held her gaze for a few seconds more, and then looked at Edward again. 'Where in Devon?' he demanded.

'The north coast, where that county marches with Somerset.'

'Is it anywhere near Valmer's lands?'

Jane's eyes cleared, and so did a little of her sexual beguilement. His interest was because of Beth. Dear Jane would be an 'also ran', as racing parlance would have it. And yet . . . His glance was upon her again, and had that certain glint that her many years of experience had taught her meant one thing.

Edward was answering. 'Valmer's land? Adjacent, but if your interest is Lady Valmer . . . ?'

'That's none of your business, Edward Welland,' Jake replied, before jerking a thumb at Jamie. 'What of him, and Phoebe Brown too, of course? Matty Brown's widow.'

Jane smiled. 'Does this mean you accept?'

'Maybe, maybe not.'

Jamie spoke up swiftly. 'Count me out. I'm staying right here. I own a share of this forge now, and have been learning my trade. I'll carry on alone.' Edward looked at him with sudden appreciation, recognizing the young smith as a man after his own heart. 'I feel like that about the Welland stud,' he said. 'If you change your mind, and want to come with us, there'll be a place for you as well.'

'Jamie, don't be too rash about managing on your own. There's a lot left to learn,' Jake warned.

'I'll take the chance.' Jamie looked at Edward. 'I'm staying here.'

Jake nodded, but addressed Edward again. 'There's still Phoebe.'

'You're free to bring whomever you wish. We want your services, Mr Mannacott.'

Edward extended a hand. 'I guess you're accepting our offer?'

'Subject to all the haggling, I suppose I do,' Jake replied, accepting the hand, but although he smiled at Jane, in his mind's eye it was Beth he saw.

*   *   *

Rosalind held her hat as the ship heeled in the ice-cold wind. Spray spattered over her as she and Rowan stood at the stern rail, gazing back at the diminishing coastline of Anglesey. Spindrift whipped through the air, and the sails cracked and swelled above them. The ship's bow plunged into a trough, and Rowan caught her firmly around the waist. 'Not a fortuitous departure, eh?' he cried, shouting above the racket.

She shrank against him, wishing he weren't so determined to see the last of Anglesey fade behind.

'Coolisk awaits, and so does our new life,'

he said.

She wondered what this vaunted new life would entail. She really didn't want to go, and resented him for forcing her. She'd begun to learn how to go on in society, and knew that if they'd stayed she would have become a true belle. Instead they were going to the back of beyond in Fermanagh.

Sensing her doubts, Rowan pulled her into his arms. 'It will be good, Rosalind, I promise.' He tilted her lips to meet his and, as they kissed, her hat was whisked away in to the spindrift.

Then, taking one last glance at the disappearing coast, Rowan ushered her from the deck and down to their cramped little cabin. He vowed to himself that he would return to England when his father died to inherit the title, and to contest anything that had been left to Ned Barker. He was the legitimate heir, and wouldn't give in meekly to his deranged father's spite!

CHAPTER TWENTY-FOUR

It was December before Guy at last persuaded Beth to take an interest in something. Feeling not a little guilty for her condition, and alarmed by her unyielding despondency, he suggested a visit to Tremoille House. At first she turned her face away from such a prospect, but then, one morning, she suddenly changed her mind. Yes, she would like to see Tremoille House again.

Jonathan had a cold, so they left him in Braddy's loving care at Greylake and set off in the travelling carriage. It took two long days to reach their destination, and after staying overnight at a Bristol inn, in separate rooms, they arrived at Tremoille late in the afternoon. The weather was clear and cold, and the deep crimson sunset cast long shadows as the carriage drove down into the valley toward the house where they'd both spent their childhood. Guy thought of the last time he'd been here, when he'd seen Beth's delightful portrait, painted at a time when she'd been carefree and happy. Small wonder he had failed to recognize her in the thin, dirty, downtrodden creature, clad in rags, to whom he had given a lift to Gloucester. And who'd concealed a thousand stolen guineas in her basket, beneath a pheasant!

'Did you ever eat that damned pheasant?' he asked suddenly, glancing across at her as she looked out at remembered scenery.

'No, because I left Gloucester that night, but I made it into a stew for Jake and Rosalind to have when I'd gone.'

'How homely of you. I can't imagine you making a stew.'

'The Devil was driving. I learned many

things when I had to.' For a moment her eyes brushed his. 'Even how to pay for my keep with my body.'

'Well, you no longer have to do that,' he replied, not without irony.

'I will if that's what you wish. I may not be much of a mother to Jonathan, but I still know that I have to guard his future.'

Brief anger glinted in his eyes. 'I have acknowledged him now, Beth.'

'Only because you could no longer deny being his father.' Her voice was flat.

'Beth, can you in all honesty say that—were you in my position—you'd have behaved differently? Have you no idea how important it is for a man to be sure his child really is his child?'

'Oh, yes, I know the importance of such things, but I also know how a man will do almost anything if he fears humiliation.'

An echo of culpability sounded deep within him, and he allowed the awkward conversation to die.

Outside, the park was shadowy, the specimen trees standing out in sharp contrast to the bitterly cold tints of the sunset. Several minutes later they alighted, and approached the heavy stone porch, which was flanked by stone Valmer lions, and then they were inside, where the temperature was scarcely better than outside because the house had been closed since the Wellands departed. The black-

391

and-white tiles and dark oak panelling of staircase hall were as they both remembered, as were the blue lions of Guy's family. The only sign of the Tremoilles was the portraits, which still hung where they'd been when Beth was last in the house. Her father gazed down, as crafty as ever, and Jane was a golden-haired bride and unlikely angel. Beth herself was there too, painted the year before Jane threw her out. She wore a *décolleté* leaf-green muslin gown, and her dark hair was in a knot with ribbon-twined ringlets.

Guy looked at the likeness. 'Oberon's daughter,' he murmured.

'I beg your pardon?'

'Well, you seem like a fey woodland spirit, or some such fanciful being not of this world.'

'I had no idea you were so poetic.'

'I have my moments,' he replied.

Their unannounced arrival had caught the servants completely unawares, and there was no small panic as they all hurried into the entrance hall to line up in haste for the new master and mistress. Mordecai Bolton had accompanied Jane back to Whitend, so a new man had been appointed, and this was the first time he'd been called upon to perform his duties. After the usual ceremony, and they had returned to their work, Guy beckoned him. 'Richards, isn't it?'

'Yes, Sir Guy.' The man bowed solemnly. He was in his forties, and looked like a clerk, in a navy coat, plain shirt and neckcloth, and fawn breeches. His mid-brown hair was tied back at the nape of his neck, his eyes were somewhere between blue and green, and his face was of regular proportions. His voice was pure Gloucestershire.

'We will obviously require the principal bedchamber to be warmed and aired as much as possible, and Lady Valmer wishes to take a bath. Appoint a suitable maid to attend her, and instruct the cook to prepare a hot supper for an hour's time, to be served to us in the bedchamber.'

Beth addressed the butler. 'Richards, is Mrs Alder still here?'

'Yes, my lady.'

'Then please request her to prepare her special Welsh rarebit on toast, and if there is still some of my father's red Burgundy, we'll have that too.'

'My lady.'

Guy nodded at him. 'That will be all.' Then, as the butler hastened away, he glanced at Beth. 'How nice that you should remember your poor old aunt's rarebit,' he murmured, in a reference to the false identity she'd given on the day he rescued her.

'Do I understand we are to share a bed tonight?'

'Yes.'

'Why?'

'Because I have no intention of feeding

393

more of my servants with tidbits. It's bad enough at Greylake, without encouraging the same here. But please don't fear my unwelcome attentions, because I intend to sleep, and that is all.'

His manner grated, stirring her out of her gloom. 'And what if I should wish to do more than sleep?' she enquired, hoping to shock him out of his infuriating calm.

'Madam, you are quite at liberty to read a book.'

Not trusting herself to respond, she began to walk away. He called after her. 'Where are you going?'

'To speak to old friends in the kitchens,' she answered without looking back. 'I will return in time for the rarebit.'

She found it pleasing to renew old acquaintances, even though she could tell that everyone knew of her scandalous cohabitation with Jake Mannacott. It seemed that wherever she went, scandal followed. Was she really such a shocking person? Or was it just that she had been unfortunate? A stir of wry humour passed through her, for it was both.

After half an hour, her temporary maid—none other than Bessie Alder, the cook's niece—informed her that her bath was ready. Fresh fires had been lit in the bedchamber and the dressing-room, but there was still an edge of damp cold in the air. Candles and firelight cast a soft, moving light over the principal

394

bedroom suite. Oak panelling graced walls that were hung with tapestries depicting the Arthurian legends, and the intricately carved four-posted bed was hung with rich dark-green velvet. The fireplace was large enough for a drawing-room, and the elaborately plastered overmantel showed a sixteenth-century hunting scene.

A small supper table and two chairs had been placed in readiness near the crackling fire, and a lacquer screen was positioned to exclude any draughts from the doors or windows. The smell of roses filled the air from two open pot-pourri jars in the hearth, and Beth had seen a number of heated bricks, each wrapped in cloth, being placed strategically among the bedclothes, so she knew that everything would be cosy for the night. Everything, that is, except the occupants of the bed.

The bath was most agreeable after the long hours on the road, and afterward she donned her nightgown and robe. Bessie then brushed her long dark hair loose around her shoulders before withdrawing. The hour was almost up and supper about to be served. Soon she would have to face Guy again, and the thought was daunting. The bed dominated the room, and her. What would happen when she and Guy lay in it together?

He entered a minute later. He too was in his robe, worn over his breeches and unbuttoned shirt, because he'd indulged in the cold plunge bath that her father had installed some fifteen years earlier. In spite of everything, she was almost overwhelmed by his intensely sexual aura. There was something so sensuous and exciting about him that she found it hard to be level headed. His unbuttoned shirt allowed her to see some of the soft hairs on his chest. They were dark, not chestnut, and almost a year ago she had rested her head upon them and listened to his heartbeats. Could it really be such a long time since they'd made love? If only they could do so again, maybe her true self would return to the empty shell she'd become since Jonathan's birth. She wanted to be well again, to take joy in their child and be mistress of Greylake, if not of its master. For all the times she'd told herself she would be better off leaving Sir Guy Valmer, there were countless more when she knew she would be more wretched away from him. She already knew how desolate her life was when he'd gone to London. It was the price of love, and, God help her, she certainly loved him. Perhaps she was beginning to be well again after all, because at least she could acknowledge that her feelings for him were undiminished. Only a week ago she could not have put two sensible thoughts together on the subject.

'Does my undress embarrass you?' he asked suddenly.

'No. Why?'

'Because you're staring at my chest as if it is something shocking.'

'I was merely thinking.'

'About what, may one ask?' He looked curiously at her.

'One may ask, but one will not receive an answer.'

The ghost of a smile passed over his lips. 'It would seem a little of your spirit has come back.' He placed a book on the supper table. It was the volume of Lesage's *Gil Blas* that she had once read to her sick father, and which she believed to be the book used for the coded letter he'd left for her. 'I saw this in the library, and thought perhaps you would like to take it back to Greylake. Actually, I found Jane Welland's book mark inside, and am amused to think she has been reading the very tome that provided directions to the whereabouts of the will she tried so hard to find and destroy.'

'So I will have bedtime reading matter, will I not.' The words lacked humour.

He frowned a little. 'Beth, I saw the book, remembered the letter, and brought it because I imagine there will come a time when you wish to see exactly what message your father left. That's all.'

'You were pleased enough to tell me I could read tonight,' she pointed out.

'Damn it all, Beth, you really are fanning the flames of your own self-pity.'

She flinched. 'Self-pity?'

397

'Yes.'

'If I am so bad, why do you bother with me?'

'God alone knows,' he answered, picking up the bottle of wine and pouring two glasses. 'I'd prefer to have the old Beth back again.'

'You think I am *glad* to be like this?' she cried.

'I don't know, Beth. Are you?'

'I don't think I will dignify that with an answer.'

He paused ruefully. 'Forgive me, for that was uncalled for. I just don't know how to cope with this. I feel you're made of the finest cut glass, and could easily shatter.'

She regarded him. 'Guy, I just can't stop myself. I feel so utterly worthless.'

'Beth, you aren't well at the moment, that's all. I'm sure you'll recover soon.'

'Too much has gone on. I thought I was strong enough for anything, but I'm not.'

'You *are* strong enough, Beth. The one thing about you of which I have always been sure is that you have great strength. You survived a year as Mannacott's mistress, and by your wits and courage managed to climb back to the social status to which you were born, so don't speak to me of being weak and useless, because I know better.'

'There's a limit to strength of character, Guy, and I have reached it!'

'Balderdash.'

'Are you attempting to jolt me out of this?'

she demanded, shaking with anger and resentment.

'At least we're having a conversation, albeit a shouting match.'

Her eyes were filled with bitterness. 'We have far too many problems and differences to indulge in pleasant chitter-chatter.'

'Nothing is insurmountable.'

'Not to someone whose answer to everything is to scuttle off to his mistress whenever things do not go according to his meticulous plans.'

He was silent for a moment. 'I probably deserved that, Beth, but can't we at least try to put the past behind us, where it belongs?'

'There was a time when I'd have given anything to put the past behind us, but no more. You have constantly resurrected it, and now it lives and breathes between us.'

'It's not the past that lives and breathes between us,' he snapped.

'What is that supposed to mean?' she demanded.

'Haldane is a free man again, and I know he still wants you.'

'And I know your mistress loves you.'

'You know she does?' He heard a note in her voice.

'She wrote to me, warning me that she intends to be my replacement. I can assure you it did very little to help my low spirits.'

Damn Maria! 'I'm sorry she did that, Beth,

and promise it was without my knowledge or consent. I don't intend to replace you.'

She turned away. 'How easy it is for you to apologize for her, yet never to apologize for yourself. You have made love to me twice now, and on both occasions you cut me with coldness afterward. That has hurt me more than you can ever imagine.'

'And you think I cannot be hurt? After that night we spent together, you awoke the following morning with Haldane's name on your lips.'

She whirled about to him again. 'I did what?'

'You stirred out of sleep as I held you in my arms, and you whispered his name.'

'I—I don't believe you!'

'Until that moment I had honestly believed that in spite of everything, you and I could make a happy and rewarding marriage. Then, in a trice it seemed, I was faced with the hard truth that Haldane still came first with you.'

'I can assure you he didn't, not then or now. Guy, I can't be held responsible for my dreams. To hold me to account for them is like bringing back the Spanish Inquisition!'

The supper chose that moment to arrive, and it was several minutes before the servants withdrew again, leaving Sir Guy and Lady Valmer seated in ominous silence over Mrs Alder's famous Welsh rarebit.

Beth regarded him steadily. 'I don't love

400

Landry,' she said, 'and that is the last time I will ever say it. I understand how you must have felt, because I would have felt the same if you'd called me Maria.'

'But I haven't, have I?'

'No, because you wear a halo, whereas I carry a pitchfork.' She indicated the Welsh rarebit. 'It will get cold.'

He inspected it. 'I trust it will be as choice as I'm led to believe?'

'You will only find out by tasting it,' she replied.

'Should I fear the inclusion of hemlock among the ingredients?' he murmured.

'I despise you, but not enough for that.'

'No, you don't. You and I both know that if we adjourned to that bed right now, we would copulate like a warren of damned rabbits. I'll warrant we do far better than you and Haldane ever did!'

She had to strike back. 'Are you sure of that? How do you know I wasn't pretending everything with you?'

'I'm not a callow boy, Beth, and certainly know when a woman is experiencing genuine sexual pleasure.'

'Sexual pleasure, but personal unhappiness, that is what you offer me, Guy. You're right about one thing, Landry is free again, and yes, I could return to him. At least then I would be loved and cherished again.' She wanted to hurt him, hurt, hurt, hurt and hurt again. Why

401

should she suffer pain when nothing seemed to touch him?

He gazed at her for a long moment, and then got up to go to the fireplace, where he placed a boot on the fender and gazed down into the flames. 'If that is truly how you feel, then go to him, I will not prevent you, but you go alone, because Jonathan will stay with me.'

'Guy—'

'Enough, Beth. I will not discuss this further. When we leave here, you can either return to Greylake with me, or go to him. I'll have no more of this.'

Footsteps ran toward the bedroom door, and then came loud knocking. 'Sir Guy? Sir Guy?'

'Yes, damn it, what is it?'

The door opened and an anxious footman came in. 'Sir Guy, my lady, a messenger has arrived from Greylake. He says this is grave and urgent news!' He brandished a sealed note that he hurried to give to Guy.

Beth's blood ran cold. Something was very wrong. Jonathan . . . ?

Guy broke the seal and read quickly, then his eyes, suddenly haunted, swung to meet Beth's. 'It's from Dr Halnaker. Jonathan's cold has worsened considerably, to the point that the doctor is certain he now has lung fever.'

Beth's hands flew to her mouth and her eyes widened with dread 'No!' she cried, stepping back involuntarily, as if by doing so she could fend off the awful news. Full-grown men often failed to fight off pneumonia; children and babies seldom survived.

Guy hurried to put a supporting arm around her. 'We're advised to return to Greylake immediately,' he said gently, and then nodded at the waiting footman. 'See that the carriage is made ready, and send a rider to Greylake ahead of us, to let them know we'll be there as swiftly as humanly possible.'

'Yes, sir.'

The footman ran away again, leaving the door open, and Guy took Beth by both arms and made her look at him. 'No vapours now, Beth, for we need to be strong.'

Her fingers dug through his sleeves. 'But Jonathan is so little, and cannot possibly survive such a—'

Guy's forefinger pressed swiftly to her lips. 'Don't say it, Beth! Don't say it. He *will* survive. We're *not* going to lose him.'

She looked at him through a blur of tears. 'But Guy, we both know—'

Again his finger pressed her lips, and she saw there were tears in his eyes too. 'Please don't say it,' he begged.

His torment was written large, and all the bitter words of moments before were suddenly immaterial. Their baby was in mortal danger, and they had to help each other through the ordeal ahead. 'Hold me, Guy,' she breathed, 'hold me as tight as you can.'

In a moment his arms were around her in a fierce embrace, and she could feel him shaking as he strove not to give in to the awful emotion that had come out of nowhere to strike them both. His voice was thick with anguish. 'God protect him, Beth, God protect our child.'

*   *   *

It was dawn when the travel-stained carriage toiled up the castle hill and finally reached the silence of the Green Court. The eastern sky was a clear yellow-orange, without any of the angry, rather frightening colours that had marred the rest of the year. On such a morning everything should have been well with the world, but as Beth and Guy alighted swiftly at the porch, they feared their baby son might be dead.

The carriage's approach had been observed, and Dr Halnaker hastened into the outer entrance hall to greet them. Guy's anxiety robbed him of courtesy. 'How is he?' he demanded without preamble.

The doctor's plump face was solemn.

'Not good, Sir Guy. I have tried everything I know, but he continues to decline.'

Beth's legs failed her, and she sank to the floor with a sob. 'No, please,' she whispered brokenly.

Guy crouched to hold her. 'He has survived thus far, Beth, and now we are here, we won't

404

let him die.' He helped her to her feet again. 'Come, we'll go to him now.'

As they went up the staircase, Guy asked the doctor what treatment had been administered so far. 'A tincture of veratrum is deemed beneficial in such cases.'

'Veratrum?'

'Hellebore, Sir Guy. I gave him as small a dose as could be prepared, and I did the same with Dove's powder, to induce sweating. Warmed goose grease has been rubbed on his throat, and hot compresses of baked onions applied to his chest, but nothing seems to reduce the fever, which continues to rage. It's proving impossible to persuade him to drink, either from the wet nurse or simply warmed water.'

'And the prognosis?' Guy asked.

The doctor paused. 'I fear there is nothing more I can do, Sir Guy. Only with God's mercy will he live.'

Beth felt faint, and was glad of Guy's arm. Every step that took them to the nursery was an agony of dread, and when they went inside, the scene that greeted them was almost too much to bear. The room was unbearably stuffy and hot, with blankets fixed at the windows and a roaring fire with flames that seemed to leap right up the chimney. Braddy was seated so close to the hearth that her hem was in danger from sparks, and she was cuddling Jonathan in her arms, crooning a lullaby.

Beth could hardly see for tears as she hurried to the housekeeper, who rose quickly and placed the sick baby in his mother's arms. He was swathed in shawls, his breathing fast and hoarse, and sometimes there was a whistling sound from his poor little lungs. He was part of her, and of Guy, and so precious that she could hardly bear to think she'd rejected him. 'I've never held him properly, Guy, I've been so selfish and . . .'

He put an arm around her shoulders. 'Don't berate yourself, Beth, for you've been ill. And we are together in this ordeal, please do not doubt it.'

'I don't,' she whispered. 'Forgive me, I'm so tired and anxious that I can't think properly.'

Braddy looked at her. 'You've been on the road for well nigh four days, my dear, so maybe the best thing you can do now is sleep.'

'I can't possibly sleep when Jonathan may be—' She broke off.

Guy's arm tightened. 'Sleep is the best thing for you, Beth. We're here now, where we should be, and if anything should happen, I will see to it that you are called immediately.'

'But what of you? You haven't slept either.'

'I managed to doze off and on during the journey, but I know you didn't. I will stay here. I'm sure that Dr Halnaker and I will be able to play a hand or two of cards. Is that not so, Doctor?'

'Yes, of course, Sir Guy.' The doctor looked

at Beth. 'All that can be done now is wait, my lady, and sleep will restore you.'

Guy took the baby from her and gave him back to Braddy, then he ushered Beth from the room.

*   *   *

Beth awakened suddenly as the clock on the mantel was striking midday. For a moment she didn't remember, but then it all swept pitilessly over her, and with a choked cry she flung the bedclothes aside to get up. Jonathan! How was he? Recovering at last? Surely that must be so if she had been left to sleep on like this.

But then she heard a slow tread approaching along the gallery. It was Guy, and she knew even before he opened the door that her pathetic hopes for Jonathan were in vain. She stood like a ghost, seeking his eyes as he entered, but she saw only cruel truth. 'No . . .' she breathed.

'He's gone, Beth. There was no time to send for you. He simply stopped breathing.'

Grief overwhelmed her and she ran to fling herself into his arms. They clung together so tightly that their hearts were surely beating in unison. She could feel him sobbing, and her love for him was so immeasurable that she would have given up her own life to spare him this cruel pain. No one else could share this terrible bereavement. They were alone, stricken and tortured, suffering the worst loss of all, that of their child.

CHAPTER TWENTY-FIVE

Christmas snow was falling as Landry rode out of Haldane for the last time. Behind him the hall was closed and shuttered, ready for Lord and Lady Welland to take up occupation early in 1817.

He rode down toward Lannermouth, and then across the bridge by the entrance to the Dower House, where earlier that day he had installed his daughters upon a bewildered Mrs Cobbett. He'd lied to her that Guy had agreed to their residence there, and she had believed him. It had all gone to his satisfaction, except for Katy's vociferous resentment.

'I won't live here, I just won't! My home is Haldane Hall, and I'll get back there! It's mine, not anyone else's! Mine! Both my mamas always told me so!'

Landry's eyes were sad as he urged his mount up Rendisbury Hill and then along the coast road toward Porworthy, but his sadness wasn't due to the children he was deserting. He was making for Greylake, and an assignation he trusted Beth would keep. Surely she couldn't deny him this one thing? A few moments of her time . . . or maybe the rest of her entire life.

He urged his mount through the snow, his thoughts only of Beth, who still dominated his entire existence. Nothing and no one else mattered. He'd lost his ancestral home and his unwanted wife, and he was abrogating his responsibilities toward his daughters, but his love for Beth endured, shining like a beacon through his stormy darkness. She was essential to his happiness, and he would move heaven and earth to take her away from Guy Valmer. He smiled grimly. It was clear to him now that the only reason she had spurned him that day in the park had been the child she was carrying. Well, that child had gone now, never to return, so there was nothing to prevent her from following her heart back to her true love.

*   *   *

Half an hour before sunset, Beth emerged from the porch, wearing a cloak over her riding habit. A groom was waiting with her horse, and helped her to mount. It was still snowing heavily, and the horse left prints as she rode away across the Green Court to keep her tryst with Haldane.

Guy watched from an upper window. He wore a loose robe and nothing more, because he had only just emerged from another of the ice cold baths that helped him forget the impotence that plagued his existence since

Jonathan's death. He left the window and returned to his bedchamber, an opulent room decorated in lemon, white and gold, with a grand bed in which it was said that Charles II had once slept. But not alone, Guy thought.

He flung himself on the coverlet, with his arms behind his head. All he could do now was wait, and hope Beth returned. She had no idea he knew about Haldane's secret note, nor would he have done had Braddy not deemed it her duty to show it to him. Now he knew every damned word.

My dearest, most beloved Beth,
I am leaving England, for there is nothing to keep me here now. My daughters are at the Dower House, in the care of Mrs Cobbett, who believes Valmer has given his consent. I pray you will use your influence with him to see they remain there in safety. You and I are both free now. After your sad bereavement, what is there to keep you at your husband's side? He has treated you abominably since your marriage, leaving you alone and uncared for, and taking up with his mistress when in London. You deserve better, my darling, and I know that you have never stopped loving me. So let us be together, in a new life, far away in America. Meet me at sunset, where the Greylake road leaves the turnpike. I must hear it from your own lips that your love for

410

me is dead.
   With heartfelt hope,
   Your adoring, Landry.

Guy gazed up at the bed hangings. He and Beth had come closer since losing Jonathan, but not close enough, for they hadn't shared a bed. The omission was of his doing, not hers. Jonathan's death had emasculated him. He'd become a cipher, a husband in title only, and the humiliation ate through him like acid. He needed to make love to Beth, but he couldn't, and rather than tell her the truth, he simply stayed away from her bed. And now Haldane's note had arrived; Haldane, who had never suffered impotency, and would give her all the sexual satisfaction her eunuch of a husband could not.

*   *   *

The jingle of harness was the first intimation Landry had of Beth's approach. He turned in the saddle and saw her appearing through the snow, which now lay deep and silent. His heart gladdened, and he dismounted to go toward her, but when he reached up to help her down from the saddle, she shook her head.

'No, Landry, for I mean to return to Greylake as soon as this has been said.'

His arms fell slowly back. 'I cannot believe you mean to stay with him after all.'

411

'He's ten times the man you will ever be, Landry.'

His face changed. 'How can you say that, when he treats you so cruelly?'

'I love him.'

Landry drew back. 'You're lying, Beth, I know it because I know you love me.'

'I *never* loved you! I love him so much that I will die if I am not near him. Oh, I've had moments of weakness, when I thought running away would be easier than facing a life of unrequited love, but since then . . . well, I know I can never leave him.'

Landry gazed at her. 'Unrequited love?' he repeated.

'Yes. He's fond of me, maybe, but he doesn't love me. So, you see, I suffer as you do. Unrequited love is a terrible thing, but if it falls to us, we have no choice but to weather it as best we can.'

'But you *did* love me,' he insisted.

'I held you in great affection, that is all. Now I no longer feel even that, because your conduct since we parted has been such that I am alienated forever. I was uncomfortable to learn about Carrie Markham and Katy, but hugely dismayed when I realized how you'd used Harriet, for whom you've shown no consideration at all. Even in death you revile her. Now you've gambled everything away, and have decided to go off to America, leaving your children behind. Why, you've even foisted

412

them on poor Mrs Cobbett, to whom you've lied. And you're actually relying on Guy's largesse to keep them.'

'To my mind it is the least he can do.'

She was filled with contempt. 'I wish I had never met you, Landry. Katy and Emily are *your* children, not Guy's, and they need you, but you're deserting them.'

'I must make my fortune again.'

'They should be with you. Have you any idea what it is to lose a child?'

'You and Greylake can have another litter,' he replied callously, abandoning all pretence.

She began to turn her horse away, but he caught the bridle. 'Damn you, Beth, and damn your husband. I'll return one day and pay you back for all you've done to me.'

'I did nothing, Landry, you did it all yourself.' She kicked her heel and the horse sprang forward, wrenching from his grasp.

*　　　*　　　*

It was dark when Beth arrived back at the castle, where she was told Guy was resting in his bedchamber. She made her way to her own room, where Braddy soon came to assist her out of her riding habit. The housekeeper was unable to meet her eyes, and at last Beth asked her what was wrong.

'I . . . I've let you down, my dear.'

'Let me down?'

413

'I was so afraid you might go with Mr Haldane, that I . . . I . . .'

'Told Sir Guy about the note?' Braddy nodded, and Beth's heart sank. 'Oh, Braddy! What did he say?'

'Only that he would not interfere, and would let you decide what you wanted. He loves you, my lady, which is something I can see clearly, even if you cannot. All he wants now is for you to be happy.'

Beth was silent for a long moment, and Braddy, becoming uncomfortable, sought to change the subject. 'What gown shall you wear this evening, my lady?'

'Gown?' Beth roused herself from thought. 'No gown, Braddy, just my loose robe.'

'But—'

'My robe,' Beth repeated.

The housekeeper brought the garment, and Beth slipped into it. Then, her hair brushed loose about her shoulders, she went to the door.

'But where are you going?' Braddy asked.

'To my husband.'

The housekeeper smiled after her. There would be no need of a love philtre tonight.

*   *   *

Guy had fallen into a dreamless sleep, and knew nothing as Beth came quietly into the firelit room. She moved silently to the foot of

414

the bed, and gazed at him as he slept. His body was relaxed, and the brocade of his robe fell softly against his chest and limbs, parting below his waist to reveal his naked loins. Oh, that splendid virility, resting gently against his thigh. It made him seem defenceless, and that was something she had never expected to think of him. He had always been so strong and in control, so . . . masterful. Yes, masterful, that was the word. But for all his strength and discipline, he had a gentler side too, a side of unexpected sensibility, as when he'd wept in her arms when Jonathan died.

She loved him all the more for this, if it were possible to increase her love. He could make her so angry and resentful enough to want to hate him, but it was just another facet of her constant love. But could he ever love her? She had thought he would come to her bed after Jonathan, but he hadn't. They had both slept alone. She prayed she wasn't making a mistake now. Braddy swore he loved her, and if he'd known about Landry's letter and yet still allowed her to leave the castle, perhaps he did. If only she knew. Perhaps there was only one sure way to find out; one way to force the truth into the open.

Looking at him now, she needed him so much that it was exquisite pain. The raw craving only he could arouse was aching between her legs and through her breasts. Taking off her robe, she went to sit on the edge of the bed. Her fingers trembled as she reached out to touch him, and feel the warmth and firmness of his skin. She remembered the first time she saw him, from her hiding place above Tremoille House, when he'd emerged after purchasing the stallion, Lancelot, from Jane. He'd been the very essence of fashionable style and grace, a man of poise and distinction, and so handsome. And now he was lying here, almost naked, and as unaware of her presence as he had been then. But he wasn't a stranger now, he was her husband, and they'd had a child together . . .

Her fingertips moved adoringly over his chest, sinking richly through the dark hairs and then tracing over his flat abdomen to the thicker hairs at his groin. It was because of him that she had first experienced ultimate pleasure through the physical act; not because she had been with him, but because he had filled her thoughts when she lay with Jake. Guy aroused a deep stirring of sexual excitement that no one else had ever imparted to her. He was the love of her life, and she longed to be the love of his.

She moved her fingers deeper into the hairs at his loins, and then gently, so gently, over the base of his slumbering member. How soft it was . . . how tender, yielding and unguarded. Her excitement intensified, stabbing through the secret muscles of her femininity, making her pulse quicken and her breath catch. A small wave of sexual pleasure washed into her deepest flesh and into her veins, like an elixir of life itself. Her voluptuous desires were leading her into temptation; fearing no evil . . .

She moved on to the bed, and then edged closer to him, so that she could rest her face on his thigh, close—so close—to the dormant maleness she craved to feel within her. She reached out to take it in her hand. It was soft and heavy, trusting almost. No, that was foolish, and yet . . . She touched the foreskin, as soft and crinkled as the finest silk, and then she massaged what was hidden beneath it. Just a little massage, to add to her forbidden enjoyment. Was it wrong to stroke him like this while he slept? Was she violating him? But she didn't want to stop, nor awaken him.

He sighed in his sleep, and his member responded in her hand, lengthening slowly, and becoming so firm and hard that her excitement was almost unbearable. She continued to stroke him, knowing that she could not stop now. Now she wanted him to awaken and want her. She put her lips to the shaft, and breathed deeply of the scent of him. Her lips moved up toward the tip, and her kisses did not cease until she was able to take him in her mouth. Then she caressed him with her tongue.

'Beth?'

His voice was sleepy, and she raised her face to gaze at him. 'Let me love you, Guy, let me love you as I need to. Please don't reject me!'

'Reject you?' He stretched a hand to her cheek. 'Oh, my darling, I want you as you want me.'

Tears sprang to her eyes. 'You do?'

'Can you doubt it when the proof stands to attention so urgently?' he said with a loving smile.

'I've sent Landry away forever,' she said.

'I know, or you would not be here now. Come, let me show you how glad I am that you've stayed with me.' He opened his arms to gather her close, and their parted lips moved together in a searing kiss that almost consumed them in flames. His potency was in no doubt as he cradled her down on to the bed and then eased himself over her. Desire pounded from his loins, and she gasped with pleasure as he slid his swollen member between her thighs. Slowly and deliberately he pushed it toward her sexual holy of holies, pausing as she arched in ecstasy. Oh, Beth, his beloved Beth. How could it have taken him so long to finally be honest with her? He had longed for her, but refused to admit it, even to himself. What a fool he was, submitting to his own imagined insecurities. He had taken refuge in coldness, when all the time his heart was on fire with love. But, no more; no more . . .

She gazed up into his eyes and smiled. 'Let us become one, Guy,' she whispered, and he thrust his quivering erection even further into the warm fastness of her sweet body. She gasped with joy. 'I love you, Guy. I've loved you all along, and will love you forever. Please tell me that you love me too.'

He penetrated her until his potency pressed the neck of her womb, and then he met her eyes again and began to move in and out. 'I love you, Beth. I love you, I love you, I love you.'